after
the
rain

Center Point
Large Print

Also by Karen White and available from
Center Point Large Print:

The Beach Trees
Falling Home

The Tradd Street series:
The Strangers on Montagu Street
The Girl on Legare Street

**This Large Print Book carries the
Seal of Approval of N.A.V.H.**

after the rain

KAREN WHITE

CENTER POINT LARGE PRINT
THORNDIKE, MAINE

This Center Point Large Print edition is published
in the year 2013 by arrangement with NAL Signet,
a member of Penguin Group (USA) Inc.

The text of this Large Print edition is unabridged.
In other aspects, this book may vary
from the original edition.
Printed in the United States of America
on permanent paper.
Set in 16-point Times New Roman type.

ISBN: 978-1-61173-622-9

Library of Congress Cataloging-in-Publication Data

White, Karen (Karen S.)
After the rain / Karen White.
pages ; cm.
ISBN 978-1-61173-622-9 (library binding : alk. paper)
1. Women photographers—Fiction. 2. Georgia—Fiction. 3. Large type books.
    I. Title.
PS3623.H5776A69 2013b
813'.6—dc23
                                                    2012035517

To my wonderful son, Connor—
I'm so proud to be your mother.

ACKNOWLEDGMENTS

My novel, *Falling Home*, was first published in 2002 and introduced my readers to the small Southern town of Walton, Georgia, and the estranged Madison sisters, Cassie and Harriet, along with the rest of the town's endearing inhabitants. Readers clamored for more, wanting to know what happened next to these people they'd laughed and cried with, and in 2003, the sequel, *After the Rain*, was published. Unfortunately, both books were soon out of print and hard to find, and readers were sending me lots of e-mails and letters asking me how they could find a copy.

Happily, in 2010 my current publisher, New American Library, gave me the chance to revamp *Falling Home* while keeping intact what my readers had enjoyed—the characters and the story. And now, in 2012, I've been given the chance to do the same with *After the Rain*.

So thank you, readers, for encouraging me to rerelease these books nearly a decade after their first publications, and for loving these characters and the town of Walton as much as I do! Thanks, too, to New American Library, for allowing these characters to continue to live on in my readers' hearts and in my own.

Last, I have to thank my constant and loyal canine companion, Quincy, who remains glued to my side as I type each word, and who makes me want to strive to be the wonderful person and writer he seems to think I am.

CHAPTER 1

Tides change. So does the moon. With the unfailing constancy of brittle autumn closing in on bright summer, things always changed. If Suzanne had ever had faith in anything, it was in knowing that all things were fleeting. And for good reason. The highway of life was littered with the roadkill of those who didn't know when to change lanes.

Almost asleep now, Suzanne brushed the pads of her fingers across her forehead, then down the bridge of her nose to the small, pointed bone of her chin. Yes, it was still her. One thousand miles, a quick dye job, and the surgical removal of her life had not completely obliterated her. Just smudged the edges.

The hissing of the bus's brakes brought Suzanne awake from her almost doze. She pushed herself away from the images of a soft bed and dark Italian suits and opened her eyes wide to stare out at the anonymous highway rolling outside her window. A waxing moon smiled down at her with a crescent grin, and she touched the glass as if to bring it closer. "God's smile," she whispered to no one, recalling something her mother had once told her. Absently she let her fingers fall to the charm on the gold chain around her neck, finding comfort in touching the small heart through her shirt.

A sign on the overpass above them beamed at her through the murky glass: WELCOME TO WALTON. WHERE EVERYBODY IS SOMEBODY. She craned her neck as the bus slid under the overpass, partially obscuring the sign, but wanting to make sure she had read it right. The bus slowed to a stop, and the door opened with a loud gasp. An older woman, wearing red high heels and with hair puffed out in a tight bouffant like a halo, stood at the back of the bus and began walking forward.

The driver followed the woman off the bus, and Suzanne listened as the luggage compartment was opened. With a squeal, the woman greeted somebody who had been waiting. Suzanne listened as a deep male voice, definitely not that of their Hispanic driver, greeted the passenger. His voice carried an accent that would have placed him in rural Georgia no matter what corner of the world he might travel. Suzanne smiled to herself, content not to be so burdened.

The driver seemed to be taking a long time pulling out the woman's luggage. From the snippets of conversation, Suzanne gathered that there was a piece missing. She rested her head on the back of her seat and continued to listen. She heard the Georgia man speak again, and there was something about his voice that pulled at her, something thick and rich like dark syrup. It soothed and cajoled, as if the voice had had years of practice.

Disturbed by the effect the man's voice was having on her, she turned away, but only to catch sight of the sign again. WELCOME TO WALTON. WHERE EVERYBODY IS SOMEBODY. She sat up, watching as the light trained on the sign dimmed, then brightened, flickering at her like a winking eye. With a hand that trembled slightly, she pulled at the chain around her neck until the charm fell on the outside of her T-shirt. Tucking in her chin to see it better, she turned the gold heart over in her hand to read the tiny, engraved words. *A LIFE WITHOUT RAIN IS LIKE THE SUN WITHOUT SHADE.* With short, unpolished nails, she scraped the charm from her palm and flipped it over. *R. MICHAEL JEWELERS. WALTON.*

She pressed her forehead against the window, forcing herself to breathe deeply and recalling the woman who had given her the necklace. *Walton.* The name shifted her jaw, as if moved by her mother's invisible hand, but she shook her head. It was a million-to-one shot that it was the same town. It would take sheer luck—something that had always run on a parallel with her life, never intersecting.

As she stared out the window, a small shape darted from the grass on the other side of the highway and onto the shoulder of the road. Headlights from an approaching car appeared on the horizon, two pinpoints gradually growing larger. The shape moved into the arc cast by a

11

streetlight, and Suzanne recognized the pointed head and thin, whiplike tail of an opossum.

Pushing her hands against the window in an impotent offer to help, she glanced again at the approaching car, then back at the animal, its quivering nose pointing into the road. *Don't,* Suzanne mouthed, but slowly the animal waddled into the lane and stopped, watching as the car bore down on it.

The entire scene was too much like her mother's fascination with the bottle, complete with Suzanne's own helplessness, and she shut her eyes on the inevitable, only opening them when she could hear the dying strains of a country song from the radio of the car as it passed. Peering out the glass, she could make out the small animal in the middle of the road, curled into a tight little ball under the crescent moon. It wasn't dead, but it wasn't doing anything to prevent another onslaught, either.

Abruptly she stood and announced to no one in particular, "I'm getting off here."

The driver looked up in surprise as she stepped off the bus, the gravel crunching under the heels of her flip-flops. "Your ticket goes all the way to Atlanta."

She gave him a half smile. "I've changed my mind." Spotting her one compact piece of baggage sitting on the pavement with the rest of the unloaded luggage, she stooped and picked it up.

Holding the oversized canvas bag by her side and adjusting her backpack-style purse over her shoulders, she glanced at the other two people standing with the driver. She recognized the lady with the big hair and nodded briefly. Standing behind her was the man who had to have been the owner of the voice.

He towered over the two people in front of him, standing somewhere around six feet four. He wore a button-down white oxford cloth shirt tucked into wrinkled khakis that looked as if he'd slept in them. A red whiteboard marker and a pencil protruded from his shirt pocket. She raised her eyes to study his face and was surprised to find him staring at her chest.

Shifting her suitcase to her other hand, she sneaked a glance down at her shirt and noticed that she hadn't tucked her necklace back in and it was now dangling over the mound of her breasts, calling attention to their size. Disgusted, she twisted away from him and turned toward the driver.

"Can you tell me if there's a place around here to call a cab?"

There was a brief silence before the tall man drawled, "You're not from around here, are you?"

Suzanne frowned up at him, wondering how he knew that about her. She briefly thought about stepping back onto the bus and its cool anonymity.

But then she remembered the petrified opossum awaiting its chance to be roadkill, and she ground her heels a little deeper into the gravel.

"No, I'm not. Could you recommend a cab company to call?"

The older woman stepped forward, her perfume reaching Suzanne first. "Sugar, are you visiting somebody in Walton? Joe and I could give you a lift—"

Suzanne cut her off. "No, thank you. I'll take a cab." She looked around, spotting a service station across the two-lane highway. She didn't have a cell phone—too expensive and too easy to trace. Surely there would be a phone at the gas station, and she could call a cab to take her to the nearest hotel. Someplace sterile and impersonal, where she could get her thoughts together and figure out what she would do next. With a brief nod good-bye, she headed across the road, avoiding looking at the opossum and making sure she checked for oncoming traffic first.

As she neared the service station, she stared at the large neon sign stuck on a pole on the edge of the highway. It read BAIT. GAS. CAPPUCCINO. Then, underneath the first line, in different lettering as if it had been added at a later date, the word DIAPERS. She hesitated again, wondering what kind of place this Walton was. She could hear the rumbling of the bus behind her as it waited on the side of the road. It wasn't too late to get back on and head to Atlanta. A big city would make it easier to disappear. Then again, they'd never think to look for her in a small town stuck in the middle of nowhere. With a deep breath of resolve, she crossed the parking lot.

The tinkling bells over the door as she entered were the last peaceful sounds she heard. A towheaded girl of about four streaked past her wearing only a shirt. Suzanne got a glimpse of the stark-naked behind of the little girl as she darted down an aisle.

"Amanda! You quit it right now or I'm gonna jar your preserves!" A tall teenage girl ran past Suzanne in hot pursuit of the pantless child, forcing Suzanne to press herself against the door so she wouldn't get run over. The girl held a small boy of about two or three against her hip, who seemed happily oblivious of the pursuit and grinned a drool-filled grin as he flopped by, apparently glad to be along for the ride.

Suzanne stayed where she was, afraid to move as the sound of more running feet approached from the second aisle. Three more children raced by, two girls and a boy, the youngest girl swinging bright red braids down her back.

Suzanne had just managed to move against a tall rack of MoonPies and drop her bag when the procession of half-naked child and pursuing teenager ran by her again. The teen paused for a moment as she spotted Suzanne, then, without preamble, handed the little boy to Suzanne. "Hold him. I can run faster."

Caught by surprise, Suzanne stuck out her arms and felt the heaviness of the child as he was placed in her hands. He looked as surprised as she was and blinked large blue eyes at her. She kept her arms extended, not knowing where to put him. Never having held a child before, she wondered briefly if it would be the same as holding a puppy. It had something to do with the scruff of the neck, but as she'd never held a puppy, either, it was all pretty vague.

The little boy let out a huge wail and began pedaling his legs as if he were on a tricycle. Just then the front door opened, and the woman from the bus and the man she had called Joe entered the store. They pressed back as the running stream of five children ran past them, the redheaded girl now carrying the pants of the escapee.

Staring after the running children, Suzanne asked, "Don't they have leash laws in this state?"

At the sound of the jingling bells, the child in her arms stopped screaming and turned his head toward the man and woman. "Daddy!" he shouted, and launched himself into the outstretched arms of the tall man.

With one smooth movement, Joe reached forward and grabbed the arm of the undressed child as she tried to make it down the MoonPie aisle again. In a stern voice he said, "You go put

16

your pants on right this minute, young lady. And don't give your sister any more trouble, you hear?"

The little girl stopped and looked up at him with somber blue eyes. "Yes, sir," she mumbled as the redheaded girl caught up and dragged her back to the bathroom.

Joe straightened and looked at Suzanne with eyes that were less than friendly. With a brief "Excuse me, ma'am," he moved past her down the aisle and toward the counter.

The older woman smiled through her reproachful glance as she followed in the man's wake.

Suzanne picked up her bag and followed them to the front counter. "I'm . . . I'm sorry. I didn't know those were your kids."

The man cut her a sharp look, effectively silencing her. She bit her tongue to hold back a retort. She'd had enough of silent, brooding men to last her a lifetime, but she couldn't make a scene. Arguing with a stranger in a gas station was not the best way to disappear into the scenery.

Instead, she hung back while she waited for them to settle up at the cash register. The man placed a case of beer, six MoonPies, a six-pack of RC Cola, and a package of diapers on the counter to be rung up. The old man in overalls behind the counter kept sneaking glances at Suzanne as if he should know who she was. She shrank back, trying not to be noticed.

But she couldn't help staring at the man in front of her. Even with a baby on his hip, there was something in the way he stood and held himself that spoke of a man comfortable in his own skin. He moved easily and with confidence—a man who knew and liked who he saw in the mirror each morning.

But his clothes were a mess, as were the mismatched ensembles of the younger children. For the first time, she looked at what the little boy was wearing—cowboy boots, a swimsuit bottom, and a pajama top with bears on it—and she surprised herself by grinning.

Unexpectedly, she raised her eyes and found the man staring back at her with hazel eyes that were more brown than green. His eyebrows lifted as if he was expecting her to make another remark about children and leash laws.

He accepted his change from the old man, then moved back to put his money in his wallet. Suzanne stepped up to the counter. "I need a cab to take me to the nearest hotel. Can you send me in the right direction?"

The white-haired man blinked bright blue eyes at her as if trying to translate a foreign language, but his smile stayed warm. "You're not from around here, are you?"

That was the second time in less than an hour somebody had said that to her, and she looked down at her flip-flops and toe ring, then up to her gauze skirt and T-shirt, and wondered what it was that made her seem so different. "No, I'm not. But I need a place to stay and a way to get there, if you could just give me a couple of numbers to call."

"Well, ma'am . . ." He paused long enough that she wondered if he had forgotten the question. "Let's see. The nearest hotel is in the town of Monroe. It's about a forty-five-minute drive, but there's no local cab service to take you there. Unless you want to ride with Hank Ripple in his truck when he takes his load of peaches. He normally passes through here around five a.m."

Suzanne smelled the heavy perfume before the woman spoke. "Honey, do you have people in Walton? Maybe somebody we could call to come get you?"

The sound of the bus rumbling past outside the store made them all turn and watch. Looking at what was probably her last chance to escape, Suzanne felt her stomach drop, thinking that maybe she had changed lanes too soon, heading right into the headlights of a Mack truck.

She shook her head. "No. I'm just passing through. Thought I could find a place to stay for a while . . ." Her voice trailed away, and she felt embarrassment as her voice trembled. It must be because she was so tired from running, exhausted from crying, and so damned mad at herself for getting off the bus. And the woman's voice was so warm and caring, and Suzanne had the most ridiculous impulse to lay her head on that sequin-covered shoulder.

The woman turned to the younger man. "Joe, there's room in the truck for one more, so we could take her into town. I figure Sam could let her stay in the old Ladue house until he's got it ready to sell."

The willowy teenager who had been eyeing Suzanne with interest stepped in front of her father and shouted, "Great idea!" at the same time Joe said, "No way." Suzanne felt nine pairs of eyes on her, but the hazel ones held her attention. They were neither warm nor inviting, and the scrutiny made her square her shoulders. Sucking in whatever pride she had left after nearly thirty years of changing lanes and saying good-bye, she said, "I'll pay you. Cash."

To her utter embarrassment, her lower lip began to tremble. She looked down at her canvas bag, neatly and efficiently packed after years of practice. It reminded her of who she had become and how she had never needed anybody's help. With a deep breath, she grabbed the strap and lifted her head. "Never mind. I'll walk."

She stomped by the cluster of people, clumped together like the caramel popcorn balls sold on a display by the register. Barely hearing the tinkling bell over the door as she pushed through it, she walked out into the parking lot, past the gas pumps, then up the small, grassy rise to the road.

She looked for the Walton sign on the overpass and began heading in the opposite direction, staying on the shoulder. As soon as she was out of sight of the people in the store, she'd stop to regroup, but right now she just wanted to disappear and be by herself again.

The sound of tires on loose gravel traveled up to her, but she ignored it and kept walking. A pickup truck sped by, the driver and passenger staring at her with open curiosity through the window. She didn't look up again until she heard the blow of a car horn. Glancing around, Suzanne spotted a large green SUV, Joe and the older woman in the front seat. The window of the truck eased its way down, and Suzanne recognized Joe's unsmiling face. She didn't stop but pushed forward.

His voice hinted of annoyance. "You're going the wrong way."

"Who says?"

"Well, Monroe's the other way."

She stubbed her toe on a large rock and stumbled but kept moving. "Maybe that's not where I want to go."

"Are you lost?"

Suzanne stopped then to change her bag into her other hand. "All who wander aren't lost, you know."

He pulled the truck to a stop behind her on the side of the road, got out with a loud slam, and began following her. The wailing cries of a small child carried on the deserted stretch of road toward them. His voice definitely had an edge to it. "Look, I don't know who you are or why you're here, and frankly, I don't care. But I just can't leave you here on the highway." She heard him trudge a few more steps in her direction. Then, as if he'd given away too much of himself, he added, "And Aunt Lucinda will not let me rest tonight until I've managed to bring you into town and seen to it that you've got a roof over your head."

She didn't slow down at all but called over her shoulder, "That's your problem. Now go away. I don't need your help."

He jogged to catch up to her and grabbed her suitcase. Reluctantly, she stopped and put her hands on her hips. He sounded as mad as she felt. "The baby's crying, the rest are hungry, and I'm getting cranky." He pushed a hand through dark brown hair in a show of frustration. "God's nightgown, woman, would you just get into the damn truck and let me drive you somewhere?"

She opened her mouth to make a retort but stopped when she realized he was staring at her chest again.

His voice softened. "Where did you get that necklace?"

Realizing her charm had fallen out of her shirt again, she immediately tucked it back in. "Somebody gave it to me. A long time ago. Now can I please have my suitcase so I can be on my way?"

In answer, he turned on his heel and headed back toward the truck. "No. You can have it back when I get you to Walton."

She jogged after him. "Hey, you can't do that! Didn't your mother ever tell you not to accept a ride from a stranger?"

He popped open the back window and threw in her bag. "In case you didn't notice, you're the stranger here. Besides, the only danger you're likely to encounter in my car is insanity from too many potty jokes." He walked in front of the truck and held open the passenger door, the baby's crying finally stopped.

Lucinda got out so Suzanne could squeeze into the middle of the front bench seat. Feeling defeated for the second time in as many months, she stepped up on the running board and climbed in.

As they pulled out onto the road, Suzanne caught sight of the opossum. It had unfurled itself but remained in the middle of the road, as if unsure which lane was safest. She pressed forward, watching him as long as she could until the truck pulled away. *I know how you feel,* she thought, then leaned back in the seat for the remainder of the ride.

CHAPTER 2

The slurping sounds of a small child sucking on a sippy cup filled the quiet interior of the truck. Suzanne sat very still, trying not to touch the man on her left, whose stiffness made it clear he didn't want her anywhere near him, either. Her nose began to tickle and she sneezed, to the quick response of seven "God bless yous." Joe didn't even turn in her direction, so she pointed her thank-you to him.

The woman next to her turned to face Suzanne, the miniature disco balls hanging from her ears doing the hustle in midair. "I'm Lucinda Madison, and this here's my nephew-in-law, Joe Warner, and his kids."

She paused, as if expecting Suzanne to follow suit. Reluctantly, she said, "I'm Suzanne."

Lucinda blinked eyes cradled by false eyelashes, waiting for Suzanne to continue.

"Um, Suzanne L . . . Paris." The name flew out of her mouth before she had a chance to figure out where it had come from. The fleeting image passed through her head as quickly as the scenery disappeared on the side of the road. It was of a page torn from an ancient magazine, with creases and holes that neatly bisected the picture of the Eiffel Tower. It had once hung on her mother's refrigerator, until it had been permanently relegated to an inside pocket of Suzanne's canvas tote, when anything as permanent as a mother or a refrigerator had disappeared from her life.

Lucinda smiled, her eyes warm but not at all guileless. With wisdom born of experience, Suzanne knew this would be a woman to be wary of. She gave the impression of being soft like a feather pillow—a nice place to lay your head. But inside, this Lucinda had a rod of steel for a spine. Her eyes saw the truth through the words, as if she'd had a great deal of experience in pulling out the weeds in the garden of her family.

"That's such a pretty name, isn't it, Joe?"

He didn't even turn his head. *"Hrum."*

The oldest, whom Suzanne had heard called Maddie, rested her elbows on the back of the front seat. "Where are you from, Miz Paris?"

Suzanne looked down at her sensible nails, neatly trimmed and filed. "No place in particular. I move around a lot."

The girl shifted her elbows so she could crane her neck to see Suzanne's face better in the overhead light that Lucinda had just turned on before ransacking her handbag. "Cool. What kind of job have you got that moves you all over the place?"

Suzanne moved in her seat to see the young girl better. She was pretty, with a narrow face and high, arched brows. Her clear skin was devoid of makeup, and her medium-brown hair was pulled

25

back into a ponytail. But it was her eyes that transformed an otherwise average face into something spectacular. They were the color of moss, accentuated by a black line around the iris. They sparkled as if holding back a joke, but there was something else there, too. Something sad and uncertain that didn't have anything to do with the everyday life of a girl on the verge of womanhood.

"I . . . I take pictures." Taking a deep breath and realizing that telling the truth about this wouldn't give anything away, she continued. "I'm a freelance photographer."

"You're kidding! Anything I might have seen?"

Suzanne shook her head. "No. I mostly work for regional newspapers and periodicals. Some ad work. But nothing around here."

Maddie pressed forward over the back of the seat. "Where's all your equipment?"

There was a long pause when Suzanne tried to figure out how much she could tell, then decided on only a partial lie. "I sold most of it. I kept my Hasselblad, though, and a few lenses to get by, but that's it. I'm not here on a job."

"You have a Hasselblad? Wow. I've only seen those in photography magazines. Is it digital?"

Suzanne smiled, impressed with the girl's knowledge. "No, it's the old V System, and it's my pride and joy."

The young girl's voice sounded incredulous.

"Why'd you have to sell all your other stuff?" Something smacked the back window, and Suzanne turned to see the redheaded girl retrieving the empty sippy cup from the seat next to her.

Lucinda's sharp voice called out a reprimand. "Maddie, I think you've forgotten your manners while I've been gone. Please apologize to Miz Paris for being so nosy."

"Sorry, ma'am," Maddie mumbled as she sat back into her own seat.

Joe angled his head toward the back without taking his gaze from the road. "You shouldn't be leaning over the front seat anyway. Put your seat belt on."

The baby screamed once before the sound was replaced with loud slurps. Maddie spoke quietly, but her annoyance was clear. "I'm not a little kid anymore, and I don't need one."

This time Joe glared directly into the rearview mirror, into the face of his oldest daughter. "As soon as you stop acting like a little kid with ants in her pants, I'll start treating you like a grown-up. Now you do as I say without arguing. Do you understand?"

Her voice was completely deflated now. "Yes, sir." Suzanne heard the metallic click of a buckle being slid home.

Suzanne felt the tension in the car like a palpable shroud, and she squirmed in her seat, anxious to be alone again and away from all the complexities of family life that had never had anything to do with her.

Lucinda broke the silence and leaned forward to see Joe as she flipped off the overhead light. "My cousin Earl sent you some of his strawberry wine. I think it's strong enough to sterilize your toilet, but he seemed right proud of it." When Joe didn't answer, she continued. "How have things been here?"

Lucinda turned around to look in the backseat, studying the children for the first time. Suzanne followed her gaze to the little boy in the car seat, one cowboy boot mysteriously absent and his pajama shirt now covered with red drool from a lollipop clutched in a grubby fist. Lucinda turned back around and faced Joe. "I can see you're pulling from the bottom of the drawers. Did the washing machine get broke?"

Joe stared out the windshield, his shoulders hunched in a defensive posture. "Um, not exactly. We, uh, I ran out of detergent and I kept forgetting to stop by the store to get some." Straightening, he faced Lucinda, his gaze deliberately overlooking Suzanne in the middle. "I've been a little busy. It's hard working full-time and taking care of six kids."

"Tell me about it," muttered Lucinda. Then, her eyes widening as if in realization, "But I've been gone for two weeks! Please tell me you did laundry at least once while I was gone."

A small voice piped up from somewhere in the back of the truck. "Daddy said if we turned our underwear inside out they'd be as good as clean."

A dead silence descended inside the vehicle, and Suzanne did her best to hide a smile. Joe reached over and flipped on the radio, turning up the volume enough to discourage conversation.

Suzanne sat forward in her seat, trying to see more of Walton and wondering distractedly where she was going. There had been so many car trips with unknown destinations for her that it didn't occur to her to care or worry where they were taking her. It didn't really matter. She never stayed long enough to make it matter.

They had driven into a residential part of the town, and as they pulled up to a stop sign she noticed a poster tacked to a telephone pole. WARNER IS WALTON, it proclaimed in broad black letters. Underneath was a picture of the man sitting next to her, in the center of six smiling and well-groomed children—none of whom seemed to resemble any of the ragtag children sitting in the back of the truck now. Beneath the picture, in bigger letters, was the admonition REELECT MAYOR JOE WARNER.

As they pulled away, the thought that had been nagging at the back of her mind finally surfaced. There was no wife or mother in the picture on the poster. Where was she? Suzanne sent a look at the man next to her. The streetlight passed light and

29

shadows over his face, like a moving picture. She studied him with the eye of somebody who spent her life seeing the world in quiet pictures—her subjects mute except for the stories they wore on their faces. She preferred it that way because it allowed her to slip in and out of people's lives without causing a stir in the air they breathed or the lives they lived. It kept her safe.

But this beautiful man with haunted eyes had a story. She just wasn't sure she wanted to hear it.

The truck turned sharply around a corner, shifting her against Joe's side. She heard his intake of breath and looked into his face. His eyes were hidden in the darkness, but she could sense the tenseness of his muscles, almost hear the gritting of his teeth. Heat seemed to fill her chest, and she shifted away from him, swallowing quickly to get the taste of whatever that had been out of her mouth.

They passed a white, steepled church with a lit sign at the edge of the parking lot that read LIFE IS FRAGILE. HANDLE WITH PRAYER. She rolled her eyes at the sheer corniness of it and sank back against her seat. Whatever kind of place this Walton was, she'd only be here a short time. Surely she could stand it for that long.

Joe looked down at the woman sitting so uncomfortably close to him. Hopefully, she was serious when she mentioned she was only passing through. What was it about her that set him on edge? It wasn't the fact that she was obviously hiding something from him, because it had less to do with who she was and more with how she made him feel. Unsettled. Not the sort of feeling a man with six kids, a job, and a mayoral campaign to deal with was used to. Back at the gas station he'd called Sam on his cell phone to okay putting this woman up in the Ladue house. The keys would be in the mailbox, and a guest room was already ready upstairs with fresh sheets on the bed. It was the closest thing to a hotel in Walton that Joe could think of. Sam was in the process of restoring the house and stayed there sometimes when his wife, Cassie, was in Atlanta on business. Joe silently thanked Sam for not questioning him further, knowing that the questions would be forthcoming in the morning when he met with his best friend for their ritual weekly breakfast at the Dixie Diner.

Suzanne stared ahead out the windshield, never once questioning where they were going. For a woman in a town full of strangers, it was odd. Not nearly as odd as the way she clutched her small bag on her lap, as if everything she owned in this life were in it. She was a mystery, all right. And not one he had any interest in trying to solve.

The headlights of his truck lit the facade of the white clapboard house, making shadows from the picket fence dance across the wraparound porch.

Suzanne sat staring at the house as if dazed. He parked the truck in the driveway and got out, then waited for her to follow.

Suzanne continued looking at the house for a long moment before Lucinda pulled gently on her arm. "Come on, sugar. Let's go on in."

Lucinda called to Maddie to watch the children, then shut her door while Joe stood holding his open. He watched as she hoisted her backpack onto her shoulder and clutched her bag close to her. Ignoring his outstretched hand, she slid across Lucinda's side, opened the door, and climbed out. Her eyes remained fixed on the small white house.

"Is this where I'm staying?" she asked, her matter-of-fact tone not completely erasing a smattering of what sounded like hope.

Joe shut his door, leaving the headlights on so he could find the key and put it in the lock. "Yep— for the duration. It's in the process of being renovated."

"Are you sure it's all right, then, that I stay here?"

He almost smiled at the look on her face. It reminded him of Maddie when he'd bought her that fancy camera she'd been mooning over for Christmas. She couldn't quite bring herself to believe that it belonged to her.

"Yeah, I'm sure. I'm good friends with the owner, and he said it's okay. We don't have any hotels in town, and I told him it would only be for a little while."

Her shoulders dropped a bit as she faced him. "I can pay. Don't think I won't."

He looked at her closely. "The thought never crossed my mind. But you'll need to speak with Sam about rent. He'll stop by in the morning."

Lucinda walked up onto the porch, and they followed. The scent of fresh paint and cut wood drifted by them on the summer air as a bullfrog, hidden behind the boxwoods, decided to serenade. The rich bubble of sound erupted in the quiet, making Suzanne jump.

"It's only a bullfrog," Joe said. "Reckon you've never heard one before, where you're from."

She turned, and her soft gray eyes met his while he waited for an answer. She said simply, "No, I haven't." She stepped closer to Lucinda while Joe fished for the key in the mailbox, then slid it into the lock.

After turning on the porch light and the foyer light, Joe looked around him. Tools and sawdust littered most of the uninhabitable downstairs, but a quick peek into the kitchen told him that there was plumbing, electricity, and a clean surface on which to eat and wash dishes. Lucinda flipped on the upstairs hall light, then climbed the stairs to fully investigate the second level.

Joe watched Suzanne as she held tightly to her possessions and slowly spun in a circle in the foyer, taking in the small rooms with high ceilings. He studied her long, straight hair, noticing the darker auburn color at the roots that the red dye hadn't quite covered. Her wary gaze came to rest on him.

"Why are you doing this? You could have left me on the highway."

He shrugged, not really believing that a person had to ask that. "I was just raised that way. I couldn't let you alone on the highway any more than I could not feed a stray cat that came to my yard."

Half of her mouth twisted up. "Gee, how flattering." They were silent a moment, taking each other's measure. Then she said, "You didn't have to. I could have made it on my own."

He looked at her tall, slender form and the way she threw her shoulders back, and knew she was probably right. Still, there was a vulnerability about her that he'd first noticed in the store, that guaranteed he wouldn't leave her struggling alone on the side of the highway. Not that he'd tell her so. He had a strong feeling that she kept that one weakness hidden carefully away, and it made him shy away from her. There was something soft and tender at her core; he knew it; he could feel it. But he didn't want to get close enough to see it.

He stared back at her blankly. "Yeah, I figured as much."

As if unused to the words, she stumbled over them. "Thank you."

Lucinda's heels interrupted as they clicked down the wooden stairs. "There's a nice little bedroom and bath up there that should do just fine. Let me go check the refrigerator before we leave, in case we have to make a trip to the grocery store tonight."

Suzanne turned to watch the older woman as she disappeared into the kitchen, her eyebrows drawn into a V. Unable to stop himself, Joe said quietly, "This is where she comes out with a large butcher knife and we have you for dinner."

She looked at him with cool gray eyes, not batting a lash and not saying anything, either.

He felt ashamed that he'd said that, considering her situation. He took a step closer to her, his hands held out to her, palms up. "Look, I'm sorry. That wasn't funny."

She brushed her hair off her shoulders, swinging it behind her. Coolly she said, "Actually, it was. I was just bracing myself to run if I heard dueling banjos."

He laughed, surprising himself. He couldn't remember the last time he'd laughed out loud like that. She turned toward the kitchen, and as she did, he noticed the lollipop stuck in the back of her hair, and his laughter died in this throat. It looked suspiciously like the one Harry had been sucking on in the truck.

"Wait," he called after her, stopping himself in time before he touched her. He pointed to the offending object. "You've got a lollipop stuck in your hair."

She put her hand on the spot and sighed. "Oh." She frowned. "Thanks for telling me."

Joe drew back and put his hands in his pockets. "I guess if I kept them on leashes, that wouldn't have happened."

Her gray eyes widened. "Look, I said I was sorry. . . ."

Before she could say more, Lucinda came from the kitchen. "There's enough beer in there for a football team, but there's also bread, cheese, and peanut butter. I'll stop by tomorrow and take you to the Piggly Wiggly to pick up a few things. Then we can chat and get to know each other better."

Joe saw an almost imperceptible shifting of Suzanne's shoulders, as if she were drawing up her lines of defense and preparing for battle. He glanced at Lucinda and noticed she saw it, too.

But all Suzanne said was "Thanks." She stood clutching her bag as Joe let Lucinda out the door, called good night, then closed it behind them.

Joe fell asleep immediately but awakened only an hour later, not sure what it was that had brought his eyes wide open. He listened to the quiet house for a moment, hearing it settling as if exhaling a deep sigh at the end of the day. He thought of his six children asleep in the rooms around him, the sound of their soft breathing his one redemption in yet another bleak and lonely night. He closed his eyes.

For a moment, Joe could almost believe that Harriet was beside him again, her warmth pressing against him in sleep, her breath touching his cheek. He even reached over to feel for her, but instead his fingers brushed the cold cotton of her pillow, his nail catching on the frayed lace on the hem. Out of habit, he pressed his nose into it, hoping to smell the scent of her one last time. But the pillow and its case had been laundered too many times since Harriet's death, and no part of her lingered in his bed anymore.

The clutch of grief squeezed his heart again, the feeling of being suddenly plunged underwater and held down, where all he could do was gasp for breath and struggle for the surface. It surprised him with its suddenness and intensity, the grief as black and all-consuming as the day he'd buried his wife and the mother of his children. These attacks had lessened in recent months, but he doubted that they'd ever go away completely. He wasn't even sure he wanted them to.

With a small groan, he climbed from the large bed, larger now that he slept alone in it, and went to the chair with the ottoman by the window. It was an old friend, and they'd spent many nights together following Harriet's death. In those first days he couldn't stand to be in the bed without her, and it had only been in the past year that he'd found his way back to it.

Until tonight. Something was bothering him that he couldn't quite put a finger on. An image of Suzanne Paris kept pushing into his thoughts—an image of the way she hunched her shoulders and folded her arms in front of her as if it was just her against the world. And one look in her eyes told him that the world was winning, despite the show of confidence she wore on her shoulders like a neon sign. She bothered him, all right, and he wasn't sure why or how. And there was certainly no room in his life to care.

He sat down in the chair and propped up his long legs, trying to find a comfortable position. He stared out into the moonless night as he tried to drift off to sleep, avoiding the ghosts in his bed and trying not to think of a lost woman with wary eyes and ghosts of her own.

CHAPTER 3

Suzanne was living in a dream. She was in a white house with a porch and picket fence, and any minute a dog would bark and lope across the immaculate green of the front lawn. She sat up and rubbed her eyes. Like all dreams, this one was destined to end. No use wasting any time wallowing in it.

She stood and straightened the white chenille bedspread, not having been able to bring herself to actually pull it back and slip inside the crisp sheets the night before. Something about that otherwise innocent gesture seemed too permanent, and she had simply lain down on top of the bed and gone to sleep.

A dog barked outside, and Suzanne started, a grin forming on her lips. Looking out the front window, she saw a sandy-haired man pull up in a pickup truck, a large mutt standing in the back. As she watched, the dog barked again, then leaped out of the truck and raced across the lawn in an apparent chase of nothing more than exuberance for life.

Slipping on her shoes and straightening her skirt, she finger-combed her long hair and braided it as she headed for the stairs and a meeting with her landlord. She swung open the door, surprising the man on the other side, who kept a hand raised in midknock. She stared at him for a long moment, taking in the bright blue eyes, jeans, and cowboy boots, and telling herself that whatever shortcomings Walton might have, it certainly knew how to raise good-looking men. If they all were like this man and Joe, she might find it difficult to leave when the time came.

The man smiled. "I'm Sam Parker. Joe told me you're Suzanne Paris." He lowered his hand, and she allowed her own to be gripped tightly and pumped up and down in a handshake. She stepped back, and he followed her into the small foyer. "Joe said you were looking for a place to stay for a while."

"Um, yeah. If you're looking for a short-term tenant, I promise you won't even know I'm here."

She frowned when she saw that his eyes were focused on a place in the middle of her chest. She folded her arms, making him shift his gaze to her face. He wasn't smiling. "Where'd you get that necklace?"

Feeling almost relieved to know it had been the charm that had caught his interest, she relaxed a fraction. "My mother gave it to me when I was fourteen." She tucked it back inside her T-shirt to end that topic of conversation. "So, I was wondering what rent would be for this house. I only want a month-to-month. And I can give you a month's deposit—in cash."

He was looking at her oddly. As if he hadn't heard her, he said, "Was your mother from around here? You don't look familiar to me." His voice had the same slow drawl that Joe's had, the words spread slowly like hot tar. She remembered how the sound of Joe's voice had affected her the night before as she sat on the bus, and she shifted her feet trying to erase the memory.

"My mother was definitely not from here. Now, about the rent . . . ?"

He shoved his hands in his back pants pockets,

40

in an identical gesture she'd seen Joe make, and looked at her closely. His eyes were sharp and intelligent, as if he could read all her secrets, and she forced herself to keep quiet and not blabber any more information. The less these people knew about her, the better. Then he gave her a ridiculously low rent quote. Without a word, she went up to the bedroom, pulled out the hem from another skirt in her bag, and retrieved the amount he'd quoted plus twenty dollars more in crisp green bills.

He raised an eyebrow when she handed them to him.

"I don't need charity, and this place is worth at least this to me. Even with sawdust covering half the house, it's still a sweet deal."

Slowly he took out his wallet and placed the bills neatly inside. "You've probably noticed that I'm still in the middle of renovations here, but I promise I won't be here all the time. I'll come up with some sort of schedule we can both live with, all right?"

She held out her hand, and he looked at it for a moment before shaking it, his white teeth showing. "I can tell you're not from around here. Otherwise, you would have offered me a pie to seal the deal."

Crossing her arms across her chest, she said, "In other parts of the country, you would have asked for references."

He gazed steadily at her, and she held her breath, realizing she had just left herself wide open to exposure. After a long pause, he said, "Your handshake is all I need. That's as good as a contract around here. If I'd kissed your hand, we would be as good as married."

Relieved, Suzanne couldn't help laughing as she walked with him to the door. As he opened it, the large dog that had been in the back of the truck leaped past him and placed his front paws on Suzanne's chest. With a scream of surprise, she clenched her eyes shut and pressed herself against the wall, crossing her arms over her face in a defensive gesture.

"Down, George. Down!" Sam shouted, and the huge dog complied, but not before he used a fat pink tongue to wedge its way between her hands and lick her cheek.

When she opened her eyes, Sam was holding the dog by its leash and trying hard not to smile. "He's big, but he's got the heart of a bunny rabbit. He's always been a sucker for a pretty face."

Embarrassed to find herself shaking, she continued to press herself against the wall. "I . . . I don't like dogs."

"I could kinda tell. I'll make sure to leave George at home next time." He glanced at her again with a curious look. "Joe mentioned you didn't like children much, either, so I'll be sure to keep all creatures—both the two- and four-legged varieties—away."

She forgot her embarrassment for a moment as his words sank in. "He said that? I mean, it's not that I don't *like* them; it's more like I don't know what to *do* with them."

Sam led the beast out the door and onto the front porch. "As with everything, they just take some getting used to, that's all. And then you find that you can't live without them. Trust me—I've seen it happen."

Suzanne frowned. "Dogs or children?"

"Both. Not much difference between the two if you ask me. And pretty likeable once you get to know them." He winked.

George barked and she shrank back against the door. "I'll have to take your word on that."

He tipped an imaginary hat. "I've got to get to work. Call me if you need anything—I left my card on the hall table. And I understand Lucinda's stopping by this morning to take you to the store. Just be prepared to buy a tube of lipstick and rouge from her, too." He winked again, then opened the door of his truck to let the dog in. After settling himself behind the wheel, he said, "See you later." With a wave, he drove off in a small puff of dirt, George's face hanging from the window with an innocent look in his soft brown eyes. He offered a good-bye bark to her as the truck pulled out of sight.

43

An involuntary laugh burst through her lips, surprising her. Hugging her arms across her chest, she walked down the steps and onto the front yard and surveyed the neat, trim house with its picket fence and rosebushes. It was certainly the stuff of her dreams, dreams that were never meant to last. But at least it was hers. For now. With the laugh still fading on her lips, she climbed the steps and went back into the house and up the stairs, having made the decision that she would at least unpack, and maybe, tonight, she'd sleep under the covers.

Sam was already waiting at the counter of the Dixie Diner, nursing a coffee, when Joe strolled in. Joe waved, self-conscious of his appearance. His blue button-down shirt had a scorch mark under the pocket, and his khaki pants had long since lost their crease. Lucinda didn't go away often, but when she did it seemed his tenuous hold on his life completely fell by the wayside. It was all he could do to drive the kids where they needed to be, help with the homework, and give them each individual attention before tucking them into bed at night and crashing on the sofa in a nearly comatose daze. Laundry, ironing, and the never-ending household chores just didn't get done when Lucinda was away. There just weren't enough hours in the day.

He greeted his childhood friend as the waitress,

Brunelle Thompkins, slid a fresh mug of coffee in his direction with a bright smile. He sipped from the hot mug, brooding over his situation. Lucinda was a godsend, but he felt guilty. Especially because he almost resented the few times she went away to visit family in North Carolina.

He'd offered many times to pay for help, but Lucinda wouldn't hear of it. She said his kids needed family and no hireling could take her place. Joe thunked his mug down on the laminate counter, sloshing some of the hot liquid over the side and scalding him. As he sucked the burned spot on his finger, he remembered that Sarah Frances had her clarinet lesson today and that the instrument was at the moment sitting on top of the TV in the family room.

"Looks like you've been rode hard and put up wet. Rough night?"

Joe sent Sam a disdainful look. "Thanks. Not that you look any better."

With a mock look of hurt, Sam said, "Cassie's been waking me up practically every hour when she goes to the bathroom." He sent Joe a wry grin. "Good practice for when Sam Junior or Juniorette arrives."

Joe stared into his cup. Softly, he said, "Yeah, I remember those days." He took a sip of his coffee but didn't say anything else.

Sam regarded his friend for a moment in silence. "If you're still not sleeping more than

45

three nights a week, let me know and I can prescribe something to help you."

Being best friends with the town doctor did have its advantages, especially with six children who were always coming down with one thing or another, but access to easy prescriptions wasn't one Joe would allow himself to take. "No, thanks. I appreciate it, but I can deal with it on my own."

Sam moved his mug out of the way to allow Brunelle to place a plate of eggs, sausage, and cheese grits in front of him.

Joe eyed Sam's plate. "Why don't you just shove that stuff directly into your arteries?"

Sam picked up the saltshaker and sprinkled it liberally over his plate. "Hey, leave me alone. Ever since she found out she was pregnant, Cassie's put us both on this health food diet. It's just about killing me. This is the only decent meal I get all week." He speared a bite of sausage and put it in his mouth, chewing with relish.

When Brunelle appeared to take his order, Joe pointed to Sam's plate. "I'll have the same as him."

"Excuse me?" Sam stopped in midchew.

"Hey, I'm allowed. I ran five miles this morning with the football team. And I haven't had a meal that I didn't pick up at a drive-through window or that came in a box in two weeks. I figure I deserve this."

Joe sipped his coffee and watched Sam eat

46

without speaking for a moment while the door chimed again and three teenage boys wearing Walton High School letter jackets strolled in. Two girls from the high school, who were drinking coffee and nibbling on dry toast at the opposite side of the counter, giggled as they sneaked glances at the boys.

"Hey, Coach Warner," the tallest boy greeted Joe, and stopped by his stool. "How's it going? Great run this morning, huh?"

Joe took his time watching Brunelle deliver his breakfast, before turning around to face the boy with the closely cropped brown hair and olive complexion. "Hello, Rob." His eyes narrowed slightly. "Shouldn't you be in class?"

Rob glanced back at his two companions. "Homeroom isn't for another twenty minutes. Have to have my java first." He grinned broadly, revealing perfect white teeth.

"Well, don't let me keep you from it." Joe took a bite of cheese grits and chewed thoughtfully, his eyes never leaving the boy's face.

Frowning, the boy said, "No, sir," then sauntered away with his friends to a nearby booth.

Sam grimaced. "You were a little rough on the kid, don't you think?"

"*Hmmph*. He's not a kid. He's a two-hundred-pound pile of muscles, testosterone, and jawline guaranteed to render senseless any girl over six and under sixty. And it's ninety degrees outside—

47

why in the hell is he wearing his letter jacket?"

Sam glanced back at the boys now crowding the booth with their broad shoulders and meaty biceps. "He asked Maddie out, didn't he?"

Joe said nothing but scowled at his companion.

"She's seventeen, Joe. Soon she'll be leaving for college. What are you going to do—send her to a convent?"

"I'm not Catholic."

"Like that would stop you. You can't keep her under your wing forever, you know."

Joe glared steadily at his friend. "Do you think I don't know that? But what am I supposed to do? I'm just a guy, and unfortunately, I know how guys think." His voice broke a bit, and he coughed to cover it. "She needs her mother."

"We all miss Harriet, Joe. But don't fool yourself—you're doing a terrific job with those kids, and you're all Maddie needs right now. Just don't smother her in your desire to protect her. It will only backfire, especially with her. She's too much like her aunt Cassie for her own good."

Joe snorted softly. "That's for damned sure. But there's so much about raising children that seems to require a woman's touch. I've been waiting for Lucinda to notice that Sarah Frances needs to start wearing a bra, but she hasn't said anything yet. I guess I'll need to bring it up."

Sam looked at his friend for a long moment. "I'm suddenly hoping that Cassie has a boy."

Joe slid his plate away from him, eyeing the boys in the corner again. "*Hrm.* You'd just be trading in one set of problems for another."

A rush of warm air fell over them again as the front door opened and two men in suits sauntered in. Joe averted his gaze and reached for his wallet. "Great. Just what I need this morning—a dose of Stinky Harden. I'm leaving." He motioned for Brunelle to bring him the check.

Sam stared openly at the two men waiting for a table to open up. "Why do you think he's so hot to run for mayor all of a sudden? It's not like he's ever had any interest before." He turned back to Joe. "He's got the look of somebody who'll play dirty—probably got that from all those years living in Atlanta. Not that he'll be able to find any dirt on you. You're so clean you squeak."

Joe raised an eyebrow. "I'm too busy to get into trouble. Kind of hard to do anything bad when you've got a small child wrapped around each leg."

Sam scooted his stool away from the counter and leaned back, pushing his plate away from him. "Well, if you're looking for trouble, you won't have to go that far. That Paris woman over at my place—good gravy, Joe. I can see why you felt you couldn't leave her at Dad's gas station." He gave a low whistle to emphasize his words. "If I weren't a happily married man, *I* might even be interested."

Joe almost spit out his coffee. "I'm not. She annoys me, that's about it. And she's hiding something. She claims she doesn't come from anywhere and doesn't have any family. How is that possible?"

"And she paid her rent in cash. Yeah, I gotta agree with you there—she's definitely hiding something. But I like her. I don't think she's trying to pull one over on us. I think she just wants to be left alone. But man, she is one good-looking woman."

Joe tried to flag down Brunelle one last time. "I'm not interested. I'm too busy and she's not my type anyway. I'm not that desperate for a roll in the hay."

A voice piped up behind them. "What's this about a roll in the hay? Joe Warner, I'm shocked to hear you speaking like that."

"Good morning, Stinky." Joe threw a ten-dollar bill on the counter, no longer willing to wait for his check. "I was just leaving." He scooted out his stool and stood.

Stinky looked at him with mock disappointment, his round face looking deceptively cherubic. "What a shame. I thought I could join you and talk about why I'd make a much better mayor for Walton."

Joe moved past him. "Would love to, but I just remembered that I forgot to floss. See you later."

Sam followed, and when they got to the door, Joe turned around to see Stinky staring after him, a calculating look on his face. Thankfully, there was nothing of substance behind his comment regarding a roll in the hay, or he knew that Stinky would be all over it like white on rice, using it to his best advantage.

Then the image of Suzanne Paris hit him so suddenly that he stopped, almost causing Sam to crash into his back. Stinky had just given him another reason to stay away from her. He shook his head as he held the door open for his friend. As if he even needed one more. Her sad, wary eyes and ridiculous toe ring were enough reasons for him.

Suzanne stood facing the house, her eye focused in the viewfinder. She hugged the cold black camera with her hands, finding her comfort in this place of still pictures. This was her world—a world of perfection and noninvolvement, a world she could walk away from as soon as she'd snapped the picture and before her feet had the chance to leave footprints in the grass.

She zoomed the lens to capture the delicate fan of the window over the front door, then moved in for a close-up of the wisteria vine climbing the mailbox with fragrant curves. A warm breeze raced across the front yard, making one of the rockers on the front porch creak. She took a few pictures of the empty chair, tempted to sit in it. But she knew if she did, she might never want to get up. There was something about this place that reminded her of that stuff she'd read about in a magazine this morning—kudzu. A leafy green vine that grew while you blinked, taking over old barns and fields in the course of a week. Already she'd found Walton—and the inhabitants she had already met—very much like kudzu vines. Suzanne looked down at her feet. She had to remember to keep them moving.

The sound of a car pulling into the driveway made her turn around, and she spotted Lucinda sitting behind the wheel of an improbably fuchsia convertible. The sun sparkled off of cat's-eye rhinestone glasses. Her bright red hair was piled high, the color clashing with the scarlet of her blouse. But nothing was as dazzling as the smile Lucinda sent her as she put the car in park. For all her flamboyance, Lucinda Madison was as genuine as they came.

Suzanne waved and smiled in return, her enthusiasm waning slightly when she spotted the two car seats in the back. In one of them sat Amanda, the streaker from the gas station store, and next to her was the little boy with no fashion sense. However, it would seem that today his ensemble of pressed blue jeans and cotton pullover with the large fire truck emblazoned on the front had been chosen with a lot more care than the previous one.

Lucinda climbed out of the car, groaning slightly.

"My goodness, I'm creaking like a rusty hinge this morning. And please excuse me if I have soap bubbles flying out of my ears. I was awake until two a.m., up to my eyeballs in laundry detergent, washing clothes." She turned toward the car and smiled at the two children in the backseat. "Harry and Amanda, I'm sure you remember Miz Paris from last night. Can you say hello?"

They stared at her blankly, matching wide blue eyes scrutinizing her openly. Lucinda walked toward Suzanne. "They're a little shy at first with strangers, but after they get to know you, you'll be wishing for earplugs."

Suzanne held up her camera. "If you don't mind, I'd like to put this inside and get my purse."

"Sure, honey. Take your time."

Suzanne raced inside. After hiding the camera under the bed and shoving her canvas bag on a high shelf in the closet, she pulled out several bills she'd stashed under a loosened corner of the rug and shoved them into her backpack.

When she came outside, Amanda shouted, "Aunt Lu, I need to go potty."

Lucinda went to the car and unbuckled the car seat. "Can we use your bathroom, Suzanne? I'll take her if you'll watch Harry."

Nodding, she said, "Sure—but go upstairs. The one on the first floor is missing a toilet. I think it's the one sitting in the backyard."

Amanda must have thought that uproariously

funny, because she began snickering, holding her hand over her mouth.

Lucinda gave her a gentle tap on her head. "I think somebody had a slice of silly pie for breakfast. Come on, let's find that bathroom."

Harry and Suzanne were left alone to assess each other. Harry apparently found something lacking, because he began to wail as soon as Lucinda and Amanda disappeared behind the front door. Suzanne looked around for a reprieve, helpless. She tried speaking to the child, even reasoning with him, but he refused to be quiet. She glanced nervously at the nearby houses, wondering if anybody would call the police and charge her with cruelty to a minor.

Near defeat, she made a face at him, complete with crossed eyes and her index finger tilting her nose up like a pig's. His crying settled to soft hiccups. When she tied her hair on top of her head like a bow, he chuckled with a surprisingly deep-throated rumble.

They were both smiling at each other when Lucinda and Amanda emerged from the house, his tears the only telltale sign of any unpleasantness.

Harry snorted, his chubby finger pushing at his nose, making Lucinda look at him oddly. "I hope you don't mind me bringing along the children to the Piggly Wiggly. They didn't have preschool today and Joe's at work and the older children are at school. They won't be any bother."

Suzanne slid into the passenger seat as Lucinda buckled the little girl into her car seat. "Please, don't worry about me. I just appreciate the lift." She examined the woman sitting next to her, noticing the surprisingly soft skin, with only fine wrinkles at the corners of her eyes. It was a beautiful face full of generosity and goodwill, sharpened slightly with what was undoubtedly a strong sense of intuition. Definitely a face she'd need to capture on film before she left.

Lucinda settled herself behind the wheel and adjusted her seat belt before moving the car onto the street. "Don't think anything of it. I'm just glad I could help."

"How come you don't have pictures on your refrigerator?" Amanda's voice piped up from the backseat.

The question startled Suzanne. "I, um, I guess because I don't have any."

There was silence for a moment, and then, "Don't you have any children to make you pictures?"

Suzanne turned to face her and shook her head. "Nope. It's just me."

Lucinda sent her a quick glance. "Have you always been alone, honey?"

Her hands plucked at her gauze skirt before she answered, "I . . . I don't like talking about myself."

The older woman stared out the windshield.

"I'm real good at keeping secrets and I promise I won't tell anybody. But it seems to me you might could use somebody to talk to." Her voice softened. "Is it man trouble?"

Suzanne squinted, the sun nearly blinding her.

Lucinda slipped off her sunglasses. "It just seems to me that there's a reason you're wanting to lie low for a while." She smiled warmly. "Anybody who comes to Walton without knowing somebody to visit must be here as a last resort." Lucinda winked, her false eyelashes waving at Suzanne like small birds.

When Suzanne didn't say anything, Lucinda asked again, "So, have you always been alone?"

With a brief pause, Suzanne nodded. "Pretty much. I have a mother, but I haven't seen her since I was fourteen. Since then it's been just me."

Lucinda slid her gaze over to Suzanne, her eyes sympathetic. "That's a sad thing for a young girl." She wiped a smudge of mascara from under her eye and replaced the sunglasses.

Suzanne straightened her shoulders, drawing in a deep breath. "It was. But I got over it. I manage fine on my own."

They drove by a house with a large wraparound porch and an elderly woman sitting in a rocking chair, a pink sweater thrown over her shoulders. Lucinda waved, and the woman waved back, a thick paperback novel in her hand. Lucinda glanced back at Suzanne, a twisted smile on her face. "Until now, I suspect."

Suzanne stared out the window at the neat, trim houses with big yards, swing sets, and roller skates on the driveways. She watched a group of small children riding tricycles down the sidewalk, following two mothers like fledgling ducks. Her fingers ached for her camera, to capture this scene somehow and make it real.

"Into each life some rain must fall."

"What?" Suzanne swung her attention back to Lucinda.

A small smile tugged at the corner of Lucinda's rouged and powdered cheek. "Oh, I don't know. It's just a little saying a friend of mine has on a cross-stitch on her wall. It reminded me of you for some reason."

Without saying anything, Suzanne returned to the window, anxious to escape this woman's close scrutiny but also somehow grateful for it. It had been a long time since anybody had cared enough to ask.

They passed through an intersection with an elementary school on the left and a large, tree-filled park on the right. A brick sign by the front gate read HARRIET MADISON WARNER MEMORIAL PARK. Even though it was August, plastic poinsettias sat in pots at the base of the sign.

"Who was Harriet?" Suzanne asked, sure she already knew.

"She was my niece and Joe's wife. She died of cancer three years ago come this Christmas. It was the saddest thing this town has had to live through in a long time."

Suzanne thought of the man whose face told stories he didn't want to tell her. If she'd been able to take his picture, she would have seen a man who wore his grief like a window on his heart. But she had spent so much of her time with him being on the defensive that she had somehow missed it.

Harry threw a toy into the front seat, and Suzanne caught it before handing it back. "But Harry could only have been . . ."

"He was born on Christmas Day and Harriet died the next week. Joe was devastated. We all were. But we're getting by."

Lucinda lifted her finger under her sunglasses, and Suzanne let the conversation drop, not knowing how to comfort. But she couldn't stop herself from thinking of Joe and of the girl Maddie. She must have been about fourteen when her mother died, and Suzanne felt her own pull of grief, knowing the toll of losing a mother while on the cusp of womanhood. "I'm sorry," she said, surprising herself by meaning it.

Lucinda pulled into the parking lot of the grocery store, sliding the large pink car in between two pickup trucks. She turned off the engine, then reached into her purse for a lipstick and began applying it. "I'm fixin' to hire me some temporary help at my lingerie store to get me through inventory and set up for Christmas. If you think you could stick around for a couple of weeks or so, you could come work for me. You won't get rich, but I can pay you over minimum." She looked expectantly at Suzanne.

With a small thrust of her chin, Suzanne said, "I know something about large-sized bras, but that's about it. Why would you want to offer me a job?"

Lucinda blotted her lipstick, leaving a bright orangey-red kiss on the tissue. "Because it looks to me like maybe you could use one to give you time to sort things out. Plus, I really do need the help." She snapped her purse shut. "You don't need to decide now, sugar, but let me know."

Suzanne climbed out of the car, then opened the back door to help Harry out of his car seat. Lucinda showed her which buttons to push and which clips to undo. When she was done, she straightened and looked around, disoriented for a moment. In her mind's eye, she saw herself in the middle of the parking lot of a store called Piggly Wiggly, holding a small child and standing next to an oversized pink convertible driven by a woman with hair a color nature never intended.

As disjointed as the image made her feel, she took consolation in the fact that nobody would recognize her here. After less than twenty-four hours in Walton, she could barely recognize herself.

CHAPTER 4

Nurse McCormick took the thermometer out of Maddie's mouth, and frowned as she examined it. "You don't have a fever, sweetie. I can't send you home if I can't find anything wrong with you."

Maddie clutched her abdomen, wishing she'd thought of it when she'd first gone to the nurse's office. "It's my time of the month and my cramps are really bad." She moaned for effect.

Nurse McCormick's round blue eyes softened in understanding. "You poor thing. I used to be the same way. All you want to do is lie in your own bed and eat chicken soup. Let me call your daddy. . . ."

Maddie sat up, remembering to still clutch her midsection. "No. You'll just make him worry and I know his AP chem class is doing some big, complicated experiment today. I'd hate to distract him."

The nurse's blond curls nodded in agreement with her head. "You're probably right. Is your aunt Lu at home?"

"Yes. I'll call her on my cell to let her know I'm on my way home so she can start making some soup."

"Perfect." Nurse McCormick gave her a look of sympathy and Maddie braced herself for what she knew was coming. "I know how hard all this girl stuff must be for you to go through without your mama. You've got Lucinda, but I just want you to know that I'm here, too, if there's anything you need to talk about that you're not comfortable talking about with your daddy or your aunt."

"Yes, ma'am," Maddie said as she stood, remembering to hunch over a bit.

"Anything," the nurse repeated, and Maddie forced a smile and nodded as if she agreed that well-meaning strangers could ever replace the mother who'd been stolen from her.

"I'll go ahead and write an excuse for your sixth- and seventh-period teachers and turn them in for you. You just run on home and get in bed. A warm compress should help, too."

"Yes, ma'am," Maddie repeated, trying not to look too eager as she headed out of the nurse's office. She walked very slowly to the front doors of the high school, belatedly realizing that she was limping, too, and hoping nobody had noticed.

She walked through the school's parking lot— where she did *not* have a car parked because her dad really believed that just because she lived within walking distance she should actually walk or ride her bike. She hadn't ridden her bike since she was fourteen, not that he noticed. She sometimes thought that in her daddy's mind she was still that same little girl she'd been when her mama died, as if all the clocks had suddenly stopped.

Maddie paused for a moment to swipe her palm across her forehead to get rid of the perspiration that threatened to drip in her eyes and found herself standing next to Lucy Spafford's red Audi convertible with KDZUQNE on the license plate. She groaned inwardly, trying to tell herself that she wasn't jealous. Maddie's mama would have made sure she had a car. A cute Volkswagen Beetle convertible. Or anything, really, that wouldn't accommodate car seats and younger siblings. Or wasn't a bike.

As soon as Maddie was sure nobody from school could see her, she broke into a sprint, not slowing until she'd reached the loading docks in the back of the Piggly Wiggly. She was panting hard and sweating so bad that at first she didn't see her two classmates lounging against one of the Dumpsters at the edge of the building.

"You got the stuff?" Ritchie Kobylt asked, his mouth barely moving as if the effort of forcing out words was too much effort. Despite the heat, he wore a black studded leather jacket draped with chains. His black hair—about six shades darker than it had been in middle school—matched his black eyeliner, jeans, and unlaced combat boots.

The girl next to him, Sandy Creek, obviously shopped at the same place since her outfit matched Ritchie's exactly, even down to the placement of the chains. Even their skin had the same vampiric paleness.

Maddie reached deep down into her purse—one that was worn and old but had been one of the last presents her mother had given her—and pulled out two packs of Marlboros before handing them to the goth pair. She'd taken them from Aunt Lucinda's stash in the laundry room. They belonged to Sheriff Adams, who'd been trying to stop smoking for about two years, with Aunt Lucinda helping him by confiscating his cigarettes. Luckily for Maddie, Lucinda was a believer in not throwing anything away since it might be useful later on.

"You got my stuff?" Maddie asked in return, trying to sound tough, too, and nearly managing it, too, except for the slight squeak on the word "stuff."

While Ritchie opened one of the cigarette packs and pulled out a lighter, Sandy groped around in her oversized backpack—black, of course, but with an attractive skull-and-crossbones motif splayed across the front—and pulled out a small stack of large envelopes. "My mom's all excited because all this stuff is coming in from schools all over the country. As if." She took a lit cigarette from Ritchie and sucked on it as if it were the last drop of water in the desert.

"You didn't tell her they're for me, right?" Maddie asked as she took the envelopes emblazoned with college logos from everywhere except Georgia. She tucked them out of sight into her bag.

"Hell no. She's been leaving me alone and not nagging me about homework or my room because she thinks they're for me." She took another drag and looked at Maddie with black-rimmed eyes. "How come you don't want your dad to know?"

Maddie shrugged as if it weren't really important. "Because he'd freak. He wants me to go to UGA or anywhere, really, that's within the state of Georgia. Not just because it's cheaper, either, but because he wants to keep me close to home. Personally, I'd rather be in a jail cell."

She glanced up at Ritchie, knowing he'd had firsthand experience with a jail cell, and hoped she hadn't insulted him. He responded by handing her a cigarette. Trying to pretend that she did this every day, she accepted it, holding it between her lips as he lit it. Holding it between her thumb and forefinger just like Ritchie and Sandy, she pulled it away from her mouth without inhaling it.

"What do you think of your dad's new girlfriend?" Sandy asked.

Maddie looked at her in surprise. They'd been best friends in elementary school, eventually drifting apart as Sandy's parents divorced and she'd started hanging around with the goth crowd, and Maddie, well, Maddie stayed the same.

Except that her mother had died. That had changed her, but only from the inside where nobody could see how much.

"She's not his girlfriend. They just met and he's helping her out. Not that I would mind my daddy getting a girlfriend. Maybe then he'd have something to distract himself with besides keeping tabs on me and where I want to go to college." This was mostly true. Her daddy hadn't so much as noticed another woman since Maddie's mama died three years earlier, so it hadn't really ever occurred to her that he might actually *want* to date again. The thought made her want to throw up a little bit in the back of her throat, but she realized that it could be to her advantage. It wasn't as if her mama was ever coming back.

They both looked at her with the same sympathetic look Nurse McCormick had given her—minus all the eyeliner—and Maddie glanced away, wondering how soon she could get away from this town and the people who would always know her as "the girl whose mother had died."

After having bypassed the fresh fruits and vegetables, Suzanne stood in the frozen food aisle, finally finding herself in familiar company. She opened a freezer case and pulled out a stack of frozen dinners and dumped them in the cart. Lucinda, following in a separate cart with the two children riding in the basket amid collard greens, sweet potatoes, and toilet paper, stopped to stare inside Suzanne's.

"Is that all you're going to be needing?"

Suzanne stared at her loot defensively. "That will last me." She reached in and held up a loaf of bread. "Plus all the peanut butter sandwiches I can eat."

Lucinda shook her head. "No wonder you're so thin. I might have to add you to the Women's Guild list of dinner donations."

Pushing her cart ahead, Suzanne called over her shoulder, "Don't be silly. There's more than enough food here to last me until I leave. I can't take the frozen food with me when I go, and I hate to be wasteful." She stopped in front of another case and pulled out a box of frozen pancakes. She held it up like a trophy. "See? I eat healthy. They say that breakfast is the most important meal of the day."

With a cluck of her tongue, Lucinda shook her head and pushed her cart toward the checkout line.

It seemed the woman knew everyone. From the checkout clerk to the man in front of her in the line, Lucinda was greeted by everybody who saw her. It wouldn't have been so bad except for Lucinda's insistence that she introduce Suzanne to every single one of them. Reaching toward a rack of sunglasses, Suzanne snagged a pair and pushed them on her nose, trying to ignore the dangling price tag. She tried on several pairs as Lucinda ran through yet another bout of introductions. She felt stupid, but it was the only thing she could think of that she could hide behind to avoid recognition. Just in case.

As she waited for Lucinda to ring up her own purchases, Suzanne casually picked up a copy of the *Atlanta Journal-Constitution* and opened it. She scanned the headlines of the first page, feeling her skin tingle in relief when she didn't see what she was looking for. Plunging head-on into the middle of the paper, she continued perusing headlines. *It's not there. Why isn't it there?* She glanced around, aware that she was breathing heavily. *Just because it's not in the Atlanta paper doesn't mean he's not looking for you.*

"Suzanne?"

She looked up, temporarily unaware of where she was.

"Sugar, could you grab a paper for me, too? I'll pay you back."

Numbly Suzanne placed the paper on the belt, then plopped a frozen lasagna behind it. As she reached into the cart for the next boxed dinner, two voices spoke in unison behind her. "You must be Joe's woman, who's staying at the old Ladue house."

Suzanne whipped around and spotted two women, well past their sixties, wearing identical yellow capri pants with matching shirts and hats with brims so big a strong wind would have made them airborne.

"Joe's woman—?"

Lucinda interrupted. "Thelma and Selma Sedgewick, I'd like you to meet Suzanne Paris. She's visiting for a little while."

The women held out gloved hands as a dazed Suzanne responded by shaking the fingertips of each woman.

Thelma—or was it Selma?—spoke first. "So, how did you and Joe meet? You know, it's about time he started to show an interest in women again. Dr. Parker said you were right pretty, too, although it's hard to tell with those sunglasses. . . ."

Not quite sure how to respond, Suzanne pulled out a bill and handed it to the cashier.

"Sorry, ma'am. I can't take anything over a fifty-dollar bill. I could call the manager. . . ."

Suzanne stared down at the crisp one-hundred-dollar bill and felt the blood flood her cheeks. She looked up and found Lucinda staring at her. Without a word, Lucinda handed the cashier two twenties.

Feeling as if she might faint, Suzanne whispered a quiet "Excuse me" and pushed through the two women dressed like canaries and walked toward the back of the store to find either a restroom or a way out. She wasn't sure which made her feel more nauseated: being referred to as "Joe's woman," whatever the hell that was supposed to mean, or remembering that Anthony was looking for her. Either way, she needed space to breathe.

She eyed two large doors with an exit sign above them at the end of the snacks and soda aisle and pushed through them, gasping for air. Blinking, trying to adjust to the bright sunlight, she spotted three figures standing about six feet in front of her.

Maddie Warner stood leaning against a back wall of the grocery store near a Dumpster, a boy and girl around the same age standing nearby, each with a hand in the other's back pocket. As soon as they heard the door shut behind Suzanne, the three looked up.

The smell of old garbage mixed with that of cigarettes, making Suzanne cough as she stared at the three teenagers. The boy tugged on his girlfriend's arm. "Come on, Sandy—we gotta go." With a quick gesture at Maddie encouraging her to follow, they walked around the Dumpster and disappeared around the corner of the building.

Maddie stayed where she was, looking at Suzanne through narrowed eyes. "What are you doing—shoplifting cheap sunglasses?"

Belatedly, Suzanne realized she was still wearing the glasses from the checkout counter. She yanked them off her nose and was about to defend herself when she noticed the cigarette trailing smoke from Maddie's fingers. "Aren't you supposed to be in school?"

Maddie took a long drag on her cigarette, and Suzanne watched in amusement as the cool and collected expression on Maddie's face quickly crumpled into a coughing fit. Suzanne reached over and grabbed the cigarette from the teenager's hand and crushed it underneath the heel of her sandal.

"Don't you know these are addictive?"

Maddie crossed her arms over her chest, a belligerent look on her face that didn't completely obliterate the expression of a deer caught in the headlights. "It's none of your business. Just go away and leave me alone." She turned her back, but not before Suzanne saw the panic in her eyes.

She studied the younger girl, recognizing the need in this child, the unspoken craving so much like her own. Softening her voice, Suzanne said, "Look, you need to be in school instead of out here polluting your lungs. If you can promise me that you'll go back to school right now, I won't tell anyone that I saw you here."

Maddie's shoulders dropped slightly. "Why?"

Suzanne shrugged. "Because it's the right thing for you to do."

The younger girl turned. "But why are you giving me a break?"

"Because you remind me of someone." She looked down at the sunglasses in her hand and concentrated on folding them up. "Now go before I change my mind."

70

Maddie paused for a moment, then turned. "Thanks," she mumbled over her shoulder before she, too, disappeared around the corner.

Suzanne stared after her, not sure what had just happened. She stood still for a long moment, feeling the hot sun beat down on her and recalling the hungry look she had seen in Maddie's eyes. It was a look Suzanne was way too familiar with.

With a sigh, she pushed the sunglasses back on her nose, then tugged on the heavy door to return to the fluorescent world of the Piggly Wiggly.

Looking both ways to make sure nobody saw him, Joe opened the door to Lucinda's Lingerie and entered. He blinked, his eyes trying to adjust from the brightness outside to the dimness of the store, created by the red fabric walls.

"Can I help you?"

He swung around to a dark corner of the store and found himself facing Suzanne Paris, a black lace teddy dangling from her one hand, a padded hanger in the other. She looked as surprised to see him as he was to see her.

"Um, uh, I'm looking for Lucinda. Is she in the back?"

Suzanne slid the teddy onto the hanger. "No. She had a few errands to run before picking up Amanda and Harry at preschool and asked if I'd watch the store."

"Oh." Joe tried to look everywhere except at her

71

and that silly black underwear thing. "Why are you here?"

"I'm working here. This is my first week. Lucinda said she needed some temporary part-time help." She raised her eyebrows expectantly.

Joe cleared his throat. "Do you know when she'll be back?"

"I have no idea. Is there something I can help you with?"

As if sensing his discomfort, she quickly stuck the hanger onto a crowded clothes rack.

"I, uh, no. I'll just wait outside until she gets back."

Suzanne widened those intriguing gray eyes. "Oh—are you looking for something for yourself?"

Joe widened his own eyes as he realized the implication. "What? No!" He shook his head, wishing he'd never stepped foot in the store. He could have waited until Lucinda came home and asked her there, but he'd been passing Lucinda's Lingerie on his way to the hardware store and decided to step in. Unfortunately, he'd completely forgotten about Lucinda's new employee. "It's for my daughter Sarah Frances. She needs a, um, a . . ."

He couldn't say that word in front of this woman. Something about her made him tongue-tied, and the subject of their conversation only made it worse.

"Bra? Your daughter needs a bra? What size?"

He looked in her eyes for any hint of amusement

and was surprised to see none. "I don't know. I thought I could just buy a couple and take them home for her to try on."

Now she smiled. "Wouldn't it be easier to bring her into the store? Lucinda has quite a selection of sizes and styles to fit any chest."

Damn. He hadn't blushed since fifth grade when he'd been caught in the girls' bathroom by Mrs. Crandall and she'd made him refill the tampon machine. He looked up at the ceiling, pretending to study the brass chandelier that hung from a pouf of red, silky fabric. "Sarah Frances is pretty much a tomboy and wouldn't be caught dead in here."

"Kinda like her dad, huh?"

She really was laughing at him. "Never mind. I'll go outside and wait."

A warm hand touched his wrist, pulling him back. Maybe it was static electricity or maybe it wasn't, but something definitely shocked him. She left her hand on his arm for another second before dropping it.

"Look, I'm sorry. I'm not making fun of you." Her face was closed and controlled, as if trying to mend fences was something she had to work hard at. "I think it's nice what you're doing." She forced a tentative smile on his face. "Come on. Let me pick a few out for you to take home. Just send back the ones she doesn't like with Lucinda."

She turned away from him toward a wall full of

small drawers. Over her shoulder she called, "Any idea how big . . . ?"

Their gazes locked for a moment, and Joe felt his cheeks flame again. *Damn.*

She turned back to the drawers and began pulling out bras. "Never mind. I saw her that once at the gas station. I'll figure it out."

He stared at the back of her, at the plain T-shirt and long, floral skirt that skimmed her legs. He shifted his gaze to her head, where she'd pulled her hair back from her face, and saw her cheeks crease in a smile. He frowned. "I'm glad you're finding this so funny."

Slowly she faced him. Her eyes were dark now, her face no longer smiling. "It's not that. It's . . ."

She averted her gaze and dug beneath the counter for tissue and a bag. As she began wrapping the first bra, she said, "It's because I was thinking of what a lucky girl Sarah Frances is to have a dad who would do this for her. I honestly didn't think they existed until now."

He was speechless for a moment, an angry retort frozen on his lips. He watched her in silence as she finished wrapping, then stowed the small tissue-wrapped packages into a shopping bag.

He was spared a response when the door swung open with a bang and Amanda rushed into the store, followed in quick pursuit by Harry and Lucinda.

"Daddy!" she squealed, launching herself into

his arms. He buried his nose in her hair, smelling the baby shampoo. Feeling a tug on his pants leg, he looked down into Harry's upturned face and lifted him up, too.

He stared into the wide blue eyes of his youngest child, feeling the old familiar ache again. Of all his children, Harry was the most like Harriet. It wasn't just his coloring. It was his quiet intensity, and his bright smile that seemed to shine light into the dark corners of one's heart. Joe's only regret about bringing Harry into the world was that his son would never have any memories of the wonderful woman who had given birth to him.

Joe squatted down and placed the children's feet firmly on the floor. Harry thrust a crumpled paper at him. "For you!"

Joe flattened out the paper on the floor and eyed the yellow and orange splotches of crayon appreciatively. "I love your use of color, Harry. I might have to frame this one in my office, if that's okay with you."

Harry responded by ducking his chin and burying his face into Joe's shoulder.

Amanda, who had been hopping around her father on one foot and then the other, stopped and thrust a paper at him. "I made this for you."

Again, Joe spent his time studying the artwork, this one with blue and green stick figures and a triangle-like structure that resembled a house.

When he looked up to compliment his daughter on her skills as an artist, he realized that she was no longer standing in front of him but was approaching Suzanne with another picture clutched in her hand.

"I made this one for you." She thrust the picture at the young woman, and from Suzanne's wide-eyed look of surprise, he thought for a moment that she might refuse it.

Stiffly, Suzanne held out her hand and took the paper, looking down at it with a tight expression on her face. She stared at the picture, not saying anything.

Joe started to move toward Amanda, to take her away before her feelings were hurt, when the little girl spoke. "It's for your 'frigerator, since you didn't have any pictures on it."

For a brief second, Joe thought he could see Suzanne's lip tremble before she said a taut thank-you and turned away to duck behind the counter.

When she emerged, she was holding her backpack in one hand and Amanda's picture in the other. Addressing Lucinda, she said, "I'll be back tomorrow morning at eight to get started on the stockroom inventory." She waited until the front door was almost closed behind her before uttering good-bye.

Joe turned to Amanda, ready to confront the tears that were sure to follow. Instead, he spotted his youngest daughter staring at the closed door with a quizzical look on her face, her head tilted to the side in the way children seemed to do when they were thinking hard.

"I don't think anybody's ever made a picture for her. She prob'ly needs to go think about it for a while."

Recognizing his own words coming out of his daughter's mouth, Joe paused, wondering if he had ever had the wisdom his children seemed to come by so easily.

Suzanne walked blindly down the sidewalk, not paying any attention to the people openly staring as she passed. She needed to reach the privacy of her own room before she began to cry. She had not shed a tear since she was fourteen, and if she were to start again now, it would not be as a public spectacle.

The six-block walk to the house she was renting took her less than ten minutes, but when she approached the front gate, she paused, staring at the beautiful wraparound porch and at the welcoming windows upstairs, where a reflection from the sun seemed like a wink.

There was something about this house that slowed her pulse and warmed her blood, much as what she imagined would happen in a mother's embrace. Maybe it was that this house had been a home to the Ladue family for almost one hundred years that made it emanate welcoming vibes. Or maybe it was the ghosts of long-dead Ladues whose Southern hospitality lasted beyond the grave.

She opened the gate and shut it behind her, no longer feeling the press of tears. She smelled the roses and the boxwoods, and above those scents, the smell of fresh sawdust telling her that Sam had already come and gone.

Slowly she walked up the front path, eyeing one of the rocking chairs. She had yet to sit in one, but today, in the late afternoon sun, the pull was strong. She imagined she saw the rocker move slightly forward, leaning down to make it easier for her to sit. Sitting in one place long enough to watch time march by wasn't something she'd ever tried before—or even wanted to do. But the soft summer scents, her tired feet, and the beautiful picture in her hand all pushed her toward the wicker-bottomed rocker on the porch.

With a deep sigh, she let herself fall into it, noticing how the wide arms of the chair wrapped around her like an embrace. She dropped her backpack with a small thud on the wooden slats of the porch and allowed herself to examine her gift more closely.

In vibrant hues of blue and green stood a stick house, with flowers in the front yard as tall as the chimney, and a mother and father stick couple surrounded by an entire brood of stick children. A horizontal block of blue crossed the top of the page—a finite sky. The endless horizon had always bothered Suzanne, as if it alone compelled her to keep moving forward. She looked at the block of blue hanging over Amanda's depiction of Walton, a heavy line of crayon marking off the boundaries of sky, and she closed her eyes. It made her feel dizzy, like the feeling of stepping onto an escalator only to find that it had stopped. For a moment she found herself envying a determinable existence, a life where leave-taking was involuntary instead of inevitable. And for one brief moment, she thought of Harriet Warner and of all the reluctant good-byes made by a wife and mother.

Abruptly, Suzanne stood, the chair rocking in her wake. She'd tape Amanda's picture to the refrigerator, next to the one of Paris. She'd be careful to only use one strip of tape, so that when she took it off when she left, it wouldn't tear the paper. She was an expert at that; she'd done it for years.

She opened the door but paused, listening to a chorus of cicadas in the large mimosa tree that bordered her yard and the neighbor's. Their sound rose and fell on a wave of late-summer air, as if heralding in the approaching change of season. She touched the charm around her neck, the cicadas bringing out a wistfulness that she seemed to harbor in her heart and couldn't shake. She wished the sound would bring her happy memories of summer evenings sitting on a porch, or chasing fireflies in the yard. But her memories were empty, like blank negatives of pictures never taken. The void was huge and could never be filled, even if she pretended it could for a few weeks in this beautiful white house with the large front porch.

Walking inside to the foyer, she shut the door with a thud, silencing the wistfulness in her heart and the soft sounds of the approaching evening.

CHAPTER 5

Suzanne shouldered her backpack, then pulled the door of the shop tightly closed before sliding the dead bolt with her key. Slipping the key ring in her pocket, she picked up the foam box holding the remains of her lunch from the Dixie Diner and began the short walk home.

The two weeks she'd been in Walton seemed more like two years. She grudgingly admitted to herself that parking her flip-flops here and lying low for a while wasn't such a bad thing. She could certainly have done worse.

At least now there were fewer open stares as she went about her business, and more waves and greetings. Perfect strangers had been bringing her food for over a week to welcome her into town, and she had learned every avenue and cul-de-sac on her journeys to return empty dishes.

She had begun to bring her camera along on her forays into Walton for the old frame houses, and their owners were willing subjects. When she realized that many of Walton's citizens were wearing their Sunday-best clothes to sit outside on their porches in the anticipation she might come by, she made an effort not to be so obvious. Still, she became known as the "picture lady" and happily obliged anyone who posed in front of her and smiled.

As Suzanne stepped off the curb, she heard her name called. Turning, she spotted Brunelle Thompkins running after her, another white foam box in her hands.

"Hey, Suzanne, wait up!" She was breathing heavily and wore a thin sheen of perspiration on her upper lip when she stopped in front of Suzanne. She held out the white box.

"It's my last piece of pecan pie, and I don't want it to go to Stinky Harden. I figured you could use the calories more than him."

Realizing that this was probably a compliment, Suzanne smiled. "Thanks, Brunelle. Would you put it on my tab?"

Brunelle shook her head. "Nuh-uh. My payment will be the look of disappointment on Stinky's face."

They both laughed for a moment; then Brunelle helped Suzanne stack the little box on top of the bigger one before heading back to the diner.

Suzanne cut through the backyard of a large house on the corner, past the bobbing heads of bright purple pansies that littered the side of the house, and emerged in the side yard of a neat and trim clapboard house that had recently been painted a pale shade of pink. The old woman who always sat on her front porch reading a thick novel and wearing a pink sweater, regardless of the temperature, glanced up. Suzanne lifted the foam boxes in greeting, and the woman waved a paperback as Suzanne passed onto the sidewalk.

When she reached her front gate, she stopped in surprise. Maddie Warner sat on the front step of the porch, leaning against a pillar, her long arms wrapped around drawn-up knees. "Hi, Miz Paris. In case you're wondering, school's out, so I'm not skipping."

Suzanne latched the gate behind her. "Since it's after five o'clock, I would hope so. Unless you had extracurricular activities."

Maddie scooted over on the step, inviting Suzanne to sit next to her. Storing her boxes and backpack on the lowest step, Suzanne sat down, placing her hands on her knees.

Maddie sniffed deeply. "Something smells good."

"Chili-cheese omelet and pecan pie. My dinner."

"*Ew.* An omelet for dinner?" She wrinkled a freckled nose.

"Well, it was my lunch, but I couldn't finish it, so now it's my dinner."

"Aunt Lucinda always makes sure we get greens at dinner. You're so lucky you get to live by yourself and eat what you want."

Suzanne contemplated the young girl, who most likely had sat down to dinner surrounded by family every night of her life. "It can be nice." She looked up as an old man and woman, their hands clasped together, strolled by on the sidewalk and waved. She waved back, the movement not as awkward as it had felt at first.

Turning back to Maddie, she said, "Speaking of dinner, shouldn't you be heading home?"

"Technically, it's not dinner—it's supper. And I'm on my way home now. I have something to show you and I just . . . well . . ." She looked down at her feet and fidgeted with the strap on her sandal. "I also wanted to thank you for not blabbing about me skipping school the other day. My dad would have grounded me for a year."

Suzanne stared at the fine bones in the girl's face, and the long, slender fingers of her hands. They were beautiful hands, the trimmed nails painted a glossy black. There was so much about this girl that was typical teenager. But there was something more, too; it was there in her beautiful hands and haunting eyes. It was this that kept Suzanne on the steps for a few minutes longer. The call for solitude was strong, but something in Maddie's eyes kept her lingering. Maybe it was because she saw the same shadows every time she looked in a mirror.

"Then why did you do it? Seems to me your dad would have found out pretty quickly since he teaches at the school."

Maddie looked down at her sandal-clad feet again, and Suzanne noticed that her black toe-nails matched her fingernails. "I just needed to check out for a day. That's all." She looked up at Suzanne, a frown puckering her brows. "Don't you ever get that way?"

"I think everybody does." She spoke slowly, trying to find the words to explain something that nobody had ever asked her about before. "I do, but mostly because I'm not used to being around lots of people. I think it also has to do with creativity. Most creative people need their space, and that's fine. Just don't go finding your space when you're supposed to be in school. I call that counter-productive." She spotted a small stack of folders on the porch, next to Maddie. "So, what did you bring to show me?"

Maddie picked up the stack and held them on her lap, looking shyly at Suzanne. "Remember in the truck you told us you were a freelance photographer? Well, I take pictures, too. I mean, I know I'm probably not that good, but my art teacher at school says I am and that I should enter some contests. I just don't want to make a fool of myself."

Suzanne looked expectantly at the stack clutched tightly in Maddie's lap. "So you want me to take a look at them."

"Yeah, if you don't mind. I mean, just glance at them, you know. Just let me know if I'd be embarrassing myself if I let anybody else see them. Like in a contest."

Suzanne repressed a smile at the earnestness of Maddie's expression. "Sure." She extended her hand.

Almost reluctantly Maddie handed over the folders. With deference, Suzanne opened the first folder and began thumbing through a collection of black-and-white glossy prints. The first few were obviously school assignments done without real imagination or skill but still with an impressive eye for shape and lighting.

It wasn't until she reached the bottom folder that she felt she held in her hands the true account of Maddie's talent. Suzanne stared at the picture on top for a long moment, and she found herself holding her breath, the scent of the boxwoods suddenly overwhelming. The photo was of a dinner table completely set with plates, food, and silverware, eight chairs surrounding the table. Seven of the chairs were occupied, but the faces were deliberately blurred, hiding their occupants' identities. The focus was the chair at the foot of the table. It was the only object in the photo that was completely focused and still—and heartbreakingly empty. It made her want to weep.

There were more, each one showing a depth of emotion rarely seen in those as young as Maddie. It was as if in exchange for a mother's life this gift had been given to her, a poignant recompense for a lifetime of absence.

When she thought she could trust her voice again, Suzanne said, "These are good. Really good. Your art teacher's right." She looked at Maddie, the young girl's face open and vulnerable. "Did your teacher tell you how to take pictures like this?"

Quietly she said, "My mama gave me my first camera and showed me how to use it. She liked to take pictures, too, and was making an album for me when she died."

Suzanne looked back down at the photographs. She had never before had the desire to help someone, to give of herself without any expectation of receiving something in return. But there was something about Maddie Warner, in her quiet gravity, that tugged at Suzanne's heart. Maybe it was because she did identify with the girl's struggling soul. Or maybe it was because her feelings were only temporary, and any bonds would be easily and quickly severed as soon as she packed her bag and left Walton when the time came for a change.

She looked into those beautiful green eyes, so different from Joe's but not like the blue eyes of her siblings, either. Smiling at Maddie, she said,

"If you'd like, I could help you with a few things. Your content is wonderful, but I think you could stand to practice a little more with lighting and shadow. And I could teach you a few techniques that I've used on jobs that you probably wouldn't learn in art class." She stacked the photos back into the folder, jostling them against her lap to straighten them. "But only if you've got the time after dinner—uh, supper—and only if your father says it's okay."

She thought Maddie would explode with excitement. Impulsively she hugged Suzanne, startling her into knocking the folders off her lap. With unbridled enthusiasm, Maddie jumped up and began gathering the photos. "Oh, thank you. I . . . thank you! I know it will be okay with my dad, but I'll ask him anyway. Can we get started tomorrow? I have to take Sarah Frances to basketball practice, but I'll be back by seven. Should I come here?"

Suzanne couldn't stop her smile. "Sure, that works fine. Just make sure you check with your dad first."

"All right. Bye!" She ran down the path, forgetting the teenage amble that appeared to be so popular with her age group.

After she slammed the front gate, Suzanne called after her, "One more thing—don't smoke. If I ever smell smoke on your breath, the deal's off, all right?"

The girl stopped, her hand on her hip, and a petulant expression on her face. "What's your problem with cigarettes? It's not like I smoke every day."

Suzanne tried to hide her grin as she recalled the image of Maddie choking on the cigarette. "It'll rot your lungs and it's addictive. I have a real problem with anything that causes a person to lose control. Just don't do it."

Maddie turned back around, waving a dismissive hand in the air. "Yeah, whatever. I'll see you later." She walked a few more steps before calling back over her shoulder, "Thanks again," then disappeared into the late-afternoon sun.

Suzanne stayed where she was for a little while longer, playing with the necklace around her throat and wondering if she had ever shown such unbridled enthusiasm over anything. Maybe a couple of times, before she was fourteen. But never afterward.

Eventually, she picked up her boxes and went inside to her solitary supper.

Joe strolled into the Dixie Diner at eleven thirty-seven exactly, just in time to beat the noon rush. He scanned the sparse late-morning crowd, looking for the tall, slim form of a woman wearing artsy-fartsy clothes and badly dyed hair. Lucinda had said Suzanne took her lunch at this time, and he could find her here. He half hoped she wasn't, remembering the scene in the lingerie shop, but knew he had to speak with her eventually.

He spotted her at a booth by herself, huddled over a chicken-salad sandwich and reading the Atlanta paper. She wore her aloneness like a shield, making him even more reluctant to approach her. Moving forward, he stood next to her. "Is it okay if I sit?"

She looked at him with startled eyes, and he wondered for a moment if she would bolt. She swallowed quickly, followed by a gulp of iced tea, before answering, "Uh, sure."

He slid in and folded his hands in front of him, his right hand playing with the wedding ring on his left. He hadn't taken it off his finger since Harriet had put it there, and he could see no reason to stop wearing it now. "I wanted to talk to you."

A look of panic settled over her face again as she quickly closed the newspaper and shoved it onto the seat beside her, out of sight. Brunelle came by with two pitchers of tea and smiled at them, and something in her eyes made Joe squirm. It was as if she was pairing him with the woman across from him. He pushed back against his seat to separate himself as far as possible from Suzanne.

"Would you like more tea?"

Suzanne nodded. "Yes, please. And make it unsweet. I just can't get used to the sweet tea that everybody around here seems to like."

Brunelle nodded and filled Suzanne's glass, then

moved to the next booth, a wide smile on her face.

Joe watched Suzanne as she dropped the unsqueezed lemon on her plate and took a delicate sip from her glass. "You're definitely not from around here."

She looked at him somberly. "I never said I was."

He looked back at her with unflinching eyes. "But you never said where you *were* from, either."

"I said I moved around a lot. That's pretty much all there is to it."

A shadow seemed to pass over her eyes, making her seem more vulnerable than defensive. What was it about this woman that made him want to reassure her? He still wasn't sure if he even liked her.

"Look. I'm not here to give you the third degree. I wanted to talk to you about Maddie."

Her mouth twitched. "Why? Does she need a bra, too?"

An involuntary laugh escaped him. "No. I think she's all squared away with her unmentionables for now. But thanks for asking." He noticed the sparkle had returned to her unusual gray eyes, and he relaxed. "It's about you helping her with her picture-taking. I'm not sure if an hour a week with you is—"

She sat up straight, interrupting him in mid-sentence. "Oh." She paused for a moment, like a strong wind gathering momentum. "I want you to know that your daughter is incredibly talented with her photography—or 'picture-taking,' as you call it. Even if you object to me giving her some pointers, I do think you should consider allowing her to pursue this interest. She could really go somewhere with it." She paused again to take a breath. "I'm disappointed that you don't take her talent seriously."

He stared at her, taken aback. "I beg your pardon? I never said any such thing."

"Well, you . . . you said you weren't sure about your daughter . . ."

He watched as the fire faded from her cheeks. "I actually came here to thank you, but I think she needs more than just once a week of instruction. She's really fired up about this. I don't know what you said to Maddie, but, well, she's excited about something for the first time since her mother died."

Suzanne tilted her head, as if trying to understand a foreign language. "She is?"

He placed his palms down on the table and stared at their backs, the gold band shining under the lights. "Yeah. Her mother died. . . ."

"I know." She said it quickly, eager to move on, like touching a bruise briefly so as not to make it hurt.

Joe continued. "Well, Maddie seemed to lose interest in most things. She pretty much stuck to home, helping out with the younger ones." He sighed and looked up. "I guess it's my fault for letting her and not pushing her out more."

Brunelle stopped by the booth again to clear the dishes and leave the bill. Joe put his hand over it just as Suzanne reached for it. Brunelle saw their hands together and smiled again, making Joe groan inwardly. Brunelle was better than CNN when it came to broadcasting late-breaking news.

Suzanne jerked her hand back. "I'll get it. I've got money."

Joe leaned forward to pull out his wallet from his back pocket. "That's not the point. I'd like to pay you for your time with Maddie. And this"— he held up the bill—"is just a thank-you." He shoved a twenty and the bill over to the edge of the table. "I must admit I'm surprised, though. I thought you didn't like children."

She frowned. "I never said that."

They stared at each other evenly for a long moment before Suzanne spoke again. "Well, then. I guess we're even. Maybe we should both stop getting our exercise from jumping to conclusions and reaching for answers."

Joe laughed out loud, making heads turn in their direction. He spotted the editor of the *Walton Sentinel*, Hal Newcomb, huddled over a booth with Stinky Harden. They were both staring at him and Suzanne with barely suppressed curiosity. His amusement died quickly. This woman had a method of disarming him in the most unexpected way. Maybe it was the way she delivered her one-liners broadside and without the hint of a smile that caught him off guard. He felt almost grateful.

A shadow fell over their booth. "Well, hey, Mayor Joe. I figure you need to keep hearing that name as much as you can for now. Won't need it after the elections."

Joe felt a throbbing begin in his temple as he watched the fleshy man in the seersucker suit wink and turn his interest to Suzanne.

She had grabbed the newspaper and was trying to slide by unnoticed out of the booth.

"I don't think we've had the pleasure of an introduction."

Stinky held out a meaty hand, making Suzanne pause at the edge of her bench. Slowly she placed her own hand in his and stood, towering over Stinky by at least a head.

"I'm Charles Harden, soon to be mayor of this town." His gaze took in the tall woman, pausing longer than necessary on her chest. He still gripped her hand, and Joe had the strangest urge to yank Suzanne away.

"Suzanne Paris," she said in a clipped tone. "Nice to meet you."

Still holding her hand in his, Stinky asked, "I hear you're new in town, but I'm having the hardest time placing your accent." He chuckled in his studied self-deprecating way. "I admit to being a bit of an expert on accents, but I have to say that

I'm completely baffled. Where are you from?"

Joe saw through Stinky's dramatics and wanted to signal Suzanne to be careful. Because if she had something to hide, his mayoral opponent would dig it out like a raccoon in a garbage can.

Suzanne didn't flinch. "I've moved around all my life, so I can't really say I'm from anywhere in particular." She hoisted her backpack on her shoulder in an obvious effort to end the conversation.

Stinky persisted. "So, how do you know Mayor Joe? Are you old friends?"

Joe interrupted. "Nope. Just new acquaintances." He glanced at his watch. "And we both have to get back to work. Wonderful seeing you again, Stinky. But you might want to go a little lighter on the aftershave next time. I think my eyebrows are singed."

Ignoring Joe, Stinky raised Suzanne's hand to his lips and placed a quick kiss on it. "May I take this opportunity, then, to welcome you to Walton? I'm sure this town appreciates a beautiful new face. I know I do."

She pulled her hand away but plastered a smile on her face. "Thank you. That's very nice of you to say."

Stinky's gaze slid down to her chest, then back to her face again. Joe clenched his fist, ready to send one flying. "Actually, I know the perfect way to get you introduced around town. Our Founder's

Day Dance is next Saturday. It would do me proud to be your escort."

Knowing his bid for reelection would be over as soon as the first punch landed on Stinky's well-fed and pompous face, Joe grabbed Suzanne's arm and pulled her toward the door. He called back over his shoulder, "She can't—she's already going with me."

Oblivious of Suzanne's protests or to all the heads turned toward them, he pushed her in front of him and led her out the door.

CHAPTER 6

Suzanne pulled her arm away as soon as they left the restaurant. "You've got a lot of nerve dragging me out of there like a belligerent child." She adjusted her backpack on her shoulder. "Next time you want to fight over toys in the sandbox, leave me out of it."

She stalked off in the direction of Lucinda's Lingerie.

"Hey, wait a minute. I'm sorry. Really." His footsteps pounded behind her until he caught up and stopped in front of her. "That was a bit childish, I admit, but Stinky sort of brings out the worst in me. Besides, you should probably be grateful."

She tried to walk past him, but he blocked her way. "What for?"

"For saving you from an evening spent with

Stinky Harden. I can't speak for myself, but I've heard others refer to dates with him as on a par with surgery without anesthesia. I think one girl had to spend time in an institution after a single evening. They say she was bored into a coma."

Suzanne stopped, trying hard not to smile. "Then thank you. Now, I've got to get back to work." She headed up the two brick steps in front of the shop and tugged on the door handle.

"Then I'll pick you up at six on Saturday."

She turned around and froze. "Excuse me?"

"For the Founder's Day Dance."

She blinked twice. "I don't think so. I already have a date with a book and my couch."

He put a foot on the bottom step. "Look, I'm not any crazier about going to this thing with you than you are, but I can't show up without you now. It would look bad."

"That's your problem." She turned the door handle.

"All right. I'll be honest with you. Maddie's going to be going with some high school jock, and the only reason I'm going is to chaperone her date. She'd find it a lot less objectionable if you were with me."

Suzanne stopped and faced him again. "But I don't have anything to wear."

"Ask Lucinda. Between her and Cassie Parker, they'll come up with something."

He was close enough that she could see the fine

lines at the corners of his hazel eyes. They were definitely laugh lines. He didn't laugh a lot now. The lines were merely old ghosts of past joys, and they softened her defense. "Why are you asking me?"

He shrugged. "Because I'm grateful to you. Because of Maddie."

"I see. I'm a pity date. How about I just pretend I'm sick and stay home?"

He touched her hand, then dropped it just as quickly. "That's not what I meant. Besides, you might surprise yourself by having a good time."

She raised an eyebrow.

"And you won't have to dance with Stinky Harden and end up in an institution."

She rolled her eyes, making him laugh. Sobering, he said, "And Maddie says you're lonely. Maybe it wouldn't hurt for you to get out."

She pulled her shoulders back. "Just because I like to be alone doesn't mean that I'm lonely."

Two men wearing overalls came out of the Dixie Diner and passed in front of Lucinda's Lingerie, waving at both Joe and Suzanne. Joe watched them as they walked away, then turned back to Suzanne. "Maybe it's not so much that you like being alone. Maybe it's just what you're used to and you don't know any other way to be."

Without answering him, she pulled the door open, the scent of rose petal sachets drifting out onto the sidewalk.

"I'll see you at six on Saturday, then."
She let the door slam behind her.

Maddie sat in the hair-washing chair at Bitsy's House of Beauty with Aunt Lucinda on her left and her aunt Cassie on her right. Being with them was the closest thing she had to being with her mother. Not the same thing at all, but as close as she'd ever get. And better than just having a dad. Maddie winced, thinking again of the birds-and-the-bees speech her father had attempted when she turned sixteen, before enlisting the help of her aunt Cassie.

Closing her eyes, she let Bitsy massage her temples. "I think giving you a few layered bangs would really soften your face, Maddie. You and your aunt Cassie have got the same head, and I can tell that it would really look precious."

Cassie spoke, her Southern accent peeking out of certain words, determined to ignore the elocution lessons she had taken during her fifteen years in New York. "I agree, Maddie. Not that I don't think you're beautiful no matter what way your hair is done, but I do think bangs would be flattering."

Maddie glanced over at her aunt, lying back to have her head shampooed, her enormous pregnant belly making her look like a blowfish stranded on the beach. Not that she'd ever tell her that, of course. Aunt Cassie was already making such a big deal about her ankles being the same size as her thighs that she knew better than even to make a joke about it.

She closed her eyes again as Bitsy used cool water to rinse out the conditioner. "This is the way Mama always did my hair. I like it the way it is."

Aunt Cassie started to say something but was interrupted by Aunt Lucinda. "Hey, Suzanne. We were wondering where you'd gone off to."

Bitsy sat Maddie up to towel-dry her hair. "Hey, Miz Paris. Aunt Lu thought you'd run off 'cause you were scared we'd cut off all your hair."

Suzanne turned up half of her mouth in that odd way she had. Almost as if she was afraid to tell the world she thought something was funny. "I thought about it, but I was actually finishing up checking in a shipment that just arrived at the store. Didn't want to leave thongs and garters all over the place." She moved her backpack off her shoulder to hang in her hand. "Then the Sedgewick sisters stopped in." She blew out a big breath. "I had to explain a few things to them. And let's just say that I was shocked to see what they bought. I haven't quite yet recovered."

Aunt Lucinda yelped out loud. "I can't believe those two. They haven't been in my shop since I opened it. They're obviously on a spy mission for the Ladies' Bridge Club." She sat up straight in her chair, hair dripping. "What did they buy?"

Suzanne slid a glance at Maddie. "I'll tell you later."

Maddie bristled. "I'm seventeen. I wish y'all would quit treating me like a kid."

Her little sister Knoxie, her bright red hair a tangled mess down her back, hobbled into the washing room, cotton balls stuck between each pink-tipped toe. "Look what Ovella did for me while I was waiting!"

Suzanne gave a real smile to Knoxie. "They look great." She slipped her feet from her flip-flops and spread her toes. "Can't say I've ever had my toenails painted before. Think they'd look good in that color?"

"Yep. It's pink. All girls look good in pink. Except for Maddie." With a dismissive look at her oldest sister, Knoxie hobbled off toward Lucinda.

Maddie watched as her aunt Cassie was hoisted to a sitting position. She tried not to think about what her aunt and Dr. Parker had to have done to get her in that situation. It was bad enough imagining her own parents doing it enough to make six children.

Holding out her hand, Cassie stepped toward Suzanne. "I'm so glad to finally meet you. I've heard so much from Lucinda and Maddie that I feel I already know you. I'm Cassie Parker, Sam's wife."

Suzanne paused, then, almost reluctantly, took Cassie's hand. "It's nice to meet you."

Cassie peered into the other woman's face. "You look familiar. Have we met?"

Pushing her hair behind an ear, Suzanne shook her head. "I don't think so. I've just got one of those faces that looks like a million other people."

Aunt Cassie continued to study Suzanne's face, her expression not completely friendly. "Maybe so. But I could swear that I've met you somewhere. I do some traveling for my job, and I'm thinking it could have been from that. Where are you from?"

"All over." Abruptly, Suzanne turned to Ovella. "You look kind of busy right now. Maybe I should come back later. . . ."

"Not at all. We're full staff on account of Founder's Day, so everybody can get taken care of. Why don't you sit down right where Cassie was, and I'll send Darlene in to shampoo you in just a second?"

Maddie watched Suzanne, who seemed to be more nervous than a worm on a hook. Maddie hadn't known her for long, but she had already learned that Suzanne was uncomfortable around a lot of people. Clutching the towel on top of her head, she moved toward Suzanne to say something, then stopped.

Reaching out, Maddie lifted a gold heart dangling from a chain around Suzanne's neck. She'd never noticed it before. "Aunt Cassie, look. It's just like yours."

Cassie came closer, peering at the small charm. "It's identical, isn't it?" Reaching below her beauty salon cape, she pulled out a longer chain, with nine gold hearts clinging to the rope of chain. A tiny key hung in the center. She held them up to Suzanne. "Maddie's mom—my sister—gave me these."

Knoxie, who up to that moment had been stomping around like Frankenstein's monster to show off her painted toenails, pushed between her aunt and Suzanne and blurted out, "My daddy dumped Aunt Cassie to marry my mama. But she gave her all those hearts anyway."

Looking down at her little sister, Maddie suddenly realized where the term "weakest link" came from. Grabbing her firmly by the hand, Maddie led her away from the washroom. "Let's go see if Ovella can find somebody to sew your lips shut."

While Knoxie hollered like a stuck pig, Maddie yanked her out of the room. After depositing her little sister in the capable hands of one of the stylists who promised she was an expert at French braids, Maddie rushed back to Cassie and Suzanne. The way they faced each other reminded her of the old Western movies her daddy liked to watch, the two women like gunslingers eyeing each other as if they were trying to see who was faster on the trigger.

Cassie smiled, her eyes tilting upward just like

Maddie's. "I guess you can always leave it up to children to fill in the holes of family history for strangers."

Suzanne squirmed just the tiniest bit, as if she were about to be tested on homework she hadn't done. "I've never had that problem."

"I guess not. Joe said you don't like children."

Suzanne's breath left her in a little puff of air. "I never said that—really. It's just that I haven't had a lot of experience being around them, that's all."

Cassie reached over to flip the heart on Suzanne's necklace to the other side. "A life without rain is like the sun without shade." She flipped it over again and read the small inscription at the bottom. "R. Michael Jewelers. Walton." Gently, she laid it back on Suzanne's shirt. "Where did you get this?"

Suzanne touched the necklace with gentle fingers, the way Maddie touched her mama's hairbrush and perfume bottles when nobody was looking. It took Suzanne a moment to speak. "My mother gave it to me. I don't know where she got it."

Cassie tilted her head. "Randy Michael is a jeweler here in Walton. His shop is on Jackson, right behind the courthouse square. Most people don't know it's there unless you're looking for it. You might want to ask him if he remembers seeing this before. He's got a memory like an elephant."

"Yeah, I'll definitely go see him. Thanks." She reached up and tucked the charm out of sight, and although Maddie was no genius it was pretty clear that Suzanne had no intention of going to see Mr. Michael.

Maddie's towel began to slide from her head, so she held still so it wouldn't fall and call attention to the fact that her hair wasn't getting dried and styled. She wasn't ready to go—not now when Aunt Cassie was starting to look like a cat waiting outside a mouse hole.

"Joe said you needed something to wear tonight. He said we were about the same size, so I brought a few dresses and shoes. I figured they could go out dancing tonight and have a good time even if I can't." Aunt Cassie grinned, rubbing her enormous belly. "They're in my car if you want to take a look."

"Thanks—that's very generous. And I will pay you back. But it's not a date. We're just chaperoning Maddie."

Maddie's head whipped around, her towel sliding to the floor. "What?"

Suzanne looked embarrassed but didn't have to say anything because Bitsy appeared to take Maddie and Cassie into the styling room. As Aunt Cassie followed, she called back, "It's none of my business, so don't feel you need to explain. Come find me when you're all done and we'll go out to my car."

Maddie allowed her aunt to go first, and settled herself in a chair in between the two rooms so she could hear both conversations, then placed a *Seventeen* magazine in her lap to use as a prop while she eavesdropped. Her mama had taught her that listening to other people's conversations was rude, but Maddie had long since found out that it was the only way to learn anything interesting.

A petite woman of about forty with dark, curly hair and wearing a large flowered smock with the words "Ask me about scrapbooking!" appeared. With a heavy Southern accent, she introduced herself as Darlene Narpone and led Suzanne to a sink. Maddie only vaguely knew Darlene since the older woman didn't have any kids at the high school. All Maddie knew was that some sort of tragedy in Darlene's hometown in Alabama had been the reason she'd come to Walton to wash hair and start over. At least that's what Maddie had overheard the Sedgewick twins discussing at the produce counter in the Piggly Wiggly.

"You're new in town, aren't you?" Darlene asked as she began shampooing Suzanne's hair.

Suzanne nodded as if she'd already been asked that same question a million times.

"I hear you're going to the dance tonight with Joe Warner. Have you got something pretty to wear? Y'all make a cute couple."

Suzanne's eyes snapped wide, her mouth open

as though she wanted to say something but couldn't because Darlene was busy spraying water and shampoo all over her face.

Darlene didn't seem to notice and continued talking. "My Albert proposed to me at a Founder's Day Dance in our own hometown. The band was playing that song 'There's a Tear in My Beer' when he just got down on his knee in the middle of the dance floor and asked me to marry him. It was so romantic."

Spitting water off her lips, Suzanne asked, "Will you and your husband be there tonight?"

Darlene shook her head as she flipped off the spray and began to squeeze-dry Suzanne's hair with a towel. "Oh no. We never got married." With a small hitch in her voice, she continued. "My Albert was just standing on a street corner, minding his own business, when a truck full of them Porta Potties took the turn too fast and one fell out. Crushed him like a bug. Couldn't even have an open casket at the funeral." She sighed. "One of those freak accidents, I guess."

"That's terrible. I'm sorry." Suzanne tightened the towel over her shoulders, looking as though she didn't know what to say. Maddie was sure her own mama had taught her about a dozen things to say when people told you bad news, but wasn't sure any of them would have been appropriate for a man who'd been squashed to death by a Porta Potti.

Darlene stood back and proudly held out her apron. "It's a good thing I have my picture albums to remind me of him and all the happy times."

With an earnest expression on her face, Darlene pumped the lever with her foot to lower the chair. She clucked her tongue as she tilted her head from side to side and examined Suzanne's hair. "You really need color. I guess I should have asked you before I washed your hair."

Maddie turned her head toward the styling room and saw Aunt Cassie with her head bent forward as Bitsy trimmed the back, but her gaze was focused on the woman in the other room. Her eyes were narrowed as if she was thinking really hard, as if she was trying to remember where she'd seen Suzanne before.

Suzanne's eyes met Cassie's in the mirror for a quick moment before she glanced away. Looking up at Darlene, she said, "I do need color. Go ahead and dry it first if you need to, but I want more red. And I want to go shorter—shoulder-length and with bangs."

Darlene's face brightened. "Sounds like a plan." She led Suzanne to a chair on the far end of the row where Cassie was getting her hair dried and reached for the blow-dryer. "Has Joe told you about Maddie's album?"

Maddie, whose attention had begun to drift to the magazine and an article about Justin Bieber, looked up again at the mention of her name.

107

Suzanne held up her hands, her palms facing out. "Look, Joe and I aren't in a relationship where we would discuss anything but the weather. I'm just going with him tonight to help him chaperone."

As if Suzanne hadn't said anything, Darlene continued. "I was helping Harriet with it—it was going to be Maddie's graduation present. It's pictures from when Maddie was a baby up until three years ago. Harriet was keeping it at my house so Maddie wouldn't find it. You know how girls are." She leaned down and shoved the plug into an outlet at the base of the chair. Straightening, she met Suzanne's eyes in the mirror. "Joe knows it's there but hasn't asked for it. Thought you'd want to know, since Maddie will be graduating in May and all."

Before Suzanne could reply, Darlene turned on the blow-dryer, blasting away Suzanne's words. Maddie's gaze froze on the glossy photo of the pop star phenom, remembering her mother gathering up Maddie's baby photos but not telling Maddie why. As if Maddie couldn't figure it out herself. As if a stupid album would somehow make her mother's absence easier to take. She'd forgotten about it, and saw no use in remembering it now.

Maddie watched as Suzanne sighed, then sat back in the chair and closed her eyes. Her fingers gripped the arms of the chair as tightly as if they were being held in place by kudzu vines that slowly grabbed hold of you without any intention of ever letting go.

Joe's hand shook as he knotted his tie, feeling like a teenager on his first date. *It's not a date,* he reminded himself. He stood back from the mirror and picked his suit jacket off the bed. His hand hovered over the cologne bottle on his dresser, the cologne Maddie had given him for Father's Day. He moved his hand back. "It's not a date," he said out loud as he stepped away from the dresser and left the room.

The children had all gone to Cassie's for the evening. All but Maddie. Rob Campbell had already come to pick her up—in his mother's Lincoln, no less. Trying to impress Maddie's father, no doubt. But Joe couldn't help noticing the roomy backseat of the Lincoln. Nothing good ever came from backseats. Except for maybe Joey, his third child.

He paused on the top step. How was he ever going to survive four daughters? That drowning feeling came over him again—the missing, the empty ache. He wasn't supposed to be doing this all alone. That had never been part of the plan. Harriet should have been here to help Maddie pin on her corsage and offer advice instead of the stilted warnings and botched pinning he had accomplished. And then he and Harriet would have lain in bed that night, talking as they always did about their day. They would have smiled over Maddie's embarrassment and Rob's awkwardness, and the way Rob had gently touched Maddie's elbow as he'd escorted her down the steps, away from them, toward his car.

He sat down on the top stair, feeling suddenly tired. With his head in his hands, he thought of Harriet. It wasn't just the role of wife and mother that he missed. It was her and her way with things. It was how she could hide her will of steel under five feet three of soft curves and sweetness. It was how she could make everything all right in his world with the touch of her hand. Lifting his head, he listened to the silence.

He didn't believe in ghosts, or in living, breathing houses. But now, even with everything silent in the absence of children, he could hear a pulse. Not a frightening feeling but one more reassuring, like the gentle hum of the clothes dryer, calling to mind familiarity, routine, and home.

Standing, he made his way down the rest of the stairs. As he picked his keys off the hall table, he caught a glimpse of himself in the mirror. He almost expected to see Harriet standing next to him, straightening his tie or picking lint from his jacket. Instead, he faced the mirror alone, the fading sun casting shadows on the opposite wall.

With quick steps, he crossed the foyer and left the house, quieting the insistent hum as he slammed the door behind him.

CHAPTER 7

Joe turned the corner and slid up to the curb in front of the Ladue house. He shut off the ignition but sat there, fidgeting with his tie, feeling stupid. With a burst of determination, he pushed open the door and got out.

Striding up to the front door, he was surprised when it was flung open before he'd had a chance to knock.

"I'm ready," she said, brushing past him and locking the door before placing the key in an impossibly small purse. A small *red* purse. One that matched the small red *dress* that she wore. He stood there for a moment, speechless, wondering absently if this was the way people felt when Publishers Clearing House appeared with a check.

As if of their own accord, his eyes slid down the length of her body, taking in the short red dress with spaghetti straps, the long legs, and those damned flip-flops. His gaze zoomed back up to her neck and the small gold charm she wore. He tried not to notice the way it dipped into her cleavage.

She dangled a pair of red high heels from the fingers of her right hand. "I've got these, but I didn't want to put them on until I knew whether or not we were going to walk there."

Somehow he found his voice. "I, um, have the truck," he said, motioning toward the large green SUV at the curb. He recalled that the third seat had been removed to make room for Lucinda's fall plantings, and he felt his cheeks warm. *What is wrong with me? I'm thinking with the brain of a teenage boy.* But there was something about that dress, and her, that made him think of large backseats and what two people could accomplish in one.

She was busy plucking at the front of her dress. "Does this look all right? Cassie and I are about the same size, but I have a feeling I might be a little bit bigger than her in the chest area."

He swallowed thickly, noticing how the tight bodice of the dress pushed up her breasts in an admirable way. "It looks, uh, fine. Come on, let's go. Rob and Maddie left half an hour ago."

"Hang on." She dropped the high heels on the porch floor, then used his arm to lean on as she quickly changed shoes. He saw the flash of her toe ring but couldn't quite remember why he'd found it so objectionable before. It looked pretty damned good, especially with the rest of the outfit. He rubbed a hand over his face, surprised to find himself perspiring.

"Thanks. Let's go." She released him and started walking toward the truck.

He watched her move down the walk, his body awkwardly reminding him how long it had been since he'd touched a woman intimately. It was going to be a very long night.

"Is something wrong?"

She had stopped and turned to face him. "Um, yes. No. Not exactly. It's, uh, your hair. It's redder."

With a long, slender arm, she reached up to pat the intricate coiled pile on top of her head. "Yeah. I think Darlene went kinda wild with the color. It's a little obnoxious."

Joe coughed, clearing his throat again. "No. It's fine. Really." He tried not to notice the bright red curls that had fallen out of the updo and now gently brushed the pale whiteness at the back of her neck.

She allowed him to help her into the truck, and he did his best not to stare at her cleavage or the way she had to hike up the short skirt to climb up the running board. He shut her door, took a deep breath, then went to his side of the truck and climbed behind the wheel.

As he started the engine, he realized she was shivering. He turned off the air-conditioning and opened the back windows, then slid out of his jacket and handed it to her. She stared at it without taking it.

"You're shivering," he said.

"Oh. Thanks." She took the jacket and placed it over her shoulders.

Buckling his seat belt, he pulled out from the curb. "If you're still cold, you can lower your window."

"I'm not c-c-c-cold."

He glanced at her with a raised eyebrow.

She looked away, as if not wanting to meet his eyes. "I'm j-j-j-just kinda nervous. I'm not used to crowds."

He looked over again at this outwardly confident woman and wondered, not for the first time, about her past and why she would be nervous about facing a group of people as amiable as Walton's citizens.

They drove the remaining three blocks to the town square and parked in his reserved spot in front of City Hall. When he helped her down from the truck, he noticed she was clenching her teeth to keep them from moving.

He glanced over at City Hall, where the dance was being held in the assembly room, trying to catch a glimpse of Maddie and Rob. Reluctantly he turned back to Suzanne. "Would you like to take a walk first? I could tell you about some of the people who will be here tonight if that would make you feel better."

Her eyes widened, and he could see the hope in them. "But shouldn't we get inside and start chaperoning?"

He took her hand and helped her off the running board. "That can wait. We need to calm you down first. Nobody will be able to understand what you're saying with your teeth chattering like that."

She stood next to him, watching him with those clear gray eyes. "Thank you," she said softly.

He held out his arm, but she folded hers across her chest instead and followed him across the square. "Where are we going?" she called out, walking quickly to catch up to him.

Stopping, he turned toward her. "Nowhere in particular. Just walking." He slowed his pace, and she fell into step beside him. The evening was warm, and he was glad to be without his jacket, but Suzanne didn't seem to notice. He steered her away from a large crack in the sidewalk as they walked past the square and down a side street.

He spoke without looking at her, finding it easier to look at his feet than at her in that dress. "Most of Walton will be there tonight, and I know just about every single one of them. And not one of them, with the exception of Stinky Harden— and you've already met him—has a mean-spirited bone in their body."

She didn't say anything, so he continued. "They'll probably talk your ear off, but it's because they've been hearing about you and want to meet you. Well, those who haven't run into you at the store or the Dixie Diner already. Lucinda said that hiring you has been the best thing for business since her two-for-one-bra-and-panty sale."

Suzanne laughed, and the sound made him smile. "Yeah, they're certainly a nosy bunch."

"Well, a new face in Walton is always news. But you certainly won't find a nicer bunch of people."

"Is that why you want to be mayor? Because your job's easy because everybody's so nice?"

He blew out a breath of air. "It's not always easy. We have our disagreements, usually about where Walton is headed. Before I became mayor, we nearly had a civil war here over keeping Walton a town or becoming a city. It got real ugly there for a while, but it's all water under the bridge now."

Suzanne slipped the jacket off her shoulders and folded it over an arm. "Why did you want to be mayor?"

He shrugged, not really knowing the answer. "It was a challenge, I guess."

"Like raising six children on your own wasn't enough?"

"I don't really know. Maybe because I wanted to serve the people who had helped out me and my family so much when I really needed it."

She didn't skip a beat. "Or maybe because you wanted to fill up any empty hours so you didn't have time to think?"

He flinched and stopped walking. She stopped, too, looking directly at him. He was surprised that in her heels she was less than an inch shorter than him. It felt odd. "You don't know anything about me. So please don't assume that you know all the answers."

Her eyes clouded, a shadow passing behind them. "I'm sorry. I shouldn't have said that. I have this bad habit of saying what I think."

They continued to stroll, past the high school and the park, until they dead-ended across the street from the Methodist church, the sign in front now reading GOD ANSWERS KNEE-MAIL.

She looked at the sign with narrowed eyes, as if trying to translate a foreign language, and it hit him again how very different she was from anybody he'd ever known. It was there in the way she talked, the way she moved, the way she kept her arms folded in front of her as if to deflect any involvement with the outside world. It made him curious about her while at the same time it warned him to stay away. "So, why don't you like crowds?"

She plopped down on the curb and began unbuckling her shoes. "Because people don't generally like me—self-preservation on my part, I guess, because of how I was raised." She stopped speaking for a moment, keeping her head lowered, her fingers stilled on the shoe's buckle. Looking up, she narrowed her eyes at him as if daring him to listen without flinching. "I grew up in and out of foster homes. I never knew my father—my mother wasn't even sure who he was. She was an alcoholic who would sober up and win custody of me until her next disappointment in life caused a bump in her road and she started drinking again."

Fighting with the buckle on her shoe, she bent back a fingernail. Cursing softly, she sucked on her finger for a moment.

"I'm sorry," he said, feeling stupid for saying something so inadequate but at a loss for any other words.

She faced him again. "I'm not telling you this for you to be sorry for me. I'm not. I just want you to understand why I am the way I am."

Leaning over again, she focused her attention on the other buckle. "The first few times I was put in foster care, I would try really hard in the beginning to get them to like me. But it never really mattered in the end. I'd always end up leaving them and moving on. So I stopped trying." She slid off the shoes and sighed. "I think I've forgotten how to fit in."

He sat down next to her, feeling as if he'd finally reached beyond her surface layer and had touched her vulnerability. "I don't think so. Maddie thinks you were sent from heaven."

She threw back her head and laughed. "Well, she's a pretty neat girl herself. You've done a great job."

He pulled away and stared across the street at the church cemetery. The white slabs and crosses stared back at him like oversized stone flowers planted permanently in God's garden. "I had help."

As she leaned over, her long fingers played with

118

the silver toe ring. She didn't answer for a while, and at first he thought she hadn't heard him. Finally, she said, "We should be getting back. Rob could have Maddie completely undressed by now."

Standing abruptly, he offered her his hand. When she took it, he pulled her up, then let go. "Believe it or not, that's not the first thought that crossed my mind. I was actually worried about what people would be saying about us."

Brushing off the back of her dress, she eyed him speculatively. "You're joking, right?"

Even standing there barefoot, her hair coming loose from its coil, she was stunning. She apparently was unaware of the effect she had on him, because of the way she kept adjusting her bodice over her breasts without turning her back to him. Clearing his throat again, he said, "I'm serious as hell."

She began marching back in the direction they had come. "By all means, then, let's dispel that rumor."

With a frown, he followed.

The light had shifted slightly, the encroaching darkness summoning shadows across the deep lawns and front porches Suzanne and Joe passed. The smells of late summer, of mown grass and hot asphalt, hovered over them, ensuring that Suzanne would think of Walton whenever she crossed paths with those scents again.

They had walked another two blocks when she realized she was still barefoot. The gravel was beginning to hurt her feet, so she paused to put her shoes back on. She searched for a stop sign to lean on so she wouldn't have to touch Joe again. After fastening the buckles, she started walking again at a brisk pace. It took a few quick steps for him to catch up. "So, is it a husband you're running from?"

She looked at him in surprise. "What would make you say that?"

"Well, it doesn't take Sherlock Holmes to figure out that you're hiding from something. Miss Lena's taking bets on your background. Some say you're hiding from a husband; a couple of others say it's from something scandalous. Only one person says you've robbed a bank."

Staring straight ahead, she kept walking. "Who's Miss Lena?"

"An old family friend. Her mind can be fuzzy, but a lot of the time she's very lucid. You'll probably meet her tonight." He stood close to her shoulder, but she still didn't look at him. He continued. "My money's on the 'something scandalous.'"

She tried not to show any reaction, but she could feel her heart beating wildly. "Sorry to disappoint, but none of the above." She kept her face straight ahead, listening to the crunching of leaves under their feet. "And why would you care anyway?"

He tugged on her arm, making her stop to face

him. "Because of Maddie." He paused, then added, "And because people are associating you with me. I'm trying to run for mayor of this town, so if there's anything in your background that you think I should know about so I can avoid any left punches, I'd appreciate your telling me."

His hand fell from her arm, and she found herself suddenly cold. His eyes were a golden green in the fading sun, the color she'd imagined the ocean would be. Taking a deep breath, she said, "An ex-fiancé. He's a controlling bastard and I needed to hide for a while until he forgets about me. That's all."

Their gazes remained locked on each other for a long moment, and she flushed. The look in his eyes told her he didn't believe that was the whole story, and he seemed to wait, giving her another chance to tell him more. "So, what? You ran off with the engagement ring and he's angry?"

"Something like that." She jerked her head in the direction of City Hall, where small clusters of people were climbing the wide front steps. "Come on—let's find Maddie before Rob gets her into a backseat."

"That's not funny." His steps quickened.

She tried not to smile, thinking of Maddie's panic-stricken face when Suzanne had asked her if she thought Rob would kiss her. "Yeah, it is."

Taking the steps two at a time, Joe paused at the top for Suzanne to catch up. "Are you ready, then?"

She nodded quickly, the gesture more confident than the way she felt.

"I'll stay with you the whole time."

"You don't have to. I can handle it."

"I know." He gave her a long, perusing look, and she wondered if all those years of being a father had given him the ability to read minds. "Come on. Let's go find out what Maddie and Rob are up to." Taking her arm, he led her inside.

Several hours later, despite having shed her shoes, her feet and head hurt. But as Suzanne sat outside on the front steps of City Hall, watching the warm wind blow the stars around in the sky, she tried to identify another hurt that pulsed somewhere inside her.

The citizens of Walton had certainly been friendly, if not openly curious about her and "her people," whatever that meant. Several times, men from the crowd had emerged to ask her to dance, but she'd refused. And Joe had stayed at her elbow for the entire time until Stinky had cornered him with a few others in a political discussion. Seeing her chance to escape, she had turned toward the door and crossed the dance floor, through the sea of sequins, chiffons, and crushed velvets. It had seemed to her, then, that this was a re-creation of her life: watching other people dance while she walked through to the other side without stopping to take a twirl or dip. It had never seemed to matter to her before. She rested her head in her hands, her elbows propped on her drawn-up knees, and wondered what had changed.

A man escorting an elderly woman appeared on the steps behind her, and the dark, well-made suit gave her a start at first before she spotted the long sideburns on the man's face. The couple surprised her by stopping on the step next to her.

The man spoke first. "You must be Suzanne Paris. We were trying to introduce ourselves all night but couldn't get through your entourage." He chuckled as if he had said something enormously funny.

Suzanne stood, trying to reconcile this man's heavy Southern accent and thick sideburns with the elegant cut of his suit. Either he really liked the mixing of styles or somebody else shopped for him.

The man shook her hand, and she was surprised to find it callused. "I'm Ed Farrell, and this here's my mama, Miz Lena Larsen."

"I've got a nice pool of money from betting on you."

Startled, Suzanne stared at the elderly woman, recognizing the pink sweater over her shoulders. It was the woman who always sat on her front porch with a book and waved to Suzanne as she cut through her yard.

She shook Miss Lena's gloved hand as the woman stared at her with wide eyes through thick glasses. " 'Something scandalous' is winning right now, if you wanted to know."

So this must be the woman Joe had told her about. She hid a smile as she pictured Miss Lena with the sleeves of her pink sweater rolled up as she collected hard cash for her betting business.

Ed patted his mother's pink-clad shoulder. "All proceeds go to charity, in case you're wondering. If 'something scandalous' wins, then the proceeds go to the beautification of the town square. It was the only way we could keep the Baptists from throwing a conniption fit."

"Oh, I see," Suzanne said, although she really didn't. She couldn't say she'd ever met a Baptist.

More people began to spill from the doors and down the steps, pushing the three to the side. Straining his neck toward the square, Ed said, "It's fireworks time. We'd best move so we can get a spot on one of the benches."

A soft touch on her neck brought Suzanne's attention to Miss Lena. The old woman had lifted the charm on the chain and was looking at it closely. Her eyes were completely hidden by the reflection in her glasses from the outside lantern flanking the door, but Suzanne could see, from the bobbing of her head, the woman's attention moving from the charm to Suzanne's face. Abruptly, Miss Lena let the charm fall.

A popping sound was followed by the soft spritz of white light as a small rocket was launched into the night sky. Miss Lena looked up, her sweater falling to the ground. "It looks like we're in for some rain."

Suzanne bent to retrieve the sweater, then followed Miss Lena's gaze toward the heavens. Only clear light from the moon and stars shone down on them, the cloudless sky showing deep blue and coal black at the same time, as if lending its color to one's own interpretation.

She handed the sweater to Ed. He shrugged and gently took his mother by the elbow. "Come on, Mama. Let's go find a seat."

She allowed him to lead her down a few steps before stopping to see another rocket shoot into the sky, showering the night with bright reds and blues. Miss Lena looked up again and then back at Suzanne, and she smiled. "Yep. Looks like we're in for nasty weather."

Over the old woman's head, Ed sent Suzanne a look of apology, then began to lead his mother down the steps.

"Good night. It was nice meeting you."

Ed waved back and continued his slow process down the steps.

She felt Joe's presence at her side before he spoke.

"Sorry. I didn't mean to leave you alone." His voice sent something shifting inside her, like a tower of neatly stacked blocks suddenly being knocked over. It disoriented her, giving her the feeling of walking blind into a familiar room in which somebody had rearranged all the furniture. She swallowed deeply and pulled back her shoulders.

"I can handle 'alone' fine. It's the barrage of people that gets to me."

He was silent for a long moment. "Right. I'd forgotten." He looked around. "Have you seen Maddie?"

Suzanne nodded, glad to be back in neutral territory. "They were talking with a group of kids by the punch bowl about half an hour ago. They all seemed to be fully dressed."

A corner of his mouth turned up. "That's a relief." His gaze shifted to her bare feet. "I guess we'll make a Southern girl out of you before long."

"Good luck," she said, bending to retrieve her shoes.

He held out his arm. "Would you like to watch the fireworks? I've got reserved seating."

Hesitantly she placed her hand on his arm, the red high heels dangling from her other hand. "Miss Lena says it's going to rain."

Joe tilted his head back to stare at the clear sky. "That's funny. She's usually right about these things. But that sky's as clear as Reverend Beasley's conscience."

As they both looked on, the sky shattered and sparkled with brilliant golds and greens, the colors raining down on them like a gentle benediction. Joe led her down the steps and across the green, the grass soft and damp under her bare feet.

She saw couples young and old, holding hands and pointing upward, a new mother holding her infant in a swaddling of pink blanket as the Sedgewick twins, in matching sequined turbans, leaned down to kiss the baby. A group of men stood in a cluster, some smoking cigarettes, some with beer bottles, trying to pretend they weren't looking at a nearby group of chattering women. She spotted Maddie and Rob, surrounded by a group of laughing teenagers, and smiled when Maddie waved.

Suzanne looked up at the bright sky and the upturned faces of Joe and the other people, and printed the picture on her heart. She would remember this night—the soft smells of summer air and burned powder, the sounds of singing crickets competing with the pop and whir of rockets. And maybe someday, when she was far away from here, she would pull the memory out, just for a moment, before tucking it back into that dark place of old hopes and disappointments she kept hidden in her heart.

She closed her eyes, but the insides of her eyelids were imprinted with the searing flash of light, seeing the explosion of color again and again. Joe touched her hand, and she pulled back.

She felt his retreat in the slant of his body next

to hers, felt his inability to understand how all this—his world—was as foreign to her as another country.

He leaned close to her ear. "Are you all right?"

She nodded, then turned back and sighed, wishing she had her camera to record a moment in her life when she stood still, her feet anchored deeply in soft grass, and stared up at the clear summer sky while allowing herself, just this once, to dream of possibilities.

CHAPTER 8

The rain tapped out a tattoo on the tin roof of the back porch of the Ladue house, lending a rhythm to the stirrings and beating of the wooden spoons in the kitchen. Suzanne paused at the threshold, taking in the scene of the women clustered about the table, stove, and sink. Their easy talk, the intimate lilts and drawls of the voices, pulled at her and made her imagine, for a while, what it would be like to be a sister, a daughter, a niece.

Cassie sat at the table, her feet propped on a chair, frosting and decorating cupcakes with candied sprinkles. The frosting was a neon blue, a custom-made concoction of Lucinda's in honor of Sarah Frances's fourteenth birthday. It was to be a surprise, which is why all the preparations were happening in Suzanne's kitchen—a place Sarah

Frances wouldn't think of looking. Maddie had told Suzanne that Sarah Frances was getting desperate, now truly believing that her own family had forgotten her birthday since nobody had even mentioned it.

Smiling to herself, Suzanne entered the kitchen and put the grocery bag on the counter next to the refrigerator, the torn picture of Paris hanging askew on the stainless steel front. "I had to go to three different stores. Nobody knew what risotto was."

Lucinda turned from the stove, where she was frying Italian sausage for a lasagna—Sarah Frances's favorite. "I'm sorry—I should have told you where to go." She wiped her hands on her apron. "I don't know why that child likes all these foreign foods. She goes to an Italian restaurant once, and now that's all she wants to eat. She won't even eat my fried chicken anymore."

Maddie looked up from the pile of dishes she was washing, dried bright blue icing stuck to her chin. "It's because she's peculiar."

Cassie stood and moved the tray of cupcakes to the counter near the sink. Licking her thumb, she wiped Maddie's chin. "I guess it's my fault. I let her eat Italian when we were in Atlanta, so you can just blame me." Winking at Maddie, she grabbed a newspaper from the recycling bin on the floor and sat back down at the table, spreading it out in front of her. "Not that a little Italian food ever hurt anybody."

Maddie flipped off the water and stacked a mixing bowl in the dish drain. "Personally, I like sushi."

Cassie raised her eyebrow and looked at her niece but didn't say anything.

Lucinda handed Suzanne a head of garlic. "Sugar, if you wouldn't mind, could you finely mince all the cloves?"

Grateful to be useful, she grabbed a knife brought from Lucinda's well-stocked kitchen and began peeling off the layers of skin before prying out the first heart-shaped clove. The sharp scent of the garlic grabbed her, pulling her into old memories that she tried not to visit too often.

She had once lived with an Italian family, the Biancas, the first time she'd been taken away from her mother, when she was about seven years old. Her mother had disappeared before, but this was the first time anybody had cared enough to notice. This time it was her second-grade teacher who observed that Suzanne had worn the same dirty dress to school for over a week and had brought a lime and a small bottle of seltzer water for lunch.

She felt a sting at the back of her eyes, and she concentrated on the chop-chop of her knife, remembering a woman with big hands and a warm smile. The Biancas had five children, all large and dark like their parents, and the kitchen was always full of loud talk and the smell of garlic. They had taken care of her, fed her, and loved her. And then her mother had said she was better, and Suzanne had packed her bag and moved back to the dark apartment on Chicago's South Side. For a while. If she'd only known then, she would have kept her bag packed and ready.

Maybe it was her happy memories of her time spent with the Biancas that had attracted her to Anthony deSalvo. Anthony with the dark hair and darker eyes, who owned a string of Italian restaurants and always smelled faintly of basil and roasted garlic. Lifting the knife high, Suzanne sliced a clove in half.

Maddie pulled off her rubber gloves and went to sit next to Cassie, sliding a section of the newspaper over to her side. Cassie leaned back in her chair and rested her hands on her round stomach, her eyes gazing speculatively at the cupcakes before switching her attention to Suzanne.

"I still can't get over how familiar you look. I've been racking my brain, but it just won't come to me. I swear this pregnancy has left me with just half of a functioning brain. Give me a year or two, and I'll figure it out."

Maddie spoke without looking up from the newspaper. "You'd better think quick, then, because Miz Suzanne won't be here that long. She's only visiting for a little while." Her voice was hesitant, as if she was waiting for Suzanne to refute her.

Cassie snorted, making Suzanne slide her a quick glance. "I've heard that one before."

Suzanne bent her head to the mincing of garlic, not saying anything.

Lucinda opened the oven and pulled out the birthday cake and stuck in the lasagna. The heat in the kitchen had made her makeup shiny and drooping, and she wore a tissue stuck in her sleeve to gently pat her forehead and cheeks whenever she started to drip.

Suzanne scraped the minced garlic into a small bowl and began on the next clove. She listened as the women spoke about neighbors, an upcoming wedding, Cassie's gardenias and swollen ankles, and Lucinda's hair color. It was all about nothing in particular, but it was everything, too. The shared memories, familiar faces, and past histories were like a web that held them together in their intimate circle of family. Suzanne remained where she was by the counter, slicing garlic and remaining quiet. She was outside the web—had always been—and the truth pressed down on her like a tender bruise on her heart.

Maddie turned a page of the newspaper and sat up with excitement. "Hey, y'all, there's an exhibit at the High Museum in Atlanta; it says here that it's a retrospective of twentieth-century photography. They're featuring photographs by the late Gertrude Hardt." She put the paper down and looked at her aunt. "Oh, Aunt Cassie, we've got to go." She pointed her finger at the black-and-white print. "It'll be there until the end of

November. I will just die if I can't go." Turning to Suzanne, she said, "Do you want to go, too? It sounds right up your alley."

Suzanne paused the knife over the garlic, her hand shaking slightly, and remembered Anthony's appeasement gift of the collection of valuable Hardt photographs. Closing her eyes, she saw his dark face and felt the first stab of fear she had felt since coming to Walton. She tried to steady her hand. "I probably have to work. And I don't have a car."

Cassie sent her a shrewd glance. "I'm sure Aunt Lu doesn't make you work seven days a week."

Lucinda placed her hands, covered with oven mitts, on her hips. "I don't. And we could all fit in my car and have us all a little girls-only road trip."

The thought of riding in the pink convertible with these women, driving down the highway, made Suzanne giddy and it embarrassed her. She was old enough to stop wanting what she had missed as a girl growing up. Way too old.

Suzanne looked at each face—Maddie's hopeful, Lucinda's expectant, and Cassie's suspicious— and knew she had no choice. "Sure. I'll go. Sounds fun."

Maddie shouted, "Yes!" and Lucinda smiled, but Cassie was busy digging in the newspaper again. "That name Gertrude Hardt seems familiar to me. Like she'd been in the paper recently."

Suzanne turned back to the garlic, forcing the knife to move.

Cassie continued. "I thought I read something about some of her photographs missing. I wonder if they'll have any mention of it at the exhibit."

Suzanne swallowed thickly, glad to have her back to Cassie Parker's discerning eyes. It hadn't taken her long to figure out where she'd seen Cassie before. It had been about a year ago, when she was doing a photo shoot in Chicago, a national print ad for a local shoe manufacturer. Anthony's connections had given her the opportunity, and she'd been nervous about working on such a high-profile job. A major New York advertising agency had sent one of their bigwigs to oversee the shoot—Cassandra Madison.

Suzanne remembered her because she hadn't been at all what she'd expected. Although she was smart and professional, Cassandra Madison's accent and mannerisms weren't New York at all. She'd been patient and soft-spoken, and had thanked them all individually when the shoot was over. But that woman bore little physical resemblance to the vastly pregnant Cassie Parker—as she was apparently known in Walton—sitting at the kitchen table behind her. Suzanne could only hope that Cassie's pregnancy would continue to make her memory fuzzy.

A tapping sounded at the front door, followed by the screen door opening, and running feet.

Amanda burst into the kitchen and threw her arms around her aunt Cassie. With a loud, smacking kiss, she grinned up at the pregnant woman. "Can I feel the baby move again?"

With a grin, Cassie moved her hands out of the way. To the women she said, "It doesn't seem as if my abdomen really belongs to me anymore."

Slowly Amanda put her hand on the bulge of Cassie's stomach and waited. After several moments, her eyes went wide and her mouth formed a perfect O. "It moved!" she squealed. "It's a girl. I can tell."

Cassie narrowed her eyes at the little girl. "How so?"

A knowing look crossed the child's face. "Because when she moves she's all gentle. Not like my daddy and Joey and Harry. Their covers are always on the floor in the morning like they've been wrassling in their sleep."

Everyone laughed except Suzanne, who had sensed Joe's presence in the kitchen and taken the opportunity to observe him without notice. His jeans and knit golf shirt were neatly pressed, the immaculate look marred only by a naked Barbie doll stuck in his shirt pocket and a bright pink barrette nestled in the dark brown of his hair. The entire ensemble made an already overwhelmingly attractive man nearly devastating.

Amanda turned and pointed at Joe with a chubby finger while her other hand tried to hide her giggle. "I forgot to take out a barrette, Daddy!"

He moved a large hand up to his head and grabbed for the offending object, but it snagged in his hair. Being the closest, Suzanne wiped her hands on her apron and moved to stand next to Joe. Standing on her tiptoes, she unfastened the barrette, noticing the thick texture of his hair while trying to keep her breathing even. She held up the clip like a prize.

"Thank you," he said with a smile she hadn't expected.

She smiled back, swallowing hard. "I think blue would be a better color choice for you."

He laughed. "Tell my hairdresser," he said, indicating Amanda, who was still giggling.

Completely unsettled now, Suzanne handed the barrette to the little girl, then retreated to the sink and began to dry the clean dishes.

Amanda walked over to the refrigerator and stood in front of it. "You hung up my picture."

"Of course I did. It's really pretty." Suzanne slid the towel around the inside of a mixing bowl, concentrating on flaking away a drop of dried blue icing that Maddie had missed.

Amanda beamed at Suzanne. "My daddy said not to be upset if you didn't, because you probably didn't have someplace to hang your pictures when you were a little girl." She eyed the bright cupcakes on the counter with interest. "But you know, if God had a refrigerator, your pictures would be on it."

Suzanne felt every pair of eyes on her and couldn't turn around. She concentrated on chasing a piece of lint on a glass measuring cup with the dish towel. When she could speak, she said, "Thanks, Amanda. I'll try and remember that."

Lucinda touched her gently on the shoulder. The concern in the elderly woman's eyes made Suzanne's ears burn. Joe must have mentioned her childhood to these people, and it shamed her. She tried to pull away and disappear, but Lucinda held on.

"I need your help with the garlic bread. If you'll butter the loaves and sprinkle on the garlic, I'll wrap them in foil. I figure we can bake them at Joe's house so they'll be warm."

Suzanne nodded and bent over her task, not risking a glance at the others in the room. She heard the bustle of people moving about, unraveling plastic wrap to stretch over the cupcakes and cake, and chairs being slid across the wooden floor as everyone prepared to leave for the surprise party.

When she finished her task, she escaped unnoticed to her room and lay in bed, listening as the door was opened and shut several times as people and food were loaded into the two cars. It was only after she heard the engines start and drive away that she ventured downstairs again. All the dishes had been put away and the floor swept, but the voices of the women still lingered like an aroma from a favorite food. Even the rain had stopped, as if conspiring to silence the world around her. Suzanne glanced around the tiny kitchen, amazed at the engulfing emptiness. She had always hoarded her solitude, reveled in her aloneness. Restless, she ran over in her mind all she could or should be doing in the welcome peace and quiet, but her body refused to propel her forward.

Instead, she sat down at the table, the chair cold on her back, and listened to the loud silence of the kitchen, watching the light slowly fade into early evening.

"Where's Suzanne?" The words were out of Joe's mouth before he considered what the others would think about his concern.

Lucinda stepped out of Cassie's car, carrying the large lasagna pan in her gloved hands. "I thought she was with you."

Maddie tugged on her dad's elbow. "I can't believe you left her."

Joe looked at his daughter. "*I* didn't leave anybody. If she'd wanted to come, she would have joined us." He avoided Maddie's eyes.

"If you give me your keys, I'll go get her."

Ignoring the hopeful note in her voice, Joe shook his head. "No. I'd better do it. It's going to take some persuasion." He turned to Cassie. "Sarah Frances won't be back for another hour, so I'm going to leave you in charge to get everything in place. I'll be back directly."

Cassie frowned. "What if she doesn't want to come?"

"I won't force her. But I feel bad that nobody even asked."

Cassie just looked at him without saying anything. He turned around and got back in his truck.

He knocked twice before Suzanne answered. Her smile was hesitant as she stood in the doorway. "I thought you had a surprise party to go to."

"I do. And I thought you'd like to come, too."

"I've got things I need to do here."

"Like what?"

She turned her head, looking into the house, as if she was trying to find something that needed doing. "Oh, you know. Ironing, laundry. That sort of thing. It stacks up all week when I'm at work. Haven't quite adopted the turn-your-underwear-inside-out philosophy yet. But I'm working on it."

He laughed out loud, the sound encouraging a chorus of cicadas in the nearby mimosa tree. "That's good to hear." The silence stretched between them, filled with the insects' whir. Finally, Joe said, "Come on. It's free food."

She turned her head again, as if listening for the

139

silence of the empty house to call to her to stay. When she faced him again she said softly, "I'll go get my bag." Leaving the door open, he watched her run up the stairs, her feet bare, the gauze skirt brushing the backs of her calves.

He held open the truck door for her and she climbed in, depositing her backpack on her lap and clutching it as he'd seen her do before—as if it held all her worldly possessions.

She stared down at her hands as she spoke. "Are there going to be a lot of people there?"

"Not too many. You've met them all before, so they'll probably leave you alone for the most part."

She glanced up at him. "That's not what I meant. I just wanted to make sure I had enough film for pictures." She patted her bag. "I brought my camera."

He nodded, checking his rearview mirror before turning left. As he drove past the cemetery, a large poster tacked on a telephone pole caught his attention. Abruptly, he swerved his truck to the side of the road and stopped.

"What's wrong?" Suzanne's hands were protectively roped around her bag.

"That damned Stinky Harden is what's wrong."

Joe leaped out of the truck, slamming the door hard. He stood in front of the telephone pole, staring up at Stinky Harden's campaign poster slapped over one of his own. Underneath the man's smug face were the words DO YOU REALLY WANT MORE OF THE SAME? Joe turned slowly, looking at the low brick wall that bordered the cemetery, and shook his head in disgust at the line of Stinky's posters somebody had tacked up. With one smooth movement, he tore the poster off the pole.

"Why does this campaign mean so much to you?"

He turned to face Suzanne, who had climbed out of the truck. "It doesn't. It's not even about me staying mayor. It's more about making sure Stinky Harden isn't mayor."

"Why, though? You're both from here. Would it really make that much of a difference?"

He looked into her gray eyes, noticing for the first time the light smattering of freckles on the bridge of her nose and the lucidity of her pale skin. He forgot for a moment what he was talking about, until he looked down at his hands and saw the poster. "Stinky has been living in Atlanta since college, and only moved back three years ago when his sister Mary Jane sold him their parents' house before she moved down to Florida. I don't know for sure, but rumor has it that Stinky pretty much gambled away a small fortune in Atlanta and was running from creditors. It wasn't until his parents died last year and left him a huge parcel of land on the outskirts of town that he started showing any interest in town politics."

He crumpled up the poster and threw it onto the floor of the truck. He looked at her again for a long moment, considering whether or not to tell her more. Finally, he said, "I've made it my business to find out that he's had some dealings with a paper manufacturer. I also happen to know that the land he inherited is mostly prime virgin forest. I may not be the most brilliant guy in the world, but I know enough to put two and two together and figure out that giving Stinky Harden a place of authority in this town would not be a good thing."

Suzanne wrinkled her nose and stared down the road, toward a distant horizon, where a smudge of green touched the sky. "I once lived near a pulp mill. You could smell it for thirty miles in every direction. Definitely not something I would recommend for Walton."

She regarded him evenly, and he realized for the first time how nice it was not to have to lean down to look somebody in the eye. He moved to the cemetery wall, his anger growing. It was damned near desecration. "This might take a while."

"I don't mean to play devil's advocate, but doesn't he have the right to advertise?"

He bit back his first word choice. "It's the cemetery. Nobody should be advertising anything here." She retreated from him, and he regretted the coldness of his words.

Her voice was quiet, hesitant almost, as if she

142

was reluctant to intrude on his anger. "It's beautiful in there, and I'd like . . ." She paused. "I'd like to take some pictures. Would that be all right? The light is really perfect right now, but it'll only last for another ten or fifteen minutes."

He looked past her for a moment, into the sun and shadows spreading beyond the gates. "Sure. Go ahead. That'll give me time to take all of these down."

She slid her backpack from her shoulder and unzipped it to remove her camera and change the lens, then tossed the bag on the floor of the truck's front seat.

Turning, she walked through the gates of the cemetery. He stared after her, wondering when she had begun to look so good to him. He hadn't quite gotten used to her accent, but he could tell he was getting there.

Shaking his head, he bent to rip another poster off the wall. As long as he kept his thoughts to himself, everything would be fine. He found it somehow comforting that he could actually look at another woman that way, and that was enough for him. He looked into the cemetery, where Suzanne had disappeared, and knew that it would have to be enough.

Large magnolia trees hovered over the graves bordered by the brick wall, their thick branches like the protective arms of a mother. Their shiny leaves lay nestled at the bottom of the trunks and over several graves like a soft blanket, forever green and warm.

She started by taking pictures of the trees and of a creeping plant that climbed the red bricks, its long, tapered blossoms closed to the world as if waiting for something more interesting than daylight. She took pictures of clusters of graves and angels as the late-afternoon sun peered through the branches and cast long shadows across the ground and the rain puddles, like timelines of lives, with a definite beginning and end.

She changed the settings on her camera and began taking pictures of headstones, some of them so old that the dates and names had been erased by time, the records of life and death gone with the memories of those who had loved them.

Standing out in the open space in the middle was a small chained area, the center of it dominated by a sculpted angel, and smaller gravestones huddled around it like a congregation bent in prayer. Her steps faltered when she saw the familiar last name: Warner. Hesitating, she scanned the graves, almost relieved when she didn't see the one she was looking for.

She felt him behind her before she heard the crack of fallen twigs. Without turning, she asked, "Is this your family?"

Joe pointed to a cluster of markers near the

angel. "My parents are there in front, and my grandparents and great-grandparents are in the row behind them. Local legend has it that Warners have owned this plot since the beginning of time." He moved forward to swipe the raindrops off the top of the chain. "Guess I'll be in here myself someday."

She studied his profile, admiring the strong curve of his chin, the way his dark hair swept over his forehead, and wondered, just for a moment, what it would be like to have roots so deep in a place that you could choose to be buried with your ancestors. It was an odd thought, sort of like her dreams where she'd be picking out an apartment in Paris to live in—pipe dreams never meant to happen but that she was reluctant to let go of. "You don't think you'll ever move away and want to be buried someplace else?"

He looked at her with a questioning expression. "Why would I want to do that?"

She shifted her feet uneasily, no longer sure she knew the answer to that. "For something different. For a change."

Joe stared off into the sweeping pinks and purples of the distant sunset. "My sister moved to Dallas with her husband when she got married twenty years ago, and she's been trying to find a way to move back ever since. When people ask her where she's from, she'll still say Walton." His eyes were troubled when he looked back at her. "I guess that's hard for you to understand."

Hurt, she turned away from him, studying a nearby gravestone to hide her feelings. "Yeah, I guess it is." Then, to change the conversation, she asked, "Does your sister have any children?"

"Three. Two boys and a girl."

"Only three?" She hadn't meant the words to come out sounding like a challenge.

Joe bent to pull a weed that had crept up alongside an ancient marker. He rubbed his hand over the crumbling inscription as he straightened. "It was never a competition. They just sort of . . . happened."

"But why so many?" She squinted at him in the bright glow of the twilight sun, the light turning his eyes to gold, and knew that he wasn't seeing her.

"They were all wanted." He looked away from her, hiding his face. "Every one of them."

"I'm sorry." She shifted uncomfortably, wondering why she always had problems with the right words. "That's not what I meant. It's only—well, most of the children I ever knew growing up weren't the wanted kind."

His face was closed as he scrutinized her. "I guess you and I are pretty different, then."

She gave him a sharp look, wondering why his words sounded like an explanation—or a dismissal. Maybe they were both. Sticking the lens cover on her camera, she turned and began walking back toward the entrance. She saw it then and wanted to pretend she hadn't, but stopped anyway.

Nestled under a giant magnolia against the brick wall was a row of three gravestones, the one in the middle decorated with a miniature pine tree and small golden heart ornaments, so much like the one on her own necklace. She read the dates on the small marker and for the first time felt her own stab of grief. She realized then that the image she'd had of Harriet had been of an older woman, a woman who had harvested years of living, loving, and family. But Harriet had been Suzanne's age when she died, and the utter emptiness of her own life seemed to reach out, grab hold, and swallow her.

Joe crouched and touched the stone, his fingers lingering on the letters of the name. "Cassie wanted her here, with their parents."

Suzanne nodded, then bent next to him. She felt his warmth, and something else, too. It was as if the memories of his dead wife were strong enough to create a palpable presence. He didn't move away but looked at her, his face unguarded, and at that moment she felt his sadness. Her heart shifted, making her fall back on her heels, and she felt the bond of a shared burden for the first time in her life.

Something her mother had once told her, something about the kindness of strangers, tugged at her, and she leaned down, too, to touch the stone and the letters of the name of the woman she would never meet but whom she felt as if she'd known all her life. She smelled the leaf mold and the damp earth and felt a part of her heart opening.

Not quite knowing where the words came from, she said, "I know that Harriet was working on an album of Maddie's life, to give to her for graduation. I could finish it, if you want me to." The words tied her down to this place, to this man next to her, and to the woman who slept beneath the arms of the magnolia. It wasn't for forever, but it was more than she had ever expected.

Joe looked at her for a long moment, as if considering his words. Then he said simply, "Thank you."

At his brief touch on her elbow, they stood and walked out of the cemetery together. A strong breeze gathered the loose raindrops and the giant magnolia's leaves and shook them together in a gentle applause.

CHAPTER 9

Suzanne tried to act undaunted when they drove up to a neat two-story brick house, the lawn littered with the accessories of childhood: roller skates, scooters, an assortment of balls, and a pitch-back net. The trim on the house was freshly painted, the grass clipped short. The flower beds were empty except for weeds, sparsely laid pine straw, and two stray golf balls. It looked exactly how Suzanne thought it would.

"Where is everybody?" Suzanne strained her neck as she unclipped her seat belt, looking for cars.

"They either walked or they parked their cars on neighboring streets. I didn't want to risk giving it away this late in the game. Sarah Frances really has no idea."

He came over to her side of the car to help her out—something she had at first been surprised by and now appreciated. She liked the feel of her hand in his and the way he helped her step over puddles near the curb. There was something about a gentleman with manners that warmed her at the core. Something even Anthony had never seemed to manage.

They left the car and walked up the brick steps to the front door. As Joe held open the screen door for her, he said, "I guess it'll come as no bolt from the blue to know that this party was all Maddie's idea. She loves to surprise people—make them do a double take. Takes after her aunt Cassie."

Suzanne thought of the stalwart Cassie, expectant mother and advertising executive. "Cassie?"

"Yep. I could tell you stories—"

They were interrupted by about fifty voices shouting, "Surprise!"

149

Suzanne jumped back, bumping into Joe. Instead of pushing her aside, he held on to her, his hands on her upper arms.

"Hey, y'all. Don't get all excited—it's just us."

Curious faces peered over the sofa and chairs, a few from inside the closet. Suzanne recognized most of the adults, but the smattering of younger people—presumably Sarah Frances's friends—were strangers. She felt only a tinge of her old nervousness and smiled at the familiar faces.

Joe continued to hold on to her as he moved her through the small foyer to the back of the house. His touch made her self-conscious but glad for it, as though he was letting her know that he was there and wasn't going to leave her alone. They passed through the kitchen, where the table and counters were loaded with food, and into the family room, where Miss Lena seemed to be holding court in a large stuffed chair.

Suzanne glanced around, noticing all the framed photographs on every available surface. The furniture was comfortable, with several antique pieces interspersed with more modern items. It was a family room in every sense of the word, complete with toy box and a tiny pair of sneakers tucked under a chair where somebody had forgotten to put them away.

Ed Farrell stood behind Miss Lena, shaking his head as she entered into an animated discussion with the Sedgewick twins. As she got closer,

Suzanne could hear that they were taking bets on something. Thinking it was about her, she started to move away but was called back by Miss Lena.

"Miss Paris, aren't you going to take a chance? We're betting on Cassie's baby and whether it's a boy or girl. Girl's winning right now, but it's not a sure thing. Proceeds go to buying a new sign for Reverend Beasley at the Methodist church. We're going to get him a lit one so that people can read his messages better at night."

One of the Sedgewick twins—Suzanne still couldn't tell them apart—spoke, the twenty or so plastic bangle bracelets on her arm clicking together as she gestured while she talked. "She's carrying it so low it's got to be a boy. I bought twenty tickets."

Her sister elbowed her in the arm. "It is most definitely a little girl. Cassie's round all over, and you know that always means a girl. Just look at her ankles! It looks like they're about to give birth, too."

The subject of their discussion, upon hearing her name, glanced over at them with narrowed eyes but was restrained from joining the conversation by Sam, who raised a beer bottle in greeting to Suzanne and Joe.

Miss Lena glared up at the twins from her chair. "Now, hush, you two. Neither one of you would know anything about carrying or having babies. I'll loan you *Wicked Tender Love* when I'm done

151

reading it, and maybe you'll learn something."

Hiding a smile, Suzanne asked, "What do I get if my guess is right?"

Miss Lena beamed. "One of Mrs. Crandall's award-winning lemon meringue pies. You'll love it. Your mama certainly did. Ate an entire one all by herself."

Suzanne froze and looked at Ed, whose quizzical expression must have matched her own. Leaning over the back of the chair, he said, "Mama, did you take your medicine today?"

Taking an envelope stuffed with money from her purse at her feet, Miss Lena answered, "Every morning, just like Dr. Parker tells me, son." She looked at Suzanne. "The boy needs to get married and settled down so he'll have somebody else to fuss over. You're single, aren't you?"

Suzanne couldn't see whose face was more red—hers or Ed's. Before she could respond, one of the Sedgewick sisters said, "She's already spoken for," and sent a meaningful glance in Joe's direction.

Clearing his throat, Joe began leading Suzanne away. "We need to confer on our bet. We'll catch you later." Glancing at his watch, he shouted, "It's time. Everybody get in your places."

As soon as the words were out of his mouth, the crunch of tires on gravel sounded out on the driveway. Unceremoniously pulling on Suzanne's arm, Joe dragged them both to the front parlor, near the door and behind the sofa, underneath the sofa table. Suzanne bumped her head, knocking over a frame, which fell in her lap. She looked down at it and stopped breathing for a moment. It was a studio picture of the entire Warner family, minus baby Harry.

The children were all smiling except for Knoxie, who was frowning at her sister Sarah Frances. Joe leaned on the arm of the chair, with Amanda in his lap, while Maddie had an arm loosely draped around his shoulders. But the entire focus of the picture was the petite blond woman in a chair in the middle—the nucleus of the family. The woman glowed with contentment and ease with her life, and Suzanne felt a momentary stab of jealousy. She could never put into words what she thought Joe was thinking whenever he looked at her, but this picture would be as good a definition as any. She and Harriet Warner were worlds apart in not only looks, but also their place on the earth—a monarch butterfly and a luna moth. Each had been dropped into lives that were polar opposites, traveling along different longitude lines destined never to intersect.

Looking up, she caught Joe watching her. Wordlessly, she replaced the frame on the table and hunched back down underneath it.

The front doorknob rattled before the door opened. There was a moment of silence before everybody jumped out and yelled, "Happy birthday!" A deadly silence ensued before Sarah Frances burst into tears and ran up the stairs without a glance behind her.

Joe looked around the room, his face stricken. "Well, that was a resounding success."

He headed toward the stairs before Cassie stopped him. "It's a female hormone thing, Joe. Better leave this up to the women." Waddling with as much grace as a hippopotamus trying to exit a swimming pool, Cassie made her slow ascent.

People gravitated back to the kitchen and the food as Sam came over and handed Joe a beer. "You're going to need this." He shook his head, his eyes following his wife's laborious process up the stairs. "Did I mention I was wanting a boy?"

Joe took the beer, and they clinked the bottles together as Maddie joined them. "Nothing's wrong with girls, Uncle Sam. Just Sarah Frances. She's retarded."

Joe gave her a warning look that she ignored. Smiling brightly at her father, she said, "Can I have a beer?"

"Last time I checked, you were only seventeen. If my math is right, that would mean you have about four years to go before you can drink. And that's about a decade before you're allowed to date." Ignoring her scowl, he turned to Suzanne. "Can I get you something to drink?"

"Just a Coke, please."

"What kind?"

She stared at him with a questioning look, wondering if Southerners really did have their own language. "A Coke."

"We've got orange, root beer, cherry, Diet Coke, regular, and Mountain Dew. Which kind do you want?"

"A Coke." She smiled, defying him to defend something as backward as giving every soft drink in the world the same brand name.

Raising an eyebrow, he left. Suzanne dug in her backpack for her Hasselblad and pulled it out. Handing it to Maddie, she said, "Here. You can use this to take pictures of the party. Just take candid ones and then we'll develop them and examine them closely for strengths and weaknesses."

As if touching something rare and precious, Maddie took the camera. "You're going to let me use your camera?"

Suzanne shrugged. "I figure there's not a lot you don't know about when it comes to using one, so you might as well. Then I can use both hands to eat."

"Which lens are you using?"

"The CB one-sixty. It has real sensitive focusing, so you don't need to manipulate it that much. Oh, and here's the flash attachment if you need it. Now go see what you can do."

Smiling broadly, Maddie said, "I will. Just you wait."

To Suzanne's amazement, Maddie headed up the stairs in the direction Cassie and Sarah Frances had gone.

"This will be interesting."

Forgetting that Sam was standing there, she was startled at his voice. "Yeah, well, I guess it's a sister thing. Always wanting to see the worst of each other."

Joe approached with a Coke for Suzanne and overheard her remark. "It's amazing, really. The girls fight like cats. But when they need each other, they circle around the wounded, armed to the teeth and ready to defend. You have to see it to believe it."

Sam took a swig from his beer. "Sort of like Cassie and Harriet were."

Joe shook his head slowly and stared down at his bottle. "Ain't that the truth!"

Before she could tell herself to keep her mouth shut, Suzanne said, "What did Knoxie mean about you dumping Cassie to marry Harriet? That must have gone over well."

Sam laughed, choking on his beer, while Joe looked at her with a strangled expression. "Well, it wasn't that way exactly." He rubbed his hand over his eyes. "We were all young and stupid, and certainly in no way mature enough to tell Cassie I wanted to marry Harriet instead of her. I even went to an engagement party with Cassie the day before Harriet and I eloped." He shook his head.

"I can't say I handled it the best way possible, but it worked out in the end."

Suzanne cradled her Coke can between her hands, feeling the cold condensation, and tried to picture the sweet-faced Harriet running off with her sister's fiancé. She couldn't. Nor could she picture Cassie and Joe together. "I'm glad you think so. But I heard that it sent Cassie into exile to New York for fifteen years. Must have been a lot harder for her to see that it was for the best."

Joe gave her a quelling look and was thankfully interrupted by Sam. "Suzanne, I wanted to let you know that I'm having an outdoor Jacuzzi delivered sometime tomorrow afternoon. Just didn't want you to be surprised when all the workmen showed up to deliver and install it." He sent her an innocent grin. "And you two are more than welcome to use it whenever you want."

Suzanne flushed as her and Joe's words tripped all over themselves, both making excuses why that would never happen, while Sam just nodded and smiled as if they were talking about what they had for lunch.

Spotting the approach of Mrs. Crandall, flanked by a Sedgewick twin on each side, Joe tugged on Suzanne's arm. "Come on, Lucinda made some of her fried chicken and famous pecan pie. Let's go get some plates."

Sam moved in front of them. "I'll run inter-ference."

With a big smile, he turned to face the elderly ladies as Joe and Suzanne made their escape to the small kitchen at the back of the house. Bright yellow chintz curtains hung at the windows, and matching yellow gingham seat covers sat on each chair. Lined up at the sink were six plastic cups, each with an initial on it, and the refrigerator wore a patchwork of brightly colored art projects. But the single object in the kitchen that marked ownership like a signature was a large ceramic plate hung over the sliding glass door. On it were five sets of handprints, each dipped in a different color of paint, ringing the outside rim. In the middle were the words "Happy Mother's Day."

It was as if Suzanne had stepped onto another planet. She could see Harriet Warner preparing meals, helping with homework, and feeding babies in the wooden high chair in the corner. Suzanne shrugged, as if being forced to wear a coat that didn't fit, and turned away.

She recognized the table from Maddie's photograph, but now every inch of its surface was covered with plates of food. She saw the lasagna and the garlic bread next to the fried chicken and collard greens, and her stomach rumbled. Joe handed her a paper plate, and she began to fill it.

Ed Farrell was already at the table, holding two heaping plates of food. He smiled at her as he took another huge helping of lasagna and dumped it on top of the fried okra on his plate. "I bet you never saw anything so good in your life, now, have you?"

"I certainly haven't. Nothing so eclectic anyway." She moved down the table and took a piece of corn bread. Looking up, she saw Cassie enter with her arm around a disgruntled Sarah Frances. Maddie poked her head between the two of them and said something that made her sister and aunt turn around and laugh. A flash erupted as Maddie snapped the picture.

Ed reached over and dumped a spoonful of something on Suzanne's plate. She looked up, surprised.

He winked. "It's my mama's fried green tomatoes. She doesn't cook so much anymore, but I used her recipe. Let me know what you think."

"Oh. Thanks. I will." She looked down at what looked like unripened tomatoes covered in a thick batter. It actually looked pretty good.

"And try some of these, too." Another spoonful of what appeared to be beans was placed on her plate.

She looked at them quizzically. "What are those?"

He tucked his chin into his neck as if he were being confronted by an alien with three heads. "You're not from around here, are you? Those are black-eyed peas cooked in fatback. It sure is good." He made the last word two syllables.

Frowning down at her plate, she said, "I'll make sure I try them, too."

159

Leaning down to whisper in her ear, Joe said, "See? I told you we would make a Southerner out of you."

Reaching across the table to grab a pat of butter, she said, "I didn't say I liked them yet." Juggling her Coke in one hand and her plate in the other, she followed Joe out the sliding glass door and into the soft summer night, whose edges were starting to wear a cool bite of autumn.

Tables had been set out, and several people were already milling about, chatting and eating. It was almost completely dark now, and children raced around the patio and the yard filled with tall pines and magnolias, chasing down fireflies. Maddie stood unnoticed among them, aiming Suzanne's camera and taking pictures.

They sat at the redwood picnic table, where Lucinda and Sheriff Hank Adams had already claimed spots. Suzanne noticed how their heads were bent together, and how they quickly sat up when they spotted Joe and Suzanne and greeted the newcomers.

Suzanne hesitated before placing her plate as far away from Sheriff Adams as possible, then quietly picked up her fork and began eating, concentrating on her food but not really tasting it, and not daring to look up or say anything that might bring attention to herself.

Joe's eight-year-old son, Joey, ran up to the table

and tapped Suzanne on the arm. "My plane's broke. Can you fix it?"

She stared as if she'd just been handed a large insect. Joe stood to take it, but she raised her hand and took the plane. After examining it for a while she said, "Here, hold this wing. Now, see the slot here? Slide it in—no, wait—make sure the wings are facing the right direction, like this. See? Now stick them in like that."

The wing slid home and Joey beamed. "Thanks."

"You're very welcome."

She turned back to her food, but her gaze caught Joe's for a brief moment before she focused her attention on her plate again.

"How's crime in Walton, Hank?"

The sheriff looked up as if noticing Joe for the first time. "Same as always, Mayor. Mostly vandalism over at the high school. And assorted bra-and-panty sets showing up on Lady Liberty in the square." He took a bite of pecan pie and closed his eyes in rapture before winking at Lucinda. It appeared the older woman might actually be blushing. "I know I only have to come to your house to get to the bottom of it when that happens."

Joe narrowed his eyes. "Now, come on, Hank. Maddie isn't responsible for that every time it happens."

Hank lowered a glance at him without saying anything, before taking another bite of pecan pie.

"Glad she's continuing the family tradition. Guess it's too hard now for Cassie to be climbing the statue in her condition. Plus, she's now a respectable married lady and all."

Suzanne heard Joe laughing, but her attention had been distracted by the scent of something so intoxicating she had to find out what it was. Leaving her plate and can on the table, she left Joe and the others to their conversation and went in search of the scent. Considering that all the flower beds were bare, it shouldn't be too hard to find a single bloom.

She crossed the lawn where tiki torches had been set out to illuminate a stone path and found herself standing next to the house by the chimney, where vines holding flat, white trumpet-shaped flowers clung to the red bricks. The scent was nearly overwhelming this close and she couldn't resist the urge to bury her face in one of the fragrant blooms.

"It was Harriet's favorite flower."

She started at the sound of Joe's voice, then held out one of the blooms, nearly six inches across. "What's this called?"

His voice sounded tight. "It's a moonflower."

"What a lovely name. It looks like a giant starfish with its five points. I wonder why they didn't call them star flowers."

He stood very close, but she didn't step back. She was done with not standing her ground;

stepping back seemed to give people the invitation to walk right over you.

"Because they only bloom at night. Nobody knows why, although they think a special moth is needed for pollination."

She looked down at the enormous bloom, feeling almost drugged by the heavy scent. "I hope they don't find out why. I like not knowing everything. Keeps life interesting."

He was silent for a moment as they both listened to the distant sound of people talking and children shouting. A warm breeze stirred the vine, shaking loose the remaining rain droplets. "Sometimes. And sometimes it works to keep people away, doesn't it?"

She glanced up, her mouth half-open with indignation, but she didn't have time to argue because Joe bent down then and pressed his lips against hers. She wanted to pull away, but the moonflowers held her spellbound, and his lips tasted of pecans and warm skin. And need. A need so deep she could feel it as she began to kiss him back.

Her hands left the moonflowers and reached around him, and he pulled her to him, neither one of them aware anymore of who they were, or where they were, or why what they were doing was so impossibly wrong.

Joe pulled back, his expression that of a man who'd just stepped out of his front door and found himself in another city instead of his front lawn. They stared at each other for a long moment, both of them breathing heavily as if they'd just run around the block.

"That can't happen again," he said as if he really believed it.

She nodded, and then tried to pretend that they both weren't thinking of when it could.

The flash from a camera startled them both momentarily, the brightness of it sealing the image of each other's expression of surprise. Suzanne spotted Maddie and the camera at the same time she heard Sarah Frances. "Daddy, it's time to sing 'Happy Birthday'. . . ." Her voice trailed off as the teen turned the corner of the house and stopped in front of Suzanne and Joe, their arms still around each other.

As if Suzanne were suddenly electrically charged, Joe jumped away from her and began walking toward Sarah Frances, who immediately ran in the opposite direction. Without a backward glance, he ran after his daughter, calling her name.

Maddie shrugged. "Sorry."

Suzanne stood with her fingertips to her lips, wondering what had just happened. Staring blankly at Maddie, she said, "I've got to go now." She began walking away before stopping and fishing something out of the pocket of her long skirt. "This is for Sarah Frances. You can tell her it's from you, if you like."

She dumped the small wrapped box in Maddie's hand, then left without waiting for Maddie to respond. She ran all the way home, seeking escape in her sparsely furnished room. She stripped off her clothes, barely pausing long enough to brush her teeth before throwing herself on the bed. She lay there for a long time, staring up at the ceiling and remembering how it had felt to belong to somebody, if just for a moment, and smelling the scent of the moonflower long after she'd drifted off to sleep.

Maddie clutched the small wrapped box in her hand looking for Sarah Frances until the wrapping paper began to get soft in the heat. She was about to give up before she recalled the place where she and Sarah Frances always ended up when the whole world seemed to be in cahoots against them. It was the one thing they had in common.

Maddie took shortcuts through backyards and driveways to her aunt Cassie's house, the house her mama and aunt had grown up in, the house with the gazebo in the back where her daddy had proposed to both sisters—although at two different times.

She heard Sarah Frances's sniffling before she reached the gazebo, but kept the camera hanging around her neck. As tempting as capturing on film her sister's suffering was, dealing with the fallout wouldn't be worth it. Besides, whether or not they liked it, they were a team, connected by the unimaginable. Although they had two other sisters, only Maddie and Sarah Frances had been old enough to really remember their mother, remember the way she smelled and what her voice sounded like. Old enough to miss more than just the memory of her.

"Go away," Sarah Frances said through sobs.

Ignoring her, Maddie climbed the steps and sat on an adjacent bench. "I'm not going to take a picture if that's what you're worried about."

She felt her sister's stare in the darkened gazebo, the blue light of the moon its only illumination. Fireflies blinked on and off around them, reminding Maddie of happier summers: summers before her world had been permanently upended.

"I want you to rip out the film and burn it." Sarah Frances hiccupped loudly.

Maddie rested her hands on the camera, feeling protective. "I can't do that. And it wouldn't change anything anyway."

Sarah Frances scooted over to the far side of her bench as if to create as much space as possible between her and Maddie. "You're on her side, aren't you? You think that . . . that . . . *woman* with the fake hair and ugly clothes can just come in here and take over and make us all forget Mama. She doesn't even like kids!"

Maddie wasn't sure what to say at first. Yeah,

she suspected that her daddy and Suzanne had taken a real shine to each other, but it had never occurred to her that Suzanne might want to take over anything, much less make them forget about their mother. She could even believe that Suzanne didn't really have any plans at all except for moving on eventually. And maybe that momentum was something they all could use.

"You should get to know her better before you start jumping to conclusions. She's actually kinda nice." She remembered the wrapped box in her now very sweaty hands. "This is a birthday present for you from Suzanne." She held up her hand.

Instead of taking it from Maddie, Sarah Frances crossed her arms over her chest and turned away. "I don't want her blood money."

Maddie rolled her eyes in the darkness, wondering if Sarah Frances needed to take a break from drama classes or Sunday school. Or maybe both. Maddie placed the box on the bench next to her, figuring she'd leave it in Sarah Frances's room. Then her sister could decide what she wanted to do with it.

"Mama's gone," Maddie said quietly, feeling that hollowed-out place in the center of her chest and knowing that Sarah Frances had a matching one. "But Daddy's not. And I think Mama would have wanted him to be happy."

Sarah Frances jerked to a stand. "We make him

happy, and that should be enough. She needs to go away and leave us alone. The sooner the better."

Maddie stood, too, the camera banging against her chest. "But what happens when we've all grown up and moved out of the house? Who will sit on the porch with him then?"

She felt more than saw her sister fumbling around for words. "You don't understand," she shouted before bounding down the steps of the gazebo and racing across the lawn in the moonlight.

But Maddie had seen her sister's eyes reflected by the moon, seen the understanding that she herself was still struggling with: the understanding that their father was still a man, and that it was still possible to be lonely in a roomful of people.

She picked up the present from the bench and followed her sister at a slower pace, pausing briefly beside the large magnolia in the front yard to watch the fireflies. She breathed in the scent of the boxwoods and the summer grass, remembering a summer from a million years ago when her mother had given them jars to collect fireflies, and Maddie had raced around the yard as if collecting as many as she could was the most important thing in the world.

Sometimes, when she was feeling much older than her seventeen years, Maddie remembered that night; remembered her mother and father and sisters and brother the way they'd once been, and a world that seemed grounded and full of possibilities. It was a place she wanted to find again, even if it no longer existed for her in Walton.

She walked the rest of the way home, her path marked by the light of the moon, and imagined her mother walking beside her, guiding the way.

Suzanne resisted the urge to smile as she stood across the counter at Lucinda's Lingerie, helping the editor in chief of the *Walton Sentinel*, Hal Newcomb, pick out a birthday present for his wife, Sugar. When he'd first said her name, images of a petite woman with delicate tastes had crossed Suzanne's mind. But when the diminutive Mr. Newcomb had asked for something in a size eighteen, the image escaped her completely.

Spread on the counter between them now was a black chiffon negligee, its voluminous pleats disguising the material's complete transparency.

"I'll take it," he said.

She wrapped it with extra tissue and watched as an extremely satisfied customer left the store. Lucinda said that sales had nearly doubled since she'd hired Suzanne. At first, it was from sheer curiosity, and then it was as if the townspeople instinctively trusted her not to divulge the secrets of the quiet little purchases they made at the lingerie store.

As she smoothed the stacks of tissue and reshelved items discarded by Mr. Newcomb, the bell chimed over the door, and Suzanne glanced up with a smile on her face.

Stinky Harden stood inside the shop, his white fedora held over his considerable belly, looking like an escaped Good Humor man with his blue-and-white-striped seersucker suit. He smiled like a frog at a fly strip. "Well, hello there, Miss Paris. What a shame you have to be working inside on a day like today. Perhaps after work you'd like to go for a walk with me and enjoy the emerging fall foliage."

Suzanne swallowed hard, his presence sending her warning signals even as he stood there in his ridiculous suit and smiled at her. "Thanks, but I'm meeting Maddie Warner at the school after work, to develop pictures in the darkroom."

He knitted his brows together. "Did you get permission for that?"

She wiped her sweaty palms against the sides of her skirt. "Yes, of course. Maddie asked Mr. Tener, and he said fine since he'd be there anyway." Suzanne wondered why she was bothering to explain this to Stinky. Grabbing a box of packaged panty hose, she moved to a far wall to begin restocking, hoping he'd see it as a sign of dismissal.

"Is Lucinda in?"

Without turning around, she shook her head.

"No. Joe had a school board meeting, so she's watching the little ones."

At the sound of the CLOSED sign being flipped in the window, she jerked upright. "What are you doing?"

He slid the dead bolt home before walking toward her.

She held the box of panty hose in front of her in a defensive gesture. "Don't come any closer."

He stopped in the middle of the shop, not close enough for him to touch her but close enough that she could smell his heavy aftershave. "Now, don't get in a snit; I'm not going to hurt you. I just want to talk to you in private. Since you're too busy to come for a walk, I figured this was the best time for it."

She started to reach for the phone on the wall, to call for help, but stopped when he pulled out a folded newspaper page and she recognized it as one she had left at the Dixie Diner. The article regarding the Hardt exhibit was on top.

"I'm not going to beat around the bush. We both know you're hiding something. Nobody comes from nowhere. And nobody just drops into Walton without a reason. So, seeing as how you're getting real cozy with the current mayor, it's in the best interests of this town to know what kind of person he's consorting with."

He placed the newspaper on the counter. "I've gone over this again and again, and I still can't figure out what article you found so important. Perhaps you'd like to enlighten me?"

With a great deal of effort, Suzanne shrugged and went back to shelving panty hose. "I read the paper every day and clip out articles I find interesting. There's no way I can remember which one caught my interest."

He folded his arms over his chest. "Uh-huh." He picked up the paper again. "There's an article in here about defective tires, and another on the Miss Monroe County Beauty Pageant. Not sure if either one of those would interest you. Then there's something about some missing photographs and the proposed hike in property taxes. . . ." He peered over the newspaper before looking back down at it. "And an article about the new exhibit at the High Museum."

Very carefully his pudgy fingers folded up the newspaper again before tucking it under his arm. "I've also made it my civic duty to follow up on your employment records. Seems Lucinda hasn't filed a W-9 for you yet. Can you think of why she'd be holding back on that?"

Suzanne bent over the box in front of her and lifted out an armful of panty hose packages. "You'll have to ask Lucinda. I just work here."

"But you did fill one out."

Moving a footstool in front of her with her foot, she stood on it and reached for the highest shelf to put away the plus sizes. "I don't recall."

"Uh-huh." He took a step closer to her. "I don't know what your game is, Miss Paris, but I'm onto you. You might want to mention to your boyfriend that he should be more careful of the company he keeps. Elections have been lost for less."

He turned to leave but paused at the door and, with a big smile, tipped his hat. "Have a nice day, you hear?" He flipped the sign to OPEN, then let the door slam behind him.

Before her knees buckled, Suzanne sat down on the footstool. She placed her head in her hands to keep them from shaking and tried to ignore the nausea boiling up from her stomach.

Leave now! her head seemed to shout. Leaving and making a change was what she was best at. But then she remembered the scent of the moonflowers and the taste of Joe's lips on hers. And she thought of Maddie and her beautiful pictures and shut her eyes. *Not yet,* her heart seemed to reply.

She sat on the footstool for a long time, wondering just when it had happened that things had changed without her even noticing.

CHAPTER 10

Suzanne held her backpack in front of her, clutching it tightly, as she approached Joe's house. She hadn't seen him since he'd kissed her. It had been a mutual avoidance, and this meeting wouldn't be easy. Except for a favor to Lucinda, nothing could have coerced her into a three-mile radius of Joe or his house.

She spotted Joe's truck in the driveway, with a bucket and running hose next to it. Her heart constricted when she realized somebody was standing behind it and, by the sound of the grunts, scrubbing hard.

Maddie's head stuck up over the back of the truck, and Suzanne tried to hide her sigh of relief. "Hey, Miss Paris." Her voice was flat, definitely not that of a happy child.

"Hi, Maddie. I thought you had a photography club meeting."

"I do, and I'm going to be late."

"So why are you washing the car?"

Maddie glowered at Suzanne. "Because Daddy said I need to wash this off before he could go to baseball practice. He didn't want anybody to see it."

Flush with indignation for this father who made his child wash his car so he wouldn't look bad, Suzanne leaned over to get a look at the bumper and then stopped, holding her breath so she wouldn't laugh.

Thoroughly sodden but still tenaciously clinging to the back bumper of the SUV were two bumper stickers that hadn't been there before. One read KEEP HONKING. I'M RELOADING and the other FISH FEAR ME. WOMEN WANT ME.

Keeping a straight face, Suzanne said, "I take it these were your idea."

With a stiff plastic sponge, Maddie used both hands to scrub side to side over the stickers. "Yeah. I was mad at him."

Suzanne dropped her bag and reached into the bucket to pluck out another sponge. She began rubbing it across the "reloading" sticker, figuring it to be the more offensive of the two for a town's mayor to be sporting on his bumper. "Why were you mad?"

Maddie lifted her shoulder to scratch a soap bubble off her chin. "Rob and a bunch of kids from school are all driving into Atlanta Friday night, and Daddy said I couldn't go."

"I see." Suzanne continued to scrub without looking at Maddie. Unfortunately, she could see— but both points of view. What those two needed was a referee, and she wasn't about to volunteer for the job.

"Why are you here? I thought you and Daddy weren't speaking since he kissed you."

Suzanne felt her cheeks flush but concentrated on rubbing off the sticker. "Lucinda has a date with Sheriff Adams, so she asked me if I wouldn't mind babysitting tonight since both you and your dad are going out." She paused and looked at the young girl. "And how is it that the whole town knows about that kiss?"

Maddie shrugged without missing a beat in her

scrubbing. "Mrs. Thompkins saw you, too. She's better than a newspaper headline."

Leaning back on her heels, Suzanne said, "I figured as much. The lingerie shop has been flooded with customers all week, dropping hints about what a wonderful guy your dad is. I don't vote, so I couldn't figure it out at first."

"People have been trying to set Daddy up since Mama died. I've learned that it's not disrespect to Mama—it's just that people here have known Daddy all his life, and they don't want him to be alone."

"And how do you feel about it?"

The last remnant of torn sticker came off with the sponge, and Maddie tossed it in the bucket, then went to the side of the house to turn off the hose. "I figure it's none of my business. I'm not going to be sticking around here long enough for it to matter, so Daddy can kiss you as much as he likes."

Suzanne stood, shocked to hear her own thoughts echoed in Maddie's words. "What do you mean?"

"I'm seventeen. I'll be heading for college next year. Heck, Sarah Frances and Joey are already fighting over my room. I'm as good as gone. I kind of think you're doing me a favor by distracting him."

Suzanne studied Maddie, seeing past the false bravado into the face of a worried and insecure child. "I'm sure there'll always be a place for you here. It's not like this stops being home when you leave."

Maddie looked at her with clear green eyes. "And how would you know what home is?"

Suzanne stooped to pick up her bag from the grass, feeling gut-punched. Teenagers always had a way of telling you what they thought regardless of how it would make you feel. "Well, I guess you got me there."

They both turned at the sound of the front door opening. When Maddie spotted her father, she quickly plucked her purse off the driver's seat of the truck. "I gotta go now. Hey, sorry about canceling today. But the darkroom's free again on Friday after school, if you can make it then."

"Sure. I need to check with Lucinda, but I'm sure it'll be fine."

With a wave, Maddie headed down the street on foot. Suzanne threw her backpack on her shoulder, preparing for the assault of nerves.

Joe was holding Harry, who clutched a tattered yellow blanket and wore footie pajamas. Joe wore sneakers and cutoff jeans shorts, and a navy blue baseball cap with the letter "W" emblazoned in red on the front. When he turned to inspect the bumper, she saw the back of the shirt: WALTON WAZZOOS.

It was the first time she'd seem him in something other than pressed pants and a button-down

177

shirt. His legs were lean and muscular—an athlete's legs. Not at all like dark and fine-boned Anthony, with his black eyes and hair that was never out of place.

"I appreciate you doing this," he said. He didn't avoid looking at her, just avoided letting their eyes meet for any length of time. He continued. "Aunt Lucinda said she's given you the scoop on everything, so I'll spare you by not going over it again. I left my cell phone number on the kitchen table—call me for anything." He looked down at Harry for a moment, smoothing the bright blond hair off the boy's forehead. "Sarah Frances has locked herself in her room and refuses to come out. That's probably for the best, so don't worry about it. And they've all been fed."

Harry let go of his father's neck and leaned toward Suzanne. Not knowing what else to do, she opened her arms and let the little boy fall into them. In the transaction, he'd managed to hang on to his bear, but the blanket had fallen onto the grass. He pointed to it and screeched, "Wooble!"

Joe picked it up and handed it to him, and Harry immediately cuddled it into his chest before nestling his head onto Suzanne's shoulder. She looked up at Joe, astonished that a child had willingly sought her out, but also at how sweet he smelled and how soft he felt nuzzled under her chin.

"This one's ready for bed." With a soft smile,

Joe stroked the baby's cheek with his finger and Suzanne knew he was seeing another face, one with the same bright blue eyes and hair the color of corn silk.

She moved away and said cheerfully, "We'll be fine. Go and have fun and don't worry about us."

He nodded, his eyes seeming to study her—as if he was making a comparison. "I won't be late. Maddie's going to a movie after the meeting, so I'll probably be home before her. And don't forget: call me if you need anything." He bent to kiss Harry on the cheek.

"Will do." She turned and walked up the steps to the front door, marveling at the soft weight of the child in her arms.

She found his room easily, following the scent of baby powder down the long hall at the top of the stairs. She was surprised to see he still slept in a crib, and wondered absently if it was because Joe was hanging on to Harry's babyhood as long as he could. Very carefully she lifted the now-sleeping child over the sides of the crib and laid him on the mattress. He burrowed into the Winnie the Pooh sheets, raising his rear end in the air and tucking his knees underneath him, the bear and blanket hugged tightly into his chest. He gave a deep sigh of contentment, then settled back into sleep.

After covering him with a blanket, Suzanne

watched him sleep for a long moment, and thought about her own mother for the first time in weeks. Had she ever watched Suzanne sleep as a baby? Harry was so beautiful lying there. It made Suzanne feel protective of him, willing to sleep on the floor by his crib just in case he needed anything. It was a strange feeling, and humbling, too. How could she have been so lacking that her mother had never felt tied to her?

She turned away and looked around the room at the hand-stenciled teddy bears that lined the tops of the walls, and the painted chest of drawers showing a landscape with a family of bears having a picnic. It was a beautiful room, stamped with love by a mother's hands.

Suzanne closed her eyes, a distant memory tugging at her brain—a memory of soothing hands and a desperate voice. A memory of a mother whose face she could barely remember. She pushed it away and opened her eyes, nearly stumbling in her surprise.

On the wall above the crib hung a cross-stitch. It was stitched with bears and bunnies bearing flowers and standing under a rainbow. And above the scene were the words "A life without rain is like the sun without shade."

She moved closer, squinting to see the tiny stitched initials in the bottom right corner of the frame: E.L. Reaching up, she let her fingertips brush the glass over the cross-stitch and searched her memory of the people in Walton for somebody with those initials.

Not able to come up with a name, she let her hand drop. Almost without thinking, she pulled the gold chain around her neck out from its hiding place beneath her shirt and looked down at the inscription: *A life without rain is like the sun without shade.* With a frown worrying her brow, she tucked the necklace back under her shirt, then left the room to go find the other children.

Out in the hallway, she spotted a closed door and assumed it to be Sarah Frances's room. Walking silently past it, she went down the stairs, softly calling out for the other children. She found Joey, Amanda, and Knoxie, already in their pajamas, on a couch in the family room, watching a Disney movie. Their eyes were riveted on her as soon as she entered the room, and for the first time she felt nervous.

"Hi, guys."

Amanda stared at her with blue eyes that were identical to Harry's. "I'm not a guy."

"Me, neither." Knoxie stared at her defiantly.

Joey rolled his eyes. "She meant 'y'all.' She's not from around here, so she says 'guys' when she means 'y'all.'"

Suzanne perched herself on the edge of a recliner and faced the children. Squeezing her hands together, she asked, "So, what would 'y'all' like to do?" She half hoped that they'd suggest they stay where they were and watch television. She was pretty sure she could handle that.

Amanda bounced up and down on the sofa. "Let's play Candy Land!"

Both Knoxie and Joey groaned.

"What's that? I've never played it before."

Knoxie and Joey looked at each other, then back at Suzanne, and smiled. "That's all right. We can teach you. Do you have any money with you?"

Suzanne nodded slowly. "Why do I need money?"

"You'll see," the children chimed in unison.

Taking Amanda's hand, Suzanne was led into the kitchen, where Knoxie was already setting out the board game. Taking her wallet out of her bag, she sat down at the table and rubbed her hands together. "Okay, y'all. Let's play."

They played for over an hour until a huge yawn from Amanda prompted an end to the game. After much stalling on the part of all three children, Suzanne finally got each one tucked in bed. Closing the last door, she stood out in the hallway, exhausted but also somehow satisfied.

Moving toward the stairs, she paused, listening to a sound from behind Sarah Frances's closed door. Walking toward the girl's room again, she put her ear closer to the door and listened. Somebody was moaning, as if ill, and Suzanne froze, filled with memories of her mother on one of her binges. She placed her hands flat on the door, feeling the coolness of the wood. Drawing a deep breath, she knocked.

"Sarah Frances? It's me—Suzanne Paris. Are you all right?"

"Go away." The voice was weak and not at all convincing.

"I can't do that. You sound like you're sick."

She heard the words again, barely audible. "Go away."

"I'm coming in." She waited for a moment, then turned the doorknob.

Sarah Frances sat on the floor by a bed canopied with a pink chiffonlike material. Suzanne stared, remembering how this was the sort of bed she had always dreamed of when she was a girl. She swung her attention back to Sarah Frances, who lay curled up on the floor, schoolwork scattered around her, her face flushed.

Pushing aside old memories, Suzanne knelt by the girl. "You don't look well." Sarah Frances offered no resistance as Suzanne felt her forehead. "You're really warm. Let's get you into a nightgown and into bed with a cloth for your forehead. Then I'll call your daddy, okay?"

Weakly Sarah Frances nodded. As Suzanne helped her stand and sit on the edge of the bed, she looked closely at the girl's face. On the pale skin of her cheeks and forehead, small pink bumps appeared just under the surface. Definitely not acne. One didn't break out with an army of pimples overnight. Frowning, she made a mental note to call Sam, too.

"Where are your nightgowns?"

Sarah Frances pointed to a white dresser, also hand-painted with a white picket fence and garden scene. Suzanne pulled out a warm flannel nightgown, knowing that when the chills came, Sarah Frances would need it.

She unbuttoned and helped Sarah Frances as much as the girl's modesty would allow, then left her to go across the hall to the bathroom, to get a cool rag and search for a thermometer. There were two sinks in the vanity: one surrounded by perfume, makeup, and heat rollers, and the other with just soap and toothpaste. A toothbrush holder sat in the center, holding about a dozen tooth-brushes, all of unknown vintage. A piece of duct tape intersected the middle of the vanity as if daring the girls to cross over into Joey's space. Shaking her head, she searched in vain for a thermometer but did find a clean washcloth, and rinsed it with cold water. Spotting a bottle of perfume, she spritzed it on the washcloth and then filled a cup with water before returning to Sarah Frances.

Her face seemed even more polka-dotted than before, the bumps redder. Suzanne gave her a sip of water, then placed the cloth on the young girl's forehead before leaving to call Joe and Sam. When she returned to the bedroom, Sarah Frances looked even worse but was now lying quietly in the bed, the covers kicked off her and the whiteness of the washcloth on her forehead accentuating the angry red of her face.

"I smell Maddie's perfume."

Cautiously Suzanne approached. "I remembered my mother doing that for me once when I was sick. Somebody had done it for her when she was little, and she said it always made her feel better. I thought it would help."

Sarah Frances turned her head away. "My mama used to do that."

Suzanne was silent for a moment, her gaze moving around the room. She spotted the birthday present she had brought to the party for Sarah Frances, still unopened, on the bedside table. Ignoring the stab of hurt, she said, "Your daddy and Dr. Parker will be here shortly. Can I do anything to help while we wait for them?"

Sarah Frances kept her eyes on the opposite wall and shook her head. "Just go."

Instead, Suzanne sat down in a desk chair and slid it closer to the bed. "I can't. You're sick, so you're stuck with me until your dad and uncle get here. So, what else did your mother do when you were sick? Did she sing?"

Sarah Frances's cheek creased as she smiled. "Mama couldn't carry a tune in a bucket. It always made us feel worse when she sang."

"Oh. Well, then. I've been told I have a nice

185

voice, so why don't I just sit here and sing quietly until you're rescued?"

The narrow shoulders shrugged. "Whatever."

Suzanne leaned back in her chair and closed her eyes, trying to pull memories of old songs from the furthest reaches of her mind. It had been so long ago that they were nearly buried under all the old hurts and resentments of a mother who wasn't always there. Settling on one, she began to hum it first until the words began to appear familiar, and then she opened her mouth to sing.

Joe heard the singing as soon as he walked in the door. Sam, who had driven up at the same moment he had, stood next to him, and they looked at each other in astonishment. Taking the stairs two at a time, they both stopped on the threshold of Sarah Frances's room, staring in.

Suzanne sat in a chair with her eyes closed, singing a familiar lullaby with the voice of an angel. Sarah Frances lay in the bed, her face turned to Suzanne, listening intently. Joe didn't want it to stop, but when he focused on his daughter's ravaged face, he must have made a noise, because Suzanne's singing stopped abruptly.

Suzanne jerked upright, then stood. "I didn't give her anything yet, figuring you'd want to see her first. I tried to make her comfortable. . . ."

Sam turned away from examining the patient to look at Joe and Suzanne. "I sure hope both of you have had the chicken pox, because I'm pretty certain that's what she's got. And trust me, you don't want to get it as an adult. It's just plain nasty."

Joe glanced over at his daughter with a worried expression. "Are you sure? All the kids got it when Knoxie was a baby. I could have sworn she had it, too."

Sam shrugged. "Sometimes a person will have a mild case the first time around that won't give her enough antibodies to fight it if she's exposed again. That could be what happened to Sarah Frances." He looked back down at the dotted face and felt the sides of her throat. "Yep, this is definitely chicken pox." Gently he spoke to the girl. "Have you been feeling feverish for a while?"

She nodded. "But I didn't want to miss school. If my grades slip, I can't play softball."

Joe grimaced and moved to stand near the bed. Taking her hand, he said, "But, peanut, if you're feeling bad, you need to stay home. You know I'll help you with the makeup work."

Her lip trembled, and Joe touched her cheek. "It'll be fine. We'll work it out."

Sam moved next to him. "You might not want to get too close if you haven't had it yet."

"No, I had it real bad as a kid, so I'm safe."

Suzanne looked at them blankly. "I have no idea if I've ever had it. I'm sure I have; doesn't every kid?"

Joe looked back at Sam. "Every kid but Harry and Amanda—they both got the vaccine."

Sam picked up his bag. "Good. It'll make your life easier having just one sick." He pulled a pen and paper from his bag. "I'm going to write down a few things that you'll need to keep her comfortable. I've already given her something for the fever. Let me know if it doesn't come down and I'll come check on her again. And by all means, tell her not to scratch."

As Sam wrote, Suzanne asked, "Will she be all right?"

Sam looked up. "Yeah, she'll be fine. She'll be miserable for a while, but she's strong and healthy and will be back to normal in a couple of weeks."

Suzanne seemed to relax. "Good. Well, I'll go get my things. Good night."

She was halfway down the stairs when Joe called out, "Wait for me. I wanted to talk about how the kids were tonight."

She paused uncertainly in the doorway. "Sure. I'll wait outside on the porch swing."

When he looked back at Sam, his friend was looking at him with amusement. "The Jacuzzi's up and running, if you're interested."

"I'm not."

"Uh-huh." With a smirk, Sam went back to writing.

"It's not what you're thinking."

"Sure it's not." Sam didn't even bother looking up.

After walking Sam to his car and then watching his friend drive away, Joe slowly walked back up the porch steps toward Suzanne. He should have just said good night and let her go, but he wasn't ready for her to leave yet. He told himself it was because he couldn't face yet another lonely night in his quiet house.

He said the first thing that popped into his head, hoping she wouldn't recognize the stupidity of it. "Do you want to go fishing?"

"Excuse me?"

"Night fishing. It's fun. I was wondering if you'd like to go."

"Um, I don't fish."

He shrugged. "Doesn't matter. I can show you. It mostly just involves patience and sitting still."

"I'm not really good at either one." She gave a push with her toe, sending the swing into a drunken arc.

"Great. Then it's time to learn."

She stopped the swing with a stomp of her foot on the floor. "What about Sarah Frances?"

"Sam gave her an antihistamine to stop the itching and make her sleep. I'll bring the baby monitor just in case. The creek's not far—right behind the house."

She stared out into the sky, where the full moon rose above the distant pines, their pointy tops

189

poking cracks into the glowing white surface. "Well, since I don't have anything else better to do, I might as well." She stood, the swing knocking into the backs of her knees.

"I'm flattered. Stay here. I'll go get a couple of rods from the garage."

She stepped toward him, her hand outstretched. "Before I forget, take this. It's Joey's and Knoxie's allowance. I won it from them playing Candy Land, but I don't feel right keeping it." She placed a fistful of coins and dollar bills into his hand.

He looked down at his hand. "You played Candy Land for money?"

Frowning, she said, "Well, yeah. That's how Joey and Knoxie explained it to me. Is something wrong?"

Nearly choking, he said, "No. I'll give it back to them. Thanks." He waited until he'd entered the garage before he let himself laugh.

When he returned, he found her standing in a pool of moonlight in the front yard, staring up at the sleeping house, a lone light in the downstairs window shining out into the night. She stood with her hands behind her back, looking like a child with her nose pressed close to a store window, wishing hard for a toy she'd never get.

He stopped in front of her, a fishing rod in each hand. "Take your pick."

She turned to face him, then tilted her head, with

a grin on her lips. "Fish fear me. Women want me."

A broad smile lifted his cheeks. "Yeah, well, maybe I shouldn't have had Maddie take that one off the bumper. At least the first part's true."

"Only the first part?" She reached over and took his favorite Shakespeare rod out of his hand. He didn't resist.

He couldn't tell if she was serious, so he said nothing. Motioning for her to follow, he headed toward the back of the house and the creek that ran between his property and Senator Thompkins's, puddling into a small swimming hole that had been a fixture in Joe's boyhood.

He'd never caught anything in the creek—something he wasn't about to admit to Suzanne—and mostly went there for thinking. He always brought a fishing pole along just in case he was caught, to give himself an alibi.

She paused in front of the small creek, gazing at the slow-moving water, its ripples reflected in the moonlight. "It's such a little creek. Does it go anywhere?"

He watched her long skirt sway around her ankles as she stood looking at the water. "You don't have to be going somewhere to be something."

He felt her cool gaze on him. "Come on. Let's sit over here, where we can watch the house."

They situated themselves on a rocky ledge, low

enough that they could dangle their feet. Suzanne sat crouched on hers, not letting her feet touch the water.

After situating the baby monitor on an adjacent rock, Joe took off his socks and sneakers and slid his feet into the chilliness of the water. "Come on, throw your flip-flops over there. The water's cool but feels nice."

She shook her head. "Not if there's fish in there."

"There's nothing in there that would want to take a bite out of your toes. Come on, give it a try."

She stared down at the water for a long time, not moving. Finally, she said, "I don't know how to swim. I've never been to a pool in my life."

Of the few things that she had told him so far about her life, this one wrenched his gut the most. He remembered hot summer days from his youth, days spent fishing and swimming in the creek with his sister and all the neighborhood children. All of his children, even Harry, could swim. It had been one of the duties of parenthood that he had relished. The thought of a child, any child, never having known the pleasure of diving into cool water on a hot summer's day pinched at his heart.

He reached into his bait bag and baited the hook on her line and then his, then showed her how to drop it into the water. He used this method a lot to speak with Maddie: *Pretend you're occupied doing something else when it's time for a serious discussion.*

Focusing on the spot where his hook disappeared into the surface of the water, he said, "Tell me about your childhood."

"It's not something I like to talk about."

"I know. That's why I'm asking."

She stared into the water, frowning. "There really isn't any more to it than what I've already told you. From the age of seven, I lived in six different foster homes. My mother never relinquished her parental rights, so I was never adopted. She disappeared from my life when I was fourteen." She snorted softly. "It's hard to believe, but she was raised in foster care, too. She always told me that she wanted it to be different for me."

They sat in the silence of the full moon, listening to the water run beneath them, and the low thrum of a nearby bullfrog. Softly, he said, "It still can be. It's not a sin to stay in one place for a while."

She shook her head, still not looking at him. "No. It's too late. I . . . well, there are reasons why I need to keep moving."

He pulled his line out of the water and rested the rod on the rocks beside him, no longer pretending to fish. He moved closer to her, smelling her soft scent that reminded him of autumn and cool nights. "What are you running from? Besides your fiancé."

Gray eyes appraised him. "I made a bad choice, mostly out of spite. I can't even say that I regret it. But that's all right. I wasn't made to stay in one place for very long."

Her words were desolate, dropped without any resolution, as if she was defying the world to tell her differently. He had no business trying, but he couldn't let her believe that. "What is the one thing that you want most of all?"

She spoke quickly, as if her words had been rehearsed over and over again. "I want to be left alone. I want my independence."

He breathed in deeply, taking in the scent of the creek, the moist grass, and her. "Then why were you ever engaged?"

She sighed. "The first of many mistakes. I thought I was tired of carrying the load my entire life. Anthony promised to take care of me, and I jumped at the chance."

"And your second mistake?"

"Believing him."

She relaxed her shoulders a bit, even let her feet dangle near the water. He stared at the smooth planes of her face and neck and the way her skin glowed in the light. He watched the grace of her arms as she held the fishing rod, her long limbs like fragile shadows in the moonlit night.

When she spoke, it startled him, and he wondered for a moment if he'd spoken his thoughts aloud.

"What is it that you want most of all?"

He thought for a long time, trying to prioritize all his wants. "I want my children to be healthy. And nurtured. I want to be a good enough parent that they don't notice the absence of their mother so much. I want to win this election and protect Walton from the likes of Stinky Harden. I want to be a better teacher and coach. I want the Walton Wazzoos to win the Monroe County Championship." He looked away and grimaced. "I want to wake up tomorrow morning not feeling so tired."

He turned his face to her and realized how close she was. As if of its own accord, his voice said, "And I want to kiss you again."

He touched her cheek, and she startled but didn't pull away. He remembered the taste of her and moved closer, bending his head until his lips touched hers.

Her body molded against his, almost as if she had been waiting for him, and her arms pulled him down with her along the rocky bank of the creek.

He rolled them over until her back was cushioned by the soft grass. His wanting of her wasn't about needing a woman; it was about needing *her*. He couldn't rationalize it; all he knew was that this beautiful woman was in his arms, responding to his touch, and he needed her in more ways than he wanted to admit.

He lifted his head to catch his breath, and looked

down at her as if she could explain why he suddenly felt as if he'd been hit head-on by an eighteen-wheeler. The gold charm around her neck winked at him in the moonlight, and a flash of memory hit him like the back of a hand—a memory of a different woman. A woman who didn't have red hair, or who wore T-shirts with long, gauzy skirts.

He sat back, stunned, and watched her sit up quickly. With a choked voice, she said, "I'm not Harriet."

He looked at her without flinching. "No. You're not."

She rolled away and stood, her back to him. "I think it would be best if we kept our distance from each other. I don't want us getting in the way of what we want the most. And there are things you don't know about me. Things that could hurt you."

His heart beat heavily as he watched her walk away. He wanted to call out to her, to make her come back, but he didn't. He wasn't sure what he would say.

She stopped but didn't turn around. "I'll stay to finish Maddie's scrapbook. But then I'm leaving, so you won't have to worry about this happening again." She continued walking, faster this time, and he watched her until she disappeared around the corner of the house.

His world darkened for a moment, and he

looked up at the sky to see a thick cloud hovering in front of the moon. The stars had disappeared, and even the crickets had silenced, as if they had sensed the change in the weather while Joe remained oblivious.

He gathered up the monitor, bait bag, and fishing rods, then walked quickly back to the house before the first raindrops began to fall.

CHAPTER 11

Maddie fumbled around in the darkroom, attempting to load the roll of film onto the metal film reel. Her fingers felt as nimble as rubber cucumbers, and she couldn't manage getting the slippery film into the slot on the danged developing tank. Suzanne had made her practice outside in broad daylight, which was difficult enough, but now she was required to do it in the dark. Maddie couldn't see her, but she envisioned Suzanne on the other side of the door, chewing on her lip and counting to ten, clenching her hands behind her back to prevent them from reaching out to do it herself.

"Dangnabit!" Maddie's voice was high-pitched and irritated.

"Is that a curse word, Maddie?"

Maddie heard the smile in Suzanne's voice through the door and stopped her fumbling for a moment. "Yeah. It's supposed to be." She sighed loudly. "The stupid film won't stay in the slot on the reel. I'm sorry."

"It's okay. I don't have anywhere I need to be, so we'll just wait until you get the hang of it." Her voice sounded controlled, as if she were practicing patience. Maddie pictured Suzanne with her arms across her chest, clutching her elbows tightly.

"Digital photos are so much easier. You just have to upload them on your computer."

Suzanne didn't say anything from the other side of the door, but Maddie pictured her frowning at Maddie's words of sacrilege.

Maddie felt for the slot on the reel and tried one more time to slide the edge of the film into it. When she felt it go in, she almost dropped it in her excitement. "I did it! It's on. I can hardly believe it."

Suzanne didn't completely hide her sigh of relief. "Great. Now put it into the film tank like I showed you and cover it so you can come out."

Maddie fumbled in the dark some more to get the lid on the small metal tank, then opened the door of the small closet before stepping out into the darkroom. Suzanne stood bathed in red from the safe light hanging overhead, and it was like looking at her through a film negative.

Suzanne indicated the dark bottles of chemicals on a shelf in the far corner. "Do you remember what each one of these is?"

Maddie ran through the list in her head from her

tutoring sessions with Suzanne and pointed to the first one, containing developer. "This one's the soup." Moving her finger from bottle to bottle, she said, "That's the stop bath, fixer with hardener, and the hypo eliminator bath." She grinned up at Suzanne. "Did I get it right?"

Suzanne smiled back. "Yeah. You're on your way. Now, do you remember what to do next?"

"Um, yeah. We've gone over it a couple of times in photography club, but I've never actually done it. Would you like to take over now?" She held her breath, afraid that Suzanne would say yes.

Suzanne shook her head but kept her arms crossed tightly over her chest. "Nope, the only way to learn how is to do it. I won't let you make a mistake—promise. Then, after you've learned how to do it the right way, I'll show you how to do it the wrong way to make some pretty neat effects."

"Cool." With studied concentration, Maddie began to move through the complicated developing process, alternating chemicals and water through the pour spout of the sealed film tank. She grinned to herself. Nobody in the photography club at school had been allowed into the darkroom yet. But, because she was the teacher's favorite, he had let her come in today with an experienced photographer. She'd try real hard not to let the dim-witted Miss Perfect, Lucy Spafford, feel bad about being left in her dust.

After she'd put in the fixer for the required ten minutes, Maddie finally found the courage to ask Suzanne what she'd been trying to ask for over a week. Being in a dimly lit room while focusing on something else helped her talk. She'd learned that method from her dad. "Have you ever heard of *Lifetime* magazine?"

"Of course I have. It's a big-time photography mag. It's also a personal favorite of mine."

Maddie kept her gaze fixed on the small metal canister. "Well, they're holding a photography contest for students. The winner's photo will be on the cover, and they'll get a scholarship to an art school in San Francisco." She tilted the canister from side to side, studying it closely. "Mr. Tener says I should enter." There. She'd said it. Now all she had to do was wait and see if Suzanne laughed.

Instead, she said, "Of course you should. You definitely have talent, Maddie, and this could give you a head start that most photographers only dream of. I mean, most photographers would kill for a *Lifetime* cover. I know I would."

Relief, mixed with doubt and anxiety, flooded through Maddie. She leaned against the wide metal sink and sighed. "But it's California. I guess that's pretty far from Walton."

Suzanne looked at her with those eyes that always seemed to calm her, and alerted Maddie that she was about to get right to the point. "Have you talked to your dad about this?"

Maddie shook her head, her ponytail shaking as if in agreement. "Not yet. I wanted to talk to you first."

Suzanne looked embarrassed and turned away to start putting the lids on the chemical bottles they had already used. "Why? What do you think he'll say?"

Maddie puckered her brows. "He sort of expects me to go to Georgia. I was even planning on applying for early admission." She looked up at Suzanne. "I don't think he could stand for me to be so far away." She shrugged slightly, trying to shake off the heavy feelings that had been following her around all week. "He needs me. And I can't stand to think of him so lonely."

Suzanne came to stand in front of her, to look her right in the eye. "But what is it that you want?"

Half of her mouth turned up in a lopsided smile as she slowly rolled the metal tank in her hands. She could tell Suzanne what she'd never been able to tell her dad. "I'd like to travel—to live some-place else besides here. I even ran away once, to New York. I didn't get past the entrance ramp to the interstate, but I had every intention of living in New York with my aunt Cassie. I just don't think I could live here forever like my mom and dad. There's more to life than that." Her grin faltered, and she felt as if she'd just denounced her own parents.

Suzanne moved out of the way so Maddie could use the sink to wash away the fixer. "Well, it sounds to me as if you're borrowing a whole passel of worry."

Maddie paused and looked over her shoulder. "You sound just like Miss Lena. She always says that."

Something like confusion passed over Suzanne's face, and she frowned. "Really? My mother used to say that, too."

Maddie turned back to the sink and began to run water through the tank as Suzanne spoke again. "You have to tell your dad, but I think you should enter the contest. Then, if you win, you can jump that hurdle. I'm sure your dad will back anything you decide to do, once he comes around to it." She paused for a moment and then said, "There's nothing wrong with wanting something different."

Maddie concentrated while she poured in the hypo eliminator and began agitating the tank. After two minutes, she began the final wash in the sink. "You don't think he'll be mad?"

"He might be hurt at first, but not mad. When the time comes, the two of you can discuss what's best for you and come to a decision. But he'll come around. He's a pretty reasonable guy."

Maddie slanted a glance over at Suzanne, remembering seeing her in the light of the porch, coming from the creek the night before with grass in her hair and skirt. Maddie had been about to call out to her from the porch when she'd spotted her dad and instead had slipped silently into the house. She hid her grin and said only, "Yeah."

Suzanne cleared her throat and reached for the tank. "I'll take the film out while you go get some photographic paper. Then, while the film's drying, we can go get something to eat at the Dixie Diner."

Glancing at her watch, Maddie shook her head. "I have to be somewhere at six. All I have to do is slide the dry film into a sleeve, right? I can do that on Monday."

A look, similar to the one she'd seen the night before, flashed over Suzanne's delicate features. It reminded Maddie of Harry when she told him there weren't any more Cheerios. "Or maybe you can do it, if you want. You might even find a picture you think is good enough for the contest."

Suzanne brightened a little. "I might. I'll let you know."

She looked so lonely, standing there with her hands behind her back. Maddie almost invited her along with her friends for the evening, and then remembered her dad and what she and her friends were planning on doing. Definitely the wrong move. "Well, I've got to go. Thanks for all your help."

Impulsively she hugged Suzanne. At first the older woman stiffened, and then relaxed enough to squeeze back and pat Maddie's shoulder. "I didn't do anything but stand around and watch. If that helped, then you're very welcome."

Maddie pulled back, glancing at her watch again. "I've really got to go. If you're going to stay, make sure you lock up or Mr. Tener will never let me in here after hours again."

"I will." Suzanne held out her hand in a little wave as she turned to leave, and a part of Maddie wanted to stay. Then she remembered Rob and her other friends who were waiting for her, and hurried to the door, ignoring the nagging pull of guilt that seemed to grab her like a fish on a hook.

She pulled open the door of the darkroom and stopped, remembering one more thing. "Charlie Harden might show up to pick up his assignment for the photography club from Mr. Tener. If he comes in here, don't let him look at my pictures."

"Is Charlie any relation to Stinky Harden?"

"His obnoxious son. Looks like a miniature version of his daddy."

Suzanne rolled her eyes. "That's a scary thought. But I didn't think Stinky was married."

Maddie stuck her fingers in her back pocket, trying not to show her impatience to leave. "He's divorced—three times, I think. He's got two other kids. Charlie's his only son, though. Thank God."

As if reading her mind, Suzanne grabbed the door and held it open for Maddie. "Don't let me keep you. You run on. I'll take care of the negatives."

"Thanks. I'll see you later." Ignoring the guilt feelings pinching at her chest, she closed the door of the darkroom and jogged the rest of the way home.

Suzanne took another sip from the Coke she'd brought back to the darkroom from her dinner at the Dixie Diner, before sliding the long strip of negatives through the enlarger and examining each print on the eight-by-ten easel below. She leaned closer, studying the shots she had taken in the cemetery. The pictures were good, if not her best, until she got to the ones taken around Harriet's grave and she found herself holding her breath. Although she was viewing the images reversed in negative form, they seemed to have a soft glow to them, as if already airbrushed by an unseen hand. There was an ethereal beauty to them, as if she had captured on film a place on earth never seen before. She went back to the first pictures on the roll to see if the flaw appeared on those, too, but they were clear.

She slid the next negative into the enlarger and turned the knob to focus it more clearly. These were the pictures Maddie had taken at the surprise birthday party. Centering the easel below the enlarger, she prepared to study them without bias to better critique Maddie's work. But she couldn't. They were wonderful.

Leaning forward, Suzanne studied a picture of

Cassie and Sarah Frances, which must have been taken after the girl had stormed up to her room. Her head rested on Cassie's shoulder, her eyes open and staring past the photographer. Only Cassie's hand was visible as it cradled the back of Sarah Frances's head, cupped in a C that symmetrically matched the curve of the girl's head. The hand was that of a mother comforting a child, and knowing the relationship of the two people in the picture didn't alter Suzanne's first impression. There was a slight shady glow in this picture, too, and she made a mental note to make a print of it to show Maddie. This one would definitely be a contender in any photography contest.

She continued to study the photos from the party, marveling at how Maddie could capture the essence of a person, the nature of the inner soul, within the frame of a camera lens. The pictures of the children leaping on the lawn in pursuit of fireflies made Suzanne smile. She was still smiling when she slid the last negative on the strip into the enlarger. Then her smile froze.

The odd glow was back in this picture, holding the same otherworldly quality as the ones in the cemetery. The frame was of her and Joe, illuminated by the radiance of the moonflowers behind them. The shot was a close-up of her face, her lips separated from Joe's by only a breath. His mouth, in an upturned smile, was the only part of him not in shadow, but her whole face, which seemed to shimmer and glow with an unspoken joy, claimed the focus of the shot. Suzanne flushed, not recognizing herself and embarrassed that Maddie had seen her this way. She felt naked staring at the woman in the frame, feeling as if she were looking at a stranger.

Her heartbeat seemed to slow to a sluggish beat as she continued to stare at the picture. *Oh God.* She let herself sag against the counter, trying to coax her thoughts in the right direction. There was no doubt in her mind that this picture could win a contest. She let her fingertip touch the cold smoothness of the easel, casting the image onto her fingers, and closed her eyes. There was no way she could ever allow her face to be plastered on the cover of a national magazine. She might as well turn herself in now.

Oh God, she thought again as she realized what was upsetting her the most. The thought of duping Maddie nearly choked the breath out of her. But the thought of the people of Walton finding out who she really was made a little piece of her die. Even if she were long gone from this place, to have them know would be more than she could bear.

She looked back up at the image and wanted to weep. When had her controlled, orderly life given way to this confusion? She used to know what she wanted. But it had changed when she wasn't looking, and she was afraid to stare at it head-on. She'd been down this road of futile hopes before, and it was littered with the carcasses of her bitter disappointments.

Change was inevitable. But she wasn't ready to leave. Not yet. She had the album to do for Maddie. And for Harriet. Then it would be time. Reaching up for the switch on the enlarger, she turned off the light.

Without hesitation she threaded the negative through the enlarger, then fumbled in the drawer beneath the enlarger and picked up the scissors. Quietly she said, "I'm sorry, Maddie," then clipped the film, watching the single frame float to the floor like a lost memory.

She stared at it for a long time without picking it up, remembering the moment in which it had been taken. She could almost smell the aroma of the moonflowers and taste Joe's lips and recall the way he made her feel. Dropping the scissors on the counter with a clatter, she crouched and retrieved the negative. If she could make just one print—one thing to pull out, later, when she was a long way from here, and remember again . . . Switching the light on the enlarger back on, she threaded the single negative into the machine, struggling to get it to stay in place. Fumbling in the drawer again for the pack of photographic paper she'd spotted, she pulled it out. After turning off the light on the enlarger again, she slid a page from the pack. It had been such a long time since she'd used anything except fiber paper in her photo development that she wasn't even sure which side to turn up on the easel. Remembering an old trick she'd learned years before, she licked a corner of the paper on each side, determining which one made her tongue drag.

After making her test strip to experiment with exposure times, she put a fresh paper on the taped-down easel and flipped on the enlarger for eight seconds.

Turning around behind her, she found the trays of chemicals she needed and slowly dropped the paper into the first tray of developer.

Stirring constantly, she watched the murky image appear through the chemical, the muted faces dreamlike but no less stunning in their intensity. It was an exquisite picture of innocent joy, the glowing whites and dusty grays contrasting nicely against the sparkle in her eyes. This picture would win any contest it was entered in. It was simply brilliant.

The recollection of a story she'd heard in a photography class years before, about how some native tribes never allowed their photographs to be taken because it captured the soul, hit her suddenly. It was only now that she knew it to be true.

Using tongs to retrieve the print from the first tray, she then carefully dropped it into the stop and fix, and finally into water to rinse off all the chemicals. Finding a roll of paper towels near the sink, she laid out a couple and placed her picture on it to dry.

As soon as she was done, she replicated the process, but this time she used the picture of Cassie and Sarah Frances. When it was done, she placed it on a paper towel next to the first one and sat down to watch it dry, placing her hands on her folded arms and closing her eyes.

She must have dozed, because the next thing she was aware of, another person was in the room with her, standing between her and the counter where the pictures lay.

"Excuse me," she said, standing, and trying to pretend to be wide-awake and alert. "Can I help you?"

When the person turned to face her, she stepped back, knocking into the chair she'd been sitting in. It was a miniature version of Stinky, a thought that amused and frightened her at the same time.

He was about her height but outweighed her by at least seventy pounds, his extra weight spilling out over the top of his blue jeans. His face was as clear and well scrubbed as his father's, making Suzanne ungraciously think of Tweedledum and Tweedledee. The memory of his father's threats kept her from smiling.

"I'm Charlie Harden. Sorry. I didn't know somebody was in here."

She moved between him and the prints, blocking his view. "That's all right. You just surprised me, that's all."

A big grin showed on his face. "Hey, aren't you Coach Warner's girlfriend?"

"No. Definitely not. We're . . . acquaintances."

He pulled a pack of Juicy Fruit gum from his back pocket and offered one to Suzanne. When she declined, he shrugged and took one himself, smacking it loudly. "That's a shame. 'Cause I was gonna give you a message to take back to him."

"Really. Like what?"

Charlie blew a small, thin bubble with his gum, popping it with a crack. A small thread of it clung to his lip as he sucked the rest of it back into his mouth. "Like, he'd better find a way to control his daughter if he wants to keep running this town."

She spotted the single negative next to the enlarger on the counter, and felt a thread of panic. "What are you talking about?"

He blew another bubble and looked up at the ceiling. "Oh, well, nothing in particular. Just that I happen to know that a certain daughter of his had better start showing a bit of restraint in her behavior."

She kept her voice calm. "Are you talking about Maddie? I seriously don't have a clue as to what you're referring to."

He looked up at the ceiling again, as if asking for divine intervention, and shook his head.

211

"You'll find out soon enough. I can't wait to see what the mayor will do. This'll be good."

Knowing that to question him further would lead nowhere, she stepped forward and swept the negative and test strip into the garbage can with a quick movement of her arm. She forced herself not to look down and turned back to Charlie.

He had moved closer to the counter and was looking at the two prints. "Wow. These are really good. Are they yours?"

She quickly rolled up Maddie's negatives and stuck them in her backpack before sliding it onto her shoulder. Then she squeezed up to the counter, nudging Charlie out of the way. Being careful to only touch the edges in case they were still wet, she picked up the pictures, holding them so that they faced her chest. "No, they're Maddie's."

He blew a huge bubble and let it pop. "Holy cow, those are really great. Is she going to enter them in that contest?"

Suzanne pretended nonchalance and shrugged. "I have no idea. It will be her decision." She moved to the blacked-out revolving door, designed to keep any light out of the darkroom. "It was nice meeting you, Charlie. Could you lock up? Maddie says Mr. Tener is real strict on that."

He waved. "Yeah. No prob. I do it all the time. I'm just supposed to sweep out the room and make sure everything's put away." He blew another bubble. "Tell Maddie that Charlie said hey."

"I will," she said, then let herself out the door.

She felt chilled as she walked out onto the front steps of the school, not stopping to wonder whether it was the early fall temperature or her feelings of guilt. Shivering slightly, she took the quickest route home, through the town square.

In the last light of the day, she crossed the green, the sun having already disappeared over the deserted town center. It was suppertime in Walton, the time when families congregated together for dinner and bowed their heads in thanksgiving.

A small breeze tumbled at her, billowing her skirt back and rustling the early leaves that had already fallen onto the close-clipped grass of the green. She looked up at the odd statue of Lady Liberty, wondering if she was the only one who thought her outstretched arm resembled a lineman's glove. She'd definitely have to get a picture of that before she left.

She glanced over at the other end of the green, to the statue of the Confederate soldier facing Lady Liberty, and stopped dead in her tracks. He wore what appeared to be a pink feather boa around his neck, and his lips seemed to be painted in a darker shade of the same hue—one eerily similar to the lipstick Lucinda was quite fond of.

As she approached, she could see the facial features of the unfortunate man more clearly, all of them having been emphasized with heavy makeup—including a set of remarkable false eyelashes.

Her first reaction was to laugh. She laughed hard enough that she had to sit on a nearby bench until the stitch in her side subsided. *Oh, Maddie,* she thought. *You are truly an original.* And that thought made Suzanne cry. Not just for what she had done to her, but for all the years of growing up that Suzanne would never see.

A stronger wind blew at her, drying the hot tears on her cheeks and making the feathers of the pink boa dance. Shivering, Suzanne cast a last glance at the decorated soldier, then stood and walked across the deserted green toward home.

CHAPTER 12

Joe tucked his cell phone into his pocket and looked over at his friend. With an expression that didn't completely erase the smile in his eyes, Sam asked, "Is it the inflatable condoms again?"

Joe shook his head, rubbing his hands over his face. "No—not the usual this time. Maddie's transformed the soldier in the green into a transvestite worthy of downtown Atlanta. Sheriff Adams is not amused. If I knew where she was, I'd wring her neck. She must have her cell phone off because all of my calls are going directly to her voice mail."

Sam sat down on the sofa next to Cassie, facing Joe. "What did she tell you?"

"That she was going to the movies with a group of her friends and that she'd be back at eleven. I already checked at the theater. Nobody's seen her." He stared blankly at Sam and Cassie, at a loss for words.

"Did you call Clarissa White? Those two are practically joined at the hip. Maybe her mother knows where they are."

Joe shook his head again. "Clarissa told her mother the same story Maddie told me. They're together, all right. We just don't know where."

Cassie patted Sam on the leg as she scooted herself to the edge of the sofa and struggled to a stand. "Well, the kids are more than welcome to stay here for the rest of the night. Especially if you're planning on having another confrontation with Maddie as soon as she walks in the door. No sense in waking the whole household."

Joe nodded sullenly. "Yeah. You're probably right. Thanks."

"I'll go make a pot of coffee. Why don't you stay and have a cup before heading home? Maybe it will give you time to cool off before you talk with Maddie."

She took his hand for a moment, and her smile reminded him suddenly of Harriet. The stab of grief wasn't unexpected, but the muffled feel of it was. It was as if something else he'd allowed into

215

his heart had cushioned the blow. He looked up at Cassie, feeling dazed. "Thank you."

She dropped his hand and disappeared into the kitchen of the old house she'd inherited when her father died. It had brought Cassie back from New York and into their lives again. Thinking back on all she had done for him and his children since Harriet's death, he had no words to express how thankful he would always be.

Sam stretched out on the sofa, propping his boots up on the peach-colored cushion.

"Keep your feet off the couch, Sam," Cassie's voice called out from the kitchen. "I happen to know that you weren't raised in a barn."

Sam immediately plopped his feet back on the floor. "I swear she's got eyes in the back of her head."

Joe grinned. "She'll need them as a mother. I think all women grow them in the last trimester of pregnancy. Didn't they teach you that in medical school?"

Sam laughed as he sat back and crossed a foot over the other knee. "So. Tell me what you found out about Stinky."

"Nothing good. My friend on the Atlanta Police Department did a little checking for me. Seems that our friend Charles Harden is up to his eyeballs in gambling debts. And that the money he borrowed wasn't from any legitimate sources that they can determine."

"So why's he in Walton?"

"Darned if I know. But it seems as if he's biding his time. He sold his house and business in Atlanta before he moved here. And I did some checking and found that the title to his parents' house is in his son's name—I guess to protect it from his creditors. That alone tells me he's got problems."

Cassie came in and handed a mug of coffee to both Sam and Joe before kissing Sam on the forehead. "Is there anything I need to give Sarah Frances before she goes to sleep?"

Joe shook his head. "Nope. I've already given her the antihistamine. Just make sure she's wearing socks on her hands so she doesn't scratch. And please keep your distance. I know you had chicken pox as a child, but I'd like to be on the safe side."

"Will do." She blew a kiss at Sam before heading upstairs to put the children to bed.

Sam leaned forward, his elbows on his knees, and continued the conversation. "Not the sort of person I'd choose to run a town."

Joe snorted. "Run it into the ground, maybe. Those sixty acres of undeveloped pine forest his parents left him is what I'm worried about. I have a strong feeling that his entire bid for mayor has to do with whatever he's got planned for that land."

"Like a pulp mill."

Joe drained his mug before putting it on a coaster on the coffee table. "Yep. Like a pulp mill. Only thing worse than the deforestation would be the smell. Of course, he'd have to convince the town council and the citizens to go along with him, but according to my friend in Atlanta, he's got friends who have strong methods of persuasion."

Joe stood, and Sam followed. "I guess you heard Stinky donated fifty thousand dollars to the library for computers and a new roof. Don't know where he got the money, but a whole bunch of people noticed."

"Yeah, I know. But I haven't got that kind of money to throw around to win an election."

Sam grabbed him by a shoulder. "Hey. You know I'm on your side and will do my best to spread the word. You've got a terrific record as mayor. People will remember that."

With a rueful grin, Joe said, "I hope so." He scratched the back of his head. "I'm going to head on home now and wait for Maddie. Tell Cassie thanks again, and I'll stop by in the morning to collect the kids and let you know how it went."

Sam walked him to the door and let him out with a wave. Joe waited for the door to close, then stood on the porch for a long time, not yet wanting to leave. This was the house Cassie and Harriet had grown up in, and where his first memories of Harriet began. He had first laid eyes on her standing on this very porch, wearing a yellow sundress. The gazebo in the back was where he'd worked up the nerve to kiss her for the first time.

It was in this old house, even more than the one they'd shared as husband and wife, that he felt her presence the most. But instead of comforting him tonight, it seemed to push at his back, sending him down the porch steps toward his truck.

Confused at the mixture of feelings, he sat in the driver's seat for a long moment. He stared out the windshield, almost seeing the pieces of his life whirling around him into a tight circle, searching for a focal point. Finally, he put the key in the ignition, started the engine, and headed for home.

A sound outside jerked Suzanne awake. She sat up, listening, the dark of the night pressing down on her. For a brief moment, she was eight years old again and her mother had just returned after a week's absence. She could almost smell the rum in the darkened bedroom. Blinking, she struggled to orient herself in the correct place and time.

She heard the noise again, and it sounded like two voices—male and female. Springing from the bed, she grabbed the red silk robe—her only splurge from Lucinda's Lingerie—and ran down the stairs to the front door as she tied the belt around her waist. Flipping on the porch lights, she flung open the door and stopped.

Maddie stood at the top of the porch steps swaying on her feet, while Robbie stood behind her with his arms on her waist as if to steady her.

"Hello, Mizz Parisss." Maddie's words slurred

together, bumping against each other like passenger cars in a train wreck.

"You're drunk." Suzanne tried to keep her voice even, to state a fact without recrimination. But images of her mother made it impossible.

"I ain't so drunk, am I, Robbie?" Her head fell backward and lolled onto Rob's shoulders.

Suzanne stayed where she was and cast an accusing glare at Rob. "I suppose you had something to do with this?"

Rob took a step forward, standing beside Maddie but still supporting her. "No, ma'am. I don't drink—and I didn't think Maddie did, either." He glanced over at his date, who was now drooling on his shoulder, but his expression held only worry and concern. "I saw her pouring Coke into an insulated water bottle. She must have had a whole fifth of rum in it already. She'd already downed a lot of it before we even reached Atlanta and I realized what it was. I drove right back."

"You went to Atlanta? I happen to know that her father told her she couldn't go."

Suzanne saw Rob's face turn ashen in the dim light. "She told me Coach Warner said it was okay. I wouldn't have gone otherwise."

She crossed her arms over her chest. "Why are you here? Shouldn't you take her home?"

Robbie struggled to move Maddie forward, but her legs seemed to refuse to cooperate and only managed bending at the knee. Robbie grabbed her before she fell face-forward on the porch. "No, ma'am. She wanted to be brought here."

Suzanne didn't move. "And I'm supposed to believe that not wanting to face her father has nothing to do with this."

He looked offended. "I kept trying to talk her out of coming here. I can handle my responsibilities . . . ma'am," he added, his inbred manners not allowed to desert him even in the wee hours of the night.

Maddie managed to lift her head. "Please, Mizz Parisss, I can't go home now. Daddy'll kill me." Her head slumped forward again, coming to rest on Robbie's shoulder.

The smell of rum wafted over to Suzanne, making her nauseated. She turned to walk into the house and call Joe, but a nagging memory stopped her—the memory of a discarded negative lying in a garbage can in a darkroom. Guilt overtook the nausea, and she turned back to the two teens. "You go on home now, Rob. I'll take care of her."

Almost reluctantly, he loosened his grip on Maddie and stepped away. With his head bent near her ear, he said, "I'll call you tomorrow."

Maddie stared in his direction with a dazed look on her face as he left them and drove away in his truck. She didn't say anything, but her eyes glistened with moisture. With a slurred voice, she said, "I think I screwed up big-time."

Maddie swayed, barely able to stand by herself,

and Suzanne found herself swaying, too, but didn't move forward. She smelled the rum again and half turned to go back into the house, leaving the girl on the porch, swaying in the storm-scented breeze.

"Please." The one word was filled with so much pain and regret that it grabbed and held on to Suzanne's heart. "I have nowhere else to go."

Suzanne started to say something, knowing that not a single house in Walton would refuse to give Maddie shelter. And then she realized what she really meant. That Suzanne's was the only house she could go to without hurting her father more. She knew that Suzanne would never share Maddie's mistake with the town. It was as if, in those brief words, Maddie had given all her trust to someone she'd known for only a short time. To Suzanne.

Suzanne took a step forward, and Maddie followed, and the two met in the middle as Suzanne moved to catch the drunk girl, and they both collapsed in a heap on the wooden floorboards of the porch.

"I think I'm going to throw up."

With practiced movements honed from years of experience, Suzanne reached for a flowerpot and held it for Maddie, pulling back her hair until the retching stopped. After moving the pot out of the way, she pulled a tissue out of the pocket of her bathrobe and handed it to Maddie.

"Feel better?"

Maddie wiped the tissue over her mouth and nodded weakly before letting her head fall on Suzanne's shoulder. "I'm sorry," she whispered.

Suzanne leaned her back against the house, pulling Maddie with her. "I'm going to have to call your father, you know. He'll be worried."

A sob erupted from the young girl. "Don't. Please. He'll be so mad."

"Then why did you do it, Maddie? Why would you deliberately get drunk?"

Maddie sniffled, her head lolling back and forth, and then hiccupped. "You wouldn't understand. Nobody does."

Suzanne took a deep breath, only a part of her wondering why it was so important to her to understand. "Try me. Maybe I'll surprise you."

Maddie was silent for a while as her fingers plucked at the short pink skirt she wore. "Because I don't want to die before I've had any fun."

Suzanne found herself patting Maddie's shoulder. "Maddie, you're only seventeen. You stand a great chance of having lots of fun."

"No." Maddie gave her head a vehement shake. "Don't you see? I'll never grow old. My grandma and my mama died young, and so will I." She began sobbing, soaking Suzanne's neck with tears.

Suzanne's heart twisted, hearing the pain and knowing how long it had been living inside this

223

young girl. "No, no, no, Maddie. That's not true. It's not a guarantee." She moved Maddie's head so that she could look into her eyes. And when Suzanne saw what was there, she recognized herself. "Don't give up, Maddie. Please don't. There are too many unknowns in life to say you know what's going to happen. You've got your whole life ahead of you, and a whole town backing you up no matter what happens. You have to live your life without fear." Suzanne started to cry now, too, remembering words her mother had told her the last time she'd seen her. "Every life holds the promise of rain. But after the rain comes the rainbow. You just have to stick around long enough to find it."

"I miss my mama!" Maddie cried, her sobs loud and choking now. Suzanne wrapped her arms around her, in a way that she must have been taught many years before, and cradled Maddie, not with the hands that had held her as a baby, but with hands that now held her heart, and it was enough. They held on to each other until their tears mixed together in a single stream of sorrow for imperfect lives and absent mothers.

As Maddie slept on the couch in the newly refurbished front parlor, Suzanne moved to the kitchen and called Joe. He answered on the first ring.

"It's Suzanne. Maddie's here."

There was no hesitation in his voice, as if he hadn't slept yet. "Thank God. I'm coming over right now to get her."

"No, Joe. Don't. She's resting right now. I think it best if we let her sleep. I'll bring her over in the morning."

"Why is she there, and why is she sleeping?" His voice held a note of agitation, no less aggravated by worry and lack of sleep.

"Can we talk about this in the morning? I really don't think—"

"Is something wrong with Maddie?"

Suzanne paused too long. Joe's voice cut in. "Has she been drinking?"

"I'd rather she tell you herself."

He cursed under his breath. "Is Rob involved?"

"Not in the way you're thinking. He did the right thing and brought her here. Joe, look, we're both tired. I just wanted to let you know that she's okay and that she's here, and I'll bring her by in the morning."

"No."

"No?"

"No. She and I go running every morning at six thirty. Tell her she better be ready and waiting to go when I come downstairs or she'll be grounded for a month longer than I'm already going to ground her."

"Joe, she's really in a bad way. I don't think—"

"I'm her father. I set the rules."

Suzanne was silent for a moment. "All right. I'll make sure she's there."

Joe didn't hang up right away. "Suzanne?"

"I'm still here."

"Thank you."

She smiled, easing the tension of the past few hours. "You're welcome." She hung the phone up slowly, hearing the click as it fell into the cradle.

When Maddie awoke an hour later to use the bathroom, Suzanne was already dressed and waiting. As Maddie emerged from the bathroom, Suzanne said, "I've made a cup of coffee for you and laid out a couple slices of bread. I'm going to walk you home now, and you can bring it all with you."

Maddie regarded her with a dazed expression. "What time is it?"

"Four o'clock in the morning."

"You talked with my dad, didn't you?"

"All I did was call to let him know where you were. I didn't want for him to worry anymore about where you were. He wants you home and ready for your morning run by six thirty. I figured if I got you home now, you could sleep in your running clothes and be ready when he is."

"I'm in big trouble, aren't I?"

"Probably. But he'll likely go a lot easier on you if you're ready for your run, which is the only reason why I'm doing this at this insane hour." She yawned loudly, not even trying to hide it.

Maddie shook her head, rubbed her eyes, then headed for the kitchen to get her coffee and bread before the short walk home.

The predawn air stung as Suzanne led the way down the front walk, remembering other early mornings spent waiting for her mother. They slowly made their way through the sleeping town, cutting through the Methodist church's parking lot. Suzanne glanced up at the sign, weakly lit by a nearby streetlight: LIFE IS A TEST. PRAY HARD.

What should have been a five-minute walk lasted almost fifteen as Maddie dragged her feet and walked as slowly as she possibly could. With more patience than she knew she had, Suzanne waited for her to catch up, then continued until they stood in front of Maddie's house.

The light in the front window shone out at them, and Suzanne stopped, marveling at the rush of warmth that flooded through her as she stared at it. No matter how mad Joe might be at Maddie, he had left the light on for his prodigal daughter.

Maddie stopped, too. "He's going to kill me."

Suzanne put her arm around her shoulders and led her up the stairs to the front door. "Nah. He might dismember you, but then he'll duct-tape you back together."

Maddie opened the unlocked door and took a deep breath. "Can you come in with me?"

Suzanne turned toward the deserted street, then back at the house with the beacon of light. "Sure.

Just for a few minutes, to make sure everything's okay."

They stepped through the door into the quiet entry hall, closing the door softly behind them. A light glowed from the kitchen, casting a small circle of light into the entranceway.

Keeping her voice to a whisper, Suzanne said, "Your dad is probably still up. You go on to bed. Neither one of you is ready to talk right now. I'll go let him know you're here."

Maddie nodded and handed Suzanne her coffee mug, then turned toward the stairs. As soon as she reached the bottom stair, she ran back to Suzanne and threw her arms around her. "Thank you. I don't care what people say about you not liking children. I don't believe it."

Suzanne rolled her eyes. "Take two aspirins before you go to bed. You won't feel as bad in the morning."

"Okay." Maddie headed up the stairs.

"And drink lots of water. The alcohol will dehydrate you and make you feel more tired than you already are."

Maddie paused on the landing and looked down at Suzanne, still lightly swaying. "How do you know all this stuff?"

Suzanne braced herself for the wave of pain that usually came when a question regarding her mother's alcoholism came up. She was surprised to feel only an old, dull ache in her heart, as if the pain had been wrapped in something soft and cushiony to protect her. Without resentment, she said, "Years of practice taking care of my mother. She was an alcoholic."

There was a long pause as Maddie stood staring at Suzanne over the banister. "I'm sorry. Not just for your mama, but for getting drunk and making you deal with it. It was really immature."

"Yeah, it was. Don't do it again."

With a nod, Maddie headed back up the stairs, and Suzanne watched her until she disappeared into the dark hallway above. Then, with a deep breath, she walked to the kitchen, preparing to do battle.

The small light over the stove was on, but the kitchen was empty. As she walked forward to turn off the light, she peered into the family room and stopped midstride.

Joe was asleep on the sofa, the TV's remote control still dangling from his hand. A muted infomercial selling cellulite cream flashed on the screen. After tiptoeing across the room, she gently took the remote from his hand and turned off the TV. She pulled an afghan off the back of the couch and covered him with it, making sure not to wake him.

Then she slid off her flip-flops and curled up in the opposite corner to wait for him to awaken. She wanted to make sure he knew Maddie was safe upstairs before she left. Feeling chilled, she pulled a corner of the afghan up over her bare feet and laid her head back on the back of the couch and watched Joe sleep.

His face was soft and relaxed, like that of a young boy, his dark hair tousled on his forehead. The lines of worry on his forehead seemed smoothed by the fingers of sleep, erasing all except pleasant dreams. A small smile twitched at the corner of his mouth, and Suzanne remembered something her mother had once told her about talking to the angels in dreams.

She smiled back, feeling how heavy her eyelids were, until she, too, fell sound asleep.

She awoke to weak daylight slapping her in the face and the smell of coffee emanating from the kitchen. Opening her eyes, she noted that Joe was gone and that the afghan had been pulled up under her chin. Sitting up quickly, she spotted Joe, perched on the coffee table in front of her, his hazel eyes watching closely.

"You look different when you sleep."

She rubbed her eyes and tried to sound coherent. "So do you."

"I meant that in a good way."

"So did I." She yawned, and he put a cup of coffee in her hand. "I was only supposed to wait until you woke up and let you know that Maddie was upstairs asleep. Sorry."

He grinned one of those heart-stopping grins, and she shifted uncomfortably. "People will be talking, you know—seeing as how you've slept with the mayor."

She blushed and looked down in her mug before taking a long sip. "Hope that doesn't ruin your chances of reelection."

He hesitated for a moment before reaching to pull something out of his back pocket. "Probably not. But this might."

He handed her ten crisp one-hundred-dollar bills, folded neatly in half. "Joey gave them to me. He saw them in your purse when you were pulling out money for Candy Land. He didn't think they were real."

She took the money and looked at the brightness of the new bills. "I . . . I didn't notice it missing. Thanks."

"We don't see wads of cash like that around here."

Still looking down, she said, "No, I don't guess that you would."

He waited for a moment to speak. Then he said, "Where did it come from?"

This time she faced him, noticing how his eyes seemed to have darkened to match the green of his shirt. "I sold something that belonged to me. For cash."

"I see." His eyes told her that he didn't. "Wouldn't that kind of money be better off in a bank?"

She shook her head. "I'm not planning on being

here much longer. It would be silly to open an account."

"Right. I forgot."

The house was completely silent except for the ticking of the hall clock. The sky outside had lightened to a pink-tinged gray, announcing a new day. "I should go," she said, putting her emptied mug on the coffee table and standing. Joe stood with her.

"Aren't you going to tell me what happened tonight with Maddie?"

She tilted her head as she looked up at him. "No. That's between you and her. But be gentle with her, Joe. She misses her mother more than she lets on."

"I know." He bowed his head for a moment. "Not that getting drunk is something I'm going to allow her to get away with."

"I'm sure you'll do the right thing. You seem to have a gift for this parenting thing."

"And so do you—which is odd, considering you don't even like children."

She rolled her eyes. "Why does everybody keep saying that?"

"You know, first impressions and all that. Not that all of mine were totally off base."

Half of her mouth turned up. "Really? Well, I'm sorry I said that thing about the leash laws. I didn't really mean it."

"Yeah, sure." He opened his mouth as if to say

something more, then stopped before starting again. "Would you like to go out with me sometime?"

Her eyebrows shot up. "Like a date, you mean? You, me, dinner, movie kind of thing?"

He shrugged. "Yeah, something like that."

"Why?"

It was his turn to raise eyebrows. "Because I think we'd have fun together."

"No."

"Why not?"

"I thought I made it clear at the creek. Because I could be bad news for you. And because it can't lead to anything."

"I know. I don't want it to. I don't have the time or energy for a relationship. Or the heart. I already gave it to someone else, and I buried it with her. I just need, oh, I don't know. I just need to get out. And I figured that you probably do, too."

She looked down and stubbed her toe into the carpet. "Aren't you worried about being seen with me?"

He touched her chin and lifted her head to face him. "I'll deal with that. Don't you think we could just go out and have fun? I think we both could use a dose of fun in our lives."

She backed away, making him drop his hand. "Good-bye, Joe."

Turning from him, she left the room. He didn't

follow, but his voice called out to her, "Is that a no?"

She paused at the front door. "I don't know."

Before he could say more, she let herself out of the house and closed the door behind her. Filling her lungs with the damp morning air, she walked down the steps to the sidewalk and noticed the dim moon above, pale against the dawn sky. It was full and heavy again, the cycles of its phases completed. She stopped and stared at it for a moment, thinking it was telling her that even change had its pattern, bringing one back to the starting place.

Pulling her sweater tight to ward off the chill, she walked down the sidewalk toward home.

CHAPTER 13

Darlene Narpone lived in a well-kept but small two-bedroom cottage that was painted an unexpected shade of pink. It was similar to the shade of Lucinda's car, and as Suzanne walked up the front walkway, she envisioned the car parked in front of the house, like one of Lucinda's matching lipstick and compact sets.

The wreath on the front door was a handcrafted concoction consisting of dried eucalyptus branches, a fat permanent marker, a fake camera, and a large pair of scissors. Suzanne reached her hand through the wreath and knocked.

Darlene answered the door after the second knock, her appearance making Suzanne stare longer than politeness allowed. Darlene wore her scrapbooking apron covering a full skirt, panty hose, and high heels. The smell of baking bread wafted from the kitchen to complete the June Cleaver effect, and Suzanne shifted her own feet to hide the scuffed flip-flops under her denim skirt.

She looked at her watch. "Hi, Darlene. Did I get the time right? It looks like you're expecting company."

Opening the door wider, Darlene said, "Don't be silly, sugar. Being forty and still single, I figure I always need to be prepared in case Prince Charming rings my doorbell. Come on in."

Suzanne felt as if she'd been thrown into an episode of *Leave It to Beaver.* Every available furniture surface was covered with crisp white doilies, and atop those were small white porcelain figurines of plump cherubs with oversized eyes. Fresh vacuum marks were lined in geometrical precision from one wall to the other like marching soldiers, and Suzanne had the feeling that if she'd had white gloves to run over the furniture, Darlene would have passed the test with flying colors.

This homey icon to domesticity had once been the sort of place she'd imagined for herself and Anthony: a home to raise a family. And now, she realized with a start, she was comparing it to the unruly clutter of Joe's house, a house whose disorder seemed to embrace you and pull you in and sit you on a worn couch before you realized what had hit you.

Straightening a doily on the coffee table, Darlene said, "My workshop's in the back of the house. Come on with me and I'll get you what you need."

With a backward glance at the immaculate front parlor, Suzanne followed Darlene into a small bedroom right off the kitchen.

"This is my workroom, where I can scrap and leave it a mess. I just close the door and don't worry about it when I have company."

Darlene smiled and folded her hands in front of her as Suzanne surveyed the room. Shelves of printed paper, markers, cutters, die cuts, and stickers covered the lower third of the four walls. A large paper cutter and other items were laid out in an orderly fashion on a card table in the corner, while a large, flat-surfaced table occupied the center of the room. Suzanne looked at a black metallic object clamped to the edge of the table, and moved to give it a closer look.

Not able to figure it out, she asked, "What is this?"

Like a kindergarten teacher empowering a student with wisdom, Darlene proudly announced, "It's an official scrapbooking cup holder. I designed it myself, and I'm applying for a patent. It's so you can drink while scrapbooking and not have to worry about spilling anything on your pages."

"Wow. I guess some people take this scrap-booking thing pretty seriously."

Darlene pursed her lips, and a stern expression came over her face. "It's about preserving your history for future generations. That's a very serious endeavor. I know that's how Harriet Warner felt about it. She was going to do an album for each of her children, showing their history. Who they were, where they came from—that sort of thing. Like I said before, she never got to finish the first one—Maddie's."

She walked over to a tall cabinet and pulled out a plastic storage bin. A large square photo album, covered in a soft blue linen, lay on top. When Suzanne looked closer, she saw a name embossed in gold on the front. She read the name out loud as her fingers fell to touch the gilded letters. "Madison Cassandra Warner." Smiling to herself, she said, "Funny, I didn't know her full name. I guess she's named after her aunt."

"Oh yes. Harriet wasn't going to let hard feelings stand in the way of doing the right thing. She and Cassie had always been close—until Joe—and it never occurred to her to name her firstborn after anybody but her sister."

Suzanne picked up the album, gingerly holding it as if she held the hopes and dreams of a mother for her child. "What was she like—Harriet?" The name felt odd on her lips.

Darlene smiled. "She was beautiful, and not just on the outside. She had a heart of gold, that one. She loved everybody and everybody loved her. Joe thought the sun rose and set over her head." Darlene looked away and dabbed at her eyes. "She also had a spine of steel. If anything ever needed to be done, Harriet Warner was always the first one in line. The Methodist church would still be without a steeple if she hadn't had the whole structure put on the National Historic Register. The entire congregation had been hemming and hawing and doing bake sales for years to raise funds, and it took Harriet less than a year."

She looked back at Suzanne, small frown lines puckering her forehead. "Joe was just about crazy with grief when she died. If it hadn't been for his kids, I think he would have just lain down beside her and passed on."

Placing the storage box in the middle of the table, she brightened. "I do think that Harriet would want Joe to find someone else. Not just to help him with the kids, but to be there for him. I'm glad you two have found each other."

Suzanne found herself violently shaking her head. "No—that's not really the way it is. See, I'm just passing through, staying in Walton for a short time. I'm not really . . ."

She paused and watched a quizzical expression appear on Darlene's face as the woman took a closer look at the lid of the storage box where the album had been.

"Well, I'll be." In the center of the white plastic lid lay a shiny new penny, the copper reflecting brightly in the overhead light. "How on earth did this get here?"

"Maybe you accidentally dropped it there the last time you looked at the album."

Darlene looked at her with wide brown eyes, her short lashes lifted in tight curls. "But I haven't touched the box or the album since Harriet died. And the penny is brand-new."

Shifting the album to one arm, Suzanne took the penny and looked at it closely. The date marked was the current year. She raised her eyebrows. "Then how . . . ?"

Darlene clutched her hands in front of her heart. "Pennies from heaven. I'm sure of it."

"What?" Suzanne tried to shrug away an uneasiness that seemed to blow down her spine, almost knowing what Darlene was going to say next.

"Pennies from heaven. When those who have gone on before us want us to know that they're still with us. Sweetpea Crandall's mother left a penny beneath an orange juice can in the freezer—a brand that only her mother drank and that had been in the freezer for over a year before Sweetpea had the heart to throw it out. That's when she found the penny, and it was like her mother telling her that she was all right and that it was okay to go on with her life. And it was a brand-new, shiny penny, too."

Suzanne plopped the penny back on the lid, afraid to touch it. "Now, surely you don't mean . . ."

Darlene nodded sagely. "I do. I think Harriet's telling you that she approves."

Staring at the shiny penny, Suzanne said, "Please don't go spreading that around. Joe and I are really just friends, with no intention to ever take it further. The children—especially Sarah Frances—would be hurt to hear that kind of thing."

Picking up the penny, Darlene slid it into her apron pocket. "I understand." She smiled a toothy grin. "But remember that Harriet approves. And if she thinks it should happen, it will."

Not wanting to continue the conversation further, Suzanne asked, "What's in the box?"

"Oh, just an assortment of things—old photos, die cuts, stickers, markers. Pretty much everything you'll need to finish the album. Except the graduation pictures, of course. Those you'll have to add later." She popped open the lid and glanced inside. "And I'm more than happy to give you ideas on how to decorate the pages. Harriet did such a beautiful job, I'm sure the ones she already did will be a perfect example for you."

She closed the box and took the album from

Suzanne. After placing it on top of the lid, she opened the cover slowly and Suzanne held her breath.

The first photo was an old class picture. The sign a boy held in the front row read WALTON ELEMENTARY, MRS. CRANDALL'S FIFTH-GRADE CLASS. She peered closely at the boy, at the slicked-back hair and the defiant cowlick, and recognized Joe. She looked back at the young girl next to the boy. She wore a white dress with ankle socks and pink Keds. A matching pink headband held back yellow-blond hair, showing small pearl earrings. She smiled shyly at the camera, leaning forward slightly as if she'd just finished saying something.

It was as if Suzanne were looking at a female version of Harry, and she knew without a doubt the girl in the picture was a young Harriet. She recognized Cassie, Sam, and Ed Farrell, though only after close consideration. They had changed a great deal since fifth grade.

"I thought Harriet was younger than Cassie. Why are they all in the same grade?"

Darlene leaned over her shoulder and looked at the picture. "Mrs. Madison wanted her girls to be in the same grade, so she held Cassie back from kindergarten so she and Harriet could go to school together. I don't think they would have wanted it any other way."

She slid a neatly manicured nail to the back row

of the picture. "This here's their older brother, Ed Farrell. Course, we didn't know back then that he was Judge Madison's son. He's two years older, but he was held back twice."

Peering closely at Cassie in the photo, Suzanne realized with a start that the young Cassie wore a gold chain on her neck. It was too small to see clearly in the picture, but Suzanne was sure small heart charms dangled from the chain. The chain was shorter, and there were only a few charms, but it was definitely the same hearts. Without thinking, Suzanne reached up and touched her own charm, feeling a connection suddenly to the children in the photo. It was a small thing, but the closest she would ever be to belonging with them.

The scrapbook's page was decorated with stickers and die cuts and labeled with neat, precise handwriting recording the history of Madison Cassandra Warner. As Suzanne turned the pages, it was as if Harriet were sitting beside her and showing Maddie's life before Suzanne had come to know her. It was as if an unseen hand helped fit the pieces of a puzzle into the correct slots to complete a picture of the young woman she'd come to know.

Suzanne remembered the conversation she'd had with Joe at the cemetery as he'd shown her the graves of his great-grandparents, and she realized that making an album of a child's history was just about the same thing as identifying people in a graveyard and picking your space between them. It was the fruit of belonging, of always knowing where you came from and where there was always a place held open for you to come back. Joe, Harriet, Maddie, and everyone else she had met in Walton were grounded here in this town, like oak trees with long, deep roots. She grimaced slightly, realizing that she was more like the dandelion seed, scattered and settled at the wind's whim, with roots no deeper than the next strong breeze.

Her thoughts made her heart ache, and for one brief moment she pictured herself standing still long enough to grow roots. And then she let it go. Holding on to dreams had only ever led to disappointment.

She turned the next page of the album and smiled at the black-and-white close-up of two feet: the sole of a man's foot and on top of that a baby's. The caption read MADDIE FOLLOWING IN DADDY'S FOOTSTEPS. The poignancy of the photo tugged again at Suzanne, and she tapped the plastic cover on the photo, guessing where Maddie's talent for photography came from. She'd have to remember to tell that to Maddie. It would bring comfort to know that she carried a part of her mother, in the same way that not knowing what traits Suzanne had received from her own mother kept her tossing in bed at night.

Closing the album, she looked up at Darlene.

"Thank you. I'll give you a call if I need help, but I think I have a pretty good idea what Harriet was trying to do. And I'll take more pictures of Maddie to add, as well as ones that Maddie has taken. She'll love it." She stacked the album on top of the storage box.

"I know she will. Especially knowing that both her mother and you worked on it."

Not really sure how to respond, Suzanne turned away and moved through the kitchen and toward the front door. As she stood on the stoop, Darlene reached into her pocket and retrieved the penny. Placing it squarely on top of the album, she said, "This is yours. Keep it in a safe place, now, you hear?"

The penny seemed to wink at her in the bright sunlight's glare. She wanted to refuse it but didn't want it to seem as though she believed Darlene's story of where it came from. She slipped the penny into the pocket of her skirt.

"Thanks," she said as she readjusted the box and album. She felt as if she held a lifetime's worth of memories, none of them hers, and more than one message from a woman who had died nearly three years before but whose presence almost seemed as palpable as the cement sidewalk under Suzanne's feet.

Joe turned the lawn mower around, then paused and whipped off his T-shirt. As summer moved into fall, the air was certainly cooler, but mowing Miss Lena's lawn using her antiquated manual lawn mower was enough to kill a man.

He blinked the sweat out of his eyes and began to push another row to the sidewalk. A quick blast from a car horn made him look up as Lucinda's long pink car swerved into the driveway, barely missing the mailbox. Suzanne Paris sat next to Lucinda in the front seat, holding a casserole dish and wearing rhinestone sunglasses that matched the ones worn by the older woman.

Lucinda waved. "Hey, Joe. I didn't know it was your turn to mow Miss Lena's lawn or I would have sent this food over with you."

He narrowed his eyes at her, trying to figure out what she was up to. For the past three years, they had been on Miss Lena's caregiving schedule together and usually gone to lunch at the Dixie Diner when Lucinda finished delivering her food offering.

When Suzanne stepped out of the car, it became obvious. She wore an electric blue short-sleeved sweater atop a lighter blue leather miniskirt. He scanned her long legs, bracing himself for her ubiquitous flip-flops, and was surprised to find high-heeled strappy sandals. Below the rhinestone sunglasses, Suzanne frowned.

"We've been shopping," Lucinda announced proudly.

"I can see that." Joe tried to peel his gaze away

from Suzanne, who was leaning into the backseat to retrieve something. He failed.

Juggling a covered basket and casserole dish, Suzanne said, "I wasn't expecting to be seen in public."

Lucinda turned toward her. "Now, honey, you know I said we needed to make just this one stop before I brought you home to change. How was I supposed to know somebody would be here?"

Studiously avoiding Joe's eyes, Lucinda gathered up a laundry basket stacked with clean and folded clothes and shut the car door with her hip. "Suzanne, just put that stuff on the porch for me to bring in. You can stay out here and chat with Joe until I'm done."

Suzanne walked past him, her heels clicking on the cement sidewalk. "That's all right. I'd like to see Miss Lena."

Lucinda raised an eyebrow at Joe.

Joe leaned on the handle of the lawn mower. "I think she wants to discuss *Love's Passionate Desire* with Miss Lena. Miss Lena already tried with me, but I couldn't get past the scene on horseback." He felt a flush of satisfaction as he noticed Suzanne glancing at his bare chest and trying to pretend as if she weren't. Not feeling at all cooperative, he slid his shirt back on and put the mower in a stopping position. "As a matter of fact, why don't I just come on in with y'all and see if I can't learn something new?"

Not waiting for an answer, he followed the women inside.

Miss Lena sat in her worn recliner, watching a movie on the Lifetime cable channel. She turned toward her visitors as they entered, and gave them a wide smile. Joe could tell she was having one of her good days by the brightness in her eyes. Using the remote to flip off the television, she slowly slid to the edge of her chair before using both arms to help her stand. "Visitors! I'll go get everybody a glass of sweet tea."

Lucinda shook her head. "No, Miss Lena. You stay right here and visit while I go get some. Have you taken your medicine today?"

Miss Lena held up her fingers in a Girl Scout salute. "Yes, I promise."

"Good." Lucinda put the laundry basket down and relieved Suzanne of her burden. "I'll be right back," she said before disappearing into the kitchen.

Suzanne stood awkwardly in the middle of the room, facing Miss Lena. "You have a lovely house."

The old woman peered closely at Suzanne. "Something scandalous won, you know. Looks like the park is getting a fall planting of panties."

Joe coughed. "I think you mean 'pansies,' Miss Lena. You know, the flowers."

She looked up at him with a confused expression. "I'm sure the book said 'panties.' He took them off of her when they were on horseback." Reaching into the wicker basket by the side of her chair, she pulled out a well-worn book with yellowed pages and a torn cover with the large-scripted title *Love's Passionate Desire* and handed it to Suzanne. "Have you read this yet? Go ahead and take it, then, and we can discuss it next time you stop by."

Joe looked at a startled Suzanne, her expression like that of a woman who'd just missed being hit by a speeding train. He moved to intercede, but Suzanne surprised him by speaking first.

"Thank you, Miss Lena. I look forward to reading it and discussing it with you." She smiled shyly. "My mother was a huge romance fan. Whenever I think of her, I always picture her with a romance book in her hand. It was the one thing in her life that truly made her happy." She turned the book over and stared at the cover. "It's been a while since I've been in the mood to read about happy endings, but this looks like a good place to start." She touched Miss Lena's arm. "Thank you," she said again.

The old woman placed a hand over Suzanne's. "It was one of your mother's favorites."

Suzanne peered closely at Miss Lena for a long moment before removing her hand. "Then I know I'll love it." She stepped back, cradling the book close to her chest.

Joe moved to sit on the footstool next to Miss

Lena, to distract her and give Suzanne some breathing space. In the short time he'd known her, he knew how important it was to Suzanne. "Has Sam been by to see you lately? You're looking really wonderful. I don't think I've seen such a pretty pink in someone's cheeks since Sue-Ellen Elmore on her wedding day."

As he chatted with Miss Lena, he kept an eye on Suzanne, who was walking around the room looking at old photos and studying the various frames hung on the wall. There was one in particular, over by the television and between the velvet-draped windows, which seemed to have captured her attention. He watched her as she studied it, her hand absently wandering to her necklace with the single gold heart charm. It no longer startled him to see it, and even now all he could think of as he watched her fingertips brush it was the way it had looked on her bare skin in the moonlight.

He turned around to find that Miss Lena was watching Suzanne, too. "That's from *Little Women*. That was my favorite book in the world until I discovered sex."

Startled, he and Suzanne swung around to look at the demure elderly woman sitting with a pink sweater on her shoulders and her hands folded in her lap. Joe made a mental note to ask Sam about limiting Miss Lena's time watching cable television.

He stood and moved next to Suzanne, peering over her shoulder at the cross-stitch framed on the wall. Within a thick border of flowers were the words "Into each life some rain must fall." The initials in the corner were the same as the ones on the cross-stitch in baby Harry's room—E.L. Miss Lena had given it to Harriet when Maddie was born, and it had hung in each child's room when they were babies. Only recently, Maddie had asked if she could take it with her to hang in her dorm room when she went away to school. It comforted him knowing that she wanted to take a piece of her childhood away with her, but it also left him hollow and aching, and wishing his oldest child weren't in such a rush to leave home.

Suzanne reached up to touch the glass, where the initials were stitched. "Who's E.L.?"

Joe looked surprised. "Miss Lena. Her first name is actually Eulene, but nobody's ever called her that."

Her hand closed over the gold heart around her neck again, and she knitted her brows together. Slowly she turned and walked toward Miss Lena, sitting down on the footstool vacated by Joe.

"My mother used to say that to me all the time. I guess she loved *Little Women*, too."

"She did. I gave her my copy to read." A shadow seemed to pass behind her eyes as the elderly woman turned to Joe. "Are you Sam? Why is Sam here?" Her gnarled fingers agitated the pink sleeves of the sweater that rested on her shoulders.

Lucinda came from the kitchen then with a tray filled with an iced-tea pitcher and three glasses. As Lucinda set the tray down on the coffee table, Joe moved next to Miss Lena. "I'm Joe Warner, Mildred and Joe Senior's boy. You taught me in Sunday school when I was in second grade, and you always gave me a toffee for memorizing Bible verses." He smiled and took her hand. "I think I was your favorite student."

Miss Lena gazed up at him, her expression mixed. He wasn't sure if she understood, and decided to give her a few moments to let it sink in. He retrieved filled glasses of sweet tea for Suzanne and Miss Lena and brought them back to where they sat. As he turned to get himself a glass, the old woman said, "I know you. You're Harriet Madison's husband. I remember now."

He glanced back in time to see the stricken look on Suzanne's face before Miss Lena continued. "Now, who's this beautiful girl? Are you single, honey? Because if you are, I know the perfect man for you."

Joe concentrated on holding his glass still as he raised it to his lips and listened to the ice cubes clink against each other.

Suzanne cleared her throat. "I've met Ed, Miss Lena. He seems like a real nice guy, but I'm not exactly in the market. . . ."

Miss Lena shook her head. "No, that's not who

I was talking about. We have a nice gentleman in town who's lost his wife. He thinks he's fine on his own, but he's really not. And he probably hasn't had any sex since she died."

Joe struggled to keep a hold of his own glass as he watched Suzanne turn a deep shade of red. She took a deep swallow of the tea and choked. Joe quickly handed her a napkin as she sputtered.

"How much sugar goes into sweet tea anyway?"

Lucinda tasted her own tea before answering, "About four cups. Why? Is there not enough in yours?"

"Yes, um, it's fine."

Miss Lena raised thin gray eyebrows. "You must not be from around here." She looked at Suzanne expectantly.

Almost recovered from Miss Lena's broadside and glad for the switch in topic, Joe took the opportunity to leave without further embarrassment. Placing his empty glass on the tray, he said good-bye to the three women, avoiding Suzanne's eyes, and went back outside to continue mowing. Maybe he could cut his foot off so that people would have something else besides his widowed status to remember him by. "Joe, the guy who cut off his foot" sounded much better than "Joe, the guy whose wife died."

Bracing his muscles, he gave the old mower a push and headed down yet another straight line of green grass. He inhaled deeply, smelling something else over the sweet scent of the cut grass. He paused, recognizing the smell of the season's change hovering in the air.

For a long time he had resisted any change, seeing it as moving him further from Harriet and the life they had shared together. But now, for the first time since her death, the thought of change no longer seemed to squeeze at his heart. He wasn't sure what was different, but he almost felt he could face Maddie's moving away, and Harry's growing older, and even another Christmas without Harriet. It was as if even the changes had a rhythm to them, bringing you back to the place you started—only the second time around you were stronger and wiser.

He pushed harder on the mower, turning his face toward the fresh fall breeze, and welcomed the change with an enthusiasm bordered by old grief and new hope.

CHAPTER 14

Suzanne lay in bed, listening to the incessant hammering downstairs. She was supposed to be at work, which was the only reason Sam was at the house working. But this morning she had awoken with a burning fever, and just getting out of bed to reach the phone had taken up her day's energy.

She had appreciated the concern in Lucinda's

voice but had assured her it was probably just a bug and she'd most likely be up and about the next day. But as the morning progressed, she felt worse and worse, and the hammering seemed to reverberate in her head until she thought her eyeballs would lose their grip in their sockets.

Wearily she struggled to a sitting position and dragged on her bathrobe. Hauling herself across the bedroom and downstairs, she went in search of Sam and the torturing hammer.

She found him in the dining room, hanging beadboard on the bottom half of the wall. He was in the middle of hammering a bottom panel in place when he must have spotted the flash of red from her robe and glanced up. He froze in place for a long moment, his hammer suspended in midair.

"Suzanne. I'm sorry—I thought you were at work. Did I get the schedule wrong?"

She shook her head, then wished she hadn't, since it felt as if her brain were sloshing inside her skull. "No. I called in sick." She leaned against the doorframe, not sure she had the energy to stand anymore.

Sam dropped the hammer and stood at the same time a movement out of the corner of her eye caught her attention. Joe, who had apparently been sawing a piece of wood on the sawhorse, quickly approached her and placed his arm around her right before her knees buckled. His lips twitched in an effort not to smile. "Have you caught a glimpse of yourself in a mirror recently?"

"No," she croaked, her voice dry.

"I'm going to carry you up to your bedroom now, all right? You're sick, and that's where you need to be."

"I can walk. Really." She shrugged away from Joe and Sam and started for the stairs. After two steps, her knees buckled and Joe grabbed her again before she fell face-first on the sawdust-covered floor.

Without asking this time, Joe grabbed her under her knees and carried her upstairs before laying her gently on the bed. Despite the crisp and clean linens, the pillowcase seemed made of itchy sandpaper, and she reached her hand up to claw at her cheek.

Joe grabbed hold of her wrist while Sam felt her forehead. "Don't scratch. Wait a minute." Joe walked over to the bureau, where a small hand-held mirror lay. He came back and sat on the edge of her bed. "Take a look."

She looked at her reflection and wasn't sure whether she wanted to gasp in horror or laugh hysterically. Small red dots covered her face as if she'd been the victim of a horrible painting accident. "Oh" was all she managed.

Sam spoke from where he sat on the other side of the bed. "Have you not been feeling well lately?"

"Um, not really. Not like today, but not myself."

"Well, it's my guess that you have chicken pox. When did you babysit Joe's kids?"

She heard Joe groan as she closed her eyes, using all her concentration in the pounding of her head. "It was two weeks ago yesterday."

Sam slapped his thighs before standing. "Yep. That would be it. Okay. I'm going to go get my bag and check you out while Joe calls Lucinda. Somebody will need to come in and take care of you. Trust me—chicken pox as an adult is not something to mess with."

"Sam, really, I can take care of myself. I'll be fine. There's no need to bother anybody on my account."

Sam ducked his head for a moment, and she could see the creases of a smile. "Suzanne, let me try to make this as plain as I can. See those bumps on your face? You're going to be crawling with them all over your body—both inside and out." He paused as if to let the mental picture sink in. "You will be miserable wanting to scratch, and the fever will make it worse. Most important, I need to make sure that somebody's here to make sure you're keeping hydrated and eating—as well as to keep an eye on your fever."

Suzanne shook her head on the pillow, feeling again the sensation of her brain meeting the sides of her skull with each movement. "I don't want anybody to take care of me. I've always—"

With a stern look, Sam said, "No more arguing. You may be used to looking out for yourself, but we here in Walton are used to taking care of those who need it. You might as well just lie back and get used to it."

Sam left, and Joe sat and took her hand. "I'm sorry. This is my fault. I shouldn't have let you near Sarah Frances with you not knowing if you'd had chicken pox before."

She tried to squeeze his hand but found she didn't have the strength. "It's all right," she mumbled, but wasn't sure she'd been coherent enough for him to understand.

Joe leaned forward, and she thought she felt a soft kiss on her forehead. "I'm calling Lucinda now. Don't worry—we'll take good care of you."

Feeling like a wilting flower, Suzanne sank back on her pillow with a groan and accepted her fate. With reluctance, she allowed her eyelids to close and was drifting off to sleep by the time she heard Joe's footsteps fading away down the stairs.

She awoke to the scent of heavy perfume and a cool hand on her forehead. Her entire body felt as if it were on fire, and she pressed her forehead against the cool hand, trying to soothe the ache. The sensation of having one thousand ants crawling on her body flicked her eyes open, and she reached for her cheeks, ready to claw off the offending intruders, and found to her surprise that her hands had been covered in soft white gloves.

Somebody leaned over into Suzanne's field of vision, and she found herself staring into the concerned face of Lucinda Madison.

"Don't scratch, honey. You've got beautiful skin, and I don't want you getting any scars."

The ants continued their march across her face, down her neck, and spread across her abdomen and down to her legs. "Please. I've got to scratch. I itch so bad. . . ."

She found her arms restrained by a surprisingly strong Lucinda. "I've drawn you a warm milk bath that will help with the itching on the outside. Dr. Parker left me with an antihistamine to give you that will help with the itching on the inside."

As if on cue, her mouth, nose, throat, and other internal areas of her body that she couldn't imagine scratching in public became invaded by the marching ants, making her fidget.

Lucinda pressed a pill to her lips. "Take this and you won't itch so bad."

Suzanne resisted, rejecting her dependence even through her fever and itch-induced haze.

Sweet, kind Lucinda forced open Suzanne's mouth, then dumped the medicine on the back of her tongue, forcing her to swallow before she could spit it out.

"Sugar, I've been tending children and sick folks all my life, so there's no use in fighting me. While you're sick, I'm stronger than you, and you're going to have to do as I say."

Suzanne turned her head away to show her displeasure, but deep inside she felt a part of herself sigh with relief that she didn't have to go through this alone.

"Are you ready for that bath, or would you like to eat something first? I brought my own homemade chicken soup. Guaranteed to make you feel better. And I promise I won't force-feed you."

Suzanne managed a smile. "This itching's about to kill me. Can I do the bath first and then have the soup?"

Lucinda's red-painted lips broadened into a wide smile. "That sounds like a good idea to me. I'll help you into the bath, and while you're soaking I'll do a load of laundry and throw in your sleep shirt, all right?"

Suzanne nodded and, for the first time in a very long while, allowed herself to be taken care of.

When she next awoke, after having been bathed and fed and put back to bed, she was surprised to find Sarah Frances sitting in a chair by the bed, reading from a math textbook and writing numbers in a notebook. She glanced up without a smile.

"How are you feeling?"

"Terrible."

Sarah Frances moved her homework to the floor and stood. "I need to take your temperature."

"Why are you here?" Suzanne's voice croaked, and Sarah Frances poured her a fresh glass of water from a pitcher on her nightstand and handed it to her before sticking the thermometer under her tongue.

"It was Aunt Cassie's turn to come sit with you, but Uncle Sam didn't think it was a good idea— with the baby and all. So I said I would." She looked down, her cheeks flushed.

"Thanks," Suzanne mumbled through the thermometer.

The girl shrugged. "Well, I felt bad since I gave it to you."

Suzanne tried to struggle to a sitting position but gave up when her head threatened to explode. "It's not your fault. I had no idea that I'd never had chicken pox as a kid."

Sarah Frances shrugged again. "Well, I still felt bad. And stop talking or you'll mess up the reading." She turned and walked toward the bureau, where she pulled something off it and returned to the bedside to show Suzanne. "Aunt Cassie sent some of her flannel nightgowns. Lucinda told her that you only had the one T-shirt, and Aunt Cassie thought that with so many visitors you might want something else to change into."

"So many visitors . . . ?"

There was a tap on the bedroom door, and the flowered top of a hat entered first before the face beneath it. It was one of the Sedgewick twins. "Can we come in?"

260

Not convinced that what she answered would matter, Suzanne said, "Yes."

Sarah Frances took the thermometer out of her mouth, looked at it, and jotted something down on a piece of paper by the bed.

The two women, dressed in matching yellow pantsuits, hats, and yellow patent leather sandals, entered the room with identical cloth bags tucked under their arms. "We're here to relieve Sarah Frances and to ask you what color you want your afghan to be."

Suzanne squinted, afraid that the fever was making her see double, but when the women came and sat on either side of her, she knew they were for real. Knowing better than to send the room spinning by trying to sit up, she stayed where she was on the pillow. "Afghan?"

"Yes, dear," said the twin on her right, the flower on top of her head bobbing in rhythm with the woman's cheeks. "Nothing warms a sickbed better than a nice afghan in a favorite color. We figured while we were sitting here during our shift, we could start making your afghan."

Sarah Frances began gathering up her things. "She'll need the ibuprofen and Benadryl in another hour or so. She hasn't had dinner yet, either." She pointed to the piece of paper she had written on earlier. "Here's her schedule—just make sure you mark down anything you give her."

The twins pulled up chairs, one on each side of the bed, and extracted fuzzy white slippers from their bags. "All right, and we brought our special vegetable soup—the one that almost won the *Good Housekeeping* contest three years ago."

Sarah Frances stood by the side of the bed and spoke, her eyes not meeting Suzanne's. "Aunt Cassie said to call if you need anything. And I left her nightgowns on the dresser."

Suzanne raised her hand to scratch her neck and noticed that the white gloves were back on.

The young girl addressed the twins. "And make sure she keeps those gloves on. I safety-pinned them to the long sleeves of her T-shirt, so make sure you take them off her before she goes to the bathroom or something."

The ladies nodded solemnly as Sarah Frances turned back to Suzanne. "It'll be pretty bad for the first five days, but you'll get used to it. And I took Aunt Lu's milk baths at least twice a day and that really helped."

"Thanks, Sarah Frances. I appreciate it. And thanks again for your help today."

The girl shrugged. "Yeah, well. I'm sorry about all this." With a small wave, she walked away with a muffled good-bye.

"Do you need to go use the lavatory, dear?"

Suzanne brought her attention back to the featherless canary at her bed and wondered which one had spoken. "The lavatory?"

The other twin leaned over the other side of the bed. "Powder your nose."

Suzanne thought hard for a moment before she figured it out. "No, I'm fine for now." She raised her hand again to scratch her chest and stared at the gloves in frustration. "But you could help me unpin these things. They're driving me crazy."

The two women stared down at her, their mouths drawn in matching frowns of disapproval. The one on the right said, "I don't think so, dear. We wouldn't want you marring your beautiful complexion. Why don't I have Selma draw you another milk bath while I entertain you? We could play 'I Spy'!"

Suzanne forced a smile as she sank lower into the bed. Using a toenail, she began to scratch mercilessly at the bumps on her other foot. The eagle eye of her current warden saw the movement under her blanket.

With a loud exhalation, Thelma stood, towering over Suzanne like a yellow apparition. "Tell me where you keep your socks, dear, and I won't have to get nasty."

Blinking rapidly, Suzanne indicated the dresser across the room, then sank farther down in her bed, pulling the blanket over her face.

The misery of the next few days passed in a blur as a stream of caretakers took their places in the armchairs across from her bed. Brunelle

Thompkins brought a pecan pie from the Dixie Diner for when she was feeling better. Mrs. Crandall brought a small portable TV with a DVD player and a few of her own favorite movies. Suzanne had never heard of most of them, never having been a fan of Humphrey Bogart or Clark Gable, but she found them a welcome relief to the boredom of being bedridden.

The purple-and-pink afghan the Sedgewick twins had made lay at the foot of the bed and had come in handy in the new, chilly fall nights. Mrs. Parker, Sam's mother, had come by several times and had sat in the chair knitting while Suzanne slept and then had helped her apply bright pink calamine lotion to the itchiest spots.

She had been pleased to see Miss Lena stop by, too. Ed had hung back in the doorway, but Miss Lena had come and sat on the edge of the bed, looking down at Suzanne with worried concern.

"Is Dr. Parker taking good care of you?"

"Yes, ma'am," Suzanne said, surprised to hear the word "ma'am" coming out of her own mouth.

A soft, warm hand touched her forehead. "You've got it bad, don't you? Your mama had it bad, too."

Suzanne glanced over at Ed for assistance, but he was busy cleaning his nails with a pocketknife.

"My Ed didn't have such a rough time with it, though. He was living with his other family then, so I guess it's a good thing. But I would have taken good care of him. I would have."

Maddie had told Suzanne about Ed's being adopted as an infant, and she knew Miss Lena was referring to Ed's adopted family. The story of them finding each other after all those years had touched Suzanne and somehow satisfied her to know that neither one of them had to be alone anymore. She glanced up at Miss Lena, and the elderly woman's eyes appeared clouded as she peered through the pages of years in her broken memory.

Miss Lena sat back and folded her hands in front of her with a wide grin. "I brought something for you." Reaching into her oversized black purse, she pulled out two dog-eared paperback books. The first, with a near-naked man and woman riding a horse on the cover, was entitled *Heaven's Passion*. With a wiggle of her eyebrows, Miss Lena pressed it into Suzanne's gloved hands.

The second book, to Suzanne's surprise, was an ancient copy of *Little Women*. "I want the other one back, but you can keep this one. I hope you enjoy it as much as your mama did. She read it three times back to back, starting page one as soon as she finished the last page."

This time Ed must have heard his mother, because he advanced into the room. "Mama, did you take your pills this morning?"

Miss Lena rolled her eyes, and Suzanne would

have laughed if her skin didn't itch so much and if she didn't feel a pang of sadness for Miss Lena.

Miss Lena pressed Suzanne's hand before she stood to leave. She allowed Ed to guide her out of the room, seeming much frailer than she had when she had spoken with animation about her beloved books.

Suzanne had then gone to sleep, her dreams chasing her from yellowed pages of books to a scene in a meadow with her and Joe on horseback. She had the distinct impression that they were naked.

Joe silently pushed the door open after hearing no response to his tapping. Suzanne lay in bed, curled on her side in what he would describe as a defensive position. When he had pictured her asleep, that was how he had seen her.

Quietly he moved to a stuffed armchair by the side of her bed and sat down, heaving his briefcase, stuffed with student papers to be graded, onto his lap. He pulled out the first paper and a red pen but just held on to them, unable to take his eyes off the woman in the bed.

Her long hair spilled over the pillow, veiling her face. But one long, elegant arm, covered with bright red and pink splotches, lay on top of the blanket, her gloved fingers clutching it in a fist under her chin as if preparing for a fight even in her sleep. His gaze wandered down the gentle slope of her body under the covers, and he was struck again by her vulnerability. It softened his heart in places he'd never expected to reach again.

She stirred, knocking off a stuffed bunny that Amanda had given to Maddie to bring to the patient. He realized the toy had been curled in Suzanne's arms, and that place in his heart pinched again, as if receiving an extra dose of softening. As he bent to retrieve the bunny, he noticed the two books on the nightstand. He picked up *Heaven's Passion* and opened it up to an earmarked page and began to read.

"Learning anything new?"

Startled, he slammed the book shut, feeling the tips of his ears burn as if he'd been caught with his pants down. He cleared his throat and looked at Suzanne. "Good morning, Sleeping Beauty."

She raised a hand to her face and stopped in dismay when she spotted the white gloves. Resigned, she lowered her hands to her lap. "Not that I can't take a compliment, but I think you need glasses."

He plopped the book down on the nightstand. "Actually, I think you need more of that pink stuff. You missed a spot."

She shifted to a sitting position, and he helped her adjust the pillow behind her back. "I think it would be easier if I just filled a bathtub with it and wallowed in it for an hour or two." With a frown, she wriggled under the covers. "I'd like to drink some, too, to reach all those places I can't scratch."

Joe glanced around the room, trying not to think of what Sam had told him about the severity of Suzanne's chicken pox. She had the itchy blisters all over her body—inside and out. It made him squirm. He sat down again in the armchair, feeling seventeen again in the scrutiny of her steel gray gaze. "Can I get anything for you? Food, water, a new DVD?"

"My camera, actually. I'd like to get a picture of everybody who sits in that chair. I think it would make a nice collage."

"I'm at your service. Just tell me where."

"It's on the top shelf of the closet, next to my backpack."

He pulled something out from his briefcase before moving it to the floor. "Oh, and I brought you a few back issues of *Lifetime* magazine. Maddie said it was your favorite. I had to barter season tickets to Walton High's football games for Mr. Harmon to release these from the library."

She held out her hands, and he placed the magazines in them. "Thanks." She smiled, making some of the dried calamine on her cheek crack. "I hope Mr. Harmon doesn't tell everybody what a pushover you are. Football coaches are supposed to be stern and admonishing."

He made a mock pass with a pretend football. "It'll be our secret."

He walked over to the closet and opened the door to the walk-in closet. As he pulled the camera from the shelf, his hand accidentally grabbed a strap from the backpack and tumbled it to the floor of the closet. When he bent to pick it up, the top flapped open and he caught sight of what was inside. He froze, staring at several bundles of crisp one-hundred-dollar bills.

"Did you find it?"

Somehow he found his voice. "Yes, coming."

He placed the bag back on the shelf and closed the closet door. He opened his mouth to question her but stopped. He'd ask her about it later, when she was feeling better. He couldn't deal with it now any more than he thought she could. And underneath it all, he trusted her. He couldn't explain it, but he did. It was in her clear gray eyes when she looked at him and in the clenched hand she placed under her chin when she slept.

Placing the camera next to her on the bed, he sat down again, pushing aside thoughts of the bag and the money. Smiling, he clasped his hands in front of him. "Well, at least let me entertain you. We could play connect the dots." He held up his red pen.

She lifted an eyebrow. "Or we could take turns reading from Miss Lena's book." After rubbing her neck with a gloved hand, she reached over and picked up *Heaven's Passion* and flipped it open to the same earmarked section that Joe had been reading. She stared at it for a moment, her eyes open as if trying to focus, and he saw the redness of her face deepen, the bumps on her face accentuated like the glow buttons on the arcade game at the Dixie Diner.

"Maybe not," she said, closing the book and letting it fall on her lap.

Joe took the book and placed it in the drawer of the nightstand, hiding it from sight. He sat down again. "Are you sure I can't get you something to eat?"

She shook her head, fiddling with her camera, then raised it to her eye before snapping a picture of him. "No, my stomach isn't feeling so great right now, and I'm afraid it will come back up. Just company is fine."

"Okay, who are you and what have you done to the real Suzanne Paris?"

"What?"

"Well, the Suzanne I know would never admit to wanting company."

She shrugged, looking down at her nightgown sleeve and fiddling with the safety pin. "Maybe I've changed my mind a bit."

He stared at her for a long moment, wondering what it had taken to let herself admit that little tidbit. "So, what would you like to talk about?"

She closed her eyes and spread her arms wide. "Oh, I don't know. How about Maddie? Have you decided on an appropriate punishment yet?"

270

He stretched his legs out in front of him, crossing them at the ankles. "Her next three or four weekends will be spent scraping and repainting the iron fence that goes around the town square."

"That's kind of rough, don't you think?"

"She's lucky I'm not sending her away to boarding school in Siberia."

"She's not a bad kid, you know. She's . . . scared."

He moved forward in his chair, resting his elbows on his knees. "What do you mean? What on earth could she be scared of?"

She paused, as if reluctant to share a confidence. Slowly, she said, "Of her own mortality. And of leaving you. She wants to go away for college but is reluctant to leave you here all alone."

"I'm hardly alone."

She raised an eyebrow. "Aren't you? You can be alone in a crowd of people, you know."

The truth stung him, and he responded before he could think. "And you'd know all about that, wouldn't you?"

She looked up at the ceiling and sank back on her pillow. "Yes, I guess I would."

"Look, I'm sorry. I didn't mean . . ."

She held up her hand. "Yes, you did—and it's true. But I want you to be gentle with Maddie. Let her spread her wings, but let her know that she still has a home to come back to. It will make all the difference."

He rubbed his hands over his face, thinking of his beloved, incorrigible eldest child. "She's been pushing at the bit ever since she was a baby, testing us, seeing how far we'd let her go before pulling her back."

"That sounds like the Maddie I know. But it's a wonder you had more children after that."

He heard the smile in her voice and decided not to take offense. "Do I need to explain the birds and bees to you, Miss Paris? Or maybe you need to read more of Miss Lena's books. But I would think that a person as well traveled as you would have some kind of understanding."

She turned away from him, hiding a small grin. "Oh, I think I understand the basics." She was silent for a moment, then said, "Did you know that there's some kind of moth that exists just to make more moths? Their mouths are too small to eat. So they just hang around, waiting to have sex before they die. Sort of a worthless existence."

"Not necessarily."

He enjoyed watching the display of bright coloring pass over her face again.

As if to change the subject, she said, "I went to Darlene Narpone's last week and picked up Maddie's album. Harriet did a beautiful job with it."

Joe paused, waiting for the jolt at the mention of Harriet's name, and was surprised that all he felt was a dull ache in his chest. "I haven't seen it."

"Would you like to look at it now? It's under the bed in case Maddie stops by again. I don't want to spoil the surprise for her."

He shook his head, knowing he wasn't ready to see it yet. "No, I'll wait until you're done."

A soft smile played on her lips, and despite her ravaged face, she still looked beautiful to him. "You were a goofy-looking fifth-grader."

He placed his hands behind his head as he leaned back. "Yep. I'm still trying to grow into my looks."

Her smile broadened. "I noticed there aren't any wedding pictures in the album. If you have any to give me, I'll be happy to add them."

The old memory hit him hard, but not with the pain he had expected. Instead, it seemed as if the old memories lay in a protective cocoon inside, waiting to be revisited but no longer able to hurt. "There aren't any. Harriet and I eloped. We always expected to have a big wedding later, with all our family and friends, but Har got pregnant with Maddie right away, and then, with Cassie being gone, it just never seemed right."

She splayed her white cotton fingers on her lap and stared down at them. "I don't think Harriet minded. It's funny, but working on the album and seeing the pictures Harriet chose to show Maddie's history and life, I feel as if I know her."

A lump lodged somewhere in his throat, and he busied himself with stacking papers and shoving them back into his briefcase. When he was able to speak again, he said, "Yeah, she was pretty special."

Those serene gray eyes regarded him keenly. "I know. I can tell just by being with her children. And with you."

He nodded, swallowing thickly. "How long do you think it will take for you to finish the album?" He wanted to add more to the question, to ask her what he really wanted to know, but he held back.

"I don't know. I need to take more pictures of her family and friends. Her house and school, too. Things for her to cherish and remember later." Her voice was filled with certainty, as if she knew the truth to her words from experience.

He ducked his head and stared at his hands. "Do you think you'll be staying through Christmas?"

She drew her knees up, scratching her legs through the blanket. "I hadn't really thought about it. There's no reason for me to hang around once the album's done." It looked as if she wanted to say more, but she stopped.

"Why?"

"I think it best I leave before the election. Stinky . . . well, let's just say that Stinky will have a harder time opposing you if I left before he did any damage."

He leaned forward. "Has Stinky been harassing you?"

She paused before answering. "He really wants

to win this election, and he'll do it any way that he can."

"You know, if you would just tell me everything, I could help you. Help you take care of Stinky. And maybe help you stay. For Maddie." He didn't know where those words came from, only that he meant them.

She shook her head, burying her forehead in her drawn-up knees. "It's too late. And knowing would only make it worse for you." She peered up at him. "When's the election?"

A surge of hope shot through him. "January."

She was silent for a long while, and he was afraid to speak. Finally, she said, "I can stay until then, if you want. For Maddie."

He reached for her hand and held it, the cotton warm under his fingers. "I'd like you to."

Her eyes, when she looked at him, were filled with such hope and loss that he wanted to shake her, make her tell him everything. But he held back and so did she.

Dropping her hand, he said, "Hey, you want to go to the bathroom or something? I could unpin your gloves."

A grateful look of relief crossed her face. "Oh, thank you! Thelma and Selma Sedgewick, those evil old women, wouldn't consider unpinning them even for a minute."

He chuckled, knowing he'd never heard the words "evil" and "Thelma" or "Selma" in the same sentence before. He leaned close and unclasped the safety pins. "I'm going to go reheat some of Lucinda's chicken soup. If it's all right with you, I'll stick around and have a bowl with you."

"I'd like that."

He moved to leave, but she pulled at his hand. "Thank you."

"You're welcome." He stood. "And don't scratch or I'm going to have to pin the gloves back on."

"Yes, sir." She sent him a mock salute. "I'll keep myself occupied while you're gone by reading a bit of *Little Women*, okay?"

He moved to the doorway and paused. "It's not so bad depending on other people, is it?"

She didn't answer, and when he turned around, he saw her with *Little Women* in one hand and the other one holding up a shiny copper penny.

"It was inside the book," she said, her voice quiet. "I didn't put it there." She pulled open the drawer of the nightstand and pulled out another, identical brand-new shiny coin.

"A lucky penny?"

She shook her head. "No. Pennies from heaven."

Her eyes shone with darkness and hope, and he wanted to walk up to her and kiss all the pain and doubt away. Her expression reminded him of the way she had looked on the creek bed, and he wondered if anything had changed. Taking a step into the room, he asked, "What do you want, right now, more than anything else in the world?"

Wrapping her hand around the pennies, she didn't hesitate. "I want to learn to swim. I want to know what it was like for you during your summers as a boy. I want to know what I missed."

He regarded her for a long moment. "I'll see what I can do." Then he made his way downstairs, in search of chicken soup.

CHAPTER 15

As Maddie approached the Ladue house, she spotted Suzanne sitting on the front porch, swaddled in a purple and pink afghan and wearing large, fluffy slippers. A book was propped on her knees as she bent her head to read, the breeze flipping the corners of the pages. It was odd to see Suzanne sitting in a rocking chair on a porch—she just didn't seem the type to want to sit still long enough. Aunt Lucinda had once told her there was something about a front porch and a rocking chair that anchored a person's soul, bringing it down to the heart of life. As Maddie watched Suzanne's face as she got nearer, she could almost believe that Suzanne had discovered that for herself.

With the sound of the front gate banging closed, Suzanne looked up from the yellowed pages and saw Maddie.

She waved. "What's up?"

277

Maddie just groaned and threw herself into the empty rocker next to Suzanne. "I can't move away soon enough. Sarah Frances is pitching a fit because Daddy says she can't go with us to the High Museum for the photography exhibit. I'm surprised you can't hear her caterwauling from here. She sounds like a stuck pig."

"Why can't she go?"

"Well, it turns out that the entire twelfth grade is going for a field trip, and I signed up you, Aunt Cassie, and Aunt Lucinda to be chaperones. Which means Sarah Frances will be in school and can't go."

Suzanne eased back in the rocking chair, her face wary. "You signed me up to chaperone?"

Maddie avoided her eyes. "Yeah. I knew you wanted to see the exhibit, so I didn't think you'd mind. There will be enough adults so you don't even have to hang out with the kids."

"Oh." She didn't sound completely thrilled. After rocking back and forth a few times, she asked, "When is it?"

"The second Tuesday in November, right before Thanksgiving break. It's the first exhibition of Gertrude Hardt's photographs in over twenty years, and nothing could stop me from being there. If I'm not in prison for killing my sister, of course."

"Well, I guess I could check with your dad and see if Sarah Frances could come along with me. If she's caught up with her schoolwork, I think it could be just as educational as a day in the classroom."

Maddie stared at her. "You'd purposely take another kid? You don't even like kids."

Suzanne stopped rocking. "Stop saying that. It's not true."

Maddie raised her eyebrows but didn't say anything.

"I'll ask your dad and see what he thinks."

Maddie snorted. "If you asked him to dye his hair purple, he'd probably do it."

Suzanne's face turned pink just as Maddie's mama's face had done when she was embarrassed. She'd never thought the two women were anything alike, but maybe she'd been wrong. And maybe her daddy had known that all along.

Suzanne noticed the folder in Maddie's hand. "What's in there?"

Maddie hesitated for a moment. "It's my contest entry. I wanted you to look at it before I sent it in. I played with the filters and burned the image a bit around the edges to make the shadows lighter, just like you showed me." She passed the folder to Suzanne. "Let me know if you think it's any good."

She'd tried not to sound so pathetic, but had definitely failed. She didn't want Suzanne to know how important this was to her, that she truly believed that her photography was her ticket out of Walton and her way of becoming more than just the girl whose mother had died.

Suzanne took the folder and opened it to the first photograph. It was the picture of Cassie and Sarah Frances that Maddie had taken on the night of Sarah Frances's party. There was no doubt that the faces in the image were what created the beauty of the photograph, but Maddie's enhancements took it up a few notches to become a piece of art, in her humble opinion. At least that's what she'd thought. Until now. She hardly dared to breathe as she waited to hear what Suzanne had to say.

Finally, Suzanne sat back, the folder still open, her eyes still focused on the photograph.

"Well?" Maddie asked, feeling close to tears.

Suzanne's gray eyes met hers. "It's perfect. I think it's a winner."

Maddie let go of her held breath, then sagged against the rocking chair. "Thank goodness. I was afraid you'd tell me it sucked."

Suzanne arched an eyebrow. "It doesn't suck—it's wonderful. And you can believe me because I'm not related to you and can't be biased."

Maddie wanted to hug the older woman, but held back. There was something about Suzanne that always made you think twice before you touched her. As if she were a fragile butterfly whose wings would break if you held her too tightly. "Well, great. I'll finish up the entry forms and get it in the mail today. Thanks. For everything." Looking down at her fingernails that were stained black with the paint from the town green's fence, she said, "Especially for what you did for me that night I went to Atlanta. That was really cool."

"You're welcome. But don't ever do it again. It destroys lives."

Maddie peered at her with dawning understanding. "Like yours?"

Suzanne looked away. "Yeah. Sort of." She didn't speak for a moment, but Maddie knew to wait. Her daddy tasted his words first before he spoke, too, not wanting anything sour to come out. Or for anything to be taken literally by the older children in his household.

Looking down at the copy of *Little Women* in her lap, Suzanne spoke very quietly. "For fourteen years, I did everything I could to make my mother love me more than she loved the alcohol. But I wasn't enough for her. It's something I don't think I'll ever get over."

Maddie's breathing felt hollow, the pain as real to her as it must still be for Suzanne. Maybe that's why she was drawn to her, two motherless girls searching the world for the one thing that would replace that loss. Swallowing, Maddie gave a big push with her feet. "Don't worry about me getting drunk again. I've never puked so much in my entire life. I can't imagine putting myself through that again."

They rocked in silence for a few moments before Maddie remembered something else she needed to tell Suzanne. "Oh, I think I'm missing a negative on the end of the roll of film. There were twenty-four exposures but only twenty-three negatives."

Suzanne's hands clutched the arms of the rocker a little tighter. "I cut it off. A strap or a finger was blocking out the entire image. So I threw it away."

"I wondered," Maddie said as she took the folder from Suzanne. "I developed that roll of film from your camera for you. I made them all into five-by-seven prints, and you can tell me if you want any enlarged. They're pretty good."

Suzanne took the envelope containing a small stack of pictures and Maddie leaned over to look at them again as Suzanne slid them out. They must have been the photographs Suzanne had taken over the past two weeks from her sickbed. There were the Sedgewick sisters holding up their sections of a pink and purple afghan for the camera, Lucinda painting Suzanne's toenails in Bingo Night Red, Mrs. Crandall laughing at a joke, and Maddie staring up at the ceiling with her chin cupped in her hands. And then there was her daddy, looking the way he did when he was about to laugh, but with a light in his eyes that Maddie hadn't seen in a long time. When Maddie looked closer, she noticed a glow surrounding the photos of her and her dad. It was as if a thin white veil had been placed between the camera and the subject, and it made the hairs rise on the back of Suzanne's neck.

"What is that?" Maddie asked, pointing to the veiled light. "Is that some special effect you haven't showed me yet? Because if it is, I want to learn how to do it."

Suzanne shook her head. "There is a way to create that effect, but I didn't do it on purpose. It just sort of showed up. I took some pictures at the cemetery and the same light appeared on those, too. I'm thinking there must have been dust or something on my lens."

Their eyes met for a brief moment before Suzanne abruptly looked away and began to slip through the pictures again as if she were trying to figure out what appeared different about these photos than her older ones that she'd shown Maddie before. Suzanne's portfolio of photographs was very good, some even brilliant. But these were special, set apart by some unknown element.

Maddie leaned back to get a better perspective and in Suzanne's third pass through the pictures, she realized what it was. Suzanne's eye behind the camera had picked up moments of interaction between the subjects of the photographs and the photographer. No longer mute, the camera seemed to sing with the rhythm of the lives these people represented. She had managed to become a part of the subject instead of simply a bystander, and it made all the difference. Suzanne sighed, then relaxed against the back of her rocking chair, and Maddie knew she'd figured it out, too.

Maddie leaned back in her own chair. "Those are really good. Do you think I could use one of them in the contest instead?"

"Now, Maddie, that wouldn't be honest, would it? Besides, yours is better than any of these."

Maddie shrugged, hoping to hide her immature giddiness that made her want to whoop and holler. "Whatever." She stood, keeping her voice normal. "But thanks." With a heavy sigh, she said, "I've got to get back to painting or my daddy will make me do the courthouse, too."

"He's only trying to make a point, Maddie. If your punishment were lenient, it wouldn't make much of an impression, would it?"

Maddie looked heavenward. "I knew you'd take his side. This love stuff is sickening."

Suzanne cleared her throat. "Excuse me? I don't think so. We're just two adults who care about you, that's all."

"Yeah, right." The only reason Maddie had even found the time to come to Suzanne's was that her dad was getting his hair cut for the second time in a month, and that never happened. Maddie stuck the folder under her arm as she zipped up her fleece jacket. "And Miss Lena's working with a full deck."

"Now, Maddie . . ."

Maddie waved her hand. "I've got to go. See ya later."

Suzanne was frowning when Maddie turned away and let herself out of the front gate. She wasn't sure what her dad felt was actually love, but sometimes she caught him looking at Suzanne in a way she wished Robbie would look at her. She wanted it to bother her, but it didn't. Maybe if her daddy was strong enough to move on, he'd understand that Maddie was, too.

She quickened her steps realizing that she'd spent too much time with Suzanne and hoping her daddy hadn't walked by the courthouse square and found her AWOL. A strong autumn wind blew leaves around her ankles, pushing at her back as if it, too, had finally decided it was time to move on.

Joe passed the red, white, and blue barber pole and held open the door to Bill's Trim & Shave for Harry. Resolutely carrying his wooble, Harry stepped inside, his blue eyes wide.

Bill Crandall stepped forward with a smile. "Well, hey there, young man. Will you be needing a shave today or just a trim?"

Joe settled back in a chair and watched the monthly ritual unfold. "Both." Harry slid a glance at his father. "Please."

"And if you have time when you're done, I'd like a little trim if you don't mind," Joe said.

Bill sent him a knowing look. "I'm sure I can fit you in, Mayor."

Settling a booster seat on one of the three barber chairs, Bill lifted the little boy into it and fastened a smock around Harry's neck, careful to keep the wooble under the protection of the bright green plastic. Tucking a warm towel into the neck of the smock, Bill then squirted a fistful of shaving cream into Harry's palm.

"Go to town with that, now, pardner."

With a shout of glee, Harry smashed the cream between both palms and slapped it on his cheeks.

Joe grinned as he watched Bill proceed to cut Harry's bright blond hair. The man must be near seventy, having cut Joe's hair since he was Harry's age, but his hands were steady and quick as he made his way around Harry's small head.

"Sweetpea tells me that Miss Paris is on the mend. I think the two of them might have had a confrontation or two about Miss Paris's inability to follow directions, but the patient made it through anyhow."

No matter how many times he heard Mrs. Crandall's nickname spoken by her contemporaries, he could never reconcile it with his recollections of his strict fifth-grade teacher. Joe crossed a foot over his other knee and leaned back in the chair. "Now, those are two personalities I don't ever want to see clashing. I'm surprised Sheriff Adams wasn't called in."

"He probably would have if Miss Paris hadn't shown my wife all those flattering pictures she'd taken of her. She let Sweetpea take one home, and I have to say it's better than that Glamour Shots photo she had taken last year at the mall." He stopped snipping and looked at Joe over the rims of his glasses. "Not that I don't think Sweetpea is naturally beautiful, of course, but that Miss Paris seems to have a way with a camera, don't ya know?"

"That she does."

"I wonder if she's thinking of opening a photography studio in town. Right now, everybody has to go into Monroe if they want those fancy pictures. It would be nice to have one right here in Walton."

"She's not planning on staying." He spoke the words quickly.

Bill glanced at him again but didn't say anything. "Well, there'll be some of us real sad to see her go. Sweetpea's been enjoying her role as mother hen. But I somehow don't see Miss Paris as someone who wants to be mothered."

Joe thought back to the Suzanne he had first seen with the wary eyes and the slumped shoulders. "You might be surprised," he said quietly.

The bells chimed over the door, and Joe held back a groan as he spotted Stinky entering the barbershop, his forehead glistening with sweat despite the cool temperature outside.

"Hey, Bill. I need a trim and a shave. Can you fit me in?"

Bill glanced over at Joe, and Joe shook his head. "I just remembered I have something to do at the office as soon as you're done with Harry."

After giving Joe a knowing look, Bill turned back to Stinky. "Have a seat and I'll be with you as soon as I finish with this very important customer."

Harry giggled as Stinky took a chair two down from Joe.

"Always a pleasure, Mayor." Stinky picked up the latest issue of the *Walton Sentinel* and spread it wide. "Just saw Maddie at the town square, scraping paint. She didn't look too happy."

"She's not supposed to be happy. She's being punished."

Stinky clucked his tongue, still focusing on the newspaper. "How's a man who can't control his own daughter supposed to run an entire town? Just to give you a heads-up, that's going to be my next campaign slogan."

Joe wobbled his foot over his knee to work out his anger. If that didn't work, he'd be obliged to send a fist into Stinky's smug, round face. "Thanks, Charles. I'll keep that in mind."

Turning a page in the newspaper and keeping his voice low so that only Joe could hear, Stinky said, "I hear you've been checking me out and sticking your nose into places it don't belong."

Joe's foot stilled, but he continued to watch Harry as he searched for a calm voice. "If you don't have anything to hide, it shouldn't worry you. However, if there is something you'd prefer the voting population of Walton not to know, then I'd say you're up shit creek without a paddle."

Stinky folded up the paper with a snap and dropped it on the low table. "What are you implying?"

Regarding him evenly, Joe said, "I know you're in debt up to your eyeballs. I also know that you own over one hundred acres of virgin pine forest out by the interstate that could be worth a modest fortune. Which leaves me wondering why you haven't openly put it on the market yet, and why you're running for mayor. If it's because as mayor you'll be on the rezoning commission, forget it. You'd have to fight all the other council members and sway public opinion. If you have any thoughts regarding deforestation and a manufacturing plant, it's not going to happen. The people won't allow it." He felt hot and angry and stuck his finger into his neckband to loosen it.

Stinky leaned in closer. "There's a way for everything, and everybody has their price. Even you, Mayor. Heck, I'll even stop my campaign if you just find it in yourself to agree with me on a few development issues."

"Is that a bribe? I can have you arrested for that."

Stinky stood suddenly but kept his voice lowered. "You don't know what you're messing with here, Mayor. Leave it be." He pointed his finger at Joe's chest. "And tell your girlfriend that I'm onto her. I don't think her past is all that lily-white. Either stop sticking your nose into my business, or stories of her lurid past are going to be on billboards up and down the interstate."

Stinky approached the barber's chair as Bill unbuttoned Harry's smock and set the little boy on the floor. His face had been wiped clean except for a smudge of cream on the tip of his nose. Swiping it off with his finger, Joe lifted the child in his arms.

"Can I have a peppermint stick now, Daddy? I was real good and didn't wiggle."

Before Joe could reach the jar on the counter, Stinky had stuck in a hand and pulled one out, handing it to Harry.

Joe jerked Harry away. "We don't take candy from strangers." Moving in front of Stinky, he pulled out another stick and handed it to his son.

"Funny. You let a stranger watch your kids. What kind of parent does that?" Stinky leaned closer, his breath smelling of onions and ketchup. "She could be some kind of a pervert—or a murderer. And you let her watch your kids, no questions asked. I think you're investigating the wrong person, Mayor."

Stinky approached the barber's chair. Stopping,

he turned around and faced Joe, his eyes hard. "You lay off my back, and I'll lay off yours. Because either way, you're not going to like what you find." He settled his bulk into the chair and closed his eyes as Bill placed a smock around his bullish neck.

Joe placed a ten and a five on the counter and waved to Bill before leaving the shop with Harry perched on his hip. He had no intention of backing off. Whatever Stinky or Suzanne might be hiding, he would continue to search until he found it. And he could only hope Stinky was wrong.

CHAPTER 16

Suzanne took the manila folder out of her backpack and stared at the eight-by-ten photograph inside. *Damn.* The folder had been bent, creasing the border of the photograph. This photo had been her favorite, the one she couldn't bear to part with, so she had stuck it in the folder and then into her bag in her rush to put Anthony deSalvo behind her, and had forgotten it until now.

She frowned at the picture, wondering what she could do. The crease wasn't deep enough to have ruined the picture, but it needed to be placed under something heavy to flatten it. She thought for a moment before heading toward the cardboard table set up in another upstairs bedroom, where she had been working on Maddie's album.

She stuck the photograph inside the back cover, making sure it was wedged tightly into the binding. Before she closed the album, she opened it to where she had left off earlier. The photos were from a family trip to the beach, with a young Maddie and her parents along with Sarah Frances and Joey. Harriet, heavily pregnant and wearing a maternity bathing suit, sat building a sand castle with the children, her eyes bright and with crinkles in the corners from smiling into the camera.

Maddie sat next to her mother, not participating in the sand castle building, but instead keeping her hands on Harriet, as if she were holding her down to the earth. Maybe it was because Maddie had been an only child for three years that she considered her siblings as stealing part of her mother away. Or maybe she knew her mother's presence in her life was only temporary, like shifting sand under the pull of the surf.

Downstairs, somebody knocked loudly on the front door.

Closing the album firmly, Suzanne went downstairs.

She flipped on the porch light and opened the door. Joe stood on the porch, with a small bag from Lucinda's Lingerie in his hand and a look on his face that did funny things inside her chest.

"If you're coming to laugh at my polka dots, you're too late. They're almost gone, and

Lucinda's given me a cover-up cream to disguise the rest. You're out of luck."

"Darn. Well, since I'm already here, I guess we'll have to find something else to do."

Trying to appear calm, Suzanne stepped back, allowing Joe to come in. She looked pointedly at the bag. "Please tell me that's slippers. I can barely walk in these things." She indicated the enormous fur balls on her feet.

He followed her gaze and grinned. "Ah, no. But I'll be sure to bring some next time." He held out the bag to Suzanne. "This is a bathing suit. Lucinda picked it out, so if it's too revealing you'll have to blame her."

Taking the bag, she looked at him with a furrowed brow. "It's fall. Why would you be bringing me a bathing suit?"

"I'm going to teach you to swim."

She tried to hand back the bag. "No way. Firstly, I'm afraid of water. Secondly, it's too cold outside."

"Well, firstly, I'll be with you so you don't need to be scared, and secondly, we'll be in the heated Jacuzzi."

"You're joking, right? I mean, you can't swim in a Jacuzzi."

"No, you can't, but you can learn other things." He paused for a moment, and she wondered if he could hear the blood swishing through her brain as she completed the sentence for him in her head.

His eyes widened as if he could read her mind.

"Like how to hold your breath in the water and float. That should pretty much cover our first lesson." He took a step toward her. "You told me you wanted to learn how to swim. To learn what it was like when I was a boy."

She felt his pull and leaned into him, brushing her forehead on his chest. "One lesson can't fill in for a whole lifetime of summers."

"No. But it's a start."

She looked into his eyes then and wanted more than ever to share a part of his life, even just this one thing. "All right. I'll go get changed." Taking the bag, she started up the stairs. "What about you? Are you going to wear your jeans?"

He started unbuckling his pants, and she stared at him in alarm. "Nope. I've got my swimming trunks on under my pants. I was a Boy Scout. I'm always prepared."

Raising an eyebrow, she ran upstairs to her bedroom to change.

When she emerged a short time later, she had already wrapped a towel around her waist and over her shoulders. The tiny yellow string bikini Lucinda had picked out for her to wear had barely enough material to make a tissue that would cover a sneeze, much less parts of her body. She stood in front of the Jacuzzi in the secluded backyard, watching as Joe took the cover off, and shivered until her teeth knocked together.

"I'm free . . . zing."

"It's nice and warm in here. Just drop your towels and we'll get in."

She didn't move.

"If you don't, I'm going to lift you and put you in the water with your towels, and then you won't have something to wrap yourself in when you get out."

That thought alone made her shiver more. With her eyes shut tight, she dropped the towels. When she opened her eyes to be able to see herself into the Jacuzzi, she couldn't help noticing Joe's stunned expression. He looked like what she imagined a guy would look like after winning the lottery. Climbing in, she quickly lowered herself down to her shoulders, loving the feeling of warmth that engulfed her.

Joe pulled off his shirt and climbed in. He moved toward her, pushing waves of hot water over her shoulders. "Are you ready?"

Teeth chattering again, she nodded.

"Cold?"

She shook her head.

"Good. Then come on." He put his hands on her bare waist under the water, and she quickly inhaled. "Now lie back. I'm holding you and I won't let you go."

He pushed her backward, keeping his hands firm on her waist. She resisted, the fear of being submerged clouding out the reality of his strong hands supporting her.

"I won't let go of you. Just lie back, and my hands will help you float."

She looked in his eyes again and felt for the first time that she could do this. Holding tightly to his upper arms, she lay back, feeling the rush of warm water in her ears and soaking her hair. With a quick movement, he let go with one hand and reached under her knees to bring her legs to the surface.

Jerking away from him, she quickly found purchase on the bottom of the Jacuzzi with her feet. "What are you doing?" she sputtered, trying to wipe the water out of her face.

He kept his voice calm, his eyes steady as he regarded her. "I was still holding you. I only released you with one hand so I could raise your legs to the surface."

She eyed him suspiciously.

"I won't let you go under. Can you trust me?"

Slowly she nodded, feeling something free up and float to the surface of her heart like tiny bubbles.

He leaned her back again, and this time she allowed him to move her legs to the surface.

"I think you're about to draw blood."

Suzanne glanced at where her nails were digging into Joe's arm and quickly released them.

"Relax, Suzanne. As long as I'm here, you don't have to worry about anything."

That hardness in her heart spewed upward again

in a myriad of bubbles as her arms slid into the water and she allowed herself to relax. She stared up at the night sky and saw her breath rise and float up into the air before disappearing. It was as if she were watching the old Suzanne take leave, creating a vacancy in her heart to fill with hope.

Closing her eyes, she listened to the steady rhythm of the jets under the water and splayed her fingers wide, as if they, too, could enjoy their newfound freedom. She looked up at Joe to see if she was dreaming, and his touch kept her earthbound, tethered like a flaming red leaf on a fall branch.

And then his fingers released her, and she was floating by herself, swimming in a pool of contentment and possibility, sure in the knowledge that Joe would never let her go.

Joe wasn't sure when Suzanne began to trust him, but he felt the lightness of her in his arms and knew she was ready. Gently removing his hands, he stared at her face in the chill moonlight, at her closed eyes and full lips, and saw her without her walls and defenses for the first time since he'd met her.

He touched her shoulder, and her eyes flew open, but not in surprise. It almost seemed as if she had been waiting for him. Taking hold of her arms, he helped her stand, feeling the goose bumps prickle her skin as the cold air hit her.

Slowly, he slid his hands down her arms, wanting to warm her, wanting to make the ghosts go away. She looked up at him, her gray eyes translucent in the cold night, and knew he wanted to do much more than that.

She took a step closer, and the tiny strips of yellow material that covered her breasts pressed against his chest. "Thank you, Aunt Lucinda," he said, his voice sounding strangled even to his own ears.

Her lips twitched upward into a grin. "Why?"

"For that bathing suit." His hands found her bare waist again, and he moved her against him.

He heard her intake of breath. "You don't think it's too small?"

Struggling to find a breath, he said, "Uh, no. It's perfect."

He caught sight of the gold heart around her neck, winking at him. It didn't startle him as it had before. Instead, it brought to mind the last time he had seen it, when she had been lying beneath him on the banks of the creek. Something long asleep inside him stirred, and he sighed, resting his forehead on hers.

Touching the charm for the first time, he pulled it closer. He could see there was something written on one side but couldn't read it from the light of the back porch. "What does it say?"

Closing her hand over his, she spoke quietly. "A life without rain is like the sun without shade."

She paused. "Somebody gave it to my mother when she was a girl, and she gave it to me the day she disappeared from my life."

He thought back on his own life, all the light and darkness of it, and felt the truth of the words. The joys could never have been as bright without the griefs that brought them to him. Like this amazing, resilient, and beautiful woman standing so close.

"It's true, you know."

Ducking her head, she said, "I'm not so sure. It never seems to stop raining."

He placed his hands on her head and gently lifted her face to the sky. "It's clear out now. You can put away your umbrella."

She laughed softly, then opened her mouth to speak, but her words were lost as he bent his head and kissed her.

He jerked his head back. "I'm sorry. That's not why I came here tonight."

She regarded him for a long moment. When she spoke, her voice was quiet. "I learned a long time ago to grab the good stuff when you can. You rarely get a second chance. If we only have tonight, what would you like to spend it doing?"

His body knew, but he wasn't sure his mind did. Yet somehow he couldn't seem to convince himself that wanting her was wrong.

Tentatively he touched her again, and her arms found their way around his neck, the force of her moving him backward in the Jacuzzi and up against the bench seat along the edge. Her long legs wrapped around him, and he sat, the warmth of the water swallowing them both as Suzanne opened her mouth and welcomed his kiss. She tasted of fall air and water and felt solid and sleek under his hands. Her limbs were long and lean— not what he was used to, but they were beautiful and perfect. They were part of Suzanne.

She pulled away and met his gaze, her voice breathless. "Where are we going with this?"

He forced his voice to remain steady. "I have a strong feeling we're on the same track here."

"I meant after this. After this, it can't go any further. I need to make sure you know that we only have tonight."

His hands stilled on her back, his chest tightening. He knew what she meant. Hadn't it been the same thing he'd told her the night of Maddie's adventure into Atlanta? She was offering him exactly what he'd asked for. His fingers toyed with the edge of the bikini bottom, feeling the firm flesh underneath. Yes, his body knew where it was going. He just wasn't sure his heart did.

Kissing her back, he murmured against her lips, "I understand. It's best for both of us." He paused for a moment, gasping for breath and wondering if there was enough air in the space between them to fill his lungs. "And if I don't make love to you right now, I'm going to die."

The only sounds were the jets in the Jacuzzi and a car passing by on the street out front. And Suzanne's breathing, tickling his neck and teasing his body. He remembered her words, *"We have all night,"* and closed his eyes with a small smile, thankful for this woman who had allowed him to forget, at least for a moment, three long years of grief and longing.

He felt a shiver go through her. "Are you cold?"

She nodded and moved her face to meet his gaze. "Let's go inside."

They moved apart, then stepped out of the Jacuzzi. Quickly grabbing the towels, he placed one on Suzanne's shoulders and wrapped the other around his waist. Taking her hand, he led her to the house, anticipating the feel of a woman sleeping in his arms again. This woman.

Suzanne awoke to the sound of somebody moving around her room. With blurry eyes, she looked at her digital clock and saw that it was after four in the morning. "Joe?"

A shadow moved and settled on the bed next to her. A soft kiss brushed her lips. "I've got to get home."

She felt disoriented for a moment, believing that she was home and that Joe belonged there with her. And then she remembered. "I know. It's just . . . so soon."

He chuckled in the darkness. "I was hoping you'd be too worn out to care."

Blood rushed to her cheeks as she remembered the Jacuzzi and the rest of the night spent in the bed. And the kitchen. And the hallway. "I like sleeping with you."

She could sense his raised eyebrows. "And the other stuff wasn't bad, either."

His knuckle brushed her jawbone as he lifted her hair and moved it behind her shoulder. "Me, too. But I've got to go before Maddie wakes up. I told her where I'd be, but I don't think either of us expected me to be gone this long." He sighed. "I'm just thankful Lucinda doesn't live with us anymore. I'd have to act like Tom Cruise in *Mission Impossible* trying to get back into the house without her knowing."

Taking his face in her hands, she kissed him, and it seemed to her that all that had once appeared so out of reach now rested solidly in the palms of her hands. She let go. "Good night. And thanks for the swimming lesson."

"Anytime." He stood. "Suzanne—"

She cut him off. "Good night, Joe."

He paused for a moment before turning from her and leaving the room. She listened as his footsteps went down the stairs and out the front door, finally dying away on the sidewalk outside.

She turned on her side, hugging the pillow to her and smelling his scent. And as the first streaks of pink painted the dawn sky, she finally fell back asleep.

A pounding on the kitchen door awakened her around ten o'clock. It was Saturday, and she wasn't due at work until one. Grumbling, she threw the covers off and stalked to the bedroom door, belatedly realizing she was stark naked. Reversing her steps, she found her red robe tangled in the bedsheets on the floor, and covered herself before running to answer the back door.

Lucinda stood at the back porch with a large Tupperware cake holder topped with a box of Krispy Kreme donuts. Around her wrist were two stuffed grocery bags from the Piggly Wiggly, one with a bright yellow tablecloth spilling out of it. Her red hair stood out in marked contrast to the overcast sky behind her. "You didn't hear me knocking on the front door, so I decided to try the back."

Suzanne frowned, staring at the donuts as her stomach grumbled. "Am I supposed to be at work?"

"No, honey. But the members of the Walton Ladies' Bridge Club will be here in half an hour, and I wanted to make sure you were prepared."

"Excuse me?" Suzanne stood at the open door while Lucinda bustled in, dropped everything on a counter, and began spreading the tablecloth over the oak kitchen table. She eyed the chairs lying on their backs and the heap of wet towels strewn on the floor without comment and went about her business. Suzanne flushed, recalling how the kitchen had become so disheveled.

Without meeting Suzanne's gaze, Lucinda said, "I'm sponsoring you for membership, so you have to give a ladies' breakfast for them all to meet you first."

"But . . . but I never said that I wanted to be a member. I don't even know how to play bridge."

Lucinda clucked her tongue as she pulled out a silver serving platter and doily from the bag and artfully arranged donuts on it. "You can learn. You're a real quick study."

"No way. This is crazy. I've never been a member of anything, and I'm not about to start now. Besides, I'm not going to be here in a few months." She walked over to where the cordless phone sat in its cradle on the counter. She handed it to Lucinda. "Call them now and tell them there's been some horrible mistake. Tell them I died. I don't care—just stop them from coming. Please."

Lucinda looked at her, her false eyelashes drooping in commiseration. "I'm sorry, sugar. I'm sure most of them have already left by now. They're very punctual." Turning her back to Suzanne, she reached back into the apparently bottomless bag and pulled out a slender glass vase with a few long stems of gladiolus. She stuck this in the middle of the table, circled the silverware around it, and opened the cake case. "Besides, you'll have all these leftovers."

Suzanne stared openmouthed at the display. "Is this April Fool's Day? Because if it is, you've got me good. If it isn't, then you've lost your mind. I'm not hosting anything."

Lucinda opened the back door. "I'm going to get the large coffeemaker out of my trunk while you go change." She stepped outside and closed the door, then opened it quickly and stuck her head inside. "And you might want to take the bathing suits out of the Jacuzzi, too, before anybody sees them."

At that moment, the sound of a car pulling into the driveway reached them. Lucinda's eyes widened. "Oh dear. Somebody's early. I'll take care of the bathing suits. You just worry about getting dressed."

With that, she closed the door in Suzanne's face.

Suzanne stood paralyzed for a moment, wondering what would be worse—entertaining the town's leading matrons wearing nothing but a red silk bathrobe, or dealing with Lucinda's disappointment at Suzanne's failure to fit in.

Grabbing up the towels and taking the stairs two at a time, she ran up to her bedroom to change.

When she came back down a little while later, it was at a much more sedate pace. The sound of women's chatter and the aroma of freshly brewed coffee drifted up to her, and she was surprised to find herself nervous.

Why am I doing this? She eyed the simple

pumps on her feet, which didn't exactly go with her long gauze skirt but which seemed much more acceptable than her flip-flops. She had no idea why the opinions of the ladies and Lucinda had become important to her, but looking down at the pumps that pinched her toes, she felt it somehow did.

The ladies were all standing around the kitchen holding small china plates and teacups supplied by Lucinda. They all stopped talking when Suzanne entered the room. Forcing a big smile, she waved. "Hey. Glad y'all could make it."

She had no idea that those words were even in her head before they appeared on her lips, and she shut her mouth, stunned, as the ladies seemed to nod in approval.

Lucinda took her around the small room, making introductions, as Mrs. Crandall supplied her with a plate of coffee cake and a cup and saucer of coffee. Suzanne recognized most of the ladies from her chicken pox confinement, and the others she had not met she had at least heard about.

They retired to the halfway-refurbished front parlor, which held a mixture of beautiful antiques and patio furniture. Suzanne took a seat in a lawn chair while the other ladies found perches on the remaining chairs and occasional tables. Sugar Newcomb, most likely on account of her height, stood next to a beautiful cherry highboy, her cup resting on the top edge as she used both hands to hold her plate and eat with a fork.

As Suzanne looked around the room, she was thankful she and Joe had never made it into the parlor. Otherwise, she wouldn't be able to look anybody in the face. Being in the kitchen had been difficult enough, but at least a tablecloth now covered the bare oak table whose hardness could be attested to by the bruises on Suzanne's shoulders.

Lula Beasley sat next to Suzanne in a mismatched dining room chair and was engrossed in a conversation with Sweetpea Crandall and Brunelle Thompkins. Their conversation caught Suzanne's attention, and she turned toward them, waiting for a lull before speaking.

"So, Mrs. Beasley. Does your husband make up those signs on the billboard? They're pretty clever."

Mrs. Beasley closed her eyes for a moment as if gathering strength. "Yes, he does. He's got a real talent for it, doesn't he? But he's having the most dreadful time right now coming up with a new one. It's like writer's block or something, because he hasn't been inspired enough to change the sign in over three weeks and people are beginning to talk." Quietly she added, "And that's after Miss Lena donated the new lit sign, too, so people are really paying attention to it." Pressing a linen handkerchief to her lips, she said, "It's dreadful."

Suzanne wasn't sure if she should laugh or offer

condolences. Instead, she said, "Well, why don't we brainstorm a few ideas and see if the reverend likes any of them?"

Lucinda clapped her hands together. "What a wonderful idea!" Several other ladies nearby said the same thing; then everybody turned toward Suzanne and quieted.

"Oh. Well . . ." She stared down at her cold cup of coffee and untouched cake, not having found a nearby surface to place either one. "Um, how about 'Under the same management for two thousand years'?"

She was met by blank stares and a worried look from Lucinda. "Give me a minute. I'm just warming up. Let's see. . . ." She racked her brain for an idea, finally coming up with "Don't give up. Moses was a basket case, too."

This was met by raised eyebrows as well as blank stares, and Lucinda stood as if ready to cause a distraction. Feeling as if she were taking a final exam, Suzanne blurted out, "Prevent truth decay. Brush up on your Bible."

Holding her breath, Suzanne glanced nervously around the room. When Lula Beasley smiled, there seemed to be a collective release of breath. The preacher's wife even clapped. "That's marvelous, dear. I can't wait to tell Clement—he'll be so thrilled." She reached over and patted Suzanne's leg.

The din in the room rose again as the members of

Walton's Ladies' Bridge Club began new conversations. Darlene Narpone greeted her warmly and asked her about the scrapbook, capturing Cassie Parker's attention. With a groan, the pregnant woman hoisted her swollen body off a low sofa and came to stand near Suzanne's lawn chair.

"It's going well—just a lot slower than I had anticipated."

Darlene patted her arm. "I know what you mean. I've been known to spend an entire week on a single page trying to get it just right."

"Yeah, but it's not only that. I saw how Harriet had documented every single picture—not only who is in each one but also what they were doing and what they were probably thinking. It's going to take a while to piece all that together, especially since I can't ask Maddie directly because it's supposed to be a surprise."

Suzanne looked up as Lula Beasley made room on the love seat and Cassie sat down with the graceful precision of an elephant. She turned back to Darlene. "I recently realized that the last three years are missing completely. It'll take some time to gather what I need."

Cassie spoke up. "You should ask me. I've taken thousands of pictures of the kids since—well, in the last three years. I can show them to you, and you can pick which ones you want and I'll have copies made."

Suzanne's eyes met Cassie's again, and she felt

the familiar panic, but this time it was sharper, more intense. As if now there was more at stake. "I guess you would. I didn't even think of it."

Cassie's eyes remained cool and assessing. "Why don't you call me and we can get together? I could also help you label the pictures. I was born and raised here in Walton, and I guarantee I know everybody in them."

Suzanne saw the challenge in Cassie's eyes, but she refused to look away. "Thanks. I will." Even as she said it, she knew she would have to. She would dread it, but she couldn't run away now. Looking over at the pregnant woman with the rounded stomach and intelligent eyes, Suzanne knew she'd have to be very, very careful.

A cell phone rang, and Cassie reached into her purse for her phone. Glancing down at the number, she said, "Excuse me. It's the New York office, and I've got to take this." She leveled her gaze at Suzanne. "Call me tomorrow morning."

Suzanne nodded. "Sure. Thanks." It felt as if her stomach had just been hollowed out, and she put her untouched plate and cup on the floor by the side of the chair.

After all the ladies had left, taking paper plates filled with leftovers and covered in pastel hues of plastic wrap, Suzanne stood with Lucinda in the kitchen, packing up Lucinda's bags. She had left the tablecloth and vase of flowers for Suzanne, saying she didn't want to haul it all back home.

But something told Suzanne it had more to do with the starkness of her kitchen, as if making it more like a home would compel Suzanne to make it permanent.

Lucinda opened the kitchen door. "I hope Sam doesn't mind, but I moved my car to the backyard to make it easier for me to cart this stuff out of here."

Suzanne peered past her shoulder at the enormous pink convertible parked in the grass between the back door and the Jacuzzi, flattened grass marking where the tires had been. "I, um, I'll let him know."

Digging behind the boxwoods that bordered the back of the house, Lucinda grabbed a handful of something colorful, then gave it to Suzanne. "You might want to hang these properly so they don't mildew."

Suzanne looked down at the cold, damp material in her hand and recognized Joe's bathing suit with her bikini top somehow threaded through one of the leg holes. She felt the color rise to her cheeks, remembering their return to the Jacuzzi sometime during the night. "Oh. Thanks."

Lucinda looked at her with innocent eyes and a warm smile. "You were marvelous this morning—I don't think there'll be any problem with every-one agreeing on letting you into the club." She leaned over and kissed Suzanne's cheek, leaving a haze of Saucy perfume. "I'll let you know just as soon as I hear anything."

"What will I have to do if they accept?"

Lucinda juggled the bags in her hand. "Oh well, you'll have to host the next meeting. And learn how to play bridge."

"How long is that going to take? I don't have that much time. Really, Lucinda, this has been fun, but it's all kind of pointless, don't you think?"

With narrowed eyes, Lucinda said, "There's a reason for everything. Just like you and me being on that same bus when it stopped in Walton. We don't always know why right away, but we seem to figure it out eventually." She smiled. "Just be patient."

A drop of rain fell on Suzanne's head, and she and Lucinda looked up to see darkening clouds tumbling across the sky.

"I'd best get to the shop. It looks like we're about to have a downpour."

They said good-bye; then Suzanne watched as Lucinda teetered on her heels crossing the grass to her car. Remembering the damp bundle in her hand, she ducked inside the back door before the deluge came, striking the tin roof of the back porch with loud knocks. As Suzanne slowly walked upstairs, she wondered if the rain was trying to jolt her with a dose of reality, reminding her who she really was. And why she could never stay in Walton, Georgia, no matter how much it began to seem she wanted to.

CHAPTER 17

Joe paused at the front gate of the Ladue house, watching Suzanne stare at four flats of mixed-colored pansies. She wore one of those filmy skirts she seemed to favor along with those awful flip-flops. He'd have to ask Lucinda to take her shopping again.

She also wore a Walton High letter jacket, and with a frown he realized it belonged to Robbie. He'd last seen Maddie wearing it, and Joe was much happier seeing it on Suzanne.

Suzanne looked up as he pushed open the gate, and she froze.

He stopped just inside the front yard. "Hey."

She gave a little wave. "Hi."

He didn't move. "What are you doing?"

"I'm planting panties." She smirked. "Trying to anyway."

He walked forward then, and her eyes turned wary. "Need some help?"

Looking down at the flower bed, where an uneven and shallow trench had been dug, she shook her head. "I don't think so. How hard can it be, right?"

"You do know you have to take the plastic pots off the plants before you put them in the dirt, right?"

Her eyes widened as she glanced up at two

313

enormous cement planters on the top porch steps brimming over with pansies. "Oh. They didn't mention that at the nursery."

Joe removed his jacket and threw it over a bush, setting a small box that he'd been carrying next to it. "Come on. I'll help you."

They bent at the same time to grab a flower flat, their hands touching. She jerked away as if he had hurt her. Joe stood, placed his hands on either side of her face, and kissed her. Hard.

She stepped back, holding her fingers to her lips and breathing heavily. "Why'd you do that?"

"To get it over with. You're acting as skittish as a long-tailed cat in a room full of rockers. I'm figuring it has to do with me and what happened between us last night, so I thought if I kissed you and got that out of the way we could get on to planting."

She looked flustered. "I wasn't thinking about last night."

"You weren't?"

"Okay. I was. But I was also thinking about . . ."

"What?"

"How maybe it wasn't such a good idea."

He watched the light in her eyes change, moving the translucent gray into shadow. He took a step toward her. "I know. Just one night, right?" He paused, trying to put his thoughts into words. "But what happens if we are given second chances? I've started to believe in them myself."

She looked down at the ground. "Trust me. They don't exist." She pierced him with a deep gray gaze, her eyes like a stormy sky. "I've learned the hard way, and I don't plan on making the same mistake twice."

He crossed his arms, blocking out thoughts of her in his arms the night before. And remembering his old life that only existed in his dreams. Still, when he looked at her, he couldn't help feeling a small glimmer of hope. That and anger at whatever had happened in her life to make her never believe in second chances.

"You think so?" He moved toward her again, taking her in his arms, and bent to kiss her, pausing before their lips met and taking a perverse satisfaction in the way she seemed to melt at his touch and tilt her head back with expectation.

Satisfied that she was now as frazzled as he was, he set her aside and went to work. Bending down, he began loosening the tender roots from the small plastic pots, setting the plants along the edge of the trench. "Why don't you come over here and let me show you how to do this? Then we'll dig up the pots you've already planted."

She came and squatted next to him, and it took all his willpower not to touch her. He showed her how to remove the plants from the green pots and to loosen the fledgling roots before burying them in the ground. He watched her slender fingers move through the dark soil, focused and capable, just as he imagined she was with everything she did.

They moved silently down the row, occasionally bumping each other or touching fingers when one of them reached for the single trowel. But they remained separate, their time together like binding air, frail and fleeting.

When the flats had been emptied, they both stood, brushing dirt from their fingers. Her face was pink from the exertion and the cold, and he wanted to kiss her again. Quickly he turned around to retrieve his jacket and spotted the small box.

"I brought you something." He picked up the rectangular box and handed it to her. "It's a wind chime. I missed hearing one last night and thought you'd like it." He didn't add that he had anticipated listening to the fall breezes ring its tune as she lay in his arms.

She took the box gently from his hands. "Thank you."

Joe pointed to a corner of the porch. "That would be a great spot for it. It's right under your bedroom window."

"Thanks. I'll hang it today."

"Do you need help?"

"I'm sure I can figure it out."

He was sure she could, but he couldn't leave it at that. "You've never held a hammer before, have you?" He climbed the stairs of the porch. "I'll go get one from Sam's toolbox and hang it for you." As he reached for the door, he bumped into the rocking chair and knocked *Little Women* onto the floor. As he bent to pick it up, something fell out of it, floating gently to the floor. It was a dried and flattened gardenia bloom, its ancient petals long since withered and yellowed.

"What is it?" Suzanne came up the porch steps to stand with him.

"It's a pressed gardenia. It looks like it's been in here for a pretty long time."

She reached for it and he placed it in her outstretched palm. She bent close to it, her nose almost touching the fragile flower. "I can almost smell its scent." A winsome smile crossed her face, and she looked as if she wanted to tell him something, but she remained silent.

"Tell me," he said quietly.

She looked past him, toward the old mimosa tree, and said, "My mother loved gardenias—everything about them: their leaves, their blooms, their scent. At Christmas, we'd go without a tree so she could buy a gardenia plant. But they always died. As much as she loved them, she'd forget to water them. She'd keep the shriveled plant on the windowsill for months, like she was trying to make it up to them by not throwing them away."

Her hand folded tightly around the dead bloom. When she opened her hand, the breeze stole the wreckage from her palm, scattering the petals across the porch and the yard, letting them fall at will. The pain he saw reflected in her eyes seemed to tighten the skin over the fragile bones of her face, and his heart in his chest.

She turned to him, a bright smile plastered on her face. "Let's go and hang the wind chime."

He lifted his hand to touch her, to smooth the faint lines between her brows, but she moved away, opening the door and leading the way into the house.

Long after Joe had left, Suzanne stayed in the front yard, soaking up the morning rays of sunshine and listening to the music of her wind chime. She turned and watched as her long shadow spilled over the bright bed of purple and red pansies that she and Joe had planted, feeling an odd tug of pride.

She moved toward the porch, her shadow following her, and it occurred to her that planting the flowers had been the most permanent thing she had ever done. Throughout her childhood and young adult life, the fleeting cast of her shadow had been the only thing she would allow to tether her to a place. But now she had the bright flowers, flowers that she and Joe had planted, which would remain when she left, to remind others that she had been there. The thought both saddened her and gave her hope.

Wiping the dirt off her hands, she went inside,

waiting for the familiar bang of the screen door shutting behind her.

After showering, she gathered up the storage box of Maddie's pictures and made her way to Cassie's house. She passed the Methodist church and checked the sign to see if Reverend Beasley had changed it.

PREVENT TRUTH DECAY. BRUSH UP ON YOUR BIBLE. Smiling to herself, she continued walking.

As she walked down the long drive to the Parkers' home, her footsteps slowed. The towering oaks, the well-tended lawn, the imposing but beautiful house did nothing to ease Suzanne's nerves. She knew that discussing pictures was not the only reason Cassie had insisted she come. She kept going over the worst-case scenario in her mind, something she'd always done in the past to make the worst that could happen seem not so bad. But for once, the trick didn't work. If the worst happened, it would shatter her.

She paused on the bottom front step, looking up at the grand columns that stretched up from the porch to the roof. Despite the impressive facade, the rockers, porch swing, and discarded shoes scattered over the floor mat gave it a welcoming feel. It was the same sensation she got every time she sat on the swing on the Ladues' front porch. As if she was home.

She knocked tentatively on the front door, then,

after arguing with herself, knocked again, louder.

To her surprise, Sam opened the door and greeted her with a wide smile. "Hey, Suzanne. We were in the kitchen having lunch. Takes a while to make it up here." He opened the door farther to allow her in.

She tried not to gape at her surroundings as she was led to the kitchen at the back of the house. The furniture was mostly antique, and beautiful oil portraits hung on the walls, but the same feeling permeated the silk-wrapped walls, the deep upholstered pieces, the velvet draperies: the feeling of welcome and of being home.

Cassie was clearing the table when they walked in. She wore the long chain with the nine gold hearts and tiny gold key. She greeted Suzanne with restraint, then turned to her husband. "Do you want any more to eat? I could pack some of the corn bread up for you to take back to the clinic."

Sam puffed out his chest and patted his flat stomach. "No, thanks. I'm full as a tick." He kissed his wife, touching her cheek and then her swollen abdomen before leaving, and the look that passed between them made Suzanne want to blush.

Cassie gestured for Suzanne to follow and led the way into an adjoining family room, an apparently new addition to the home. A playpen stuffed with toys and baby paraphernalia filled it, most of the items still sporting bows of pale green and yellow.

"Forgive the mess. I've had two baby showers in the past month, and I haven't had a chance to put everything away."

Suzanne offered a tentative smile. "It doesn't bother me. Actually, you should probably throw it all around the room to get the real feel of a baby in the house. Joe's kids seem to like it that way."

She had meant it as a light comment, but Cassie just looked at her strangely. Without saying anything, Cassie moved a stack of magazines and newspapers, along with a box for a breast pump, off the low coffee table.

Suzanne placed her box on the cleared table, then sat down. She folded her hands in her lap, wondering why she felt as if she were being interviewed for a job. "I just brought the pictures I need help identifying, and I also brought the album, in case you wanted to look at it."

Cassie looked at the blue album, her eyes hesitant. "Great. I keep meaning to stop by and take a look, but I haven't gotten around to it yet."

Suzanne handed the album to Cassie and watched as she opened the front cover.

On the inside front cover were the words "Congratulations to my daughter, Madison. With all my love, Mama." The words were written in light blue ink, the handwriting gently sloped and tilting, dancing their way with loops and swirls across the top of the page.

Cassie touched the writing with her fingertips, her voice quiet when she spoke. "This is going to be a lot harder than I thought it would be."

Suzanne cleared her throat. "I could leave the album with you, if you'd prefer to look at it in private."

"No, that's not necessary," Cassie said as she looked up briefly before focusing again on the album. "Joe said you were waiting to finish the album before you left town." She turned to the first page. "I wouldn't want to hold you up."

Suzanne sat back, her skin heating. Despite the cool reception, Suzanne liked Cassie Parker. If only things could have been different.

"I remember this picture." As if forgetting who she was talking to, Cassie opened the album farther to show Suzanne. "It was the first year Harriet was Kudzu Queen. Aunt Lu did our hair in matching Princess Leia braids." She smiled, passing her hand over the smooth plastic page protector. "Harriet looked beautiful. I just looked like somebody had stuck two breakfast Danishes onto each side of my head."

Suzanne leaned forward, trying not to laugh. "Nah, they're more like biscuits, I think."

Cassie laughed and Suzanne pressed closer, studying the picture as she had done before. "You can tell you're related. Except for the coloring, I'd think you were twins."

"Really? No one's ever said that before." She studied Suzanne closely. "Maybe because you never saw us together. We were as different as night and day."

"Maybe. Or maybe because I've only ever seen the pictures I'm not influenced by your different personalities."

"How would you know that? You don't really know me."

"No, but I know Maddie. The whole town thinks she's your clone. That's usually followed with a 'God help us.'"

Cassie's cheek creased as she smiled and bent again to study the album. "Maddie's going to love this. And I appreciate you doing it. Darlene approached me several times about taking up where Harriet finished, but I couldn't. It was . . . it was too hard for me." She closed the album and patted the cover. "I think it's best that an outsider do it. Somebody who's not emotionally involved."

Suzanne looked away, the need to explain too strong to keep her quiet. "That's not exactly true, you know. I have a special fondness for Maddie. She's . . . special."

"Just Maddie?"

"For all of them. They've been through so much, but they're sticking together. I've never known kids to be so loved by a parent."

"I was talking about Joe."

Suzanne glanced down at her hands, the nails short and clean. "I'm doing the album for Maddie. She's hurting a lot more than I think anybody realizes."

Cassie sat back. "I'm her aunt. I think I know her better than most people."

Suzanne met her gaze. "I'm not trying to compete with you. But because she's related to you, she might not be as forthcoming as she would be to a total stranger." The last word left a bitter taste in her mouth. It would seem that even after three months in this town, she was still considered an outsider.

Suzanne stood and walked across the room to the fireplace where there were framed pictures of Cassie in a wedding dress, as well as more pictures of Harriet and her children. "Joe mentioned that he told you about the night Maddie got drunk. What I didn't tell him, but that I think you should know, is that Maddie told me that she thinks she's going to die young—like her grandmother and mother. It scares her. Enough to act out, I think. She needs to be reassured—often. This has probably been eating at her since her mother died."

Cassie stared at her, her mouth slightly agape. "She never told me that. Never even gave an indication that that's how she felt."

Crossing her arms over her chest and turning to

face Cassie, she said, "It's probably because she thinks you're in the same boat and doesn't want to upset you."

She could see the stunned expression on Cassie's face turn to anger. "But why would she tell you?"

Suzanne folded her arms over her chest again, trying hard not to take offense. She'd never before been confided in, and it had hit her as being strange, too. Nice, but strange. "Well, like I said, probably because she considers me safe. I won't be around long enough to point fingers and tell her, 'I told you so.'"

Cassie stared at her for a long moment. Then, stiffly, she said, "Thank you. For telling me. I really had no idea."

Suzanne came and sat down next to her again. "You're welcome. I just wanted to make sure somebody else would know after I'm gone."

Cassie continued to study her closely. Uncomfortable, Suzanne reached and opened the storage box. "Here's where I need the help. I don't have a clue as to who all these people are. I recognized Sam with the glasses and Joe with the cowlick, but most of the old shots are completely unidentifiable."

Cassie picked up a small snapshot and laughed. "This was after I came home. We were at the Kudzu Festival Parade, and Maddie had decorated Lucy Spafford's float with condoms."

"Is decorating with condoms a recurrent theme in Walton?"

With a broad smile, Cassie said, "Yeah, it's pretty popular down here. Can't exactly remember how it started, but Maddie's taking over the reins rather nicely."

She passed the picture to Suzanne and picked up another one and smiled. "This is going to be a lot more fun than I thought. Hope you didn't have someplace to go."

Suzanne shrugged. "I've got nothing planned for the rest of the day."

"Great." Cassie struggled to a stand. "Let me go get us some sweet tea and we'll get started."

The two women spent the next three hours poring over the pictures, labeling and documenting the ones that Harriet and Suzanne had chosen to be included in Maddie's album. As they worked, Cassie became more animated, sharing old stories of her growing-up years in Walton. She surprised Suzanne by even sharing her estrangement from her family and her years spent in New York.

They sat with their heads bent together, giggling over candid photos and gossiping about the people who filled the peripheries of the photographs. To Suzanne, it was like watching a movie. She became one of the characters—a sister, a friend, a loved one—a thread in the weave of the story. But when the movie ended and the credits played, she was by herself again, a bystander behind the camera, watching other people's lives.

By the time Suzanne started packing up and getting ready to leave, they had consumed almost a gallon of iced tea and an entire package of Oreo cookies. Cassie looked down at the empty wrapper and frowned. "Don't tell Sam. He'll kill me."

"I promise. At least you have a reason to be eating the extra calories."

"Well, maybe not *that* many." She eyed Suzanne. "You can certainly afford a few more calories. Don't they have food in Chicago?"

"They do. I just never had much interest in it." She stopped suddenly, glancing up at Cassie. "How did you know I lived in Chicago?"

Cassie's eyes were sharp. "I didn't. Until now. Chicago was the last business trip I took. I figured I must have seen you there."

Suzanne busied herself with sorting and packing away the pictures in the correct order. "Yeah, well, I've lived in Chicago off and on since I was little. There's a good chance you've seen me there. Or someplace else. I've lived in Florida and Minnesota and just about every place in between in the last five years. It could have been anywhere."

Cassie didn't respond but bent over to help Suzanne pick up. When they were done, Cassie walked her to the door. As she held it open, she said, "By the way, in case Aunt Lu hasn't already called you, the members of the Ladies' Bridge Club voted to add you as a member."

"They did?" Suzanne wondered at the odd tingle at the back of her head, as if she had just won an award.

"Yep. Only one dissenting member."

Suzanne thought back on the Methodist church's sign. "Was it Lula Beasley? She seemed to like my quotation suggestions, though."

"No, actually. It was me."

The two women stood face-to-face in the threshold of the old house, sizing each other up. "Why?"

"Don't get me wrong. I like you. I like you a lot. And I like how you are with Maddie. I've been distracted with this pregnancy, and she's really needed you." She rested her hands on her abdomen, and Suzanne watched as a small roiling motion appeared beneath the drapes of her maternity dress. "But you're not what Joe needs. And because of that, I don't want you to hang around Walton one minute longer than you have to. Joe's been hurt a great deal. I couldn't stand to see him hurt again."

"How do you know what he needs? He's so good at pretending he doesn't need anything."

"Well, from what I can see, that's the only thing you two have in common. But you're not . . ." She stopped herself, a horrified expression eclipsing her face.

Suzanne stilled. "I know. I'm not Harriet." She pushed back at the pain in her heart. "I would never want to hurt him." She looked away, staring out at the lawn, the blades of grass gradually surrendering their green coats for brown. "And Joe and I have an . . . understanding. We won't let it go too far."

Cassie gave an unladylike snort. "Right. Gosh, that sounds familiar."

"I could never stay here. I'm not meant to live forever in the same place."

"I've definitely heard that one before, too." She spread her arms wide, indicating the beautiful old house and the wide lawn with the giant magnolia in the front. "This town and the people who live here have a way of sneaking up on your heart when you least expect it." She leveled Suzanne with a hard stare. "Just don't let it happen to you."

Suzanne moved onto the porch and pulled back her shoulders. "Good-bye, Cassie. Thanks for all your help."

Cassie smiled. "Good-bye, Suzanne." She then closed the door.

Suzanne stared at the door for a long moment. "If it's not already too late," she said out loud to the stately columns and the boxwoods that bordered the front walkway. She got halfway down the walk when a prickling feeling on the back of her neck made her turn around. She saw nobody, but she felt as if she should send a huge wave, as if saying good-bye to a friend. Her gaze scanned the wide front porch, but she saw no one—just a soft rocking of the porch swing.

"Good-bye, Harriet," she said softly, feeling odd for saying it out loud but knowing she had to anyway.

Adjusting her load in her arms, she turned around and walked quickly the rest of the way home.

Joe pulled a stray weed from Harriet's grave, noticing again how empty his left hand was without the wedding band he had worn for so long. He couldn't remember exactly when he had taken it off, only that he had. He mourned it but also felt like a snake shedding its skin when he looked at the plain paleness of his empty finger. It made him think of new beginnings.

He shivered in the coolness of the evening as he stood. He hadn't been back to the cemetery since his last visit with Suzanne, and it surprised him. He usually came once a week to check on the upkeep of the grave. And to talk.

He cleared his throat. "Maddie's thinking about going to art school in San Francisco. It's going to kill me a little bit to think of her so far away." He smelled the rich earth and the distant scent of burning leaves and moved his feet on the hard-packed dirt. "You'd be so proud of her. She's beautiful, and smart, and talented. Suzanne thinks she's got a great future as a photographer. We all agree that she gets it from you."

Smiling, he looked around at the neighboring graves, lined up in stark white and listening patiently to him while he spoke to ghosts. "Sarah Frances is tackling puberty, but we're managing. Joey's doing well with football, and Knoxie shows a lot of promise with piano. She's still unhappy about her red hair and wants to change it blond like yours. I think Suzanne has held her off for a few years, though. She's a redhead, too."

He caught himself thinking of Suzanne again and quickly reined in his thoughts. "Amanda and Harry are such good kids, Har. I can't believe they're mine. I guess God knew that I couldn't take more like the first four or it would have killed me." He gave a crooked grin. "I have to think you have a hand in it. Thank you."

He felt the old familiar sting behind his eyes, and he looked up into the murky sky, watching as the moon crept out behind strips of early-evening clouds. "I slept with another woman, Har. With Suzanne. I didn't think I ever would, but it felt right. And I had the funniest feeling when I left her house that night that you somehow approved. It was the oddest thing."

Shoving his hands deep into his pockets, he ducked his chin into his chest to ward off the fall chill. It was then that he noticed the small object lying atop Harriet's gravestone. He reached over and picked it up to examine it more closely. In his palm lay a shiny copper penny, Abe Lincoln's head etched deep and clear in the fading light.

He folded his fingers over it and stuck it in his pocket. Kissing his fingertips, he laid them on the stone. "Good night, Harriet. I love you."

Turning, he picked his way down the walkway to the entranceway of the cemetery, feeling the fall wind push at his back, steering him from one place to another, as if he had no say whatsoever in where he was heading.

CHAPTER 18

Suzanne watched as the long pink car slid to a stop in front of her house, looking like the stretch version of a powder puff. Cassie was stuffed behind the wheel and Sarah Frances behind her. As Cassie approached, the girl offered a tentative smile from the backseat.

"Where's Lucinda?"

The question had been addressed to Cassie, but Sarah Frances offered, "She was puking her guts out all night. It's probably that stomach bug that's going around. My friend Brittany said that it makes your stomach turn to soup and squirt out both ends."

Cassie cast her a sidelong glance. "Lucinda's not feeling well and said we should go without her. She let me take her car because I fit in it better."

Suzanne stepped down the porch steps toward the car. "Shouldn't somebody stay here to keep an eye on her?"

"Actually, Sam took her to the clinic with him so he could make sure she wasn't getting dehydrated. She'll be fine."

Suzanne opened the door and scooted over the wide leather seat. "Um, is it all right for you to drive?"

Cassie avoided her eyes. "I prefer to be behind the wheel. It's probably a control issue left over from my years in New York." She turned to Suzanne. "It's a warm day, especially for November. How would you feel about putting the top down?"

Suzanne couldn't suppress her wide grin. "I think that's a great idea."

Cassie pushed a release button, then wedged herself out of the car. Sarah Frances leaped from the backseat and helped her fold down the enormous top and secure it behind the backseat. When they had settled back into the car, they both pulled out matching rhinestone cat's-eye sunglasses. Cassie smiled. "Aunt Lu gave these to us. She said you already had a pair."

After fumbling in her backpack, Suzanne pulled out her glasses and slid them on. They all looked at each other and burst out laughing. Cassie put the car in reverse and backed out of the driveway. "This is going to be fun, y'all."

They headed out through town, waving and smiling at people, and Suzanne felt like a beauty queen in a parade, minus the tiara. This was girl fun, a real *Thelma and Louise* adventure, and something that in the past she would have scoffed at. But if somebody had tried to take away her glasses and make her leave the pink car, she would have fought tooth and nail.

As they pulled into the parking lot at the high school to wait until the school buses were loaded with the senior class field trip to the High Museum, they passed Joe and the football team, out for their morning run. Joe motioned for the team to go ahead as he approached the car and rested his forearms on Suzanne's door, a grin on his face. "Nobody pinch me. I don't want to wake up from this dream."

"Daddy!" Sarah Frances's groan couldn't mask her wide smile.

Cassie adjusted her belly behind the wheel. "We're going to go pick up men. I hope you don't mind."

"Don't mind at all. Just have Sarah Frances back by bedtime."

He straightened, and Suzanne took advantage of the dark sunglasses to stare at him, her thoughts wandering into dangerous territory. She looked up, realizing that Joe and Cassie were staring at her as if waiting for her to speak.

"I'm sorry. Did you say something?"

Cassie put something in her lap. "I asked if you'd had a chance to read one of the brochures Maddie brought home. It tells a little bit about the photographer and some of the best-known photographs. Just in case you weren't already familiar with her."

"No. Not yet," she said, staring down at the brochures. Suzanne picked them up, her fingers suddenly cold. The title of the first one read *Gertrude Hardt: Behind the Camera.* Her gaze dropped to the paragraph below. *This exhibit showcases a world of scientific and academic inquiry far removed from the heroic and transcendent portraitures; a world of astonishing experiments, extraordinary apparatus, and surprising photographic inquiry.*

And then her gaze fell to the photograph featured at the bottom of the brochure. It was of a barefoot child wearing a winter jacket, the child's face pinched with cold. The dirty face stared out under filthy hair, but the small hand held a bright white daisy. The intensity of the white was what drew the eye, showing that through all the filth and poverty that imbued this child, the story of the photograph was in the hope and brightness of the one fragile daisy.

Suzanne knew the photograph well. It had once hung on the wall of her tiny apartment and was the one thing she had owned that she cherished. It had reminded her of her own buried hopes, and she thought that was why Anthony had given it to her. Too late, she realized he owned it solely for its monetary value. And he despised it simply because it reminded him too much of where he'd been. Flipping open the brochure, she spotted the rest of the pictures—with one glaring omission—from her collection, the same collection she had sold as quickly as she had changed her hair color and her address. She could only imagine how angry Anthony must have been when he found out what she'd done. And she knew without a doubt that Anthony wouldn't be very far behind this exhibit of Gertrude Hardt's famous photographs.

She looked up, startled to hear Joe speaking. "We were hoping you could translate what 'transcendent portraitures' means."

Suzanne swallowed the bile that had risen in her throat and forced a smile. "I haven't a clue." Her world seemed to spin for a moment, and she thought she might throw up. "You know, I probably shouldn't go. Lucinda's sick, and there's only Brunelle's daughter Cordella to watch the store."

Cassie put the car in drive. "Cordella will be fine. Let's just have some fun and enjoy the trip."

Joe touched her arm, and when she looked at him his eyes were shadowed with worry. "Are you all right?"

"I'm fine. Really."

She glanced over at Cassie and saw that she was

watching her closely. The roar of the bus engines caught their attention. Cassie waved. "They're leaving. We'll see you later, Joe."

Suzanne pushed away the feeling of uneasiness as she said good-bye to Joe. As the long pink car slid away, she couldn't help wondering if all the running she had done had been in circles and if she had finally, simply, come to the place where she was supposed to be.

The car sped down the interstate, drawing stares and waves from passersby and from the Walton High School buses. She saw Maddie at the back of one of the buses, waving wildly and wearing a wistful look that said she'd rather be in the pink car. Suzanne felt relieved when she spotted Rob sitting next to her.

Cassie flipped on the car radio, and a country music station blared out a song about "wherever you go, there you are." Cassie turned to Suzanne, the sun glinting off the rhinestones in her sunglasses. "So, what do you think, Louise?"

Suzanne smiled as some of her worry slipped away. "It's great, Thelma. Just great."

Sarah Frances leaned as far forward as her seat belt would allow. "Who's Thelma and Louise?" she shouted over the din of the radio and the rushing wind.

Cassie and Suzanne gave each other conspiratorial looks. Cassie spoke first. "Just two friends out for a ride."

Suzanne rested her head back against the seat, letting the wind rush at her face and hair, and tried to forget, just for a while, the photograph of the child with the flower, and that it had ever meant anything to her.

Maddie caught up with them as soon as they reached the main entrance to the High Museum. She and Rob were holding hands, but she immediately pulled apart when she spotted Cassie and Sarah Frances. She appeared to hum at a high pitch that only Suzanne seemed able to hear. Even then, she wasn't sure if it was the excitement of seeing the exhibit or the proximity to Rob.

The long line of students and chaperones filed quickly into the building, then up the wide, winding walkway that took them to the main exhibit hall. A large picture of Gertrude Hardt hung on the main wall, with her birth and death dates, along with her biography, written on a large panel hung next to the frame.

Suzanne knew it all by heart and didn't press forward to read the plaque. Instead, she stared at the picture of the artist, looking in the weathered face and pale blue eyes for a hint of the genius within. She watched as Maddie did the same, her tall figure buffeted by the throng of teenagers moving to the front of the group.

Suzanne accepted a headset from a museum staffer, then hung back as the rest of the group received theirs, the earphones resting around her neck. She felt suspended in time, with a horrifying sense of déjà vu, but she felt powerless to back up and start over. As she walked into the first exhibit room, she felt herself propelled forward but not against her will. Glancing over her shoulder, she wished for nothing more than to let it be over.

As she waited for Maddie, Cassie, and Sarah Frances to catch up, she placed the headphones over her ears and flipped the recorder to the on position. A woman's voice, with a crisp, British accent, spoke. "Despite the forty years Hardt spent photographing American cities and their occupants, she left behind a relatively small body of work. Until recently, a large portion of her collection had remained unseen by the public eye. Reported missing and assumed stolen from the estate of the late art enthusiast Caldwell Winthorpe of Chicago, the photographs remained underground for nearly fifteen years until unearthed recently and lent anonymously to this exhibit. An investigation is pending concerning the ownership of the photographs."

Rewinding the tape recorder, she listened again to the woman's chipper voice: ". . . photographs remained underground for nearly fifteen years until unearthed recently . . ." She rewound and listened to the same words four more times. Something was wrong. Really wrong. How could they have been missing or presumed stolen? They had been given to her as an engagement gift. From

Anthony—a year and a half ago. Right after he had hit her for the first time and she had told him she was leaving. He had given her the photographs, knowing her weakness. And she had taken them.

She moved slowly with the crowd as they meandered from picture to picture, her eyes not really seeing but her mind working furiously. If they had been stolen fifteen years before, then how did Anthony own them to be able to give them to her?

She stopped suddenly, causing Sarah Frances to bump into her. *Because they had never really belonged to him.*

She felt sick, afraid she'd throw up right there on the glossy wooden floors of the High Museum's exhibit room. Forcing her way through the crowd, she found a cushioned bench seat against a wall and sat down. Her head felt cold and clammy as she leaned forward, resting her head in her hands. *He's won. All this time I thought that I had succeeded in besting him, and all along he knew he'd won.* It wouldn't be a matter of his word against hers. If they were stolen, and she had sold them, Anthony would never be implicated. All it would take would be one anonymous tip from him to the authorities.

She swallowed heavily, forcing down the rising tide of panic. All this time she'd been thinking he was after her, trying to reclaim his property. Not the pictures, but her. The pictures were merely a means to an end.

How predictable she must have seemed to him. He knew what she would do. And now he didn't need to chase her to find her. He could let the police do it for him. The threat alone would be enough to make her return to him. It wouldn't matter what she told the police. Anthony had money. And friends in high places. Either way, she'd end up back with him or in jail. Each choice would be a prison of her own making.

Somebody sat on the bench beside her, and she looked up, immediately knowing that things really could get worse. Stinky Harden, wearing a light blue seersucker suit, sat next to her, a look of mock concern on his face. "I didn't know you were chaperoning. You weren't on the bus."

She forced herself to remain civil. "I rode with Cassie Parker. They said they had enough chaperones on the bus." She looked around for Cassie, or anybody she knew, to rescue her. Her party must already have passed into the next room.

"You don't look like you're feeling so well. You worried about Maddie not winning that photography contest?"

She looked at him oddly, wondering how he even knew about the contest. And then she remembered his son, Charlie, was a photographer, too. "I'm not worried. I think she has a pretty good chance at winning."

He leaned his considerable bulk against the wall behind them. "If I were a betting man, I'd say Charlie had an even better chance of winning." He pretended to think for a minute. "For the sake of argument, let's pretend that I am a betting man. You interested in making a wager?"

"No. I'm not."

"Not even if the odds are in your favor? And by winning you'd be doing something for Joe?"

That got her attention, and when she looked at him, she realized that had been his intention. She was so damned predictable. "What are you talking about?"

"How about we make a little bet between the two of us? Let's just say that if Maddie wins, I'll drop out of the mayoral race."

Her stomach roiled but she ignored it, pretending to be only half listening. "And if Charlie wins?"

The hardness in his eyes belied the doughy cheeks and rosy skin. "Then you tell me everything I want to know."

"What makes you think that either Charlie or Maddie will win? There's bound to be thousands of kids entering this contest."

"Because I've seen both entries. Now, I'm not an art con-wa-sur or nothin', but I know good picture-taking when I see it."

"And you're so sure that you'd bet your run for

342

mayor on it?" She still wasn't convinced he wasn't joking. And she certainly had nothing left to lose.

He nodded. "Yessirreebobtail."

"But what happens if neither of them wins?"

Pulling a toothpick out of his shirt pocket, he stuck it in his mouth. "Then all bets are off."

She spotted Charlie with a group of kids huddled around a photograph of a seminude woman sitting in a small metal tub in front of a kitchen fire. Her haunted eyes held hunger and hopelessness; her sloped shoulders, defeat. But Charlie was snickering, pointing at the bare breasts and making ribald comments.

She stared into Stinky's florid face and thought of Joe, and her heart ached for him, for them, and for what he would feel when he finally knew. And now Stinky was giving her the chance to do something to make it up to him—something for which she'd expect no repayment, a final gesture to him to give him thanks and to say good-bye.

Hell. She had nothing to lose, and Joe had everything to gain. Facing him, she shook his hand. "It's a deal, then."

His hand lingered on hers more than necessary and she drew it back, wiping it unobtrusively on her skirt. Without another word, she stood and moved quickly out of the room into the next, looking for Maddie.

She found her with Rob, standing close together

343

but not touching. Suzanne saw the reason why when she spotted Cassie and Sarah Frances at the adjacent photograph. Suzanne moved to stand behind Maddie and gazed over the girl's shoulder at a once-familiar scene. It showed a mother in a Depression-era dress with two small children, neither one of them older than five, going through a garbage can on a street corner. The picture was dark, but a fine halo of bright light seemed to outline the mother, like a beacon guiding the way for her children.

The photo had always reminded Suzanne of her own mother, which is why she'd kept it in the protective folder under her bed—so she'd never have to be reminded of her mother and how she'd never allowed light into her daughter's life.

Maddie said something, and Rob laughed as Maddie ducked her head onto his shoulder. Cassie called out a familiar name behind her, but it sounded muffled through the headphones. Turning slowly, Suzanne watched as Cassie called out again, this time raising her hand, and when Suzanne's gaze followed Cassie's, she thought the world had stopped spinning.

Anthony—tall, dark, and brooding in his black Italian suit—had stopped in front of Cassie and was kissing her cheek, European-style.

With shaking fingers, Suzanne managed to turn off her headset and focus her attention on the scene being played out before her. She allowed the crowd of teenagers to move her along to the next photograph, so that now she was standing facing Cassie, with Anthony's back to her.

"Pregnancy becomes you, Cassandra. Will you be returning to the agency after the baby is born?" His words were dark and smooth, like his hands. They could also turn hard and biting without provocation. She'd had the bruises on her heart and on her face to prove it.

"Thank you, Anthony. And yes, I will be returning to work when the baby's old enough, but I'm not planning on traveling—at least for the first couple of years. I'll leave that up to Andrew. But please feel free to call me anytime. I'll remain the account manager and will be overseeing things from my home office."

"That's wonderful news. You've done such a marvelous job so far that I'd hate to lose you. The print ads you shot in Chicago last year were wonderful. I was hoping we could schedule something similar for the spring, when we open up our new restaurant."

Cassie's eyes seemed to glaze over at the mention of Chicago. Her eyes darted over to the crowd behind Anthony, finally settling on Suzanne. *She knows,* Suzanne's mind calmly realized. Her gaze met Cassie's, and she felt the battle between them. *Don't,* she tried to say, but she remained silent and unmoving, her eyes pleading.

With a perceptible struggle, Cassie turned her attention from Suzanne back to Anthony. "What brings you here to Atlanta?"

Anthony swept an arm through the air. "This exhibit. It's the opening day, and I didn't want to miss it. I'm a huge fan of Ms. Hardt's, and when I heard that there would be photographs displayed that had never been seen in public before, I knew I had to come."

Even though his back was to her, Suzanne could picture his black eyes, hollow of all emotion and filled with an empty chill. She found the courage to move and began to back away. And then Cassie looked at her, and Suzanne saw the confusion in her eyes before hearing Cassie say, "I just realized that you probably know . . ." And then she stopped.

Before Suzanne could turn and run, Cassie clutched at her heavy abdomen. "Wow. That was a big one. I think I'm carrying a linebacker for the Georgia Bulldogs."

Suzanne could sense Anthony's revulsion by the way he stepped back from Cassie. "Are you all right? Would you like me to get somebody?"

Cassie shook her head, her hands still clutched over the baby. "No. Really. I'm not due for another three weeks, so I'm not worried. I think he was just stretching or something."

"Well, then." He took Cassie's hand in his own and gently kissed it. "I must be going. I have a plane to catch back to Chicago. It was wonderful seeing you again, and I will call you about the new campaign sometime next week."

Suzanne didn't wait to hear Cassie's response. She turned and ran the rest of the way to the end of the exhibit, then ducked into the first women's bathroom. She made it to a stall and threw up, continuing to retch until there was nothing left. After rinsing her mouth, she began to wash her face with icy-cold water as her hands shook. The water slid down her face and into the neck of the blouse, but she didn't feel it at all.

The door opened and Cassie walked in, their gazes meeting in the mirror as the cold water dripped down Suzanne's face, stinging her eyes.

Cassie's expression gave nothing away. "We need to talk. I've bribed Sarah Frances to go back with Maddie on the bus so we can have some time alone."

Without waiting to see if Suzanne followed, Cassie left, the door swinging shut behind her. After staring at the stranger in the mirror for a moment, Suzanne had no other choice but to follow.

Wearing her sunglasses and keeping her head ducked, Suzanne caught up to Cassie in the parking garage as she stood next to the large pink convertible. Cassie reached for the door handle, then stopped, her eyes clenched tightly.

Alarmed, Suzanne ran over to her. "Are you all right? Do you want me to call Sam?"

Cassie shook her head. "No, I'm fine. The baby's not due for a while yet. These are just those fake contractions—what are they called? Braxton Hicks or something."

Suzanne hesitated, not convinced. "Give me your cell phone and I'll call Sam just to be on the safe side."

Cassie shook her head again. "I'm not going to get Sam panicking over nothing. I'm sure these contractions will stop before we even get home." She glanced up at Suzanne. "You'll just have to drive."

A fat pillow of panic and guilt lodged itself halfway between her mouth and her stomach and wouldn't budge. She opened her mouth to tell Cassie that she didn't have a driver's license, but Cassie was already climbing into the passenger seat, her hands clutching her protruding belly.

She slid in next to Cassie and looked at the steering wheel. She knew how to drive; she just didn't have a current license. Taking a deep breath, she started the engine, vowing to stay within the speed limit and avoid attention from any traffic cops who might be lurking between Atlanta and Walton.

Suzanne made it out of the garage and back to the interstate before Cassie spoke, her voice strained. "So, why are you hiding from Anthony deSalvo?"

Clutching the steering wheel a little tighter,

Suzanne answered, "Because he's not a very nice man. It would be a lot healthier for me if he didn't know where I was."

"You were engaged, weren't you?"

Embarrassment and regret settled over Suzanne again, as if he'd beaten her again with his fists and then with his gifts that made her stay. "Yeah. For a while. And then I left him."

Cassie was quiet for a moment, and Suzanne glanced over to see her eyes shut tightly again as she grimaced. "Look, Cassie, let me call Sam. You're making me nervous."

"No. I'm fine. And you're just looking for an excuse to end this conversation. Why did you leave him?"

Because he hurt me. And the hurt goes much deeper than the bruises. He made me see the ugly truth of the person I really am. "He's got a bad temper. I didn't want to be the brunt of it anymore."

"What about the pictures? There's got to be a reason why he showed up today and why you were so jittery about coming here. What's the connection?"

Suzanne focused on the road in front of her. "He gave them to me. When I left him, I sold them for a lot of money."

"That's understandable. So why all the secrecy?"

"Because before I left, he said all the documentation said that they belonged to him and that if I took them, it would be stealing. But I swear to you, he gave them to me. As an engagement present."

Cassie was silent, and Suzanne looked over to find the other woman breathing deeply, her head bowed as if deep in thought. After a moment, she said, "So it's basically your word against his."

Suzanne paused for a moment, wondering how much she should tell, then realized that she had to continue. "It's much worse than that. I found out today at the exhibit that those pictures were probably stolen fifteen years ago. Before he gave them to me. He used me to launder them. All he has to do is tell the authorities I sold them. They would never believe me in a million years if I told them Anthony had given them to me. I'm sure he wants to find me to make me come back to him. Or he'll send me to jail."

Cassie shook her head slowly. "You could be in a lot of trouble, you know." She rubbed her hands over her abdomen. "Why would you ever agree to marry somebody like that?"

Suzanne slammed her hands against the steering wheel, making the car swerve slightly into the next lane. She jerked it back. "Stop asking me these questions. You don't know anything about me. And it's none of your business."

Cassie gritted her teeth through a contraction and shouted, "It damn well is my business. Harriet was my sister."

Suzanne's eyes smarted. "What has that got to do with me?" She wished she hadn't said it, because she already knew.

"Because, unfortunately, what happens to you will adversely affect Joe. That's why it's my business. I knew it was too soon for him to get involved with somebody. And then he just happened to pick the absolutely wrong person."

The words hurt more than Suzanne wanted to admit, and she said the first thing that came to her, knowing they'd hurt Cassie just as badly. "Harriet's dead, Cassie. Joe isn't."

A groan of pain came from Cassie as she twisted herself on the seat and threw her head back. "Damn it, Suzanne. Don't you think I see that every day of my life?"

Suzanne pushed the gas pedal down harder. "Just because Joe's getting on with his life doesn't mean that there's no more room for Harriet. Is that what you're afraid of, Cassie? Because making Joe a martyr will not bring her back."

"You could never love him like Harriet did. Never."

Tears blurred Suzanne's vision, and she blinked rapidly as she approached a solid wall of Atlanta traffic. She stopped behind a large office supply store truck as other cars filled in the gaps around her and engines idled.

"Maybe I already do."

"No." Cassie's voice sounded strangled, full of pain.

Suzanne continued to stare straight ahead, not able to face Cassie. She felt the truth of her words before they appeared on her lips, but they gave her cold comfort. "I do. Not in the same way Harriet did. She fell in the love with the man he was. I love him for who he is now."

"No!"

This time the word was nearly a scream, and Suzanne jerked her head toward Cassie. "What?"

Cassie's amber eyes were filled with pain and . . . surprise. "My water just broke."

CHAPTER 19

Suzanne thought her neck would snap as she jerked her head toward the laboring Cassie, then toward the metal ocean of stopped cars, then back again. "No." She repeated Cassie's words, the pain in them no less acute.

"The baby's coming. I can feel it."

"No, it's not. Just hang on until I can get you to a hospital." Her foot hovered over the gas pedal as she prepared to move. Unfortunately, nobody else in the lane in front of her or on either side seemed to be of like mind. A man in a small BMW with the window down was looking over at them in curiosity but raised a newspaper when Suzanne looked in his direction.

Cassie grunted. "I think I need to push. I need to push!"

"Don't you push. Whatever you do, don't you push."

Suzanne turned off the ignition and searched under the seat until she found the "recline" button and tilted the seat backward to give them more room. Then she lunged past Cassie and grabbed Cassie's purse, yanking out her cell phone. Too panicked to realize that his number was probably on speed dial, she shouted, "What's Sam's number?"

Through gritted teeth, Cassie gave her the number, pausing after the first three numbers to allow for a contraction to pass. "They're coming faster now. I swear I can feel the head."

Suzanne's fingers shook so badly while she dialed the phone that she had to hang up twice and try again. Sam answered on the third ring.

"Sam, it's Suzanne. I'm with Cassie and I think she's gone into labor."

Sam's voice was calm, probably from years of dealing with emergencies. "Where are you?"

"Somewhere on I-Twenty in the middle of a traffic jam. There must have been an accident or something, because we haven't moved in about ten minutes." She stood on the seat to peer over the line of cars. Two teenagers in a vintage Beetle to her left looked at her with curiosity while the BMW guy just shook his head. "We just passed Exit Nineteen."

She glanced over at Cassie, and her panic rose a notch. "What are you doing? Put your underwear back on!"

The hair around Cassie's face stuck to her sweat-soaked cheeks. "I'm getting ready to deliver this baby. It's not going to wait."

Suzanne thought she could detect a note of panic in Sam's voice as he responded, "How far apart are the contractions?"

"It's hard to tell—I'm not using a stopwatch. But I think about every two to three minutes."

There was a brief pause. "Tell her not to push. I'm calling an ambulance now on my other line. Don't hang up the phone."

"Right. Like I would." Sam had already put her on hold.

Cassie was now bracing herself against her door, her legs up on the bench seat, and she was pushing—hard. Suzanne looked up and caught the wide-eyed stare of Mr. BMW before he looked back at his paper.

She turned back to Cassie. "Don't push! You are not having that baby now. An ambulance is on the way."

Cassie's face reminded Suzanne of that girl in *The Exorcist*, but instead of green, her skin was a vivid red. "Damn it, this baby is coming now!" She rolled her head back and forth. "Aunt Lu's going to be so mad about her car."

Sam came back on the line. "Tell her to hang on;

the ambulance should be there within fifteen minutes."

Suzanne's voice shook. "I don't know, Sam. She's pretty insistent that that baby is going to be born any minute now."

An excruciating wail shot up over the sound of idling engines, and for a moment Suzanne didn't realize that the sound had come from Cassie. One of the teenagers in the Beetle called to her, "You okay in there, lady?"

"Sam? Are you there? I think Cassie's in a lot of pain."

Cassie let out another wail, as if for good measure.

Sam's voice was strained. "I'm going to have to walk you through this."

She thought her head would spin off its shoulders. "No way, Miss Scarlett. I don't know nothin' 'bout birthin' babies."

"Look, Suzanne. The ambulance isn't going to get there in time. You're the only one who can help her."

Cassie began panting heavily, her face reddening. Then she gasped out, "I know you can do this."

Suzanne glanced over at Cassie's face, red and sweaty in the midst of the contraction, and she knew she didn't have a choice. "I was afraid you were going to say that." She forced herself to take three deep breaths. "What do I do first?"

"Do you have any hand wipes? You want your

hands to be as clean as you can get them."

She cradled the phone under her chin. "Yeah. I've got some in my backpack." Her backpack sat on the floor of the backseat behind her, and she reached back and pulled them out. She emptied half the box onto the dash before opening the first one and scrubbing her hands.

Cassie shouted as another contraction took hold of her, and Sam sounded shaken when she heard his voice again. "Can you see anything?"

Trying not to appear squeamish, she peered past the raised skirt of the maternity dress. "I . . . I see the baby's head."

"Shit." His voice was quiet, as if she wasn't supposed to have heard him curse.

She seemed to draw strength from his helplessness, feeling a real need to help for the first time in her life. "Look, Sam, I can do this. Just tell me what to do and I'll do it."

"I need to talk to Sam." Cassie reached for the phone, but as she did, her fingers caught in the long chain she always wore around her neck. The delicate chain snapped, scattering gold hearts all over the seat and floor of the car. Suzanne could see panic in Cassie's face for the first time since the labor had begun. Cassie tried to hoist herself up to capture all the hearts, but another contraction seized her and she bore down on the child attempting to be born, another guttural scream pealing out of her mouth.

Suzanne kept her voice calm. "Don't worry about the hearts. I'll keep them safe and make sure they're all put together again. Promise. Just concentrate on this baby." She watched as more of the head appeared, and she waited to see what would happen.

Cassie gripped her wrist hard enough to make it hurt, her breathing labored and pausing between the words to gasp for air. "Make . . . sure . . . you . . . do. Joe and his kids . . . mean more to me . . . than you'll ever know."

Suzanne just nodded, wondering if Cassie was still talking about the necklace. She didn't release Cassie's hold until the contraction had passed, then held the phone to Cassie's ear so she could speak to Sam.

It was then she realized that she had an audience. A middle-aged man wearing a golf visor and a knit shirt was peering inside the car.

"Need some help? My wife and I are in the van behind you, and it looks like you might be having some difficulties. . . ." When he saw what was in the front seat, he averted his gaze.

"Are you a doctor?" Even she recognized the note of hysteria in her voice.

"No."

"Then I need you to run up and down these lanes and see if you can find one." She glanced back down at Cassie. "Even a veterinarian would work. Just go. Run!"

The man nodded and headed off, his expression one of relief.

A near scream erupted from Cassie's mouth, following by grunting. "This baby is coming *now!*"

Sam's voice faded in and out as he spoke. "She always means what she says. You're going to have to put the phone down, Suzanne, and be ready . . . guide the baby out."

"Sam? I can't hear you. Tell me what I'm supposed to do next."

"Support . . . head . . . shoulders . . . keep baby . . . on stomach." She turned and aimed the cell phone toward the back of the car, trying to get a clearer signal. "Clear the nose . . . mouth . . . wait . . . ambulance . . . umbilical cord . . ." And then the phone went dead.

She glanced out the window, looking for the man who'd approached her earlier, but didn't see him or any would-be rescuer and tried to suppress the panic that was about to make her head explode. *You have to stay calm. She needs you.* She turned back to Cassie, who was now wedged up against the side of the car, sweat rolling down her cheeks and a clear look of panic and pain etched on her face.

Suzanne did the first thing that came to mind. She took her hand. She tried hard to keep the fear out of her voice but wasn't completely successful. "Cassie, we can do this, okay? You do whatever you're supposed to do, and I'll be here waiting to catch the baby. We'll be fine. You'll see."

Their eyes met, and for a brief moment, Suzanne felt the bond of sisters, of implicit trust. It shot like adrenaline through her system, making her stronger.

Cassie responded by bearing down, the silence of her effort deafening in the small space of the front seat. Suzanne knelt on the seat, watching with awed fascination as the tiny head emerged. She ignored the blood and fluid and saw only this beautiful new life.

Cassie screamed, then yelled before collapsing back against the side of the door. Gasping, she asked, "Is it out? I don't hear anything."

"Not yet. I think you're going to need to push again to get the shoulders out."

"Oh God." She breathed heavily, gathering strength. "They didn't go over car deliveries in Lamaze class."

Suzanne grimaced. "Maybe you can talk to them about adding it."

Another contraction hit, and Suzanne reached for the baby's head as tiny shoulders emerged, followed by the rest of an impossibly small human being. It slid neatly into her hands, and she stared at it for a moment, wondering if this had really just happened. Cassie threw her head back and screamed like a dying animal, and Suzanne thought for a moment that Cassie had lost her mind. Nobody could stand that kind of pain. And if she did, this was sure to be an only child.

Remembering what Sam had said, she began clearing the mucus from the baby's nose and mouth and was rewarded by a resounding squawk from the bundle in her arms.

Cassie was now slumped against her side of the car, her head barely raised. Weakly, she asked, "Is it a girl or boy?"

Momentarily confused, Suzanne stared at the baby. "I don't know."

Cassie's eyes closed for a moment as if to summon the last of her energy. "Look between the legs, Suzanne!"

Feeling stupid but pleased with herself at the same time, she did as she'd been told. "It's a girl."

Cassie reached for the baby, and Suzanne laid her on her mother's chest. Reaching in the backseat, she grabbed one of Lucinda's sweaters and put it over mother and child.

A tapping sounded on her car door at the same time she heard the wail of a siren. The man she'd spoken with earlier stood with a tall woman wearing glasses and carrying a small black bag. Weak with relief, Suzanne moved to get out of the car, but Cassie's voice called her back.

"Thank you."

The baby made mewing noises under the sweater, and Suzanne smiled. "You're welcome." Then she left the car, allowing the doctor to take over. She stood by the side of the car, leaning on it to keep from falling, and waited until the ambulance arrived, unable to shake the silly grin off her face—or the feeling that she had just changed lanes on the highway of her life. She could only hope that a tractor-trailer truck wasn't headed her way. The sky rumbled overhead as storm clouds smothered the sun, and she huddled in her thin sweater as the first raindrops began to fall.

Joe touched the glass on the observation window of the nursery, looking at the rows of pink and blue bundles in the clear plastic bassinets. He closed his eyes, the poignant memories of his six trips to this same hospital almost overwhelming. Until the last time, with Harry, this had been his favorite place in the world. Even the sterile smell and bland walls couldn't wipe away the way he'd felt in the halls of the maternity ward. It was a place of unbelievable joy, affirmed love, and new beginnings. And then, the last time, of endings.

He opened his eyes and saw baby Parker, swaddled in pink and mewling like a kitten for attention. *Already acting like Cassie,* Joe thought, and smiled, wondering at how this miracle of life continued to surprise him. Life went on, no matter how much you dared the sun not to rise again. He wouldn't have believed it three years ago, but things did change. He still missed Harriet, still loved her. He always would. But now she was a part of his past—a happy past but still the past. The future was his to live and to fill with whatever he chose out of life.

A nurse walked into the room, and Joe tapped on the window and pointed at the Parker bassinet. Picking up the baby, the nurse moved closer to the window to show him. He marveled at the tiny, perfect fingers, the minute nose, the delicate eyebrows and lashes. She let out a loud cry, much bigger and louder than such a small human being was expected to make, and Joe smiled again. This was definitely Cassie's daughter.

He thanked the nurse and waved at his niece, the joy and nostalgia melding together and sending a warm glow into his heart. He watched the nurse put the baby back into the bassinet. *New beginnings.* If only he could convince Suzanne that every life held the possibility of new beginnings, of second chances. He touched the glass again, then turned away and headed for home.

As Joe pulled the truck into his driveway, he spotted Suzanne on the front steps wearing a tall princess hat with streamers that came down over the waist of his old ski jacket that she wore. Amanda was in the process of galloping toward her at full speed. By the time he'd left his vehicle and made it to the front walk, Amanda was happily ensconced in Suzanne's lap. As he approached, he realized that not only had Amanda dressed Suzanne, but she'd also done her makeup.

Resisting a smile as he viewed their matching matte blue eye shadow and round circles of rouge on their cheeks, he bowed deeply, sweeping his hand over the ground. "Your Royal Highnesses."

"Hi, Daddy! Miss Suzanne and I were playing Pretty Princess."

He grinned down at Suzanne. "Let me guess: you lost?"

She stuck out a foot and playfully kicked him in the shin. "At least I knew better this time than to bring any money."

The front door popped open as Knoxie ran out chasing after Harry, his hands covered in oozing red goo. He launched himself at his father, but Joe managed to evade him with a well-placed hand on the little chest. "Whoa there, buddy. What's this on your hands?"

Knoxie sighed loudly. "I was making lunch and I asked him to hold the tomatoes while I got the bread out of the fridge."

Suzanne stood, plopping Amanda on the porch. "Come on, Harry. Let's go get cleaned up and I'll help Knoxie with lunch."

Joe eyed the clownlike makeup on Suzanne's face and knew that he'd never seen her looking quite as beautiful. "I'll help."

They all moved into the kitchen. Suzanne lifted

Harry up to the sink and began rinsing his hands. "How're Cassie and the baby doing?"

Joe reached up and removed Suzanne's princess hat. "They're both doing great—better than Lucinda's car anyway. Her car will be at the detailer's for another week, but Cassie and the baby are supposed to leave the hospital tomorrow."

Suzanne grinned as she dried Harry's hands on a paper towel and set him back on the ground. "Sorry to hear about the car, but it's good news about Cassie. Have they named the baby yet?"

Sarah Frances entered the kitchen, wearing a pretty silver bangle on her arm and a toe ring on her bare foot. Joe frowned but caught Suzanne's grin out of the corner of his eye.

He tried to keep the censure out of his voice. "What are you wearing, Sarah Frances?"

"It's my birthday present from Suzanne." She smiled shyly at the older woman.

"I haven't seen you wear it before."

She shrugged as she opened a drawer in the hutch and pulled out place mats. "I hadn't gotten around to it yet."

A small glance passed between his daughter and Suzanne, and he knew enough to know that things were okay between them and that it was none of his business.

He turned to Sarah Frances. "Can you help Knoxie with lunch? I need to talk to Suzanne."

She nodded, and he led Suzanne outside, where

they sat on the top step. The sun shone brightly but hardly put a dent in the chill of the late November day. He looked at his jacket, nearly swallowing her slender frame, and realized it had probably never looked better. "Thanks for watching the kids while I was at the hospital. Hope they didn't wear you out too much."

"I had fun." She squinted up at him with a questioning look, one that mixed curiosity and wariness in equal measure. "You didn't tell me if they'd named the baby yet."

"They did." He paused, watching the play of light and shadow in her gray eyes. "Harriet Suzanne Parker."

"What?"

He laughed at the expression on her face. "You've been made immortal."

"Was this Sam's idea?"

"Nope. Cassie's. I supposed after what you went through, you deserved a little recognition."

Suzanne hugged her arms to her chest, her breaths coming out in puffs of white. "I hope this means she's not still mad at me."

"Why would she be mad?"

"We were arguing when her water broke. I was hoping that I hadn't caused the baby to come early."

"Actually, since the baby was almost nine pounds, Cassie should be thankful it came three weeks early." He peered at her closely. "What were you arguing about?"

She glanced up, and her lips, heavy with bright fuchsia lipstick, were almost touching his. "You," she said softly.

"What about me?"

She fiddled with her fingernails for a minute before answering, "How much you like to pretend that you don't need anybody in your life. She said it was the only thing we have in common."

He sat back, leaning against the railing. "Do you believe that's the only thing?"

"No." She reached up and tentatively touched his face. "We both have these empty places inside." She placed her hands on his chest. "And we both wish we had more time to fill them in with what needs to be there."

She really had no idea. Reaching behind her head, he pulled her to him, tasting the sweet fullness of her lips and not caring that they were on the front porch of his house for everyone to see. He wanted her, mind, body, and soul, and it was about time he told the world about it.

The sound of a car door shutting jerked both their heads up. Maddie was getting out of Rob's car, and they both waved when they spotted him and Suzanne on the front steps. Joe kept his arm around Suzanne as Maddie made her way toward them.

She gave them a nonchalant hello before opening the door. Turning back to them for a moment before going inside, she said, "You might want to take the lipstick off before you go anywhere, Daddy."

Suzanne ducked her head into his chest and laughed, the sound warming him to his very core.

He waved Maddie away. "Why don't you go help your siblings get lunch ready?"

When the door banged shut, he turned back to Suzanne. "Oh, before I forget—Cassie gave me something to give to you. She said it was stuck in the folds of her dress when she got to the hospital."

Joe dug in his back pocket and pulled out a small gold heart charm. She lifted her palm, and he placed the heart in it. "She said you'd know what to do with it."

She looked at him again with those incredible eyes. "Tell Cassie that I do and that I'll take care of it."

He wondered why those words made her appear so small and vulnerable, and as she bent to look closely at the heart, he leaned over and kissed the top of her head.

She glanced up quickly. "Why did you do that?"

"Because I wanted to. And because you seemed to need it."

He thought she was about to argue. Instead, she took his hand. "Thank you. You're a pretty nice guy, Joe Warner."

"Shh. Not too loud. It's bad for my reputation." He put his hands over hers to warm them, one of hers fisted in a ball to hold the heart. "You need to come to one of our football games. They call me 'Mean-ass Joe.' To my back, of course." He reached out to smooth a strand of bright red hair behind her ear—hair that was a dark auburn at the roots. He almost asked her then about the money in her backpack that he'd seen in her closet, but didn't. Things were still so fragile between them. She was like a butterfly in his hands; if he squeezed too tight, he'd damage her wings. But if he opened up too much, she'd fly away.

Instead, he said, "I guess a lot of people wear two faces. To protect those who know and love us from seeing our other half."

Smoky gray eyes stared into his. "Maybe." She pulled away from him and tucked the charm into the pocket of her oversized jacket. Then she giggled. It was light and frivolous and definitely not a sound he'd heard come from her before. It made him smile. "Mean-ass Joe, huh?"

He elbowed her gently. "Hey, that's better than 'Sweet Potato Joe,' you know what I mean? I've got to put the fear of God in them."

She elbowed him back. "Mean-ass Joe," she said again. Then she snorted.

He leaned close to her. "What should your nickname be? 'Sexy Suzanne'? Or maybe 'Sweet Suzanne'?" He watched her closely. "I know. What about 'Secretive Suzanne'?"

She pulled away, and he knew he'd gone too far.

She stood abruptly. "I've got to get back to work on Maddie's album. And take care of Cassie's necklace."

He stood to face her, and when she looked at him, she smiled. "You look like you belong in a circus." She pulled a clean tissue from a pocket and handed it to him. "You might want to use this before anybody sees you."

He took the tissue as she kissed him on the mouth, her lips chilled against his. Then she walked away from him without another word, looking small and lost in his oversized jacket. He watched her as she headed down the street, willing her in his mind to look back—just once. He was about to give up when she neared the end of the block and looked back with a small wave. Then she turned her back on him again and disappeared from his view.

A cold wind blew down his spine, like an odd premonition, and he couldn't help thinking that this wasn't the first time he'd watched her walk out of his life—and that it probably wouldn't be the last, either. Sticking his hands deep inside his pockets, he turned and entered the house, listening to the fall wind batter the door shut behind him.

Maddie listened as her daddy moved around the downstairs of the house, turning off lights, clearing a path through toys and checking doors to make sure they were locked. He and Mama had once done it together, but now it was a lonely ritual, and one that he'd postpone as long as he could. He usually fell asleep on the couch first, as if an old lumpy couch was more appealing than an empty bed.

Maddie fished a Barbie doll from a dark corner of her closet and tossed it into a pile she was making for Knoxie and Amanda. She waited as her father's footsteps paused in the hallway outside her door before he knocked softly.

"Come in," she said, not at all ready to explain why she was sitting cross-legged on the floor by her closet, its contents strewn in neat piles around her, a packing box filled to the top and pushed against her dresser.

"Shouldn't you be in bed, Maddie?"

She didn't look up. "I wanted to finish this first."

He stepped closer and saw the old school program from a fifth-grade play that lay open in her lap. She closed it and stuffed it in an overflowing garbage can.

"What are you doing?"

"I'm cleaning out my closet. I figured I'd better get this over with now so you don't have to deal with it after I'm gone."

He sat on the edge of the bed. "What do you mean? You're only going away for college, Maddie. This will still be your bedroom. And if you're accepted at UGA, you'll be coming home a lot."

She shrugged, still not looking up at him. "Yeah. Whatever. But just in case . . ." Her voice trailed away as she picked up a stack of old birthday cards and dumped them on top of the play program.

"Just in case what?"

Finally, she turned her eyes up to him, embarrassed that they were wet. "In case . . . well, I remember after Mama died. Aunt Cassie and Aunt Lucinda came by and cleared out Mama's closet and dresser drawers, and they cried the whole time." She sniffed and looked at the pile in front of her on the floor. "It was like she was dying all over again. I didn't want you to have to go through that with my stuff."

Her daddy slid to the floor to sit next to her, and put his arm around her shoulders. "You're not dying, Maddie. You're just going to college. And as long as I'm alive, there will be a place for you in my house. Always."

Maddie buried her face in his shoulder, wishing she was small enough to fit in his lap again. But she was too big for that now, but not too big to need a father's shoulder to cry on. He placed his hand on her head. "What's wrong, Maddie? Are you missing your mother? I miss her, too, you know."

She sniffed and nodded. "Yeah. But it's not just that."

She didn't say anything more for a long time,

trying hard to find the right words. She'd learned that from him. Her voice was small and feeble when she finally spoke. "I'm scared. Scared about college. Scared about making the wrong decision." She stilled, bracing herself for her father's reaction. "Scared about dying young. Like Mama. And Grandma."

He hugged her tightly, making her remember how he and her mama used to spray a can of Lysol under their beds to kill all the monsters she imagined lingered in all the dark spaces. She wanted so badly now to still believe that all monsters were so easily vanquished.

Lifting her head from his shoulder, he brought her face in front of his. "We don't always know what's in store for us. We do what we can to control our futures, and that's all that we can do. I know you'll do that. Heck, I know fifteen people who will remind you every year about getting a mammogram and doing self-exams just in case you forget. Beyond that, it's out of our hands."

He swallowed as if fighting back his own tears, then said, "Your mother gave you so much—your beauty, your brains, your awesome talent. But most of all, she gave you life. Her only dream for you, and for all her children, was for you to take your lives and live them to the fullest."

Maddie laid her head on his shoulder and sobbed, her tears soaking his shirt, and she felt her daddy's tears falling in her hair. "Don't be a prisoner to your fears, Maddie. Reach as far as you can. But always remember that there will always be a home for you here, wherever I am. Whenever you're give out and tired, and feeling more like the bug than the windshield, you can come home. Even if it's just for a little while to catch your breath."

He leaned back against the side of the bed and held her to his chest as they looked out of her window and watched the cold winter moon climb higher in the sky. "Your mama once told me that every life would have some rain in it, but that's the only way you'd ever get to see the rainbow."

Maddie lifted her head and looked at him, her face wet. "Suzanne told me the same thing."

"Well, then. It must be true. If two of the smartest women I've ever known are in agreement, then it's fact."

She smiled, her heart lighter until she saw the old sadness in her father's eyes. *How can I ever leave?* Swallowing back her doubts, she kissed his cheek and moved away. "Thanks, Daddy. I feel better."

"Me, too." He glanced around the mess on the floor. "It's late. Why don't you get some beauty sleep and I'll help you put this stuff away in the morning?"

Yawning loudly, she said, "All right."

He stood and pulled her up with him, and she realized for the first time that she now reached his shoulders. When had she grown so tall?

He hugged her, then kissed her on the forehead before saying good night. After he'd closed her door, she listened as he slowly walked down the hallway toward his empty bedroom, his footsteps echoing in the sleeping house.

CHAPTER 20

Joe slapped the newspaper on the laminated counter at the Dixie Diner, almost making Sam spill his coffee in surprise. "Well, good morning to you, too."

"Look at this."

Sam glanced down at the page in front of him. "Police called to residence on Maple Lane because of dog barking?"

Joe shook his head with impatience. "No. Here." He pointed to the top of the page, and Sam read aloud, "City of Mapleton Notice of Public Hearing. Consideration of annexing one hundred and thirty unincorporated acres into the city limits of Mapleton. The property is located off the I-Twenty access road east of Walton in proximity to Highway Nine."

Sam wrinkled his forehead. "What are they talking about?"

Joe sat on a stool and nodded at Brunelle, who held up a pot of coffee. "That's Stinky's property— all of it pine forest. The city administrator in

Mapleton was his college roommate at Tech, who also happens to be a major stockholder in Wright Paper Products. Are you getting the connection?"

"Yeah. But why the annexation? Isn't that just an additional unnecessary step?"

"Not at all. The zoning regulations in Mapleton are a lot less stringent than here in Walton. Which won't matter much to Walton, since we'd bear the brunt of the deforestation and pollution of a pulp mill."

Sam rubbed his forehead. "Why haven't we heard about this before? The hearing is next Wednesday."

"That's what I want to know. I'm the mayor of this town, and this is the first I'm hearing about it, too. My guess is, Stinky's been greasing some palms."

"Nothing you can prove, huh?"

Joe took a gulp of his coffee, burning his tongue. Cursing, he slammed it down on the counter, spilling some over the side. "Nope. Can't prove a damned thing. Thank God I know about it now. It's not a lot of time, but I bet I can get enough support here in Walton and in Mapleton to oppose. I'm the mayor—it's time to start throwing some weight around."

Sam's forehead creased. "There's an activist group I've heard of—something like 'Reach for the Unbleached' or something like that—who might be able to help you out. I've got their Web site bookmarked on my computer. I'll e-mail the URL to you."

"Great. Do it today. I need to get on this as soon as possible."

They both sat in silence for a moment as Brunelle brought them their breakfasts. Brunelle had long since forgone the ritual of showing them the menu since they always ordered the same thing. Sam took a bite of cheese grits, washing it down with a swallow of coffee. He turned to Joe. "I don't want to sound negative, but I think we need to consider everything. What's going to happen if Stinky wins this election? Imagine all the information he'll be privy to that he won't bother sharing with the rest of us. I think a pulp mill could be the least of our worries."

"I won't let that happen. Hal Newcomb's last survey had me with a ninety-four percent approval rating. Unless I screw up real bad between now and the election, I don't think Stinky stands a chance—no matter how much money he gives to the Daughters of the Confederacy." He took a quick gulp of coffee, burning his tongue again.

The bell over the front door rang, and Suzanne walked in. She wore one of the outfits Lucinda had helped her buy on their shopping expedition. It was a lot less revealing than the blue leather miniskirt getup, but it created the same reaction as men along the counter turned their heads.

The cropped pants revealed long, slender calves and ankles, her narrow feet in high-heeled strappy sandals, the toe ring visible on her right foot. None of the men seemed to care that it was too cold for sandals. A formfitting orange sweater outlined her slim waist and ample breasts, the gold heart necklace bouncing over them, as if a man needed a piece of jewelry to draw his attention to her chest. Joe wanted to throw his jacket over her.

Her face brightened when she spotted him, but she waited until he waved her over to walk toward him and take the adjacent seat at the counter. He forgot all about what she was wearing when he saw her eyes and lost himself in their gray depths. To her surprise and his, he leaned over and kissed her lightly on the lips, his mouth lingering over hers for a long moment. It wasn't enough that people had been gossiping over backyard fences about the night he'd left her house at four a.m. He wanted people to be able to talk about him and Suzanne in front of him.

"Coffee?" Brunelle held the pot up in front of Suzanne, and she nodded.

Sam cleared his throat. "Well, I'd better be going. Cassie asked me to tell you to stop by and see her and the baby when you got the chance."

Suzanne looked uncomfortable and concentrated on unfolding a paper napkin and placing it in her lap. "Yes, well, I've been meaning to, but I've been busy at the store with getting ready for Christmas and everything."

Sam leveled a gaze on her. "She says you two need to finish your conversation."

Joe could tell she was avoiding Sam's eyes. "Tell her I'll come when I can."

"All right." He kissed her on the cheek. "Let me know if you plan on delivering any more babies, so I can start planning my retirement."

She blushed as he squeezed her shoulders and waved to Joe before leaving. Noticing the paper spread in front of Joe, she asked, "What's this all about?"

Joe shook his head while folding up the paper. He wasn't about to let Stinky Harden ruin his time with Suzanne. "Just bad news. Stinky Harden is hell-bent on destroying this town. I just have to make sure I stay mayor long enough to ensure that doesn't happen. If I don't win this election, there will be hell to pay."

Her face looked pinched, and when he moved to take her hand on top of the counter, she moved it to her lap.

"What's wrong?"

She smiled brightly, but her eyes didn't match her smile. "Nothing. Just tired, I guess. Lucinda's really working us hard, trying to get all the new merchandise on the shelves. You'd think there was a run on red silk slips for Christmas or something. Nobody wears a slip anymore."

She took a sip of her coffee, and Joe watched her delicate profile, the pale skin on her cheeks, and the way her hand shook slightly as she lifted her mug. He wanted to pull her into his arms, to feel her against him, right there in the middle of the Dixie Diner. But she'd shut him out again, and he'd never been a glutton for punishment. All of his bruises had been accidental.

"Don't be so sure, Suzanne. There's something about a slip under a woman's dress, especially a red one. . . ." He let her imagination fill in the rest while he took a sip of coffee. He was rewarded with a slight flush on her cheeks.

The bell over the door rang again, and a gust of cold air hit the back of Joe's neck. He could feel who it was before he'd even turned around.

"Well, hey there, Mayor. And Miz Paris. Don't y'all look like a pair of roosting ducks sitting here together like that?" Stinky smirked. "Better make sure some hunter doesn't come by and pluck you two off."

He threw back his head and laughed. "Hey, y'all remember my son, Charlie, right? Miz Paris, he said he met you once at the school. You were tidying up or something in the darkroom."

Stinky tugged on the arm of the younger version of himself, pulling him in front to face Suzanne and Joe. Suzanne had gone very still, her face even paler than usual. Her voice sounded thin. "Yes, I remember. Good to see you again, Charlie."

Charlie looked up at the ceiling and mumbled something.

Stinky creased his brows in mock sincerity. "Haven't heard anything from that *Lifetime* contest yet, have you? I keep calling, but no decision's been made yet. They said by the end of the week." He elbowed his son, and Joe wondered why the boy looked so miserable and wouldn't look at Suzanne.

Suzanne cleared her throat. "Yes, well, I guess we'll find out when they're good and ready."

"Well, I'd better get back to it. Good to see y'all." He patted Joe's shoulder a little too firmly. "Happy mayoring, Joe. Enjoy it while you can."

Motioning for his son to follow, Stinky led the way around the room, pressing flesh and handing out campaign buttons. Joe squinted to read the one Stinky had just placed on Bill Crandall's suspenders: I CAN CONTROL MY CHILDREN *AND* THIS TOWN.

Joe moved to get off his stool, but Suzanne's hand held him back. "Don't. People will admire your restraint more than your ability to knock the opponent out cold at the Dixie Diner."

He sat back down, knowing she was right, and wondered again what kind of life she must have led to have been granted so much wisdom.

She laid a bill and some change on the counter and pushed back her stool. "I've got to go. Lucinda will be wondering what's keeping me."

He touched her arm, and she looked at him. "What are you doing tonight?"

He thought he saw an almost imperceptible move toward him before she caught herself. "I'll be working on Maddie's album. I'm way behind."

"Do you need company?"

She looked down at his hand on her arm. "No. Not tonight. I'll get more work done if I'm by myself."

He released her, hiding his disappointment. "Good-bye, then. Have a good day."

She nodded and left without looking behind her. As Joe stood to take his wallet out of his back pocket, he looked over to find Stinky watching him closely. His opponent had a knowing look on his face, and it gave Joe chill bumps. Without acknowledging the other man, Joe turned and left the diner, thinking it was time for Suzanne to give up a few secrets.

Suzanne sat on her front porch with a book her in hand, her feet resting on the porch railing, and sobbed. She wore Joe's old jacket, and the pockets were stuffed with Kleenex. She'd seen the movie version of *Little Women* twice, and she knew she'd need them for the last few chapters of the book. It felt good to cry. It was something she rarely allowed herself to indulge in.

She tilted her head back, letting the feeble warmth of the sun soak into her winter-weary skin, and thought fleetingly of Joe, and of how he made her warm with just a touch. She snuggled deeply into her coat, feeling like a hibernating animal—safe and warm for now, but heading toward the inevitable moment when she would have to stick her neck out and move into the world again. The thought made her ill. *How can I leave? How can I stay?*

Blowing her nose loudly, she turned the last page of the book and froze. She stared for a long moment at the name scrawled in childish handwriting on the inside back cover in fading blue ink. *Michelle Lewis.* She ran her finger lightly over the inscription, as if trying to touch a face that had long since faded from her memory. *How long has this been here?*

But Suzanne knew. She realized then that she had probably already known, ever since Miss Lena had given her the book. She sat staring at the immature lettering for almost an hour, old memories and past conversations flitting through her brain. Memories of her mother telling Suzanne about her past, about growing up in so many foster homes. And of living with the one person who had made a difference in her life. The woman who had given her mother the necklace with the charm.

Reaching under her jacket, Suzanne pulled the necklace out to look at it more closely. She read the words out loud, her voice quiet in the chill air. "A life without rain is like the sun without shade."

And under that were the words "R. Michael Jewelers. Walton."

She had known it all along, but had refused to acknowledge it. At first, she'd been afraid the knowledge would suck her in, making it harder to leave. But now she knew it was simply a matter of fitting in the last piece of the puzzle showing a journey that had come full circle, the end still nowhere in sight.

Closing the book gently, she went inside to the drawer in the hall table and pulled out the bag that contained Cassie's broken chain and loose charms. She had put it off long enough, but it was time now. Shoving the bag into a pocket, Suzanne left the house, heading to the place she'd been avoiding since she arrived in Walton in what seemed another lifetime.

The late-afternoon sun slanted its dying rays across the doorway of the brightly shingled shop, the gold lettering on the door reading R. MICHAEL JEWELERS. SINCE 1939. A bell over the door announced her arrival, and a man of around sixty appeared from the back of the small store. He had a shock of salt-and-pepper hair that fell over his forehead and framed bright blue eyes. He wore a loupe on a band over his forehead, the creases in the skin around his eyes indicating that he'd just pushed it up when he'd heard her enter.

He gave her a friendly grin, and she couldn't

help smiling back. "Is there something I can help you with today?"

She took the bag out of her pocket and laid it on the glass counter over a display of diamond engagement rings. "I need to have this fixed."

He nodded. "Ah yes. Cassie Parker was in here the other day with that sweet little baby. She said you'd be in here soon and went ahead and paid for it."

"Excuse me?"

Bright blue eyes looked innocently at her. "Pardon me?"

"She already paid for it?"

"Sure did." He slid the jeweler's loupe back over his eye and examined the break in the chain. "Just like she said. A simple repair job, and then we can put all those hearts back on track."

Suzanne shook her head, wondering why Cassie hadn't simply come and picked up the broken necklace from her first.

"If you have a few minutes, I can fix this while you wait."

"Sure. No rush."

While he disappeared into the back, Suzanne looked around the store, admiring the beautifully colored gemstones and creamy strands of pearls that lay under glass in cabinets against the walls, and in a square display in the middle of the store. She studied a picture on the wall, of a younger version of the man who had helped her. He stood with two older versions of himself. He wore a cap and gown and was holding a diploma. Hanging next to the photograph were three gemologist certificates bearing the names of Randy Michael, Randy Michael Jr., and Randy Michael III, respectively. Whatever the family lacked in originality, they made up for in perseverance. She imagined a Randy Michael opening and closing the shop each day for the past six decades, and she felt a small stab of wistfulness. How wonderful to know your place in the world before you're even born.

Mr. Michael came out from the back. "It's as good as new. I even polished it up a bit, too." Gently he lowered the necklace into a small cotton pouch. "I remember when Harriet came in to order those last six charms. Nearly broke my heart." He slid the pouch across the counter and smiled. "Seems like they're in good hands now."

Frowning, she put the pouch in her pocket. "Would you mind taking a look at something and telling me if you remember seeing it before?"

"Sure thing. Let me have a look." He peered at her through his loupe, his blue eye enlarged like a giant housefly's.

She reached around her neck and undid the clasp of her own necklace. Gently she placed it on the counter, the quiet clicking noise it made when it touched the glass sounding loud in the empty shop.

He raised the heart up close to his face, peering at it closely. "Hmm," he said as he studied one side, then flipped it over.

Handing the necklace back over to her, he pushed the loupe up again. "Yep. I've definitely seen that before. That one would be hard to forget."

"Really? Why is that?"

"Because my daddy and me got in a huge fight about it. It was right after I graduated from college and I was working here in the store. My daddy said not to engrave it because the words were too long and it would be too hard to read. But the lady insisted and I did it anyway. Glad I did, too."

Suzanne listened to the sound of her own breathing for a moment, feeling empty but somehow full, too. "What year was that?"

"It was nineteen sixty-nine. And I know that for a fact." He nodded as if to punctuate the sentence with his long chin.

She knew the answer to her next question, too, but she had to ask it anyway. "Do you remember the lady who had it made?"

"Now, that's another one that would be hard to forget. Miss Eulene Larsen. She's been a regular since my granddaddy ran the store. Sweetest thing, too. It's such a shame about her mind. She was always sharp as a raccoon's tooth. And now . . ."

His words drifted off, and Suzanne finished the sentence for him. "And now she's usually just as sharp, but people don't always want to listen to what she has to say."

He raised bushy eyebrows. "Well, you just might be right about that, honey."

"Yes, well, thanks, Mr. Michael."

"You're very welcome. Stop by anytime."

She waved good-bye and listened for the ring of the bell as she opened the door to leave. Tucking her hands deep in the pockets of the coat, she headed for Miss Lena's house.

It was almost dusk by the time Suzanne stood in front of Miss Lena's door and rang the doorbell. She was ready to ring it again when she heard the slow shuffle of steps and then the front door was pulled open.

"Well, this is such a nice surprise. Come on in, sugar. I was just getting ready to watch *Wheel of Fortune*. I think that Mr. Sajak is so good-looking, don't you?"

She stepped back and allowed Suzanne to enter. A dinner tray holding the remainders of Miss Lena's dinner sat parked next to the well-worn recliner, and the opening music for the game show was starting on the television.

Suzanne took off her backpack and jacket and hung them on the coatrack by the door. "Let me clean up your dinner for you while you watch your show. We can talk when it's over."

"Why, thank you. I do appreciate it. Dr. Parker checks every day to make sure I've watched my

Wheel of Fortune. He says it's good for my memory, even though I tell him there's nothing wrong with it at all."

Suzanne smiled, then picked up the dirty plates and took them to the kitchen. She noticed the plastic flowers in the vase of water, the coupons nailed to the pale blue wall, and the stacks of toilet paper by the back door. At first glance, she thought it strange. Then she remembered that her own mother had stockpiled Charmin by the back door, too. It was cheaper than Kleenex, and you never forgot to grab a bundle of sheets to stuff in your pockets on the way out. She smiled wanly to herself. Just one more clue she'd been oblivious of.

After cleaning up, she joined the older woman in the front room, taking a seat on the ottoman near the foot of the recliner. When the show was over and the winner had finished squealing and hugging the show's host, Miss Lena turned to Suzanne.

"Can I get you some sweet tea while we chat?"

"No, thank you." She opened the copy of *Little Women* that she had pulled from her backpack, and held up the back cover to show Miss Lena. "Do you know who this was?"

Miss Lena adjusted her bifocals to see the faded print, then smiled as she read the name. "Michelle Lewis. Of course I remember her. She was a very dear child." She looked over the book at Suzanne and frowned. "You look so much like her, too, although her hair wasn't as red as yours."

Suzanne touched her hair self-consciously. "Yeah, well, me and Miss Clairol had a hand in that. It's not supposed to be this bright."

Miss Lena leaned closer to Suzanne and spoke in a conspiratorial whisper. "So, did you come here tonight to tell me about your scandalous past?"

She shook her head. "No. I wanted to talk about my mother."

Miss Lena nodded slowly and sat back in her chair, the old springs squeaking. "I wanted to adopt her, you know. But I wasn't married, and back then they wouldn't allow that. So they took her away." Her eyes held a faraway look to them, as if focused on a lost little redheaded girl. "I wanted a daughter so badly. And Michelle and I were like two peas in a pod. We would sit out on the porch for hours, just reading. We'd talk about the books we'd read, and I think that's what helped her the most. She could talk on and on about other people's troubles, because I think it was too hard for her to talk about her own."

Suzanne tried to reconcile Miss Lena's image of a vulnerable young girl with the mother she'd known, but couldn't. "What sort of troubles did she have?"

"Did I ask you if you'd like some sweet tea? It's

no bother. Did you say that Miss Clairol would be stopping by?"

"No, and no, thank you." She waited patiently for Miss Lena to answer her question and had almost given up when the faraway look came back to Miss Lena's eyes.

"She had such a big heart, filled with so much love. But she didn't know how to give it away. Nobody had ever shown her."

Suzanne swallowed the bitter taste in her throat. "She never did learn how."

A soft smile transformed Miss Lena's face, making her look much younger. "Now, dear, that's not true. I've seen you with Joe's babies, and with Joe himself. You had to have learned that from somewhere, don't you think?"

Suzanne sat back on the ottoman, stunned. She opened her mouth to protest, but no words would come out. She remembered cradling Maddie that night on her porch, and the tight feeling in her chest she'd experienced while watching Harry sleep in his crib. And even the need to make the hurt go away when Sarah Frances had been sick with chicken pox. And somewhere, in the back of her mind, was the feel of her mother's hand on her cheek.

There was nothing she could say, because it was true.

Taking the old woman's hand again, she said, "You showed her, didn't you?"

"I tried, sugar. I tried. But that child had troubles so deep that I couldn't draw them out of her." She squeezed Suzanne's hand. "That doesn't mean she had no love for you." Miss Lena leaned forward and touched the charm around Suzanne's neck. "She'd saved this all those years and then gave it to you. It was her heart and the only thing she had to give. Do you see that now?"

Suzanne sat in silence, listening to the quiet tick of the clock, and her heart seemed to beat louder in her chest. She did see. For the first time in her life, she didn't see her mother's abandonment as something she was responsible for. She grasped the small charm in her fingers. Her mother had loved her enough to set her free, to unbind her from the demons that had chased her mother all her life. The necklace had just been part of the gift.

"Is *Wheel of Fortune* on yet? I just love that Pat Sajak."

Suzanne looked up at Miss Lena in confusion. "You already—"

A brief tapping sounded on the door. Suzanne walked to the door and opened it, surprised to see Mrs. Crandall standing on the other side.

The older woman spoke in a whisper as she addressed Suzanne. "How's she doing? I've come to chat and see her safely to bed. I didn't know she was expecting company."

"I just stopped by for a little while. She seems to

be fine, but I think she's getting tired. I'll go say good-bye and let you take over."

She kissed Miss Lena on the cheek and the old woman called her Michelle. Then Suzanne let herself out the door, feeling suddenly exhausted. She sat down on the porch steps, amid the ceramic planters filled with plastic flowers, and clutched the gold heart charm tightly. *A life without rain is like the sun without shade.* She finally knew what her mother had been trying to tell her all these years. *Oh, Mom. I wish I'd known sooner.*

She stared up at the cold, white stars in the blackness of the winter sky, her breath rising like an offering to the heavens. She thought of the earth spinning on its axis and the moon revolving around it, twenty-four hours and three hundred and sixty-five days of light and shadow, bringing you back to the starting point.

Smiling to herself, she rested her forehead on her drawn-up knees. Things never really changed, and journeys never took you someplace new. The road had a way of circling back behind you, leaving you not changed but certainly wiser.

She wondered if her mother had ever sat on this very porch and wished on faraway stars in this section of sky above Walton, Georgia, and the thought brought her comfort, like seeing an old friend after a long separation.

"Thanks, Mom," she whispered, and the words carried up to the stars that never changed but watched as the world spun beneath them, turning night into day, summer into fall, and a woman's wary heart to one filled with hope.

CHAPTER 21

The door to Lucinda's Lingerie swung open, bringing with it cold air, the scent of burning leaves, and Cassie Parker wearing an infant carrier strapped across her chest. Small pink-booted feet stuck out of the leg holes of the carrier, and their kicking was accompanied by a loud mewling sound.

Suzanne, in the midst of folding yet another stack of red silk slips, looked up in surprise. "Hi, Cassie. I've been meaning—"

"I know. I figured I'd beat you to it. I wanted you to see the baby before she graduated from high school."

"I'm sorry. Really. It's just . . ."

"Don't worry about it. I'm here now." She dropped her purse to the floor and began to fumble with unhooking the carrier. "Could you give me a hand here? You need to be an octopus to manage this thing."

Suzanne came around the counter and stood in front of Cassie, not knowing exactly what she could do.

"Take the baby under the arms and lift her out."

Feeling nervous, Suzanne did as she was told and gently lifted the baby into her arms. "Oh," she said, not really knowing why but completely surprised by the warmth of the small bundle in her arms. "She's so tiny."

Cassie raised her eyebrows. "She's a whole two pounds heavier than when you last saw her."

"Wow. What a porker. She looks different in her street clothes."

Cassie reached over and took off the pink knit cap the baby wore, then looked at Suzanne as if she'd just unveiled a masterpiece. "What do you think?"

Suzanne fumbled with the baby in her arms until she held her in a cradling position and could look at the tiny face. Bright blue eyes were framed with dark lashes against pink-and-white skin, a peach fuzz of white-blond hair covering the round head. The baby cooed and stuck a tiny fist into her rosebud mouth and began to suck loudly.

"She's perfection." Suzanne smiled down at the baby, inhaling deeply of that unique baby scent that made seemingly normal people go weak at the knees and suddenly speak gibberish.

Cassie smiled, looking pleased. "I think so, but I'm her mother. It's nice of you to say."

Suzanne pulled the baby up to her shoulder to snuggle her better. "I'm not just saying that. She really is."

"We're calling her Susie. Harriet seemed like a big name for such a little girl. I hope you don't object."

"No. Of course not. I . . . I think it's pretty neat."

"Good." Cassie frowned. "We need to talk."

"I don't think . . ."

"I remember what you said in the car, before my water broke. You said you loved Joe."

Suzanne felt her face heat and looked down at the fuzz-topped head of the baby. "I do. But I don't think that has anything to do with us needing to talk."

"Yeah, it does. Because Joe's like a brother to me. And I have a strong suspicion that he feels the same way about you."

Suzanne tried to keep her voice calm. "Then can't we just let it be? This is between me and Joe."

Cassie slid off her jacket and sat down on the plush couch situated outside the dressing room and indicated for Suzanne to join her. "Actually, it's not. Sorry." She forced a smile. "You know, before Susie was born, I was prepared to just let you run your course with Joe, then leave. But things are different now."

A gnaw of worry settled at the back of Suzanne's neck. "What do you mean?"

"It's not that I like you any better—I've never had a problem with that. And it's not even that you helped deliver my baby, although I'll always be grateful." She looked down at the baby as if trying to compose herself. "It's more because you love Joe—and how hard it was for you to take that risk. And to be willing to walk away from it for his sake. You've given me a well-deserved lesson in unselfishness."

"You don't really know me. . . ."

"Yeah, I do. I'm a quick study." Cassie took a deep breath. "So, what are you going to do now? It's only a matter of time before Anthony finds you, you know."

The baby began to fret, and Suzanne patted her gently on the back as Cassie dug in the diaper bag for a bottle. She took off the lid and handed the bottle to Suzanne, along with a burp cloth. "It's breast milk. I'm trying to get her used to the bottle, though, so Sam can feed her, too."

Suzanne looked at the bottle for a moment, then moved the fretting baby into position. She gave the baby the bottle and settled back against the couch, amazed at how easy it seemed. Her eyes met Cassie's. "I'm not . . . I haven't decided to do anything yet. But I can't tell Joe. I don't want him to know—ever."

"Know what? That you were engaged to the wrong guy?" She grimaced. "It's happened before, you know. Joe and I could tell you that."

Suzanne shook her head. "No. Not that."

Cassie put her hand on her arm. "Then what?

Look, you've got to tell somebody sometime. It's not going to go away just because you keep it to yourself."

Suzanne focused on the baby in her arms, listening to the quiet slurpings she made as she drank the formula. "You don't understand. You, and Joe, and everybody else here—you're all good and decent people. I'm not. I did things that I'm ashamed of. Things that if you knew, you . . . you wouldn't want to know me. And so would Joe. I'd rather leave than have you all find out what kind of person I really am."

Cassie's voice was soft. "But I do know. So does Joe. That's what kind of person you are. That's all that matters."

Suzanne shook her head. "You wouldn't say that if you knew the truth."

The baby began to whimper, and Cassie reached for her, then put Susie on her shoulder and began to pat her back. "What truth, Suzanne? What are you afraid to let us know?"

Suzanne stood, not able to face this woman whose opinion of her suddenly seemed to matter so much. She faced the window, staring out at the square with the soldier atop his horse. "That I had the morals of a prostitute? I pretty much sold myself to the highest bidder. I saw a man with money who offered to take care of me, and I hopped into his bed so fast it would have made your head spin. And even after, when he started to hurt me, I'd threaten to leave and he'd give me an expensive gift. What did I do? I accepted them all—all of them. And then I'd sleep with him again. Until the next time he'd hit me, and it would start all over again." She turned around to face Cassie. "There. Now you know what kind of person I really am."

She expected to find revulsion in the other woman's eyes, but all she saw was sympathy. Cassie's eyes met hers. "My opinion hasn't changed. I see a woman who was lonely and desperate and needed somebody to love her. You did the best you could with what you were given. Nobody could fault you for that."

"I do. And that's not all. I . . . I've made mistakes since I've come here." She stopped herself before she mentioned Maddie's name, remembering the photograph negative she'd thrown away. No one could ever know the truth.

A soft burp escaped from the baby, and Cassie cradled her again to feed her the rest of the bottle. "There's something here that you're not getting, Suzanne. You're not alone anymore. If Anthony showed up in Walton tomorrow, do you think we'd all desert you? First, the Ladies' Bridge Club would stuff him with lemon meringue pie and buttermilk biscuits until he couldn't run, and then we'd have Bitsy give him a big hairdo before sending him off for a weekend of fishing with Stinky Harden. He wouldn't know what hit him.

He'd want out of here so fast that he'd forget all about bothering you again."

Suzanne couldn't help smiling at the mental picture conjured by Cassie's words. "There's still the matter of me facing jail time. And Joe running for reelection. In one fell swoop I could turn everybody against me and stick them with a mayor who'd like to turn the town into an industrial wasteland. Even I'd have a hard time sticking with me."

Cassie took the empty bottle out of the baby's mouth. "It wouldn't matter if you grew horns. Joe would stand behind you. We all would. But it would go a lot easier for you if you'd come clean first." She stood. "Come help me put the baby back in her carrier. Sam's waiting for us at the clinic."

Suzanne came and held the baby up while Cassie positioned the little feet in the leg holes at the bottom and placed the pink cap on Susie's head. Then she turned to Suzanne.

"Look, I'm not going to tell you what to do. But you can't hide from your past forever. One day it will come sneaking up behind you and hit you upside the head. Believe me—I speak from experience." She zipped up the carrier and Suzanne helped her with her coat. "But we're a lot more forgiving than you give us credit for. And I doubt that leaving is really what you want to do."

Suzanne turned away, not sure what to say.

There were no easy answers to anything anymore. Then she remembered Cassie's gold charms. "Wait. Before you go—I have your necklace."

Cassie waited while Suzanne went to her backpack behind the counter and pulled out the cotton pouch with Cassie's necklace. "It's all put together again."

Cassie took the bag and held it. "If it were only that easy." She turned to go, her hand on the doorknob. "You should tell Joe. He would help you."

Suzanne shook her head. "I can't. Helping me would really screw up his life. And he'd do it anyway."

"Yeah, but not as screwed up as he'd be if you left town. You know, you must not think a lot of him if you believe he'd love you any less once he knows the truth."

"He's never said he loved me."

"You're taking the easy way out. He doesn't have to." Cassie opened the door.

"Are you going to tell him?"

"No. That's your job."

"And if I don't?"

"He'll find out eventually. But not from me."

The cold air from the open door filled Suzanne with desperation. "Maybe Anthony will never find me here. Maybe I could stay indefinitely, and nobody would ever have to know."

"Never say never."

The baby began to cry, and Suzanne reached

over to stroke her cheek, smiling into the little face. Susie quieted, finding her fist and sucking loudly.

Cassie smiled down at her daughter. "I don't care what people say about you and kids. I think you're a natural."

Suzanne was about to respond when Sugar Newcomb, all six feet of her, approached the shop. Suzanne retreated as Sugar gushed over the baby before following Suzanne into the shop.

"I've come to get a Christmas gift for my husband."

"We don't sell men's underclothes, Mrs. Newcomb. Have you tried Harold's Men's Shoppe?"

Sugar winked. "Trust me. This is for Hal. I've come to see if you have a red silk slip in a size eighteen." She walked past Suzanne toward the new arrival of red silk lingerie.

Suzanne kept the mental images at bay as she turned to the red stack she'd just finished folding. She felt as if she were in a holding pattern, unsure of where she would land, but hoping for a soft place to fall. It was the most she'd allowed herself to hope for a long time. She didn't have to do anything right now. She wasn't so naive as to believe that staying in Walton could be anything permanent. As long as Anthony deSalvo was part of her past, the past would always be lurking, right behind her shoulder.

● ● ●

Maddie sat in her fifth-period American history class, her foot wobbling anxiously as Mr. Dorgan drummed on endlessly about manifest destiny and the acquisition of Texas. She kept glancing at the huge metal clock that hung over his head, the minute hand dragging slowly over the small black marks.

The mail would have been delivered by now, and it would be sitting in the mailbox, undisturbed, the most important letter of her lifetime stuck inside. She glanced back at the clock. Only one minute had passed since she'd last looked at it.

Something hit her in the side of the head and fell onto the top of her desk. It was a rolled-up ball of paper, and she knew it had come from her best friend, Clarissa White. Clarissa had been ordered to sit on the exact opposite end of the class from Maddie in every class they shared together. It seemed the teachers didn't appreciate their need to communicate in loud whispers through the boring lectures.

She glanced up to make sure Mr. Dorgan hadn't noticed before unfolding the note. *What's up with you? Your wiggling like you need to go pee.* Maddie noticed that the *you're* was missing a contraction, but spelling and grammar had never been Clarissa's strongest subjects. Boys and gossip were.

402

Maddie looked at her friend and widened her eyes, hoping Clarissa would know that she was being completely oblivious of the important things in Maddie's life. Like that letter from *Lifetime* magazine that was now sitting in her mailbox at home, unopened.

Finally, she raised her hand and tried to make her voice sound as pathetic as possible. "I don't feel very good. May I be excused to go to the nurse's office?"

Mr. Dorgan narrowed his eyes behind thick glasses and stroked his beard, which Maddie suspected he grew only to make him look older than his twenty-four years. "What's wrong?"

She looked down in her lap, trying to look embarrassed. "It's female problems."

"We'll see you Monday."

Without looking up again, Maddie grabbed her books and headed out the door. She waited for Mr. Dorgan to peek his head out of the classroom to make sure she was headed in the direction of the nurse's office. Then she took a turn down a hallway and sprinted toward the exit, ducking under the window of the door of her dad's science classroom.

She ran all the way home, ignoring the waves of passersby and the stitch in her side. She dumped her books on the sidewalk in front of her house and stared at the closed mailbox while she caught her breath.

Slowly she reached up and opened the small door. Peering inside, she saw a small stack of several magazines, two letter-sized envelopes, and one large manila clasp envelope. Her heart seemed to throb so loudly that she thought if she looked at her chest she could see it move.

With a shaking hand, she reached in and grabbed the mail, leaving her books on the ground as she walked to the front steps of her house and sat down. She tossed the envelopes aside with the issues of *Field and Stream* and *Time*. Only the larger envelope was left in her lap. Printed in the top left corner was the name and logo for *Lifetime* magazine.

She held it for a long moment before ripping it open, feeling stupid for thinking she held her future in her hands, but feeling it anyway. Then she tore at the envelope, and a letter fell out and she quickly opened it to read. And then she felt as if somebody had punched her in the stomach, taking all the air from her lungs. She stared at the words on the page, the black letters floating like dead fish in a polluted creek.

Second place. Okay. She'd won second place. She could almost hear her dad saying that second place was still an accomplishment considering it was a national contest. Then her gaze moved to the picture below the text. It was the picture of the winning entry and the winner's name, and they kept swimming in and out of focus. She found that she couldn't breathe, that she was gasping for breath, and she was okay with that. Because she wanted to die.

Feeling almost numb, she pulled out the preview copy of the magazine with the winning entry plastered on the front. She tried to cry but couldn't. There was a ball of anger, hurt, and disappointment wound so tightly and stuffed into her chest that nothing would come out.

She looked back down at the cover of the magazine. Plastered across the front was the picture of Suzanne with Maddie's father's profile on the edge of the picture. Maddie remembered taking the photograph at Sarah Frances's birthday party, but this was the first time she'd seen it. With a sick feeling in the pit of her stomach, she remembered the cut edge of her film, and Suzanne saying it had been a picture of a camera strap and she'd thrown it away.

Then why was Charlie Harden's name printed below the picture, and beside his name the words "Grand Prize Winner"? It was *her* picture. How had Charlie won with *her* picture?

And then she remembered showing Suzanne the picture of Cassie and Sarah Frances, and Suzanne saying that it was perfect, that it was a winner. *A second-place winner,* Maddie reminded herself.

She shoved the magazine and letter back into the envelope, unwilling to let anybody see her hurt and humiliation. She let herself into the empty house and ran up to her room before tossing the envelope under her bed and burying her face in the flowered pillow.

It was a long time before the tears came, and when they did, they shook her entire body, leaving her drained and empty when she was finished.

And then the rage came. Hot, angry waves of it, renewing her energy and giving her purpose to get out of the bed. She sat on the edge of her ruffled bedspread for a long time, long enough to think and plan. And when the anger had completely obliterated all traces of hurt, she was ready. She rose, wrote a note to her dad saying that she was spending the night with Clarissa, then left the house.

First, she'd deal with Charlie, since that would be the easy part. She'd leave Suzanne for last. Mostly because she wasn't sure what she would do. And second, because she knew that whatever she would do or say to Suzanne could never hurt Suzanne as much as Maddie's own hurt was eating her alive.

Taping her note to the foyer mirror, she left the house, letting the door slam behind her.

In the dim overhead light in the kitchen, Suzanne stared down at Maddie's album, at the soft blue linen and gold-embossed name, and smoothed her hand over it. She was done. The story of Maddie's life, from before her birth to the present, was done. There was still her high school graduation, and all the wonderful things in her future to be placed in the empty pages in the back, but Suzanne's job was done.

It thrilled her and saddened her at the same time. Harriet would have been proud of the work Suzanne had done, of the story she'd continued, of the woman Maddie was becoming. She hoped that Maddie would treasure the album, adding pictures to the pages like days in the year, each one contributing to the story.

But now that the album was finished, she knew she had to make a decision. The minutes of her borrowed time were flitting away, irretrievable movements on the clock. Cassie was right—sooner or later Anthony would find her. It would be better that, when he caught up to her, she was no longer in Walton. She could not bear to see the look of disappointment on the faces of the people she'd grown to know and love. She could give it all up if she knew they would never know the truth.

But the squeeze on her heart that she felt when she thought of Joe was nearly more than she could bear. He had shown her that she could feel, that her heart was big enough to allow another person in. And she loved him for that, and for the way he touched her, and the way he had let her into his life.

Whatever happened between them, she wanted

him to know this. In the days, weeks, and months to come, it would be important for him to know this.

She stood abruptly, and without stopping to brush her hair or pull on a jacket, she bolted down the stairs two at a time and ran out of the house. She almost didn't see him standing on the other side of the gate and would have run into him if he hadn't reached out for her and called her name.

"Joe," she said, breathless.

"I couldn't sleep," he said, his voice thick as if holding back more words he was afraid to let go.

"Me, neither."

His hands slid down to her waist as he moved her closer, and the stars seemed to burn more brightly in the sky.

"I was thinking how I didn't want another night to go by without you. And then I realized that I didn't have to."

She pressed herself against him, laying her head on his chest, and felt his heartbeat beneath her jaw. "Funny. I was just thinking the same thing."

He kissed her then, his lips soft on hers. "I can't pretend anymore. I know you think this is completely out of your ballpark, but I want to be with you."

She held her breath, not wanting him to go on, not wanting him to say the words she knew he would.

"I was lying in bed tonight, thinking about how

much I had changed since you came to town. Remember when we talked out by the creek, when we told each other the things we wanted the most in life? And tonight, just lying there in bed, I realized that there were a few more things I needed to add." He touched her cheek. "That I want you next to me at the dinner table, at church—at the Piggly Wiggly, strolling down the frozen-food aisle. I know you can't see it, but I wanted to know if you could at least try it on for size."

She put his head in her hands and saw it all, saw it all with such clarity that it sucked the air from her lungs. She stared into his eyes in the bright moonlight, and all the hope and longing that she felt in her heart were mirrored there. Then the angry tears came, hot and blurry, and she knew without a doubt that a lifetime of not having could never equal the pain in this single moment of impotent wanting.

She kissed him to hide her tears as she blinked them away, then pulled back. "I love you, Joe Warner."

He kissed her eyes, taking away the tears, and when his mouth touched hers again, she could taste the salt. It tasted bitter and left her wanting.

She held him tightly. "Come upstairs with me."

He pulled back and stared in her eyes for a long moment, and she knew he was thinking of the words she had omitted, of the answer she had not given. She remembered Cassie telling her that she wouldn't make it easy for Suzanne by telling Joe. Nor would Joe make it easy for her by asking her to stay. Something moved in his eyes, and she knew he was making his own compromises, envisioning a night spent in her arms but a lifetime of not having her.

As he had done on the day she'd come down with chicken pox, Joe lifted her in his arms and carried her upstairs to the bedroom, leaving all promises and untold secrets outside in the cold night air.

CHAPTER 22

Joe kicked the door shut behind them, then set her down on the bedroom floor.

Suzanne spoke against his mouth. "Why'd you do that? There's nobody else here."

"Habit," he said, then moved his hands up under her sweater and paused. "What's that?"

"A slip."

He breathed heavily into her ear. "What color is it?"

"Red."

"Wow." His hands removed her sweater and skirt and she stood there in only the red silk slip. "Don't turn on the light. I don't think I could last long."

She held her arms out to him and he came into

them, pushing them both backward onto the bed. Their lips touched and held, and their hands worked the buttons on his shirt and the zipper on his pants until Joe's clothes joined Suzanne's in a heap on the floor.

He pushed his weight off her, leaning on his elbows and staring down at her in the pale moonlight from the window. His face was all dark planes and shadows, but his touch was real and sure, a part of her and of this new life she didn't want to part with. He touched her cheek and breathed deeply. "You're beautiful in your skin."

She sighed in the darkness, not wanting to break the spell spun by his words, and she pressed up against him, feeling the red silk move against her skin. She reached for his hands, letting his weight fall on her, and pressed their arms over her head. She needed to feel him, to feel his weight, knowing that his inevitable absence later would crush her even more. He lifted the gold heart from her chest in an unspoken question.

"My mother gave it to me."

Their eyes met in the dim glow of the moon. "Why?"

"Because she loved me. I just never realized how much. It took my coming here and finding Miss Lena to figure that out."

He raised an eyebrow. "Nothing happens by chance, you know. There's always a reason."

"I know," she whispered. She thought of the

411

beautiful moonflowers and of the moths that pollinated them in the anonymity of the night. She stared up into Joe's face, wanting no more secrets between them.

"My real name is Suzanne Lewis."

He kissed her neck, his breath soft and warm on her skin. "Why 'Paris'?"

"Because I always wanted to go there."

He lifted himself up on his elbows so he could look in her eyes. "What else do you want that you haven't told me?"

I want you forever. "I want you. For as long as we have."

He kissed her then and all she could think of was how much she wanted him, and how much they needed each other, and how it could never be enough for either of them.

The phone rang, shrill and loud in the darkened room, and Suzanne picked it up before the third ring. She felt Joe's chest behind her as she moved the phone to her ear.

It was Lucinda. "Suzanne? I need to speak to Joe. Right away."

Suzanne didn't stop to think how Lucinda would know Joe was with her, and handed over the phone. "It's Aunt Lucinda."

Joe nodded and took the phone. "It's Joe."

Suzanne heard Lucinda's voice but not what she was saying, but she could see Joe's knuckles grasping the phone tighter and tighter as he listened.

Finally, Joe spoke. "Do you know where she is? Okay. I'll be there in fifteen minutes."

Suzanne took the phone as Joe leaped out of the bed. "What's wrong?"

He hopped on one foot as he put his underwear on while reaching for his jeans. "Somebody stole Charlie Harden's PT Cruiser. The good news is that they found it. The bad news is that they found it in the middle of the Walton High Cafeteria. On its back."

"Why are they calling you? Isn't that more the sheriff's job than the mayor's?"

He stared at her for a moment without speaking.

Her eyes opened in realization. "Oh my gosh. Maddie." Suzanne jumped out of bed and flipped on the light, doing her best to find the discarded clothing and put it on. "I'm coming with you."

As she was putting her arms into the sweater, Joe grabbed her and led her out of the house. When they reached the sidewalk, Suzanne had a hard time keeping up with Joe's long stride. She ran to catch up to him. "She couldn't have done this, Joe. I can't imagine that she'd know how to hot-wire a car, break into a school without setting off the alarm, and then flip a small car on its back. There's no way."

He didn't stop to answer. "She had help. And I have a pretty good idea who."

"Rob? Oh no. He wouldn't do anything like that."

Joe looked grim as he kept up his grueling pace. "Not unless he had good reason. Something must have set her off."

"But what? I saw her yesterday and she was fine." She jogged a bit to catch up, her thoughts clearing in the cold air. She stopped, and Joe did, too.

"Oh no. Did she get the photography contest results today in the mail?"

"I don't think so. It wasn't with the rest of the mail."

"How was she acting when you got home from school?"

"I didn't see her. She beat me home and left a note that she was at Clarissa's, which is why Lucinda was watching the kids." He paused for a moment, thinking. "Oh no," he echoed.

He grabbed Suzanne's hand and began to walk faster.

A feeling, dark and sinister, crept around the base of Suzanne's neck. Maddie had been prepared to lose. She'd wanted to win, but she had spoken openly about her plans if she didn't. Something was really wrong. Another thought struck her. "But how would either one of them have gotten past the alarm at the school? And how on earth did they get it through the doors?"

He shook his head, his breath coming out in fat white puffs. "She's always asking to play Angry

Birds on my phone. All my codes and passwords are on it. She's the kind of person who would store information like that for future use." He clenched his teeth, and she could see his jaw working furiously. "And I'm assuming she used the loading doors in the back. They're wide enough that a small car could fit through them."

As they approached his block, she tugged on his arm, making him stop again. "Joe, take a deep breath and calm down. Whatever this is about, Maddie feels deeply about it. Find out why first. It might help you control your anger. She's not the kind of person to do something like this without good reason."

Joe took his hand back and raked both hands through his hair. "She could have just cost me the election. This is really, really bad."

He turned toward the house, and she called him back. "She's your daughter, Joe. Don't forget that. She's young and vulnerable and prone to rash behavior. Be gentle with her. Her disappointment in you could never be worth winning an election." She kissed him gently on the lips. "Things have a way of working themselves out."

"Thanks. I'll try to remember that." He held out his hand. "Come on. I need you with me."

The feeling of dread continued to press on her as she took his hand and followed him past the parked sheriff's car, Joe's SUV, Sam's pickup truck, and Lucinda's pink convertible.

The porch lights were on, as was every light in the downstairs. For a fleeting moment, she wondered why she didn't feel the need to pull away and run back to the quiet aloneness of her house.

Joe opened the front door and held it for her, then led the way to the kitchen, in the back of the house.

The small room was crowded to overflowing, with the large bulk of Sheriff Adams taking up one corner of the room, while Sam, Lucinda—wearing bright pink curlers in her hair—and Maddie sat at the table with dripping iced-tea glasses weeping onto the table in front of them. Robbie and Clarissa stood behind Maddie's chair, and Suzanne could tell the two girls had been crying, and Robbie looked as if he wanted to.

All eyes turned to them as they approached the table and Maddie stood.

"So, Daddy. Looks like we've both screwed up again."

He dropped Suzanne's hand and moved closer to the table. Suzanne could see him working to control his temper. "What do you mean? I'm not the one who's been picked up by the sheriff. You've got a lot of answering to do."

Maddie reached across the table for a large manila envelope. "You're sleeping with her, right? Take a look at this and tell me which one of us has done the worse thing."

She pulled out a magazine and slapped it on the table in front of her father. There was a stunned silence in the room as everyone caught sight of the front-cover picture of Suzanne and Joe. It looked like a picture taken in the afterglow of sex, and the ethereal light from behind their faces made it even more obvious.

Suzanne started to shake, her world slowly spinning off its axis.

Joe picked up the magazine. "So you didn't win. But that's no reason to vandalize somebody's car."

Maddie stood, her chair almost tipping over. Her voice rose a degree. "Look who won first place." She stabbed a finger at Charlie's name on the cover.

He looked, his forehead furrowed in confusion, then turned back to Maddie. "Charlie took this picture?"

"No!" Maddie nearly screamed, and Suzanne wanted to melt away, to die, to do anything to keep Maddie from continuing. But she stood where she was, waiting. It was what she deserved. She could almost hear Anthony's voice shouting at her. *"You always get what you deserve, Suzanne. Nothing ever happened to you that you didn't already have coming to you."*

She touched the necklace around her neck, hoping to find strength in it. All it did was give her the courage to stay where she was. *A life without rain is like the sun without shade.* She closed her eyes. Would it ever stop raining?

She opened her eyes and met Maddie's, and waited for the sharp blow of the ax to fall.

Maddie was nearly screaming now. "This was *my* picture. I took it and it was on a roll of film I gave to Suzanne to develop. So tell me, now, how did Charlie get it? How? And why would you do this to me?"

She started to cry, great, racking sobs, and Cassie stood and cradled Maddie's head on her shoulder. Cassie's eyes met Suzanne's over Maddie's head. But they weren't accusing. Instead, they were opened wide, as if waiting for Suzanne to explain herself, to make it all go away.

Suzanne couldn't look at Joe but felt him stiffen beside her. She faced Maddie, her voice amazingly calm. "I . . . I didn't give it to him. I threw it away, and he must have found it in the garbage after I left."

Maddie cried harder and kept her face buried in Cassie's chest. It was Cassie who asked, "Why would you throw it away? Surely you could see that it could win. It's an amazing photograph."

Suzanne resisted the urge to look away, to run. *This is what happens when you don't change lanes fast enough.* She could barely force the words out. "Because I couldn't risk having my picture plastered across the cover of a national magazine."

Maddie tore away from Cassie. "But why? Could whatever you're hiding be worse than what's happened? I thought you liked me. I could even see you as my stepmother—you were that convincing. But not now. Not ever. I'd rather die than ever see your face again."

She ran from the room, her feet hard on the stairs and the hallway above them. A bedroom door slammed, and all was silent for a moment.

Suzanne swallowed hard, still avoiding looking at Joe, and feeling all eyes on her. She couldn't face seeing their accusing glares. She already felt as if she were at the gates of hell. The looks on their faces could only push her over the brink.

She turned to leave, then stopped. She couldn't leave. Not yet. Not that she could make them forgive her, but she could at least make them understand. "I did it because I loved her. And Joe. And the rest of you. That wasn't supposed to happen, but it did. All I wanted to do was to buy some time because I didn't want to leave." She swallowed thickly, not wanting to cry. Not yet. "Looks like my time's up."

She turned and ran from the room and out of the house, not stopping until she'd reached the Ladue house. She closed the door and leaned against it for a long time, breathing heavily and forcing herself not to cry. Her fingers found the heart around her neck and she touched it, needing comfort but finding only cold metal. She tried to remember what Miss Lena had told her about being worthy of her mother's love. She looked up at the ceiling as if she might find her mother there to argue with. *I'm glad you're not here to see this, Mom. I've done everything wrong. Maybe Anthony was right. Maybe I did have it coming to me.*

She started to cry then, her knees buckling as she slid down the door to the floor. She couldn't wipe the picture of Maddie's face out of her mind. It would haunt her for the rest of her life. How could she let Maddie know that the person who had thrown away the negative was not the person she was now? She was stronger. Miss Lena had helped her see that. She could almost believe that Cassie and Joe and the rest would stand behind her and help her fight this. But the look on Maddie's face told her differently. She could never go back.

Slowly she went upstairs and opened the drawers of the dresser and began pulling out everything that belonged to her. The wind picked up outside, tossing the wind chimes and their music out into the winter night, and it made her cry again as she thought of Joe and all the hopes they had had. After shoving in everything that would fit into her backpack and canvas tote, she went to the spare bedroom and took Maddie's album. Then she went down to the kitchen and took off the picture of the Eiffel Tower and

Amanda's picture from the refrigerator before leaving the house for the last time.

After locking the front door, she shoved the key under the doormat and walked out the front gate to the sidewalk. She didn't dare look back at the beautiful white house with the wind chime hanging from the front porch, and the picket fence wrapping around the yard like arms in an embrace. She itched to take a picture of it, to store it away for later, when the horror of this night had faded. But she couldn't. It had been the only place she'd ever called home, and having a one-dimensional record of it would only make it less real.

She headed toward Cassie's house, the album tucked under her arm, listening as her feet beat a lonely echo on the deserted streets.

Suzanne was surprised when she reached the house and Cassie was sitting in the porch swing, bundled inside a thick afghan.

Suzanne paused on the bottom step. "What are you doing?"

"I was about to ask you the same thing. It's four o'clock in the morning. Only nursing mothers are supposed to be up at this hour."

"I was going to leave this on the porch, but since you're here . . ." She walked up the steps and handed Cassie the album. "It's done. You can give it to Maddie. Now or on her graduation day—I don't suppose it matters."

Cassie stopped the swing and took the album. "Why don't you stick around and give it to her yourself?"

Suzanne snorted, not completely hiding the sob in the back of her throat. "She doesn't want to see me. Not that I can't blame her. What I did was unforgivable."

Cassie was quiet for a moment, looking up at Suzanne. "No. Maybe what *we* did was unforgivable. We accepted you too easily. We didn't give any consideration as to who you were or where you were from."

"What—so you would have stayed away from me?"

Cassie shook her head. "No. So we would have realized how fragile you really are. We would have taken better care of you."

Tears ran down Suzanne's cheeks, and she gave them an angry wipe. "Don't try to be nice to me now, Cassie Parker. I don't deserve it. I've really messed things up, and there's no going back."

Cassie surprised Suzanne by throwing her head back and laughing. "You remind me of me three years ago. Next you're going to tell me that you're leaving for good."

Hurt, Suzanne stared back at Cassie, feeling the freezing air numb her nose as she breathed in heavily. "I am. There's no way I can stay now—not after what I did to Maddie. And there's the matter of my picture on the cover of *Lifetime*.

Anthony will take the first flight down, and I'll be facing a jail sentence. I'm leaving tonight."

Sobering, Cassie stood. "Don't make another mistake to try and fix the first one. You'll regret it the rest of your life. I know I do. I got hurt really bad once. Instead of staying to face it, I ran away and didn't come back for fifteen years. And when I came back, my sister was dying. I had lost all that time with her, and I could never get it back. Don't make the same mistake I did, Suzanne."

Suzanne turned away. "It's not the same. This is where you belonged. I don't. I've never belonged anywhere, and it's too late to start now." She began to walk down the steps. "You don't have to tell Maddie who did the album if you don't want to."

Cassie moved toward her. "Don't go, Suzanne. What about Joe?"

Suzanne stared out into the interminable night, the darkness swallowing everything. "He'll win the election and get on with his life. He'll find somebody else."

"No, he won't. He loves you."

Suzanne paused. When she spoke, she had a catch in her voice. "Not after tonight. Not after seeing Maddie . . ."

"Then you don't know him. You might love him, but you certainly don't know him."

"I know him enough to know that it would kill him to lose the election to Stinky and let Walton down. Having a girlfriend who betrayed his daughter and faces time in a jail cell will not induce people to vote for him. He'll probably be relieved to see me leave." She tried not to think of the warmth of his arms, the fullness of his heart, and the way he loved the people in his life without holding back.

"But where will you go?"

Suzanne shrugged without turning around. "I'll catch the bus I came in on and just stay on it as long as I can. I've done it before."

"Will you at least call me if you need anything?"

"Probably not." She began walking down the front path toward the avenue of oaks.

Cassie called out to her, "This isn't good-bye, so I'm not going to say it."

Suzanne kept walking. "Good-bye, Cassie." And she continued walking, staring at the stars that were forever beyond her reach, until the thick darkness blocked Cassie and the big white house from her sight.

CHAPTER 23

Maddie splashed cold water over her face again, then stared at her reflection in the bathroom mirror. It didn't help. Her eyes were still puffy and red from crying. Not that it mattered. Nothing mattered anymore. She remembered how hopeless she had felt after her mother died, and how she thought nothing could ever hurt that much again. She'd been wrong. At least her mother's dying hadn't been intentional.

She heard the front door shut downstairs in the empty house, and her aunt Cassie calling up to her, "Maddie? Are you here?"

Slowly Maddie pulled open the bathroom door and peered over the banister at her aunt in the foyer below. "I'm here. I'm skipping school, but my dad knows about it."

Aunt Cassie wore a sympathetic look on her face, and Maddie relaxed a bit with relief. After last night, she could have sworn that her aunt was siding with Suzanne. She loved her aunt Cassie and would have hated not speaking to her for the rest of her life.

Maddie came down the stairs one at a time, and when she reached the bottom, her aunt gave her a warm, one-armed hug. It was then that she realized that Cassie was carrying something under her other arm.

"What's that?"

"Come on into the living room and I'll show you."

She followed her aunt into the pale yellow room that was only used for company and special occasions—and Aunt Cassie knew that. A tickle of uneasiness brushed the back of Maddie's neck as she walked into the living room.

They sat down on a cream love seat, and her

aunt placed a large scrapbook album on Maddie's lap. Maddie noticed with a start that her own name was embossed across the front.

"I know this is a little early to be giving it to you, but I figured you needed to see it now. It's supposed to be a graduation present."

Maddie stared uneasily at the pale blue linen cover, remembering the conversation she'd overheard at Bitsy's salon between Darlene Narpone and Suzanne about a surprise for her. Maddie's preoccupation with the photography contest had made her forget all about it until now. Something thick and heavy settled into the bottom of her stomach. "Who's it from?"

"Your mother. And Suzanne. It was a labor of love. From both of them."

Maddie tried to shove the album off her lap, but Aunt Cassie grabbed it and pushed it back. "We're going to look at it now together. You need to see it."

"I don't want to. I don't want to have anything to do with that woman. I'll look at the parts my mom did, but not anything else."

"But all the pages are intertwined; there's really no place to distinguish where your mother's work stopped and Suzanne's started. You'll just have to look at it and see the whole picture."

"I'm not going to do it."

Cassie put her hand on Maddie's arm. "Yes, you are. I know you're angry at Suzanne. She made a terrible mistake—she knows that. But she did it out of love. If her ex-fiancé saw her picture on that magazine, he'd come after her. His name is Anthony deSalvo, and he's not a very nice man. She didn't do anything wrong, but he could make her go to jail. And she didn't want to leave you. Can you understand that's why she did it?"

Maddie shook her head, not wanting to listen. "I don't care. She lied to me. She betrayed me. I don't ever want to see her or hear her name again."

Cassie sighed heavily, as if searching for patience that Maddie knew was in short supply with her aunt. "Look, I want you to do this as a favor for me. Just look at the album. How you feel afterward is completely up to you."

Maddie stared down at the album, feeling nothing but revulsion. She picked it up, ready to hand it back to her aunt, when something slipped out from the back cover. Cassie leaned over and picked it off the floor, and Maddie saw it was an eight-by-ten black-and-white photograph.

Cassie held it in front of her so both of them could study it closely. It was a picture of a rainstorm in the desert, the gray sheets of rain thundering down on the cracked floor of sand, the stiff earth rolling on and on, with no beginning and no end. But the rain poured down, filling and softening the cracks of the hard ground. And there, as if accidentally caught on film, was the

427

form of a woman sitting on a large boulder, her back to the camera. Her arms were open, her face turned toward the angry sky, her eyes closed against the unforgiving beat of the rain.

It was stunning in its beauty and reminded Maddie of some of the photographs she'd seen at the Gertrude Hardt exhibit at the High.

She turned to her aunt. "Where did this come from?"

Cassie creased her brow. "I don't know. I wonder if Suzanne forgot it was here." She placed the old photograph on the coffee table. "I'm going to leave this here for now, and we'll worry about it later. Right now we need to look at the album."

Maddie glanced at her aunt, at her determined expression and the hard set of her mouth. Her aunt's stubbornness was something mules envied, and she knew she'd better give in now, because it would happen eventually. Besides, she wanted to see what her mother had done. She'd just pretend she'd done the entire album.

Maddie slowly opened the album and saw her mother's handwriting. A tight ball formed in her chest, and she felt her aunt's arm around her shoulders.

"This will be hard at first, but you'll be glad you saw it when you're done."

Maddie nodded, knowing she couldn't speak, and began turning the pages, soon forgetting her anger and her heavy heart. Each page showed her a chapter of her life, the life of a child who was loved and cherished. She looked at her baby pictures, at the photos of her with her mother and father and then with each of her baby siblings, and her heart cried out for the years that were gone, while at the same time it sang for the joy those years had given her.

Then she came to the more recent pages: the pictures Suzanne had taken of her at football games, at her sister's party, and in the photography lab with Suzanne. She looked at the pictures of the two of them together taken with the timer set on the camera, their heads held close as they examined proof sheets.

These, too, were photos of a daughter and friend, a girl who was still greatly loved by the people who filled her life. She recognized Suzanne's fine handwriting documenting the events and people in the photographs, along with Maddie's accomplishments and thoughts. Thoughts Maddie had never voiced to anyone, but that Suzanne seemed to know anyway.

The pages showed her the years and the people that had made her into the person she'd become. The bad times along with the good had shaped her, and the two people who had made this album had shown her this. They also showed her where her foundation was, how indestructible it was, and how she would always have a soft place to fall.

She knew now why her aunt had made her look at the album. It wasn't to make her anger and hurt go away. It was to help her see beyond it to the woman who loved her like a mother, a woman who knew her as well as the people who had known her since birth, and loved her anyway.

She looked up at her aunt, unsure.

Cassie's voice was gentle, but her words were not. "Be a more mature person than I was, Maddie. Don't let resentment and anger cloud your love for Suzanne. What you two had was special, and you'll never get it back if you let her go. Never." There were tears in her eyes, and Maddie knew she was thinking of the fifteen years of wounded pride that had separated her from her sister. Fifteen years that could never be brought back.

Maddie leaned forward and took the black-and-white photograph off the coffee table. "This must have been a favorite of Suzanne's. It's like a picture of her, isn't it? She's sitting all alone out in this desert, and the rain's practically drowning her. She sits there and takes it because there's nobody there to protect her."

Cassie took the photograph from her hands and put it back on the table. "I think you're right. But I also think that's more how she feels about herself than how things really are now. I think it's time that we showed her."

Tears stung Maddie's eyes, and she looked down at the album. "She has a lot of explaining to do. And a lot of begging for forgiveness, too."

Her aunt's voice held a note of relief. "She knows that. But you have to make the first step."

Maddie looked at her in surprise. "I'm not the one who screwed up."

Cassie stood. "No. But you're the one with the support system. Suzanne thinks she's alone."

Maddie swallowed. "Where's Suzanne now?"

"She's gone. She left last night."

Maddie stood, feeling a tide of rising panic. "Will she be coming back?"

"I don't think she's planning to."

Maddie dropped the album on the coffee table. "We can't just let her leave like that. Do you think we can make her come back?"

Cassie shrugged. "It'll be tough, but if we can find her, I'm sure we can find a way to bring her back." Her aunt watched her shrewdly.

Maddie threw her hands over her face. "I've really screwed up, haven't I?"

Cassie brushed Maddie's hair off her forehead. "Nothing that can't be fixed if you set your mind to it. I have great faith that you'll figure something out."

"What if I can't? Daddy will be miserable without her. We'll all be miserable without her."

"You'll find a way. You are your mother's daughter, you know."

Maddie smiled for the first time. "Yeah. I know. I just need to think."

"You do that. Just make sure it's nothing illegal. And run it by me first."

"Okay. I can do that. Anything else?"

"Yes. Let me know if I can help. If we put our heads together, we can do anything."

Maddie hugged her aunt tightly, so glad to have her in her life. "Thanks, Aunt Cassie."

Her aunt nodded, her eyes suspiciously moist. "Right now I need to go find your father. Is he at school?"

"Yeah. He's trying to pretend that nothing's changed."

"I'll see if I can catch him there. But if you see your dad first, tell him I need to talk to him as soon as possible. He needs to know about Suzanne and Anthony deSalvo. Mr. deSalvo will probably be visiting Walton as soon as that issue of *Lifetime* hits newsstands next week. It'll probably get ugly, and I know Stinky Harden will want to get involved, so he'll need to be prepared."

With a quick kiss on Maddie's forehead, Aunt Cassie left. Maddie sat on the sofa for a long time, looking at the album and thinking. When her gaze fell on a picture of the Walton High football team, the idea hit her and she smiled. Then she ran upstairs for a notebook and her cell phone. She had at least a week's worth of planning to do, and she couldn't waste any of it. It was time to save Suzanne from Anthony deSalvo, save the town from Stinky Harden, and have a little fun doing it at the same time.

With a determined grin, she raced back down the stairs, not bothering to lock the door that banged shut behind her.

Joe sat in his office at City Hall, feeling as if he were having an out-of-body experience. In the week since Suzanne had gone, that same sensation had enveloped him more than once. It was different from the way he had felt when Harriet died, but the sense of desolation and grief was the same. But this time it was all his fault. He'd made the mistake of trusting someone, of letting someone in. And then she had left him.

He tried to focus on the paperwork in front of him, along with the press releases on another annexation hearing in Mapleton that he'd just had faxed over from Hal Newcomb at the *Sentinel.* Stinky Harden was on the move, as if he'd just found a new weapon in his arsenal, and he was aiming it right at Walton. Stinky had something up his sleeve, and damned if Joe wasn't going to find out what it was.

As if conjured by the devil, Stinky strolled into the office, not bothering to knock. Rolled up in his hands was a magazine. He tossed it on top of Joe's desk, and Suzanne's face unfurled.

"Hey, there, Mayor. Look what hit the stands this week."

Joe didn't bother looking down. "I've seen it. Congratulations to Charlie. Must feel real good to win by cheating."

Stinky spread his hands in the air, as if offering them for an inspection of cleanliness. "Hey, he won fair and square. Ain't nobody can tell me he didn't take the picture. He's got the negative."

"I'm still working on it. But you can rest assured that I'm going to have a little talk with the folks over at *Lifetime*."

"Don't be so sure of that, Mayor. If you're thinking you're going to get something out of Suzanne, think again. If the lady's as smart as I think she is, I'd say she's left town for good."

Joe leaned back in his chair, feeling that he should have taken two more aspirins than the four he'd taken earlier. "What are you getting at?"

"Well, a real city slicker just drove into town in a rental car from the airport. Says he's looking for a Suzanne Lewis. Something about her being a thief. I believe he's gone to go talk to Sheriff Adams." Stinky pulled a toothpick out of his shirt pocket and stuck it between his teeth. "Sounds like she's my campaign dream. I already got my boys working on my next campaign button. 'I don't date cons.'"

Joe stood abruptly, his chair rolling on its wheels until it slammed into the wall behind him. He didn't stop to wonder why he was trying to protect the woman who had deserted him. "You son of a bitch." He came around the desk to stand in front of Stinky, his face within inches of the other man's. "You don't know anything about her."

Sweat spotted Stinky's forehead, but his eyes didn't pull away from Joe's. "A lot more than you, apparently. She even reneged on a deal we had."

Joe backed up, still wary. "What kind of deal?"

Stinky looked uncomfortable for the first time since he'd entered Joe's office. "She agreed that if Charlie won the contest, she'd tell me everything I wanted to know about herself."

"And if he lost?"

"Then I'd drop out of the election." A smug smile sat on Stinky's face as he chewed on his toothpick.

This time, Joe grabbed him by his collar, seeing clearly for the first time in a week. "You did this to Maddie, didn't you? And to Suzanne. You've damaged two people just to win this election. No, you might not have taken that negative out of the garbage can, but you sure as hell made Charlie enter it as his own, thinking he'd win, didn't you?" Joe released him, pushing him backward as he did.

Stinky straightened his collar and tie. "Now, wait just a minute, here. Charlie won that contest with his own picture. And nobody can prove otherwise."

Joe grabbed his coat off the antique rack by the door. "You haven't heard the last of this. I know what you're up to, and you're not going to get away with it." He swung open the door, letting it bang into the inner wall of his office, and strode out into the hallway.

Stinky followed him. "You might want to check at your house first. I told Mr. deSalvo that you were sleeping with her."

Joe paused on the landing. "Go to hell, Stinky." Then he ran the rest of the way down the stairs and out onto the street.

When he pulled up in front of his house, he recognized Sheriff Adams's cruiser and a red Mustang convertible he'd never seen before. As he walked behind it, he spotted the rental agency's bumper sticker.

They were in the yellow living room, and Lucinda was bustling about in a bright pink apron, handing out refreshments. Joey was chasing Sarah Frances and Knoxie with a rubber snake while Harry and Amanda flanked the dark stranger on the love seat, each of them squeezed up to his sides, eating lemon bars with powdered sugar that was now liberally covering the man's pants. The man looked miserable and annoyed. *God bless Lucinda.*

Joe nodded to Hank Adams. "Sheriff," he said, then turned to the stranger but didn't offer him his hand. "I'm Joe Warner. Is there something you want with me?"

The man extricated himself from the love seat. "Where's Suzanne?"

Hank turned to Joe as Joe gave the children "the look" that sent them scurrying out of the room. "Joe, this is Anthony deSalvo from Chicago. He says Suzanne stole something from him."

Joe remembered what Cassie had told him, how the pictures had probably been stolen before they were given to Suzanne. He faced the man and kept his face expressionless. "She didn't steal them. This man gave them to her as an engagement present."

Hank shook his head, looking uncomfortable. "He says Suzanne stole a collection of Gertrude Hardt photographs. I did make a few phone calls and verified his story."

Joe's gaze didn't flinch. "Can he prove that Suzanne did it?"

"That's why we need to find her and ask some questions. Do you know where she is?"

"No. But she's not here."

Lucinda appeared again, wobbling in red high heels and carrying a tray of iced-tea glasses and a pitcher. She placed it on a bookshelf before leaning over the coffee table to move a stack of books, to make room for the tray. Something slid off the stack and floated to the floor, and deSalvo moved to pick it up as Lucinda turned back to get the tray.

DeSalvo held up an eight-by-ten photograph, a satisfied look on his face. "I have proof now."

Hank stuck out his hand, and deSalvo handed it to him. As Hank looked at the photograph, the other man snapped open a briefcase at his feet and pulled out a folder, a look of surprised satisfaction resting on his face. "Here's a catalog of the missing photographs. The one you're holding is at the bottom of the second page."

Hank took the catalog while Joe moved to his side to look. It was definitely the same photograph.

"What does this prove?"

"It, ah . . ." Hank coughed and looked over at Lucinda, who was regarding him with narrow eyes. He quickly looked back to the photograph. "I'm sorry to say it, Joe, but you're in possession of stolen property. I'm going to have to take you in for questioning."

"You've got to be kidding me! Hank, you know I didn't steal this. I've never even seen it before."

"Don't make me use the cuffs, Joe. Just cooperate and I'm sure we'll get this settled in no time. But you might want to call your lawyer."

"My lawyer? Hank, this is *me* you're talking to. Your daddy is my lawyer. *You* call him. And tell him to get down to the station just as quick as his lumbago will allow him."

As Hank led Joe out of the house, followed by Anthony deSalvo and a glaring Lucinda, Knoxie

438

ran out of the house following them, her red hair held back in one long braid. "Daddy! Don't let them take you to jail! Who's going to feed us?"

Joe did a double take at his daughter and saw Lucinda elbowing her to be quiet. Knoxie glanced over at deSalvo and saw that he'd had no reaction to her theatrics, and immediately stopped. She waved to Joe. "Don't worry, Daddy. I'll help Aunt Lu with Amanda and Harry. Just don't let them keep you in jail too long."

Hank rubbed her head as he passed. "Don't worry, sugar. I'm sure this is just a huge misunderstanding and we'll have your daddy home before suppertime."

"Now, just a minute, Sheriff—"

Hank cut off deSalvo. "I'm following the law by the book here, mister, as much as I know Joe is innocent. So just cut us some slack, all right?"

With that, he opened the back door to his cruiser and Joe got in. After the door had shut, Joe rested his head on the back of the seat. Being taken to jail was just par for the course of his life lately. It had all started when he'd first seen Suzanne at the gas station, and life hadn't been the same since. He winced. It had been better. Until she left. *Where are you, Suzanne? And how did that damned picture end up in my house?*

He waved to Lucinda and his kids, knowing they'd be well cared for in his absence, and sat back to endure the ride to the police station.

Suzanne pulled the stopper from the small motel sink and watched the water and soapsuds disappear down the drain. She missed having a laundry room. And a kitchen. And a big bedroom with a view of a wide front lawn. And the voices of people who filled all those rooms.

She caught sight of her reflection in the overhead mirror again and winced. Her eyes were still pink and swollen, as if she hadn't stopped crying in over a week. Then again, she realized, she probably hadn't.

There was a loud knock on the door, and Suzanne called out, "I'm not ready for housekeeping yet. Come back later."

There was no answer except for another knock, louder this time. And then a familiar voice. "Miz Paris? It's me—Rob Campbell. Maddie's friend. Can I come in?"

Suzanne froze for a moment, then opened the door and allowed him to enter.

"Rob. It's good to see you." She looked past him to the empty hallway, then closed the door. "How did you find me?"

He gave her an endearing smile that Suzanne knew had probably melted Maddie's heart at least once. "People answer questions from a kid a lot quicker than they would from an adult."

She tried to keep her voice light and only half

succeeded. "You mean you're not the only one who's tried to find me?"

He looked embarrassed. "So far. But I'm sure as soon as Coach Warner comes to his senses, he'll be looking, too. But he's been a real pain in the ass ever since you left. It would be a lot better for all of us if you'd come back."

She tried her best to hide her disappointment. "Is that why you came? Because I can't go back. Not ever. And Maddie doesn't want me to, either."

"Oh no, Miz Paris. You're wrong. She was real mad at you and all, and I think she still has issues, but she wants you to come back to Walton. That's why we're here in Myrtle Beach. We've come to bring you home."

"She's here now? With you?" Hope surged inside her, like water on a dry creek bed. Then a sick thought hit her. "Does her father know? I mean, you're pretty far from home, and I can't see her dad agreeing to an overnight trip with a boy."

Robbie coughed and looked at his sneakers. "Um, actually, he doesn't know. He's, uh, he's in jail. Which is part of the reason why we've come."

"What? Joe's in jail? What happened?"

"It's not that bad. They haven't set bail yet, because Coach Warner refuses to talk, but Dr. Parker says he'll post bail as soon as he changes his mind. But I'd rather have Maddie go over the stuff with you. Can I go get her?"

Suzanne nodded, feeling numb. As soon as

Robbie left, she began to pace the room, unsure of Maddie's reception. She couldn't forget Maddie's last words to her, or the look on her face.

Hearing noises outside, Suzanne opened the door and stepped back as Maddie and Robbie entered the room and closed the door quietly behind them.

Maddie regarded her intently, her green eyes sharp, her mouth firm. *You've grown up, Maddie.* It was as if, in a week, she had gracefully given up the things of childhood and had discovered all the joys and burdens of growing up. The young woman in front of her was beautiful, smart, and strong and Suzanne felt a surge of pride as if she somehow was partly responsible.

Without a word, Maddie moved forward and put her arms around Suzanne, hugging her tightly. "I'm sorry. I didn't mean what I said to you."

Suzanne bit back tears. "Yes, you did, and that's all right. I deserved them."

Maddie pulled back, shaking her head. "Aunt Cassie told me everything. Why you did it. And why you wanted to stay."

Suzanne looked down, no longer able to hold back the tears. "It was still unforgivable."

Maddie squeezed her again, her own eyes bright with unshed tears. "If you love somebody, there's nothing that can't be forgiven. My mama would have told you the same thing."

"So you're not mad at me anymore?"

Maddie pulled back with a frown. "I'm still pissed. But I'll get over it."

"That's a relief." Suzanne took a deep breath. "I wrote to *Lifetime*, by the way, to let them know the whole story and, hopefully, disqualify Charlie."

Maddie and Rob exchanged a quick glance. "Thanks, that's really great, but we need you to help us out with something else now."

"Like what?"

"It's a long story, but Daddy's in jail and they're saying that he's in possession of stolen property. The official charge is theft by receiving. They found one of those missing photographs in our house."

Suzanne couldn't breathe for a moment as she fell onto one of the double beds and put her head in her hands. She remembered the photograph she'd stuck in the back of the album—and forgotten until at that moment. *How could I be so stupid?* "It's a Gertrude Hardt."

A crooked smile lit Maddie's face. "Yeah. Anthony deSalvo told us that."

"He's in Walton?" Suzanne shook her head. "Of course he is. He saw my picture on the magazine. I knew it wouldn't take him long."

Maddie sat down next to her. "I know that's why you took the negative. And now he's in Walton, making everybody's life hell."

Suzanne met her eyes. "But how did Joe get the picture, and how did Anthony find it?"

"It fell out of my album when I was looking at it with Aunt Cassie. I'm sure if I hadn't been so blind with anger, I would have realized what it was and not left it hanging around. Instead, I just put it on the coffee table in the living room and forgot about it. Sheriff Adams and Mr. deSalvo saw it when they came to question my dad about you."

"This gets worse and worse, doesn't it?"

"It will only get worse if you don't come with us. Daddy's figured out where the picture came from, but he refuses to tell the sheriff. They've proven it's an authentic photograph and part of the missing collection."

Suzanne stared at them numbly. "I didn't mean for this to happen. I just wanted to go and let you all get on with your lives."

Maddie took her hand. "But you are a part of our lives. Daddy won't admit it, but he's half out of his head with grief. I haven't seen him like this since Mama died. He's so angry with you, too, for not telling him the truth. And for . . . for what happened with my picture."

Robbie sat down on the other bed. "Miz Paris, I know that it's going to be hard coming back and facing Mr. deSalvo and his charges. And you might even have to spend a night in jail. But Maddie's got a plan, and if everything goes the way it's supposed to, nobody will end up facing a jail sentence, and Coach Warner will still be mayor."

She didn't even stop to think before answering. She would go back to save Joe, even if it meant having to face the one thing she'd been running from. But it would be worth it if she could make up for all her mistakes to Joe. And Maddie. Besides, she had nothing left to lose.

"I'll go. I should never have let it get this far. If I've done something wrong, then I'll have to deal with the consequences."

Maddie stood and faced Suzanne, her hands on her hips the way Suzanne had seen Lucinda do when she was giving one of the children a dressing-down. "Look, Miz Paris. If *I* can figure out a way to forgive you, then *you* got to find a way to forgive yourself. Everything bad that's ever happened in your life is not your fault, okay? So stop trying to punish yourself for things you didn't do. Nobody likes a martyr."

Suzanne stood up, anger pulsing in her veins. "I'm not being a martyr. . . ."

Maddie smiled. "Great. You're mad. Keep that thought, because you're going to need it. Come on, let's go. I've got a great plan. . . ."

As Suzanne sat in the back of Robbie's Jeep while it flew down the interstate, she played with the gold charm around her neck and stared up at the overcast sky and at the sun struggling to come out from behind the clouds.

CHAPTER 24

Maddie hung back in the shadows off the side of the road, looking for headlights to spring up from the long stretch of asphalt. She checked her watch again. Ten forty. They should be along any minute now. She coughed quietly, choking on the heavy aroma of manure that hung in the air.

She looked down the road again and this time was rewarded by two pinpricks of light. She put her cell phone to her ear and heard Rob say, "It's them." Ending the call, she turned her head and yelled, "Go!"

Brake lights and headlights came to life as an engine was cranked, and a large, lumbering truck pulled out into the middle of the road, straddling the center line of the deserted highway.

As the red Mustang came up behind the truck, Maddie said a silent thank-you to Kenny Northcutt, who knew more about cars than he did about anything else. He'd said he could rig the convertible so that the top couldn't be closed. Thankfully, the December weather had been balmy enough that a person from frigid Chicago wouldn't complain too much about not being able to close the roof.

The little car's tires screeched as it braked hard, then swerved as it avoided the slow-moving truck. It stopped almost perpendicular to the back of the truck, the passenger close enough to touch the mud-splattered license plate. The car honked with three bright yaps as Maddie jogged down the shoulder of the road, keeping out of the light from the overhead billboard, her hands holding her camera close to her chest to keep it from bouncing.

The truck stopped completely, causing two more bleeps from the impatient sports car behind them. Then a loud squealing pealed out into the night as the tailgate of the truck slid back and the dump bed rose in the air on a high incline.

Before the men in the car could gather what was about to happen, an entire load of fresh cow manure slid from the truck over and into the passenger compartment, coating all with thick black dung.

Maddie struggled hard not to laugh, not wanting anything to ruin her plan. The men in the car were now standing on the front seat, yelling and cursing at the top of their lungs.

As if on cue, Arnie and Chip Slappey got out of the truck. Both of them were football players for Walton High, and they stood well over six feet and weighed close to two hundred and fifty pounds apiece—and all of it muscle, thanks to the manual labor they did on their daddy's farm. The fact that they both wore overalls didn't lessen their formidable presence at all.

Maddie watched, mesmerized, as they began to

talk like those boys from *The Dukes of Hazzard.* As long as she wasn't expected to go parading around in short-short cutoffs, she didn't care. They were being too damned effective.

Arnie spoke first as he came around to the driver's side of the car. "Oh man. We're sorry, sir. I told my daddy to get that truck fixed weeks ago. The level for the dump bed keeps activating by itself every time we stop the truck. That's the second time it's done it in a week."

Anthony deSalvo let out an expletive Maddie had never heard, followed by "You asshole! Look what you've done!"

Stinky Harden, in the passenger seat beside deSalvo, was busy wiping manure off his face with his coat sleeve. "Son of a bitch!" he yelled, slinging cow dung.

Chip stared up at the two dung-covered men with a speculative look. "Well, gosh. This is terrible."

DeSalvo glared at him. "You're damned right, it's terrible. And you're going to pay for this. We're late for a meeting already, and I certainly don't want to show up anywhere like this. What the hell are we going to do?" He turned to Stinky, who looked in the dim light like a fat, dark pinecone.

"Shit," was all he said.

The brothers chuckled as Chip stepped forward. "You got that right."

His brother moved next to him. "Hey. We might

be able to help you out some, seeing as how you're in a hurry and all. Why don't I call Mr. Parker to come tow your car, and we'll drive you to wherever you're going in our truck?"

DeSalvo and Stinky climbed out of the car, each wincing as his hands smeared more dung onto the car as he touched it for help in getting out.

Chip looked at his brother. "I don't know about you, but I don't want that stuff in the cab of the truck. Daddy just had it cleaned, and he'll have our hides." They looked in unison at the two dung-covered men. Then Chip spoke again. "We got those blankets in the front cab. They could use those until we got them home to change."

DeSalvo began unbuttoning his light-colored jacket, which was now smeared with dark patches. "I don't care. I've got to get out of these clothes before I die from smelling this shit."

Chip pointed to the side of the road where Maddie was hiding, and she ducked back farther into the overgrowth, out from under the billboard's glare. "Why don't y'all go over there into the bushes and take off your clothes and I'll bring the blankets? I got an oil rag, too, to get off some of the stuff in your hair. You'll just need to share, 'cause I got only the one."

"Just do it," deSalvo grunted as he headed off toward the side of the road and out of view of the road.

Maddie moved into position with her camera,

trying not to look away in disgust when bare flesh was exposed. She didn't want to miss any shots.

When their clothes had been thrown into heaps as far away from them as possible, they stood, naked and shivering. DeSalvo called up to the road, "Hey, where are our blankets? We're freezing down here!"

In answer, they heard the sound of the truck's engine start, and Maddie looked up to see the truck moving faster than she'd ever known the ancient vehicle could move.

In their haste to make it back up to the highway, the nude men bumped into each other and fell, then tripped over each other again as they tried to make it up the slight embankment.

Neither of them seemed to notice the whirring click of Maddie's camera going undetected in the overgrowth behind them. Then, when she was sure she had enough shots, she backed up from her spot and ran back down the road to where Rob was waiting to pick her up. With a thumbs-up, she jumped into his car, and he peeled out down the road in the opposite direction of the stranded car and headed toward the photography lab at Walton High School.

"You're free to go."

Hank Adams stood at Joe's cell door, holding it wide open.

"What's going on?"

"My deputy is bringing in Suzanne. She's turned herself in and explained how the picture got in your house."

Joe stood, uncertain. "Suzanne's coming here?"

Hank nodded. "Yeah. Did you want to stick around and talk to her?"

Feeling a renewed sense of hurt and anger, Joe followed Hank out of the cell. "Yeah. I'd like that very much."

Joe had fallen asleep in the waiting room at the front of the station when Suzanne arrived. Hank and his deputy discreetly retired behind the desk, giving Joe and Suzanne some privacy.

She stopped and stared at him, those gray eyes wide with uncertainty. "Hi, Joe."

Just the sound of her voice made him want to pull her into his arms and tell her he would make it better. But then he remembered what she had done to Maddie. And how she had left without a glance behind her to see the devastation. A thought niggled at the back of his mind, but he pushed it away. Maybe he was making it easier to end their relationship, to go back to the half life he'd been living before she'd ever arrived. It was safe, it was familiar. Maybe everything that had happened was just enough to tell him that he wasn't ready for another relationship. And probably wouldn't be for a very long time.

"Welcome back, Suzanne. Thanks for all the letters."

She looked down at her feet, and he saw her cheeks flush. "I did write you. But I tore up all the letters. I didn't think you'd want to hear from me again."

He stared at her, at her pale skin and the way her red hair brushed her cheeks, and he couldn't speak. Mostly because he didn't want her to know the truth. Instead, he said, "Maddie seems to have lost a lot of her anger at you. I don't think I'll ever get there, but I'm really proud of her."

"You should be. She's a remarkable person. She's the one who found me in Myrtle Beach and told me you were in jail."

He looked at her, surprised. "Maddie found you?"

"Yeah. She and Rob."

"What in the hell was she doing in Myrtle Beach?"

Suzanne took a deep breath, and he could tell she was getting angry. "Trying to save your ass."

"I guess she learned that from you, huh? I'm surprised you didn't take the next bus to the West Coast."

She stared at him solemnly, her chest rising and falling, and he hated himself for hurting her so deliberately. He wasn't even sure why he was doing it. It could have been hurt or humiliation—he could take his pick. Didn't matter. He still felt like a jerk.

He was surprised when she answered calmly,

"No, instead I drove down here with Maddie and Rob and turned myself in."

His throat dried as the guilt hit him. "I guess I should thank you, then."

"Don't bother. Besides, Maddie promises me that it won't be for long."

Joe recalled deSalvo telling him that he would drop the charges if Suzanne would go back to Chicago with him. Joe regarded her closely, his heart thudding sluggishly in his chest. Slowly he asked, "What does Maddie know about it?"

"She's got a plan. She hasn't told me all of the details, but she's implementing it now as we speak."

"She's what? I don't want her to get into any more trouble because of you. Don't you think she's been through enough?"

Suzanne glared at him, and it was almost a relief to see her old fire coming back. "I tried to talk her out of it, but she wouldn't listen. You know how she is. She said she was doing it for you as much as for me. And she promised that it wasn't illegal." She swallowed, and he could see she was trying hard to keep control. "She wanted to thank us both for all that we had done for her."

He didn't want to listen. "Where is she?"

"I don't know. Cassie does, though. She's been helping Maddie."

He rubbed his forehead, feeling another head-ache beginning to pound at his temples. "Oh no.

453

There's no telling what the two of them could come up with."

Suzanne lifted her hand as if to touch him, then dropped it. "She's all right, okay? Rob's with her as well as a few of the guys from the football team. They won't let anything happen to her."

He looked at her as relief at seeing her, then worry and anger over Maddie, rushed over him. "Don't try to help me with Maddie anymore, okay? We don't need your help. Last time you tried, I ended up in jail, and my daughter with a broken heart."

She looked at him with so much hurt in her eyes that he wanted to take the words back. Instead, he fought the niggling thoughts in his head and simply stared at her, mute.

"You know something, Joe? All my life, I have wanted what I have found here in Walton these past few months. More than anything else in the world, I wanted a family, a place to belong. And I guess I shouldn't be greedy and want it for more than my allotted time. I'm sorry. Really, I am. I won't interfere with your life anymore."

Feeling gut-punched, he turned away from her, not able to look in her eyes. He motioned to Hank to let him know he was through. But before he left, he faced her again. "If I don't see you again before you leave, good-bye, Suzanne."

She didn't answer, and he left quickly, pushing hard on the glass door of the police station and making it swing open with a bang. Then he used the pay phone outside to call Cassie, wondering what in the hell had happened to his cell phone.

Joe banged loudly on the door of the photography lab until Maddie opened it and let him in.

"How did you find me?"

"I just had a long and illuminating conversation with your aunt Cassie. She told me everything. Where's Rob?"

"Looking for you, to tell you I'm fine and not to worry. And now that you know, you'll let me get back to developing these pictures."

"What are you planning to do with them?"

"We need deSalvo to drop the charges against you and Suzanne and get his butt on the next plane to Chicago as soon as possible."

"This isn't some kid's prank, Maddie. Extortion is not a joke."

"This isn't extortion. It's just getting somebody to pay attention to you while you make a point. Suzanne didn't steal those pictures. We want to make sure Mr. deSalvo agrees."

"I'm not going to let you do this."

"You can't stop me. And before you even try, remember that Suzanne only came back to Walton to get you out of jail. She didn't have to, but she did. The least you can do for her is to help us get Anthony deSalvo off her back forever."

He was silent a moment, the fact that Suzanne

was in jail instead of him starting to sink in. "But I thought you said you'd rather die than ever have to speak to her again."

She regarded him with such fire that for a moment she looked just like Harriet with all her strength, spirit, and determination, and it tugged at his heart. Maddie had grown up into a woman, and he was just noticing it now. "A moment of forgiveness is a whole lot easier than a lifetime of loss, Daddy. I would have thought that Mama and Aunt Cassie had taught you that by now."

He felt a little sick, remembering the hurt in Suzanne's eyes when he'd left her at the jail. He'd been angry at her—for leaving him, for hurting Maddie. In his heart, he'd known why she had done it, but it was so easy to push her away. So much easier to go back to the comfort of his loneliness, where the business of his days kept grief and loss out of reach.

He and his daughter stared each other down for a long moment, and he knew that he was losing this battle. When had she learned to be so strong?

"Daddy, Suzanne didn't leave you to desert you. She left because she thought it would save you. Don't let her go. Can you really imagine the rest of your life without her?"

He looked away, ashamed. "No," he said quietly. "I can't." And he couldn't. How could he have been so stupid, and why had it taken a seventeen-year-old girl to point it out to him?

He faced her again. "Can I see the pictures?"

"Only if you promise not to touch them."

"I'll try."

Maddie regarded him with narrowed eyes.

"Okay, I won't touch them. But I can't promise you that I'll go along with all this."

He followed Maddie through the revolving door and to the counter, where a dozen or so photographs were propped on paper towels as they dried. "Wouldn't a digital camera have been quicker?"

"Yeah, but the only camera I had quick access to with a high-end lens that could take pictures at night without a flash wasn't digital."

He hardly heard her as his attention was captured by the photographs. He looked up at Maddie. "You took pictures of naked men."

She rolled her eyes, and it reminded him so much of Suzanne for a moment. "I'd hardly call those 'men,' Daddy. It's Mr. Harden and Mr. deSalvo. Please."

"And what, exactly, are you planning on doing with these pictures?"

"Not me—Aunt Cassie. I already scanned and e-mailed the worst of them to her. She and Uncle Sam are on their way over to Mr. deSalvo's hotel room in Monroe right now."

The words were out of his mouth before he'd even had a chance to think about it. "Give me a few pictures."

"What?"

"Give me some pictures. I'm going to go pay a visit to Mr. deSalvo, too. But I want to be prepared in case I get there before Cassie and Sam."

"What are you going to do?"

He paused for a moment, admiring this beautiful girl he had somehow helped bring into the world. "I'm going to try and show the world that I can be half as forgiving as you."

He took the pictures and looked at them closely. "You're going to have a lot of explaining to do, missy."

"Not as much as you are if you don't get Suzanne to stay."

Without another word, he kissed her on the forehead and left, hoping he wouldn't be too late to show Mr. deSalvo a little Southern hospitality.

Suzanne sat in the Dixie Diner, opposite Cassie and Sam, and stirred her coffee. She'd been surprised when Sheriff Adams had told her that Anthony had dropped all charges, and even more surprised when the Parkers had shown up to take her to breakfast.

Tired of waiting for either of them to tell her, Suzanne finally asked, "So, what happened last night? How did you get Anthony to give in so easily?"

Cassie handed her a stack of photographs, and Suzanne took them and began to go through them, one by one. They were dark and some were too blurry to see the subjects' faces clearly, but the majority were clear enough that she could make out who was in the photos.

"Oh . . . my . . . ," was all she could say at first. Then: "Um, I'm assuming Maddie did the photography?" Suzanne smiled weakly. "I'm so proud to say I taught her everything she knows, although it's definitely not her best work."

Sam winked. "Yep, the girl's an avid learner, that's for sure. Said it was a real challenge to get the photos at night without a flash."

"I bet." Suzanne brought one of the photos closer to her face to see it better. "What're all those dark splotches on their skin?" Suzanne asked.

"That would be mostly cow manure on their heads and necks, but some of it's mud from the embankment," Sam said.

"And they're naked," Suzanne said.

"Yep. Like a couple of jaybirds." Sam grinned.

"It looks like they're having dirty sex together."

"It sure does, doesn't it?" Sam stacked the coffee mugs and moved them over to the counter.

"How on earth did Maddie get these?"

"All it took was a note, presumably from you, to both men, telling them that you were in jail and willing to discuss things with them. You suggested they come together since what you had to say would benefit them both. Unfortunately, they had a little accident with the Slappeys' manure truck." He smiled amiably. "The rest, as they say, is history."

"Joe's going to be so mad when he finds out how involved Maddie was in all this."

Cassie and Sam looked at each other before Cassie spoke. "He already knows. He was at the hotel when we got there, and we filled him in. He's the one who spoke to Mr. deSalvo."

Worry tightened in her chest. "He spoke with Anthony?"

"Sure did. Joe was able to overlook the stench long enough to show him a few pictures and have a conversation. He said Mr. deSalvo was most impressed by Maddie's talent. Joe also said that it wasn't hard to convince him that releasing the pictures to all the Chicago papers, as well as sending them to his competitors, could really hurt business, not to mention officially end any political aspirations I happen to know he harbors. Joe also mentioned that I had mailed the negatives to my lawyer in New York with a letter explaining that it should only be opened if instructed to do so by someone here in Walton, who shall remain nameless. He was most agreeable to Joe's suggestion that he make it clear that the Gertrude Hardt photographs were a gift to Suzanne, that he drop all charges, and that he return to Chicago first thing this morning." Cassie took a deep breath and smiled. "I think that pretty much covers it."

The diner was completely silent for a moment, and Suzanne could almost hear her blood race through her veins. "But he stole those photographs from the Winthorpe estate. All he needs to do is contact the heirs, and they'll do all the dirty work for him."

Cassie nodded. "Good point, and one I'd already considered, which is why I called my lawyer in New York. He has contacted the estate's heirs, and they have agreed that a payment at today's fair market value from Mr. deSalvo would be agreeable. And Mr. deSalvo was kind enough to agree, thanks to Joe's insistence. They also mentioned that they had already received a significant, although anonymous, cash payment for almost the entire amount."

Suzanne looked away. "Yeah, well, I didn't feel it belonged to me." She regarded Cassie and Sam again. "Thank you—for everything. I don't know what else to say."

"Don't say anything. Just stay." Cassie took Sam's hand and held it.

Suzanne took a deep breath. "Is Joe going to use these pictures to get Stinky to back off from the mayoral race?"

Sam shook his head. "He did say that he'd use them just to help convince Stinky not to press charges against the Slappey boys. They were the ones driving the manure truck that accidentally let go of its load on Mr. deSalvo's car. But Joe won't use the pictures to help him with the election. He says he can win it fair and square. He said that if this town could rally around you when you needed it, then he hasn't been giving them enough credit for how smart they are."

"He said that?"

"Believe it or not. Joe's not always as dumb as he looks."

Cassie elbowed Sam. "So, what are you going to do now—now that you're free from deSalvo?"

Ignoring the heaviness in her heart, Suzanne smiled. "I think I'd like to travel awhile, see more of the South. Maybe find a town to set up a photography studio, do some freelance work. That kind of thing."

Cassie regarded her closely. "Sounds like something you could do here in Walton. We don't have a local photographer. And you know that I'd be more than happy to give you some of the agency's business."

"Thank you, Cassie. I know you would. But I don't think I could face Joe every day of my life. He made it very clear that there's no room in his life for me."

Cassie took her hand. "That's not the way he feels, Suzanne. You two can work this out. I know you can."

Suzanne grabbed her backpack and hoisted it on her shoulder. "I think my job here in Walton is done. I'm calling the *Lifetime* people tomorrow to follow up on the letter I sent them last week. Hopefully, they'll disqualify Charlie, and Maddie will win with her second-place entry. I still have the photograph that I made from the negative—maybe that will be enough proof for them. Then I'm getting on the nine-thirty bus and heading south." She tried to smile but only halfway succeeded. "Things always seem to work out in the end, don't they?"

Cassie gave her husband a long look before turning back to Suzanne with a mischievous smile. "Yes, they do, don't they?"

Suzanne stood. "I guess you're not going to say good-bye again, so I'll do it for both of us." She leaned across the table and kissed each of them on the cheek. "Good-bye, Cassie and Sam. I'm going to miss you. I'm going to miss you all." She turned and fled from the diner before the tears came. It was one thing to be stranded between two busy lanes in the middle of the road and looking like a fool; it was another thing entirely to have witnesses.

CHAPTER 25

Suzanne smiled at Mr. Parker as she put her MoonPie and RC Cola bottle on the counter.

"Well, hey there, Miz Paris. Didn't expect to see you back so soon."

"To be honest, I didn't expect to be back so

soon, either. Would you mind making change for me so I can buy my bus ticket?"

As she slid her money across the counter, a loud commotion erupted from the front of the store. Amanda Warner, joined by Joey, Knoxie, and Sarah Frances, ran through the door and toward the candy aisle, not slowing down to call out a greeting.

She turned back to Mr. Parker, a question on her lips, when a deep Southern voice spoke behind her. "Don't they have leash laws in this state?"

Her heart seemed to freeze in her chest. She turned around and saw the face that she had tried so hard to forget, but which always seemed to be permanently lodged in her memory. Harry, wearing cowboy boots, training pants, and nothing else, stood next to him, clutching Joe's jeans. It was hard squeezing her voice out of her frozen chest. "What happened? Did Lucinda desert you again?"

"Not exactly. She says she's on strike until I come to my senses."

Suzanne spotted Maddie in the MoonPie aisle, trying to pretend she wasn't listening.

"Come to your senses?"

"Yeah. She said something about me forgetting all about forgiveness and understanding somewhere back in preschool and that I needed to get a life. Or maybe that was Maddie who said that. Either way, they're both right."

Her breath was coming in shallow gulps now. "They are?"

He sighed, as if he'd been working up to this performance for a long time and wasn't getting the audience reaction he'd anticipated.

Finally, he said, simply, "Stay. Please. I know I've been a real ass, and I don't deserve you to even ever talk to me again, but I want you to stay." His warm brown-green eyes bored into hers, and she had the unlikely sensation of being torn from the wreckage of a highway collision by strong arms.

She tried to straighten her shoulders, as was her old habit, only to find they were already straightened. With a tilt of her chin, she asked, "Why?"

"Because I love you. Because I want to spend the rest of my life with you."

She continued to focus on breathing normally. "But we're not anything alike."

Half of his mouth turned up in a grin. "That's for sure."

"And I wear a toe ring that really seems to bother you."

"I'll get one, too."

She tried to force back a smile as she crossed her arms in front of her. "What can I give you that you don't already have?"

"You." He stepped closer, dragging Harry with him.

It was then she noticed that the other children, with the exception of Maddie, had come to stand behind Joe. Amanda piped up, "Marry us, Suzanne."

Joe's eyes were deep and solemn as he tilted his face down to hers. "She's stealing my thunder, but the sentiment's the same."

Suzanne had the sudden picture in her head of her and Joe in the frozen food aisle of the Piggly Wiggly, and her heart seemed to leap in her chest. *Yes,* she thought, and then, "Yes," she said out loud.

Joe's lips touched hers, and they were warm and soft and real. And then she heard a whoop from Maddie, and Joey saying, "I think I'm going to be sick," and Harry buried his face in his father's pants leg with a giggle.

Suzanne sat with Joe on the porch swing at the Ladue house, the smell of wet grass and fresh paint strong in the air. Not that it would be called the Ladue house much longer. After the wedding, it would become the new Warner house, a place for new beginnings and fresh dreams—dreams Suzanne had finally allowed herself to have.

The storm had remained unabated all during the graduation ceremony, but it hadn't succeeded in dampening the spirits of seniors as they'd stood in the high school gymnasium in caps and gowns and received their diplomas. The freshly waxed floors of the gym, courtesy of Maddie's community service for what she'd done to Charlie's car, gleamed with the same brightness of the young people's faces as they turned toward their futures.

More people arriving for the post-graduation party at the house hurried up the stairs, huddling under wet umbrellas. After stacking them in the corner of the porch, Joe opened the door and let the guests in before rejoining Suzanne on the swing.

Bill and Sweetpea Crandall emerged from the house just as Joe sat down. Bill came over and shook Joe's hand as he stood up again. "Well, Mayor, congratulations on the annexation of that pine forest acreage. I don't know how you managed it, but you did."

"Thanks, Bill. It wasn't too hard, once the people of Walton knew what was at stake. Now our city limits have just expanded a bit."

"Heard ol' Stinky Harden hightailed it on down to Mexico to hide from his creditors. Hated to see him go. The way he waddled in those seersucker suits was always good for a laugh."

Sweetpea moved to stand next to them and addressed Suzanne. "I just saw Maddie's album, and it's simply the most beautiful thing I've ever seen!"

"Thanks, Mrs. Crandall, although I can't take full credit. It was Harriet's idea, and she started it."

"Oh, I know. But it's like you two worked

together on it, you know? It was hard to tell where her part ended and yours began."

Joe squeezed Suzanne's hand. "Yes," she said. "I know."

Mrs. Crandall continued. "I loved that studio portrait you did of Cassie and the baby. I swear it belongs on a Pampers TV commercial." She lowered her voice a notch. "You know, if you could make me that beautiful in a photograph, your studio will have more business than it could ever handle!"

"She's a photographer, Sweetpea. Not a miracle worker." Bill Crandall winked broadly.

Mrs. Crandall slapped her husband on the arm with her handbag. "Thanks so much for inviting us to the party. I got Maddie a waffle iron, but I'm not sure she's going to need anything like that in San Francisco. Tell her I have the gift receipt from Target if she wants to return it for a sushi slicer or something."

"I will, Mrs. Crandall. Thank you."

Mr. Crandall opened the umbrella over their heads and pulled his wife closer with his arm around her shoulders. "Come on, dear, cuddle up tight, now. Sugar melts when it's wet, and we can't have you making a slippery mess all over the porch steps." He kissed her temple and led her down the walk.

Joe sat back down and turned to Suzanne. "Are you ready to go in yet?"

She shook her head. "A few more minutes. All that youthful energy pretty much wears me out. But Lucinda seems to be in her element—especially with the sheriff at her every beck and call." She rested her head on Joe's shoulder and stared out at the rain dripping from the lush and green mimosa tree. "Besides, I like sitting out here with you and listening to the rain. I don't think I've ever done that before."

They rocked in silence for a while longer until the front door opened again and Ed and Miss Lena came out. Joe stood again, always the Southern gentleman, as Ed helped his mother put on her pink sweater before approaching Suzanne.

"Did you give it to her yet?" Miss Lena asked.

Suzanne shook her head. "Not yet. I haven't had the opportunity."

The old woman winked. "She's going to love it."

"Yeah, I know." Suzanne gave her a wistful smile.

Miss Lena moved her face closer to Suzanne's. "You don't need it anymore, you know. You've found your own heart."

"I did, didn't I?" She took Joe's hand and held it close to her chest.

Ed grinned broadly. "Mama tells me you're going to Paris on your honeymoon."

Joe gave an exaggerated sigh. "That was Suzanne's idea. She assures me I won't starve to death if I don't have grits and bacon for two weeks. I hope she's right."

With a bright smile, Miss Lena said, "Which reminds me. I have something for you." She dove into her oversized handbag and pulled out a thick novel entitled *Desire*. With a wicked gleam in her eye, she handed it to Suzanne. "For your honeymoon. I earmarked all the juicy bits." She elbowed Joe in the ribs. "So glad to hear he's having sex again. I just knew it would work out between the two of you."

Ed tugged on her arm. "Let's go, Mama. You need to take your medicine."

Ed opened an umbrella and began escorting her away, and they listened to her protests as she was led down the walk. "I don't need to take my medicine. My mind's as sharp as a tack." She turned around and winked at Suzanne before continuing her tirade. "Just because I mention the word 'sex' and I'm eighty-three years old, people think I've lost my mind."

Joe laughed out loud as he sat down again next to Suzanne. "Are you sure you want to stay here in Walton with me?"

She kissed him lightly on the lips. "Absolutely. They make me feel perfectly normal."

He kissed her back, harder, and only stopped when Maddie came out of the house.

"I was looking for you two. I guess I should have figured you'd be out here alone."

Suzanne moved over to make room for Maddie between her and Joe. "Come sit. I've been waiting to give you your graduation present."

"I already got the album. People are looking at it inside and going just gaga over it. Darlene Narpone is handing out business cards like they're going out of style."

"No. This is something else."

Maddie held up her hand. "Hold that thought. I wanted to give you something first. I found this on my dresser this morning, and it wasn't there last night. I asked Lucinda about it, but she'd never seen it before, either. She said it was a penny from heaven. So I decided to give it to you. As a sort of early wedding present for good luck."

Suzanne held out her hand and took the penny. Somehow she managed to control her voice. "Thank you." She shifted in her seat so she could face Maddie, then reached behind her neck and unclasped the gold heart necklace.

As she put it on Maddie and began fastening it, Suzanne said, "I want you to have this. My mother gave it to me when I most needed it, and now I'm giving it to you."

Suzanne looked at the gold charm again and saw all of a mother's love, hopes, and dreams. She had found them all, and it was time to pass them on to Maddie.

Maddie held the charm up and read the inscription out loud. "A life without rain is like the sun without shade." She smiled brightly, belying the tears sparkling in her green eyes. "Your mother was right."

Maddie hugged her, and Suzanne rested her head on Maddie's, blinking back her own tears. Things had changed. She had finally accepted her mother's love, as well as her own need to love and be loved, and Joe and Maddie had come to terms with the loss of a beloved wife and mother. But they were the same people, really. That much hadn't changed. Their paths had merely intersected at a crossroads, bringing them back to the starting place.

"Wow, look at that." Maddie pointed to the sky and stood to move toward the edge of the porch, and Suzanne joined her.

It was then that Suzanne noticed that the rain had finally stopped and a bright rainbow was now straddling the sky as if illuminating the dark corners of the earth.

Quietly Maddie said, "You have to get through the rain if you're ever going to see a rainbow. It's true, isn't it?"

Joe came to stand behind Suzanne and put his arms around her. He kissed the back of her head. "I imagine so."

And the world continued to spin on its axis, bringing rain and sun, joys and sorrows. Suzanne realized that life had always been this way, and probably always would be. But now she'd found her place in the great vastness of the world, and Joe's arms held her to it. She looked up again at the bright hues of the rainbow, almost believing that she could feel the turning of the earth. A journey come full circle.

Maddie stepped off the porch and moved away from them, intent on her own thoughts. Joe turned Suzanne around to face him and kissed her. "Thank you."

"For what?"

"For what you've done for Maddie. For what you've done for me. I'll spend the rest of my life showing you how thankful I am."

She put his face in her hands. "I think it's the other way around, but I'm willing to let you try."

He kissed her again and then led her into the house, letting the door close behind them.

It began to rain again, the drops splattering against the roof and windows, but the sun continued to shine, its bright light casting hope in the shades of a rainbow across the fathomless Georgia sky.

QUESTIONS FOR DISCUSSION

1. *After the Rain* is a sequel to the author's earlier work *Falling Home*. If you've read *Falling Home*, do you remember these characters? How have they changed? Is it a pleasurable experience to reunite with them? Did you have any suspicions about Suzanne's true identity?

2. How does the author create such a vivid sense of place? How would you describe Walton? Do you recognize your own hometown in this special corner of the world?

3. The women of Walton keep the community strong, and literally are the caretakers of memories (as with Maddie's scrapbook). In what other ways are women the soul of the town?

4. How have Harriet's children dealt with the loss of their mother? How have the adults?

5. Does Suzanne do the right thing by prolonging her exit from Walton, even as it begins to put Joe's career in jeopardy?

6. What prevents Suzanne and Joe from moving forward in a romantic relationship? How does

Harriet's presence still inhabit the day-to-day lives of her family and home?

7. Why do you think Maddie chooses to confide in Suzanne, a stranger to town, over her own family, and especially Cassie? How is Suzanne safe or more objective? How does she help in the situation?

8. Had you heard of "pennies from heaven" before? Do you think such a phenomenon is real? Or have you experienced it?

9. Do you think Harriet would have (or does) give her blessing to Joe to move on? Would you want your loved one to find love again after you pass on?

10. Could you have destroyed the negative? What do you think you would have done in this situation? How does Suzanne attempt to make up the loss to Maddie?

11. Do you think Cassie's objections, and guarded behavior, to Suzanne were justified? Are Joe's personal life and affairs really her business? Does Cassie see a little of herself in Suzanne?

12. "She remembered cradling Maddie that night on her porch, and the tight feeling in her chest

she'd experienced while watching Harry sleep in his crib. And even the need to make the hurt go away when Sarah Frances had been sick with chicken pox." Do you find this description accurately paints "maternal feelings"? Would you add any others? Do you think Suzanne is ready to assume a maternal role?

13. Where do you see the main characters of this book in five years? In thirty?

Karen White is the *New York Times* bestselling author of fourteen previous books. She grew up in London but now lives with her husband and two children near Atlanta, Georgia.

CONNECT ONLINE
www.karen-white.com
facebook.com/authorkarenwhite

Center Point Large Print
600 Brooks Road / PO Box 1
Thorndike ME 04986-0001 USA

(207) 568-3717

US & Canada:
1 800 929-9108
www.centerpointlargeprint.com